Thirsty Thursdays

Thirsty Thursdays

ELENA GRAF

PURPLE HAND PRESS

© 2020 by Elena Graf

All rights reserved. No part of this book may be reproduced, scanned, or distributed in any printed or electronic form without permission.

This is a work of fiction. Names, characters, places and incidents are the product of the author's imagination or used fictitiously, and any resemblance to actual persons, living or dead, businesses, institutions, companies, events, or locales is entirely coincidental.

Trade Paperback Edition
ISBN-13 978-1-953195-03-6
Kindle Edition
ISBN-13 978-1-953195-04-3
ePub Edition
ISBN-13 978-1-953195-05-0

Cover design by Corrie Kuipers

Purple Hand Press
www.elenagraf.com

03.10.2025

*To my brother, Richard (1955-2015), whose Thirsty Thursdays
with his friends inspired this book*

1

Sam McKinnon flipped open her leather folio to make sure she had enough grid paper. Although she'd used AutoCAD to design everything from high-rises to monuments, she still liked to draw rough sketches on paper. Since she'd first learned drafting in high school—the only girl in her class—she'd preferred a certain brand of mechanical pencil. She checked the supply of lead under the eraser, replaced the pencil in its leather loop, and tossed the folio on the seat of her truck.

She didn't need the GPS to find the address. Her destination was one of the biggest houses on Gull Island, a three-story Victorian reproduction right on the ocean. Whenever Sam passed it, she rolled her eyes. *Why does money make people lose their aesthetics?*

The email inquiry indicated the referral had come from the owner's doctor. Hobbs Family Practice was the only game in town. Liz Stolz, the senior partner, was always sending clients Sam's way, usually more than she could handle.

Now, Sam could really use the work. Business had been slow since the shutdown. The summer people had stayed away, and construction work had abruptly dried up during what should have been Sam's busiest season. Activity finally began to pick up around Memorial Day. People were returning to their summer homes, despite the governor's fourteen-day quarantine.

Cars with out-of-state tags jammed the roads as Sam drove through town. She was relieved to pull into her client's driveway and see a Maine plate, the pink-bow, breast-cancer series. *Does that mean something,* Sam wondered, *or is it just another rich girl's charity?* The people who owned the waterfront houses on Gull Island certainly had plenty of money to give away.

The paved driveway was level, but out of habit, Sam yanked up the parking brake. She opened the console and took out the mask Maggie Fitzgerald had made from colorful quilting squares. She sewed them by the dozens to benefit the Webhanet Playhouse, but she offered the prettiest ones to her friends. Pretty wasn't Sam's style, so she'd chosen a blue-and-khaki, checked gingham.

Sam rang the bell and stepped back the recommended six feet. It took a few minutes, but the door finally opened. An elegant woman with penetrating, blue eyes and carefully styled, dark hair stood there. She wore no mask.

"Oh, you're one of those," she said irritably.

It didn't take Sam long to figure out the woman was referring to the mask. There had been a minor war in the Hobbs community Facebook group about the masks. The people who swayed right thought they were unnecessary because the pandemic was a hoax. Everyone else was trying to comply with the CDC guidelines. Sam wasn't about to get into a pissing contest over a mask, so she said, "We had an appointment for a bathroom estimate."

"Yes, but I was expecting Sam McKinnon."

"I am Sam McKinnon." Sam opened her folio and took out a business card.

The woman scrutinized it at arm's length. "Samantha McKinnon, AIA, ALA, FAIA, LEED, Licensed General Contractor, State of Maine," she read aloud. "You certainly have enough initials after your name." She peered at Sam suspiciously. "Why is a fellow of the American Institute of Architects doing bathroom renovations? Can't you get better work?"

"I'm semi-retired. I can pick and choose what I do. I like doing projects with tile work."

"You do? Why?"

"It's creative and fun. I enjoy getting my hands dirty."

The woman frowned disapprovingly. She looked like the kind who never got her hands dirty. "Well, come in." She stood back. Sam slipped by her, keeping as much distance as possible.

"I'm Olivia Enright." She offered her hand, but Sam didn't get close enough to shake it. "Oh, come on now. This is ridiculous," Ms. Enright said, her hand hanging in the air.

"I'm sorry, but it's for your safety as well as mine. I hope we're not getting off on the wrong foot."

"I hope not either." Ms. Enright lowered her hand to her side. "Let me show you what I want done."

Sam followed the woman, noticing that she had a shapely backside. *Stop it*, Sam told herself. *She's a client*. But it hadn't escaped Sam's notice that when Olivia Enright wasn't scowling or challenging her about wearing a mask, she was a damn good-looking woman. Her hair was probably dyed. The color was too monochromatic to be natural. Her features were refined and so regular that her face was indistinguishable from a host of other attractive women. Like the face of a model, it was a blank canvas on which to paint.

Sam distracted herself from rating the woman's looks by taking in the bones of the house. It was obviously a custom build. There were some nice features—not over-the-top pseudo-Victorian, mostly just a nod to the style. Sam figured the house couldn't be more than five or six years old, given the condition of the surface materials.

Ms. Enright led her up the stairs to the second floor and down a hallway to what appeared to be the master suite. Here, the Victorian style gave way to modern engineering. Enormous windows offered a spectacular view of the ocean below, and there was a clever, cantilevered balcony accessed by a sliding glass door. Sam paused to admire the ingenuity of the design.

"This way," said Ms. Enright, impatiently gesturing in the opposite direction. She showed Sam into a large en-suite bathroom. All the fixtures and materials were high-end, including the shower with expensive marble walls.

"Why do you want to renovate this bathroom?" asked Sam, turning to the client. "It looks great."

"It has no tub. I like a good soak from time to time."

Sam glanced around. There was no space in the room for a bathtub. Judging from the bathroom's location in the house, adding on could be quite a challenge.

"I've always wanted a claw-foot tub," said Ms. Enright.

"I'm sure we can find you one, but there are other styles that would fit in with the design of this bathroom."

"It's a Victorian house."

"It's a Victorian-style house, not a Victorian-era house. That means you don't need to choose period-exact details."

Ms. Enright did not look convinced by the explanation.

"I can bring some catalogs," said Sam. "You have a lot of options, including Victorian reproductions."

"Money is no object."

"That's great, but I believe in spending money efficiently."

Ms. Enright obviously sized her up. "Good to know."

Sam pulled a tape measure off her waistband. "Would you mind if I look around and take some measurements and photos?"

"Fine. I'll wait in the bedroom."

The comment made Sam uneasy. She didn't mind the woman hanging around to answer questions, but she hated the idea that she didn't trust her. Sam shrugged off the thought and opened her folio.

No expense had been spared in building the bathroom, and Sam hated to waste such beautiful materials. She tapped the walls to see where there might be room for expansion. As her knuckles moved along, the sound changed, indicating a large cavity. Tapping across the wall, she mentally measured off six feet—perfect for a tub.

Sam came into the bedroom and found Ms. Enright sitting on the bed, scanning her phone.

"Do you mind if I take a look at this wall? I think I might have found some space for expansion."

"No, go right ahead," said the woman, not looking up.

Sam turned around and saw the reason for the wall cavity. It was a closet. "Okay if I take a look in this closet? Do you use it much?"

"It's mostly empty. I store extra blankets in there."

"Do you have other closet space?" asked Sam, glancing around the room.

Ms. Enright absently gestured over her shoulder. "There's an enormous walk-in over there."

"So, you wouldn't miss this closet if I used the space for a bathtub?"

"I didn't say that," replied Ms. Enright, finally looking up with a challenging stare.

Sam's eyes scanned the room and fell on a vacant wall. "What about other storage? Maybe a Victorian armoire? I see you have room over there." Sam nodded in that direction.

"Now, you're a decorator too?"

Sam had learned to hold her tongue with clients, but the woman's attitude irked her. After a deep breath, Sam said, "Just a suggestion." Despite the mask, Sam instinctively smiled to lower the temperature of the conversation. "I'm going to take some measurements and see what other options I can come up with. Would you consider converting to a shower-tub combination?"

"No," said the woman flatly.

"Okay. Scratch that. One question. Why didn't you include a tub in the original design?"

"I wasn't involved in the construction. I inherited the house from someone."

The woman glanced at her watch.

"I won't be much longer," Sam assured her.

"Don't hurry. I want it done right."

As Sam reeled out her tape measure on the bathroom floor, she wondered why the woman had to be so bitchy. That seemed to be a quality of the affluent, the newly wealthy in particular. Everyone else was beneath them, especially the people they hired to do work on their houses. Sam had witnessed that attitude firsthand when she'd spent a year as a carpenter's apprentice. A contractor had told her that a building she'd designed was impractical, adding, "Architects are all theory, no practical experience. You're the air heads of construction."

At first, Sam prickled with irritation. Then, she realized the man had a point, so she asked him to take her on as an apprentice. Some people thought Sam was crazy when she took leave from her office job and put on a tool belt. Secretly, she'd always wanted to work in the trades. She loved building things—one of the reasons she had been drawn to architecture.

Sam transferred all her measurements to the grid paper, made some quick sketches, and photographed everything in the room for later reference. She went into the bedroom to measure the closet. While she was on her hands and knees to position the tape, she had the strange feeling that someone was staring at her ass, but she didn't dare look over her shoulder to see if she was right.

After making a few more notes, Sam flipped closed the folio. The sound caused the woman to look up from her phone. "All done?" she asked.

"For now. I'll drop off some catalogs and send some links to websites that sell renovators' supplies. What's your time frame?"

"As soon as possible."

Sam tried to be patient. "I mean, do you have a specific date?"

"I really miss having a tub."

"Don't you have one in another bathroom?"

"No, only showers."

"Usually, there's at least one tub in the house, in case the owner has small children."

At that, a shadow seemed to pass over Ms. Enright's face. "There are no tubs in this house," she reiterated firmly.

"Don't worry. We'll figure out how to put one in," said Sam in a reassuring tone. "I'm finishing up another job. I can be available next week, but first we need to settle on the plans. If you choose me to do the work, I'll need time to pull a permit, which could take a while. Technically, you don't need one for an interior job like this, but I always like to get one, in case there are questions later." Sam noted a subtle look of approval on Ms. Enright's face. Otherwise, it was totally neutral. "I can send over a rough estimate by close of business tomorrow. I'll need a day or two to refine it. Will that work for you?"

"That's earlier than I expected," said the woman, looking pleased. "Yes, that will be fine."

Once Sam was back in her truck, she made a few more notes and checked the time on the dashboard clock. Estimates were free, but if the job went live, she charged for the time. In all, she'd spent less than an hour in Olivia Enright's pseudo-Victorian. She'd be in plenty of time to join the gang at Liz's place for a drink.

As soon as the weather had begun to warm, Liz had instituted "Thirsty Thursdays," a weekly cocktail hour for her Hobbs friends. The name, a nod to rowdy college parties, made them all feel silly and young, but the intent was serious.

"We're going to become weird if we don't socialize," Liz had said, "I mean weirder than we are already." Lucy Bartlett, who was a psychotherapist as well as the rector of the local Episcopal church agreed wholeheartedly. To maintain their sanity, they needed to be with other people. Liz's enormous wrap-around deck had become the setting for their weekly gatherings. The snacks were usually so plentiful and filling that eating dinner afterward was optional.

Sam didn't want to arrive empty-handed, so she called Maggie Fitzgerald. "Do you need anything?" she asked. "How about some beer?"

"Are you kidding me?" Sam could imagine Maggie rolling her eyes. Her wife, Liz, was a craft brew aficionado. Their refrigerator in the garage was always filled with beer. "Get some chips if you absolutely must bring something," said Maggie, "but we really have everything we need."

As Sam started the engine, she had the feeling she was being watched. She glanced up to see Olivia Enright standing at a second-story window overlooking the driveway.

"Don't worry, lady, I'm leaving," Sam said aloud as she backed up her truck.

2

Liz Stolz stacked the red, plastic beer cups on the table at the center of the deck. She'd calculated the exact distance that allowed everyone to access the food and drinks and still be safely apart. On one side of the deck, she'd set up a cluster of chairs for those who'd been in the same social bubble since the shutdown. Lucy and Erika had only recently moved back to their beach house after spending almost three months in Liz's garage apartment. They were still working remotely, so Liz considered them safe. She missed their company at dinner and especially missed hearing Lucy's beautiful soprano on their talent nights, but she understood the couple's need for privacy. They'd only been married since October, barely eight months ago.

Liz remembered when she and Maggie couldn't keep their hands off each other. They'd been reunited after forty years, college lovers separated by family disapproval and Maggie's marriage to a man. Maggie's cancer diagnosis got their relationship off to a rough start. For a while, it didn't look like they would make it. Liz hadn't considered herself marriage material until she realized Maggie needed the commitment. There were still rocky times. Somehow, they got through them. Lucy, whose specialty was marriage and family counseling, liked to say, "The perfect marriage is just two imperfect people who refuse to give up on one another."

Erika Bultmann came up the deck stairs. "Am I the first?" she asked in her distinctive, German-tinged, British accent.

"You are indeed," said Liz, allowing Erika to set down a plate of stuffed mushrooms before clapping her into a hug. "Where's your better half?"

"I left Lucy in an emergency session with one of her clients. The isolation is very traumatic for some people." Erika looped her blond hair over her ears. It had grown during the lockdown and become noticeably whiter. Maybe the stress had gotten to her too. The political environment was becoming tenser as the election neared. Erika's specialty as a philosopher and an expert on Habermas was political communication. Although she'd hoped to retire, her expertise was suddenly in high demand.

"Aren't we lucky to be introverts?" Liz said.

"You really think we are? We enjoy people when we choose their company. Look at you with your houseful of people all summer. Is that the behavior of an introvert?"

"Leave it to you, Professor Bultmann, to require precision. All right, I'm a serial introvert. Good enough?"

"It will do. Now, let me get a drink. I'm finding this article I'm writing on political argument vexing. I need to rest my brain for a bit."

"I thought you were taking the summer off."

"In this political climate, I couldn't possibly keep my mouth shut. It would be unethical."

"Hello? Where's the rest of the gang?"

Liz turned around to see Brenda Harrison. She was still wearing her police uniform but had taken off her tie and service belt.

"And where's *your* better half?" asked Liz as Brenda helped herself to a beer.

"She's not coming tonight."

Liz waited for Brenda to elaborate. When she didn't, Liz asked, "Does this have anything to do with rescheduling the move?"

"Let's be honest. It's not rescheduled. It's canceled."

Erika turned to Brenda with a look of concern. "You mean, for now?"

Brenda shrugged. "Who knows?"

"It's not that serious?" Erika pressed gently.

Brenda idly glanced over the railing at the garden below. "With the police killing people of color one after the other, I'm a bad guy again."

"But you're one of the good guys!" exclaimed Erika. "One of the very best!"

"Doesn't matter. To Cherie, all cops are the same."

"Have you talked to Lucy about this?" asked Liz, frowning.

"No, I really can't. She's still seeing Cherie as a client."

"That sucks, Brenda. I'm really sorry." Liz gave Brenda's shoulder a comforting pat. "Let me call Cherie. That will get her ass over here—stat!"

"Please don't. You're her boss. She'll take it as an order. I don't want everyone to see we're not getting along."

"Okay, if that's what you want, but I will ask tomorrow why she didn't show up. Maybe she'll talk to me."

"Liz, please. Just leave it alone," said Brenda in a sad voice.

Liz hated to see her friend hurting, especially because this was the first time Brenda had been in a real relationship since her wife had died. She certainly didn't deserve to be rejected just because she wore a badge. Besides, Brenda had literally written the book on police work in minority communities.

Out of the corner of her eye, Liz saw Sam McKinnon ascending the stairs. Her face was sour. *Why is everyone in such a bad mood tonight?*

Sam's short, dark hair was in disarray, which meant she'd been too busy to deal with it. That was a good sign because Liz had been worried about her. Sitting around with nothing to do had taken its toll on Sam. The machines in her woodworking shop sat idle. Her mental state had gotten bad enough for Liz to suggest medication. Fortunately, a few chats with Lucy had gotten Sam back on track, but her brown eyes didn't have their usual sparkle of optimism. Even her freckles seemed pale. Liz suddenly thought of how the beautiful colors of a mackerel faded after it was caught and dumped into a pail for bait fish.

"Another cheerful reveler," said Erika, noticing the new arrival. "What's the matter, love? You look like shit."

"Well, your friend here," said Sam, thumbing over her shoulder toward Liz, "referred me to some bitch on Gull Island. I just came from measuring for the estimate."

"Who are you talking about?" asked Liz, trying to remember any recent referrals.

"Olivia Enright."

"Ayuh," agreed Liz, "she's a bitch all right."

"Then why did you give her my name?" Sam threw up her hands in frustration.

"You needed work." Liz thought about it for a moment and made a face. "Took her long enough. I gave her that recommendation before Christmas. I figured you could use a job during your slow season."

"Thanks, I guess," said Sam, flipping the top off a beer. She started to pick up a plastic cup, then left it on the pile and drank straight from the bottle.

"Oh, no. Regression," Liz observed.

"It's just us," said Sam, looking around. "Who cares?"

"How do you two know each other?" asked Brenda, watching them curiously. "Maybe you told me, but I forgot."

"We were in the same woodworking club in New Haven," said Liz. "Eons ago."

"Yes, Neolithic era," said Sam with a perfectly straight face. "Before iron tools. Back then, we cut wood with stone axes."

Liz was glad to see Sam's quick humor easily bubble to the surface. One of the things that had attracted her to Samantha McKinnon was her sunny personality. Even her approach to furniture design was open and light-hearted. Fortunately, she wasn't the precious type who made art furniture. You could actually sit in the chairs she built, although her cabinets were tiny and basically useless for storage.

"I'm sorry if I steered you wrong with Olivia Enright," said Liz. "She certainly hasn't made many friends in town."

"That's for sure," Brenda said. "She annoys the shit out of everyone in the town council meetings. Even the die-hard Republicans can't stand her."

"She also has a lot to say in the Rotary meetings, but I haven't a clue what her deal is, and I'm her doctor."

Olivia Enright had come in last fall for a UTI. She'd refused to let Cherie, Liz's physician's assistant, touch her. In her words, she wanted "to see a real doctor." Cherie, whose training as a psychotherapist enabled her to handle almost anyone, had to interrupt Liz to deal with her.

The patient had waited until she was bleeding to see a doctor, and she was abrasive and prickly. UTIs could be extremely painful, so Liz was willing to give her a pass. The "real doctor" remark was unforgivable. Fortunately, Cherie was gracious about it.

Maggie and Stefan came out to join them. Liz was relieved because she could easily get into a full-fledged grousing session with her buddies. The presence of Maggie and Erika's father would force them into more sociable conversation.

Erika kissed Stefan. "Hello, Papi. I see that Maggie and Liz are feeding you well."

"Yes, I think I've put on some weight. Maggie and Liz are excellent cooks."

"Better than I?"

"Different," replied Stefan diplomatically. "Liz tries, but no one can cook your mother's recipes the way you do."

"Well, let's see," said Liz, glancing around. "Who are we waiting for? Cherie's not coming, so only Tom and Lucy."

"I'm here!" Lucy called. Liz glanced over the railing and saw a familiar redhead heading up the stairs.

"Hello, gorgeous. About time you showed up. We're all waiting for you."

"Yeah, right," said Lucy in a friendly tease. She had taken off her collar and opened her clerical blouse a few buttons, which gave Liz a view into her cleavage. *I shouldn't be looking*, Liz told herself, but she couldn't tear her eyes away.

Lucy gave Maggie a hug and Liz a sweet kiss on the lips. Liz caught Maggie's eye roll in Erika's direction. Good thing everyone knew Liz's flirtation with Lucy was innocent…mostly. Sometimes, her lizard brain wanted that beautiful redhead in the worst way. Fortunately, her frontal lobe still worked.

Lucy was an equal-opportunity kisser. She offered hugs and kisses to the other members of their social bubble, ending with Stefan, whose eyes twinkled when she kissed him. There wasn't a man…or woman in Hobbs who wasn't charmed by St. Margaret's rector. Lucy blew kisses to Brenda and Sam before settling in a chair next to her wife. Erika put her arm around her in a little, territory-claiming gesture. "No kiss for me?"

"Close your eyes, everyone," said Liz. "This one will be X-rated."

Playing along, Lucy held up her hand to block the view as she kissed Erika.

Tom Simmons poked his head up from the stairwell. "She's the only priest I know who can make a kiss seem like a sacrament." Unlike Lucy, the associate rector of St. Margaret's wasn't looking like a priest. Tom was wearing a violet polo shirt and Bermuda shorts.

"Good one, Thomas," said Liz. "Coming from a golf game?"

"Yes, and I enjoyed it immensely. Beautiful weather."

"Everyone here now?" asked Maggie. "I'll light the grill."

Tom helped himself to a glass of chardonnay. "It's so nice to see real people. I'm so tired of Zoom. Zoom pastoral counseling. Zoom home visits. Zoom worship. I feel like I could just zoom away!" He moved a sling chair six feet away from Sam and raised his glass. "Cheers, dear friends."

Liz raised her glass. "If someone had told me before I met Lucy that I'd be hosting two priests on my deck, I'd have said they were crazy."

"It's all right," Lucy said. "You're our favorite atheist. Right, Tom?"

"She is indeed. Too bad I missed out on her company all those years. Erika too. We used to have such good times together." The friendship went back almost forty years, when Tom and Erika were graduate students at Yale, and Liz a surgical resident. After Tom left his PhD program, they'd lost touch.

"I don't think you want to get us started on that subject, Tom," said Liz, thinking of some priceless stories from their mutual past.

Tom laughed merrily. "You're right. I certainly don't. I have a reputation to uphold in this town."

Erika got up to get more wine, and Liz appropriated her seat. "Lucy, I need you for a consult."

Lucy turned her green eyes on her. "Sure, Liz. What for?"

"I have a patient who wants Alprazolam for panic attacks, but I don't know her very well. I've only seen her for an emergency visit and a cold. I told her I would only prescribe benzos with a psych consult. She threatened to get a script from her previous doc, but I told her I'd write one if she saw you, and you agreed. Will you see her?"

"Sure. Tell her to call Jodi for an appointment."

Erika stood over Liz and gave her a look of faux menace. "That's *my* seat."

"Take it easy. I was just leaving."

Liz saw Maggie beckoning her to the grill. She handed Liz the tongs to take the shrimp off the grate. As Liz arranged them on a platter, Maggie leaned over to speak confidentially. "This is another expensive party. You really should consider reining in our Thirsty Thursdays now that you're not drawing a salary."

"We have plenty of money," grumbled Liz.

"I know," said Maggie, "but you're also helping Alina and your niece. You can't support everyone."

Liz leaned closer to Maggie's ear. "Maggie, I appreciate your concern about my finances, but it's my business, and if I choose to pay the support staff's salary instead of my own, that's my decision."

Maggie drew back. Her hazel eyes studied Liz. "I'm not trying to interfere in your business, but I know how generous you are. You need to take care of us too. You lost a lot of money in the downturn."

"Don't worry. I know my limits."

"Honey, you can't carry everyone. This pandemic could last a long time."

"As soon as people realize it's safe to go to the doctor, and money starts coming in, we'll be fine. My partners have young families. The support staff and Cherie have no other income. I can manage it for now."

Maggie gave her a skeptical look.

"Hey, you two, we're hungry," called Brenda. "That shrimp smells so good!"

Liz took the tail of Maggie's long, white braid and tickled the back of her neck with it. "Relax, Mag. I've got it covered." She gave her wife a quick kiss. "Trust me."

3

Despite her dislike for Olivia Enright, Sam had spent a good hour sticking Post-It tags in catalogs for her. She'd also sent an email with links to websites, but there had been no reply. Sam briefly wondered why she was going out of her way to be so accommodating. Then she realized she was trying to prove that, no matter how much the woman irked her, she could be professional.

Difficult clients were the norm in Sam's business. She'd strictly been a C-suite-level architect and often had to deal with hostile boards of directors, officious CEOs, and know-it-all design committees. Many of her clients were arm-chair designers, or they tried to nickel and dime her on the costs. She always expected resistance, ignorant suggestions, and interference. If only her clients would just let her do her job.

As Sam thought back over her career, she wondered when the approval process had soured her on architecture. Winning the contract to design the Grayson Building had brought her fame and her photo on the cover of *Architectural Digest*. That was twenty-five years ago, when she was thirty-four. After that, her career had skyrocketed. She'd reached the pinnacle around ten years later and had a wall of awards to prove her talent. She'd had a good long run, but now, her aesthetic had fallen out of fashion. In thirty years or so, it might come around again and be trendy and retro. At fifty-nine, Sam didn't have time to wait for a renaissance in her career.

She'd been doing small projects in the New York metro area when Liz had asked her to oversee the renovation of her house and design her new medical office. Sam was smitten by Hobbs, like all visitors, so she'd bought herself a small place on Jimson Pond. At first, it was just a summer and weekend house, but last year, Sam had decided to make it permanent.

The sale of Sam's house in New Haven had earned a nice profit. The upgrades she'd made had turned the old townhouse into a showplace. At the peak of her career, she'd made good money and invested it wisely. Plus, she had the income from the trust fund. She could have retired years ago, but she needed to be busy. When she began talking about moving to Maine, Liz suggested woodworking as a second career. They even talked about opening a gallery together in Webhanet, but it was just talk. Sam knew that custom furniture was as outdated a concept as her architecture.

Sam collected the catalogs and her notes. She double checked to make sure she had the estimate in her folio and headed out to her truck. As she drove down to Gull Island, she admitted to herself that she didn't look forward to seeing Olivia Enright again. The job could be lucrative, but part of her hoped the annoying woman would reject the estimate and find someone else.

After pulling into the driveway, Sam gazed at the house, trying to motivate herself to get out of the truck. "Just do it," she said aloud. She rang the bell and stood back. When the door opened, Ms. Enright smiled, not a cold, formal smile like before, but a friendly, welcoming one. She stepped back, so that Sam could enter without violating the safe distance between them.

"Thank you for coming personally," Ms. Enright said. "You could have sent the estimate by email."

"I know, but I wanted to drop off these catalogs and get some feedback on my suggestions. If you hire me for the job, I have to start hunting down materials. Sourcing is sometimes the hardest part of a project."

"Come in and sit down," said Ms. Enright, leading the way. "Can I get you something to drink?"

Sam studied the woman. *Had she had a brain transplant?* "I don't really need anything. Thank you."

"I was about to have a glass of pinot grigio. Any interest?"

It was a warm afternoon, and the thought of some cold, white wine brought on a sudden thirst. "Sure. If you're having one," said Sam. "Thank you."

"Have a seat there in the living room. I'll be right with you."

She seems almost pleasant today, thought Sam, *what the hell happened to her?* From her seat on the plush sofa, Sam gazed around the room, trying to figure out the woman's design aesthetic. The informal furniture was obviously expensive, a cut above the casual-style retailers that catered to the elite. The details—the paintings, the accent pieces, even the throw pillows—were too well-coordinated to be anything but the choice of an interior designer. There was nothing personal to glean from the objects in the room. It was all work for hire.

Ms. Enright came in with a tray bearing two glasses and a bottle of wine in a chiller. She poured the wine to exactly the right level in the glasses, took one, and left the other on the tray for Sam. "You're going to have to take off that mask to drink the wine," she said, as if Sam hadn't already figured that out.

Sam's eyes could estimate length almost as well as the tape measure at her belt. She calculated the distance between her and the wine to be five-and-a-half feet, give or take an inch. After Sam picked up the glass and returned to her seat, she took off her mask and put it in her pocket.

"That's better," said Ms. Enright. "I like to see people's faces when I negotiate. Here's to a successful project," she said, raising her glass.

"But you haven't seen my sketches or the final estimate."

"I'm sure they're fine." Ms. Enright glanced at Sam's glass. "Your wine will get warm. Right now, it's at exactly the right temperature. I just removed it from the wine cooler."

Sam took a quick sip of wine. "Very good."

The woman recited the name of the wine and the year. *Is she trying to impress me?* Sam wondered, but she smiled pleasantly. "Did you have a chance to look at those websites? I sent the links in my email."

"Briefly. I spent more time looking at your website and researching your background." Ms. Enright gave Sam a probing look. "Why did you give up architecture?"

The direct question put Sam off balance. She wouldn't have expected a renovation client to take such an interest in her credentials. "I still work as an architect. Light commercial mostly."

"You've won awards. You're famous all over the world. Why did you give it up?"

"My style is no longer in vogue. Every designer has their time. Trying to prolong it or adapt to changes in taste only works up to a point. Sometimes the results are just plain sad. I never wanted to be a parody of myself, but mostly I wanted to do something else."

"And what was that?"

Sam recognized that Ms. Enright was interviewing her, but she stifled her annoyance and remained polite. "I love tile work. That's why I do bathrooms. Sometimes, kitchens, or even bigger installations."

"And you do the work yourself?"

"Some of it. For code reasons, I don't do rough plumbing and leave electrical work to the pros."

Ms. Enright sat back in her seat. She gestured to Sam's wine glass. "You should drink it while it's cold."

Sam nodded and picked up her glass.

"I had no idea who you were when you came the other day," said Ms. Enright. "I apologize if I seemed rude."

Sam didn't like the idea that her client thought she was due more respect because she used to be famous, but she nodded to acknowledge the apology.

"I'd like to go over the estimate with you." Sam slid the paper across the table and carefully sat back.

Ms. Enright put on reading glasses and picked up the paper. Sam expected the review to take a few minutes. She always gave detailed estimates, breaking down the costs into separate line items for demolition, labor, and materials. After a brief scan of the spreadsheet, Ms. Enright took off her glasses. "More reasonable than I'd expected."

"Labor is less expensive here in Maine."

"Yes, I've noticed."

"I gave you a range for the fixtures and materials. I'd really like you to look through those catalogs I brought, so we can zero in on what you're looking for. Of course, we can get you a claw foot, but we can also get you a composite soaker tub. It will be deeper and hold more water. When you get older, it will be easier to get into. I bet we could even match the marble of the shower surround."

Ms. Enright put on her glasses again and flipped through the catalogs, carefully studying the pages Sam had tagged. "These are quite nice. I hadn't realized there were so many possibilities."

"Some are more expensive than others, but I'm sure we can find something that fits your budget."

"I told you. Money is no object."

Sam always hated it when the wealthy said that. It was so arrogant and usually, a lie. Everyone had a budget.

While her client was occupied with flipping through the catalogs, Sam took the opportunity to study her. Sam guessed they were about the same age. The haircut was expensive, her makeup quietly elegant. When she wasn't scowling, she was a damn good-looking woman. Today, she was wearing capris, and Sam noticed that her legs were shapely. Her feet were long and slender. Her red toenails peeked out through her sandals. Sam glanced up at the coffered ceiling for relief from the surprise flash of sexual excitement.

"I like this one," said Ms. Enright, holding up the catalog. "It looks comfortable. I like the clean lines."

Sam smiled. She especially liked that tub. It took its inspiration from nineteenth century bathtubs with a high side at the back so that the bather could sit back and relax. "Do you want me to try to match the shower surround?"

"No, the white is simple and elegant, but do you think we can get more of that marble for the walls?"

"I'll try."

Ms. Enright picked up the drawing for the project and frowned. "Your plan still puts the tub in the closet."

"That's the only place that makes sense."

"What about the storage?"

"If you agree to that design, I will personally help you find an armoire to make up for the lost space." *Why did I say that? I'm not that desperate for the work.*

Ms. Enright looked delighted. "You will?"

"Yes, of course. There are wonderful second-hand furniture shops up and down Route 1. I'm sure we can find something that looks right and provides the lost storage."

"Maybe we could go together," said Ms. Enright, her voice rising on a hopeful note.

"Sure…" said Sam slowly. Now, she was really sorry she'd blurted out the armoire idea. "Once the job is done, I'll set up a time for us to shop, but now, Ms. Enright, you should look at faucet handles."

"Call me Olivia."

"Olivia, then."

"May I call you Samantha?"

"My friends call me Sam."

Olivia shook her head. "You're much too pretty to have a man's name. You'll be Samantha to me." Her tone made it sound like a command. Only Sam's mother called her by her full name, but it wasn't important enough to make a fuss.

"I'll leave these catalogs for you to browse," said Sam, getting up. "You'll have to decide soon, so I can order the fixtures."

"When can you start?"

"Once I get through the punch list of the job I'm working on now, I'll be available. Next week?"

"Wonderful. I'll make my decision on the faucet handles by tomorrow."

That was music to Sam's ears. She loved decisive clients. As she took her mask out of her pocket, she noticed Olivia's look of disapproval. "Do you really have a problem with the mask?"

"No, of course not. I'm an intelligent woman. I've read the science. Of course, masks will help slow the spread of the virus."

Sam wanted to ask, *so why did you carry on about the mask when I arrived the other day?*

"Everything is so charged right now," Olivia explained with a sigh. "I find myself angry over things that wouldn't usually bother me. This quarantine thing. Being shut inside for almost three months! I'm so sick of it!"

"I understand," said Sam. "We're all sick of it. We all wish things could just go back to normal."

Olivia shook her head. "Things will never be the same again."

As Sam gazed into Olivia's blue eyes, she realized that the woman was highly intelligent, and the belligerence was a bad habit more than anything. Then, Olivia gave her the strangest look.

Could she be attracted to me?

Sam took a quick breath and decided she needed to get out of there. Pronto!

4

Lucy Bartlett gazed around her rectory office. She'd been away from it so long it looked strange. The walls, her desk, the visitors' chairs were objects she once took for granted. Now they seemed alien. Even the air felt somehow different.

Lucy didn't need Liz's approval for in-person meetings at the rectory, but she trusted her advice. Until now, Liz had hedged. Where Lucy was concerned, Liz was always overprotective. Finally, they'd agreed on practices to keep both St. Margaret's rector and her parishioners safe. Liz measured off the distance from the desk and put masking tape on the floor to establish the safety zone. She did the same in Tom's office. She gave the parish admin a box of disposable surgical masks with strict orders to offer one to anyone who showed up without a face covering. Listening to Liz sternly lecture Jodi on how to sanitize the surfaces, Lucy could almost imagine her friend in her former role as chief of surgery at Yale.

Lucy put on one of the black masks decorated with a little, white, embroidered cross that Mrs. Reardon had hand-stitched for the priests of St. Margaret's. The double-layer cloth masks were a bit warm for summer temperatures, but Lucy wore them to show appreciation for the long hours the old woman had put into sewing them.

Smiling, Lucy settled back in her chair. Video chat technology had been a godsend during the shutdown, but there was no substitute for being in the same room with her clients. When she saw only a face on a screen, she missed so many subtle clues to her clients' thoughts and feelings—a sudden shift in the sitting position, clutching the other hand, a wagging foot—all those little motions that told a story beyond the words the client spoke. Now, a mask would cover part of the face, a different deficit. No matter. Lucy would pay closer attention to everything else, especially the eyes.

She said a little prayer as she always did before she began counseling sessions. She asked God for the grace to be patient and kind and to reflect

Her divine love. When the knock at the door came, Lucy ended her prayer and crossed herself.

"Mother Lucy, your eleven o'clock is here."

"Send her in, please."

Jodi looked sheepish. "She refuses to wear a mask."

"We can't force them." Lucy sighed. "Let her in." Fortunately, the visitors' chairs were positioned beyond the recommended distance, so there was less risk.

Olivia Enright entered the room with a frown. She had perfect posture. Her summer-weight pants suit fit perfectly. Her hair and makeup were perfect. *It must take a lot of effort to be that perfect*, thought Lucy.

The client attempted to approach, presumably to shake hands, but Lucy raised her hand like a crossing guard. "If you don't mind staying behind the tape on the floor, I'd appreciate it. We're trying to keep everyone safe."

Ms. Enright made a face but retreated to the other side of the tape. "You people are really being ridiculous, you know. We have to learn to live with this virus."

"Yes, we do, but I'd rather learn to live with it than die from it."

Ms. Enright gave Lucy a pointed once-over. "You look pretty healthy, Reverend Bartlett…and young. I doubt you're even in the high-risk group."

"No, I'm a little younger, but my doctor gives me advice about safe practices, and I try to follow them."

"Your doctor? Dr. Stolz?"

"Yes."

"She referred me to you."

"Yes, I know. She wanted a psych consult before she prescribed benzodiazepines."

"A formality really. I could get them from my New York physician."

"But you came for an appointment anyway. Didn't you?"

"Yes, it seemed more efficient."

"Spending an hour with me doesn't seem very efficient, but let's see." Lucy gestured to a chair. "Have a seat and we'll talk."

Ms. Enright sat down. She took in the room in a glance, then focused on Lucy's framed diplomas and licenses on the wall. "So, you're another one."

"Another one what?"

"Someone who switched careers. I remember you as a principal soprano at the Metropolitan Opera."

Lucy braced herself. She hated when this subject came up. "Yes, I sang at the Met."

"I was on the board for a time. Not in your era, however." Ms. Enright squinted as she studied Lucy's theology and social work degrees. She scrutinized the bachelor of music diploma from Juilliard. "At least, you don't try to hide it. I've had to dig to find out about the others. I've come to learn that my doctor was a famous breast surgeon, my bathroom renovator was an award-winning architect. Now, I learn my therapist was an opera star. This town is full of has-beens."

With effort, Lucy restrained her reaction. Her clients weren't usually so provocative. "We don't think of it that way. We see it as walking a new path. It's good to reinvent yourself from time to time."

"Yes, I'm sure, but I've yet to discover what my new path will be."

"I hear you're on the town council and very active in the Rotary and other civic activities."

"I am. I believe in keeping busy. Now that I'm a full-time resident, I've taken an interest in the town."

"What did you do before you came to Hobbs?"

"I founded the Enright Fund, one of the most successful hedge funds on Wall Street."

"But you're retired now?" Lucy asked, gently leading.

"Not voluntarily. My son was involved in some questionable trading practices, and my family sold our shares, some of it for damages."

"I'm sorry. That must have been difficult."

Ms. Enright smirked. "Difficult is an understatement. I'm surprised you don't know about the scandal. It was the headline in the financial news for months."

"I have my portfolio managed professionally, so I don't usually read the financial news."

"You should, you know," said Ms. Enright with a scolding look. "It doesn't matter who manages your portfolio." That sounded exactly like the kind of advice Liz liked to give, but there were many more interesting things to read about than money.

Lucy settled back in her chair and studied her client. "Tell me why you need tranquilizers. Dr. Stolz mentioned panic attacks."

"Yes, although, I don't have them quite as often now. Mostly, I can't sleep at night. I wake up and then, I can't get back to sleep, especially when I start thinking about something."

"Thinking about what for example?"

"We're in a recession. The markets are being propped up with toothpicks. Once the reality of the pandemic fully cycles through the economy, there will be another downturn."

"Why does that worry you? Do you have a lot of money in the stock market?"

"Only a reasonable amount as a hedge against inflation. The country can't keep printing money. I've retreated to bonds, cash, precious metals… secure investments."

"So, a crash is not an imminent threat to you personally."

"No, but I spent my entire career thinking about the markets. I can't just stop."

Lucy studied the woman. She seemed much less hostile than when she had first arrived. Lucy could see from the set of her face and the level of her shoulders that she was more at ease. "This scandal that you alluded to, does it still trouble you?"

"Yes, of course. I left Wall Street in shame. My son killed himself."

"What?" Lucy hadn't meant to react so obviously, but she was stunned by the information and the casual way the woman had delivered it.

"That was also reported in the financial press that you don't read." Again, the scolding tone. "My son overdosed on drugs when his trading issues were discovered."

"Is that when the panic attacks began?"

"Yes, as a matter of fact."

"The suicide of a child is a horrible burden for any mother."

"Yes, especially because I was the one who pushed him into the questionable trades…not directly, of course, but I put pressure on him to perform. I was his boss."

"That must make it even harder. I'm so sorry for your loss."

Ms. Enright glanced away. "I admit I wasn't a very good mother. Certainly, not a very attentive one. He was away at boarding school from the time he was old enough. I was busy building the business."

Lucy was beginning to realize Olivia Enright had enough issues to keep a therapist busy for years.

"Losing both your son and your business must have been devastating. Do you feel you properly mourned those losses?"

Ms. Enright's perfectly neutral expression suddenly changed to disdain. "I don't believe in such self-indulgence."

Lucy couldn't stop her brows from rising. She hated stereotypes, but her client certainly fit the myth that Wall Street traders were ruthless. Unfortunately, ruthless people were often equally hard on themselves and the people they loved.

"Ms. Enright, I think you could benefit from one of my bereavement groups. There's one for parents who have lost–"

"No groups! I'm not going to air my problems in front of the people in this town."

"But you're telling me."

"Only because Dr. Stolz insisted."

"But you could have called your New York doctor and avoided all this. So, why come to me?"

Ms. Enright gave Lucy a long, measuring look. "I've heard good things about you, as a priest and a counselor. I'm an Episcopalian. I always meant to come to one of your services. I've been curious."

"Why curious?"

"I hear that you're married to a woman."

"That's true. I am," Lucy confirmed.

"I'm a lesbian."

"Oh," said Lucy. This time she managed to keep her eyebrows from jumping up.

"That information is obviously not for public consumption."

"I'm ethically bound as a priest and a therapist to keep everything you tell me confidential."

"I assumed as much, but you never know. And I assume, since Dr. Stolz referred me, that you will share what I'm telling you."

"Not necessarily. I only tell her what she needs to know to make a medical diagnosis and decide on a prescription. The other details are irrelevant."

"I'm glad to hear that."

"But I don't think drugs will solve your problem. In my opinion, you could benefit from counseling."

Ms. Enright's lips curled into a supercilious smile. "Do you need business, Reverend Bartlett?"

Lucy was surprisingly insulted by the question, especially because it was uncomfortably close to the truth. Since the church had been closed for the pandemic, revenue to the parish had dropped off sharply. But the thought of recommending therapy for profit would never cross Lucy's mind. She tried to think of a way to respond without sounding defensive.

"I wasn't suggesting that *I* be your therapist. I could recommend therapists in Portsmouth or Portland, where no one would know you."

Ms. Enright frowned as she studied Lucy. "In fact, I think you are exactly the right person to be my therapist. When can we begin?"

Despite the niggling reluctance in the back of her mind, Lucy said, "We can begin now, if you wish."

"I do, as a matter of fact."

Lucy sat back in her chair. "All right. Let's start with the basics. How old are you?"

"I'm sixty."

"Do you have a partner?"

"No, I'm single."

"Family?"

"No. My parents are deceased. I haven't spoken to my siblings in years. I am estranged from my daughter-in-law and my grandchildren. I took my son's side in the separation. We haven't spoken since."

"Does that make you sad?"

"The woman is a bitch. No. But I do miss the children."

"Tell me about them."

"The older one is twelve. Her younger sister is ten."

"What are their names?"

"Sharon and Jessica. I haven't seen them in three years. I can scarcely imagine what they look like now."

For a moment, Lucy saw a flash of vulnerability. Then her client's face resumed its deadpan expression.

"So, you live alone. You don't have close family," Lucy recapped. "What about friends?"

Ms. Enright smiled sadly and glanced away. "Not many. I had a lot of casual acquaintances when I was in business, but they've mostly abandoned me. I suppose they were embarrassed by the scandal. The boards of charities removed me so fast my head spun. I wasn't even involved in the questionable trading. Guilt by association, I suppose."

Even while describing what for anyone would be painful and extremely difficult, Olivia remained remarkably calm. She never squirmed. Her hands were perfectly still and relaxed. Her face was a mask of composure. Lucy realized this must be a deliberately learned behavior useful for business negotiations.

"How do you occupy your time?" Lucy asked.

"I read. I am teaching myself Italian with online courses. Before this miserable pandemic, I planned to go to Italy. I rented a restored villa in Tuscany, and I was very much looking forward to an extended vacation."

"Anything else that gives you pleasure?"

"I listen to music. I'm very fond of opera. I have some of your recordings, by the way. I enjoy them very much."

"I'm glad to hear it."

"A shame you quit singing. I suppose now you sing in church. When will you reopen?"

"I don't know. Soon, I hope. Once the bishop says we can."

"Good. I'll be there for your 'grand reopening.' Now, will you tell Dr. Stolz I can have the Alprazolam?"

The abrupt switch of topic startled Lucy. Apparently, Ms. Enright had decided the conversation had gone on long enough and wanted to get down to business.

"I'll recommend that you get the prescription, if you agree to come to a few more sessions with me."

"That's blackmail."

"Maybe, but you can always call your doctor in New York. You'd be on my pastoral counseling time for another four sessions. There will be no charge."

"I'll pay, nonetheless, because I can."

"Thank you. We are grateful. These are difficult times."

"Yes, they are." Ms. Enright studied her for a long moment, then smiled. "You're quite a remarkable woman, Reverend Bartlett. What do your parishioners call you?"

"Most call me Mother Lucy."

"'Mother Lucy' it is, then."

❖❖❖

After a long day of sessions, Lucy was glad to hear that Erika had accepted an invitation from Sam for a cookout. The weather had turned suddenly warm, so Lucy looked forward to a swim in the pond. The water was still cold but warm enough for a quick dip.

Lucy felt the cares of the day seep away as she floated on her back and looked at the brilliantly blue sky overhead. For the exercise, she swam out to the floating dock and back again. After a dozen laps, the chilly temperature of the pond finally got to her. She hauled herself out of the water. Erika got up to hand her a towel.

"Oh, that felt so good!" After Lucy dried herself, she spread out the towel and lay down on it. The filtered sunlight felt good, but even through closed eyes, she could feel Erika admiring her.

"Lust is one of the deadly sins," Lucy said, turning her face in Erika's direction and opening one eye.

"I don't think that applies to one's wife," Erika replied, grinning. "It's criminal that a priest can be so sexy."

Sam glanced at Lucy. "I have to agree with Erika. In a bikini, you are X-rated."

"Don't be silly. I'm fifty-six and fat."

"You're not fat," protested Sam. "Are you crazy?"

"She's vain," said Erika. "Don't encourage her."

Lucy sat up. "I'm thinking about asking Liz for a referral about my jowls."

"What jowls?" asked Erika. "You're can't be serious. If you weren't a priest, you could be a model!"

"My mother was a model…before she became an opera singer."

"I remember you telling me."

"I'm beginning to sag," said Lucy, feeling her jawline.

"You are not!" Erika protested.

"Yes, I am. I noticed this morning in the mirror."

"Don't be ridiculous. You look fine!"

"I'll leave you two to duke it out while I put the burgers on," Sam said, getting up. "Thank you for bringing the potato salad, Erika, and the cole slaw."

"German-style. I hope you don't mind. My mother's recipes."

"Looks delicious." Sam headed into the house.

"You don't think Liz will be angry that we're socializing outside of our social bubble?" asked Lucy, sitting cross-legged. She arranged her towel around her shoulders. The little breeze off the pond was cool.

"Oh, I'm sure she knows. Everyone is so tired of this bloody pandemic. We need to be with other people. Besides, Sam is really careful." Erika tossed her towel in Lucy's direction. "Put it over your legs. I can see the goose bumps."

"She's so excited about this contract with Olivia Enright."

"Yes, it's a nice commission," said Erika. "Good for her. That woman knows a lot of wealthy people in this town. The right referrals could really help Sam's business." Erika studied Lucy with a cool look. "You aren't really thinking about plastic surgery?"

Lucy laughed. "No, I'm not serious. I'm not that vain."

"I didn't think so, but nothing you do or say surprises me anymore."

"Good. I like to keep you guessing. Makes our relationship more interesting, don't you think?"

"It does, but you shouldn't do that in front of people who don't know you as well as I do. They might get the wrong idea."

"I don't care." Lucy wrapped the towel tighter and hugged herself.

"Is everything all right, love? You are a bit muted tonight."

"It was a tough day. Olivia Enright is going to be my client too."

"Really?" said Erika. Her pale, blue eyes were large with curiosity. "Does she have problems?"

"You know I can't talk about it," scolded Lucy.

"Yes, of course." Erika looked pensive. "The way Sam was going on about the woman's looks, I think she may be interested in her. Is she a lesbian?"

Lucy shrugged.

Erika frowned. "All right, Mother Lucy. You know something. What is it?"

"I can't say."

"I know you can't. But you don't want Sam to get into trouble, do you?"

"No, but there's nothing we can do. Unfortunately."

"Oh, dear," said Erika, glancing toward the house.

5

Brenda Harrison turned the corner and noticed a familiar SUV parked in her driveway. As Hobbs' chief of police, Brenda always tried to set a good example, but she stepped on the gas pedal and deliberately exceeded the speed limit.

She'd given Cherie the key when they'd decided to move in together. Back then, everything had been going so well. Brenda had cleaned out a bedroom in her Colonial, so Cherie could have a room of her own. Brenda had lined up her friends with trucks to help move Cherie's things. Everything had been put in place for a Memorial Day weekend move. Then a black man in Minneapolis was killed by a cop, who knelt on the poor man's neck until he couldn't breathe.

When the story broke on the evening news, Cherie was triggered by her own sad experience of police violence. A trooper had pulled over Cherie's obviously black half-sister for a broken taillight. When she didn't move fast enough, he shot her. He apologized profusely to Cherie, who could pass for white, for hitting her with the bullet that went right through her sister. Ever since, Cherie had hated guns and cops.

In an instant, all the careful work of the people who had helped Cherie get over her PTSD—Lucy, Liz, and Brenda—had become unraveled. Panicked, Cherie lashed out at Brenda, who vainly tried to calm her. Then she stormed out of the house. They'd barely spoken since. For over a week, they'd been communicating in texts that said just three words: *I love you.* If they loved each other, why were they apart?

The Floyd case was somehow different from the countless others that had come before it. The images were shocking, even to Brenda. The murder of a black man, who later turned out to be innocent, was so obviously callous and hateful that it made a powerful impression. There were demonstrations against racism all over the world, but, in Brenda's house in the small Maine town of Hobbs, two new lovers had been torn apart.

When Brenda opened the front door, she could hear Cherie singing in the kitchen. She sang well enough to qualify for solos in the church choir, but just the sound of Cherie's voice was music to Brenda's ears. The enticing aroma of spicy, Cajun beef stew cooking on the stove confirmed that Cherie was *really* home.

Brenda hung her hat and keys on the hooks by the door and took off her service belt. She dropped the magazine out of her gun, ejected the round from the chamber, and locked the pistol in the handgun safe in the closet. She performed each of these end-of-the-workday rituals carefully and slowly to prolong the sweet anticipation.

When Brenda turned around, she saw Cherie gazing at her with shining blue-green eyes. The next moment, she was in her arms, hugging her with all her might.

"Welcome, home, Chief Harrison," she said, turning her face up for a kiss.

"Welcome home to you, girlfriend." Brenda allowed herself to get lost in the feel of Cherie's sweet, warm mouth until she had to reach out to the wall for balance.

"Oh! I've missed you," said Cherie, hugging her close. Her soft breasts below Brenda's felt so good.

"I'm so surprised to see you. What happened?"

"This." Cherie whipped her phone out of her pocket. She flipped to a news story from *The Portland Press Herald*.

Brenda took the phone and held it back a little because, as much as she hated to admit it, she'd soon need reading glasses. The headline proclaimed "Maine Police Chiefs Protest Brutality." The lead photo showed a contingent of Cumberland and York County police chiefs assembled on the steps of the Portland City Hall. Brenda expanded the photo to see the detail. Along with the other chiefs, she stood at parade rest behind Westbrook's Chief Roberts as she addressed the crowd. The other photo in the story showed Brenda at the podium, making a speech in support of Black Lives Matter. She decided that, despite the extra pounds a wide-angle lens added in photos, she didn't look bad.

"You're my hero!" said Cherie, throwing her arms around her and squeezing her until she could barely breathe.

As she returned the hug, Brenda silently thanked the publicity director of the Maine Police Chiefs Association for recommending the photo op. The publicity was good for the department, but Cherie's return was a welcome side benefit.

"Aren't you hot in that tie?" asked Cherie, her sensitive fingers teasing the knot open and pulling the tie through Brenda's collar. She tossed it over her shoulder. "You don't need that anymore. And look at all these buttons!" Cherie smiled playfully as she unbuttoned Brenda's police blouse.

"Are you undressing me?" asked Brenda incredulously.

"That's one way to get you out of this damn uniform."

Brenda tried to stop Cherie from unfastening more buttons by grasping her hands. "I haven't showered since this morning."

Hanging on to the button she was opening, Cherie sniffed Brenda's armpit. "You don't smell bad. It's your scent. Kind of sexy actually. Your pheromones." She gave the armpit another sniff. "You're excited, aren't you?"

"Pent-up demand."

"Oh, baby, I know what you mean!"

Brenda let Cherie's hands go, and she continued unbuttoning her blouse. As she pulled the shirt tails out of her pants, she kissed the top of Brenda's breasts.

"This is kind of fun," said Cherie, licking in the cleavage. "A little salty there, but nice. Let's see what else you got." When Cherie looked up, those beautiful, blue-green eyes were full of mischief. She held Brenda's gaze while she opened the tab of her pants and unzipped the fly. "This is one of my therapy assignments from Mother Lucy, you know. I'm supposed to undress a cop."

"Just any cop?"

"No, only the Hobbs police chief. She's the only cop I'm interested in." Cherie nudged Brenda's trousers down her hips and let them drop to the floor. She backed her up to the bench they used to put on their shoes. "Have a seat, Chief Harrison. I need to help you out of your pants and shoes. Wait. Let's get rid of the panties while we're at it."

"Have you lost your mind?" asked Brenda, grinning, as Cherie pulled them down.

"Sh, girl. Sit down and let's get rid of these shoes." Brenda sat down. After Cherie untied and pulled off the service shoes, Brenda was embarrassed to see one of her black socks was threadbare at the heel. Cherie picked it up and stared at it. "Well, that can go away." She tossed it aside and pulled off Brenda's pants and panties. "Now, sit back and relax."

Brenda leaned against the wall. Her eyes grew wide when Cherie took her legs and put them over her shoulders. "What have we here?" asked Cherie, stroking her gently. "Nice. Very nice. Very wet too." She watched Brenda's face as she stroked her. "Feel good, baby?"

Brenda could hardly speak, it felt so good. "Yes. Good," she choked out.

"Now, I'm going to give you a nice, deep, welcome-home kiss." Cherie took Brenda's clit in her mouth and sucked gently. Her tongue teased for a moment before slipping into her vagina. It emerged to lick outside, gently circling but not quite touching the most sensitive spots. She stroked with her fingers again. "I like your scent. You're always so clean, most of the time the only thing I can smell is soap. You know that vaginas clean themselves, don't you? And pretty efficiently too."

"Cherie, please don't give me a medical lecture while you've got me so hot."

"Sorry, sweetie. I just don't want you to come too fast."

"You're torturing me."

"I know. Do you like it?"

"No. I mean yes. Please…"

"All right. You're one of *those* girls. No patience." Cherie slid her fingers inside Brenda and then licked her clit delicately. Brenda clutched the edge of the bench. When the orgasm came, she saw stars. But Cherie continued her efforts and Brenda came again. Twice, in fact. Cherie gave her clit a little peck of a kiss, and slid Brenda's legs off her shoulders. "I'll have to try that undressing trick again soon. It worked better than I expected."

"What about you?" asked Brenda reaching for her.

Smiling, Cherie gently slid out of her arms. "You'll have to wait 'til after dinner. A little, sweet dessert for my best girl. Now, go put some clothes on. You're half naked!"

It was true. The only thing Brenda was wearing was her open shirt and bra. She got up to pick up the parts of her uniform scattered all over the floor. Cherie yanked back the socks. "These are going in the trash." As Brenda bent to pick up her panties, Cherie gave her behind an appreciative caress, then put her fingers inside her.

"That's wicked," said Brenda. "Now, you're taking unfair advantage."

"You're right." Cherie withdrew her fingers and gave them a seductive lick. "Get dressed. I'll pour you a glass of wine."

Brenda ran upstairs. After she hung up her uniform, she decided to take a quick shower. Despite what Cherie said, she felt sweaty after the busy day, and the beating water refreshed her. As she reached between her legs to wash, she could feel how swollen she was, which made her think of Cherie's skillful tongue and fingers. What an incredible lover she was, and they were just beginning!

It was a warm evening, so Brenda put on a pair of shorts and a T-shirt. She skipped the bra because she was home now and wanted to be comfortable. Barefoot, she went down to the kitchen.

"Your dinner smells so good," said Brenda. Cherie smiled and handed her a glass of red wine.

"This is the same wine you brought over as a peace offering. Remember? The day after you almost got into a fight in that bar."

Brenda blushed a little at the memory. Bringing a guy-magnet like Cherie into a rowdy, country-western bar for their first date ranked as one of Brenda's all-time worst misfires. Fortunately, they'd gotten past that episode. Lucy had talked Cherie through her fear of cops, and Liz had helped her get over her fear of guns. Cherie was still afraid of them, but not so terrified that she couldn't be in the same room with one. A good thing. It's hard to be a cop's girlfriend and not encounter guns.

Cherie tapped her glass against Brenda's. "Welcome home, Chief Harrison."

"I thought you did that already."

"That was just the appetizer. Wait till you see the dessert!" Cherie raised a blond brow. "I heard you taking a shower up there. Don't you believe me?"

"I thought you were the clean freak. You're the one who told me about the dirty lime wedges I stuff into my beer bottles."

"That's different." Cherie reached under Brenda's T-shirt and gave her breast a caress. "I like it when you don't wear a bra. Easy access." She pinched her nipple and the sensation went straight to Brenda's brain, where it exploded like fireworks.

Brenda swallowed hard. She'd never been with a woman as sexy as Cherie. Marcia had always let Brenda initiate sex. This was a new experience. Brenda wasn't sure what she thought about it, but she was willing to see where it led.

Cherie gestured to a chair. "Tell me about your day while I put up the rice."

Brenda took a sip of wine and gave Cherie a running commentary on her day. It had been busy, but pretty average, with meetings and the usual fires to put out. Cherie listened attentively, as if what Brenda was telling her was the most amazing news she'd ever heard.

"What about your day? How is it being back in the office?"

Cherie made a little face. "It's hard maintaining the hygiene protocol so carefully. The patients call on the phone when they're in the parking lot, and we let them in one at a time. They wear masks. We wear masks and gloves. I feel so detached from my patients. But it's good to see them in person."

"Do you think this Telehealth thing will catch on?"

"I do. And for some things it's just fine. Most of the time, I can diagnose someone from hearing them recite their symptoms. Sometimes, an examination is really important. You can ask someone to open their mouths and show their throat and tongue, but I can't shine a light down it to really see. It's a mixed bag."

"I get it," said Brenda.

"You do?" Cherie looked delighted at the idea.

"Sometimes, you just need to be there."

"Yes," said Cherie. "Thank you for understanding."

"I try. I don't know what your job is like, but I listen."

Cherie reached across the table and took Brenda's hand. "Thank you. That's what I love about you. I'm sorry I've shut you out."

"It's a hard time for you. This police violence must be terrifying for someone who's witnessed it firsthand. But please, give me the benefit of the doubt. I'm on your side."

Cherie squeezed Brenda's hand. "I have an enormous request."

"Yes?"

"There is a Black Lives Matter demonstration in Portland next Saturday. Will you come and wear your uniform?"

Brenda took a deep breath. "I'll come, but I can't wear my uniform."

"But I want people to see there are good cops like my Brenda."

"There are many good cops like me, but when I wear my uniform, I'm representing the Hobbs PD. I can't wear it to a public demonstration. And I can't get arrested."

"I can't either," Cherie admitted. "I could lose my license."

"Then, I hope you understand. I can go to represent myself, Brenda Harrison, ally and friend to the Black Lives Matter movement, but not as a police officer. If the demonstration were in Hobbs, and I was on duty, that would be different."

"Then what would you do?"

"Apart from supervising my officers policing the crowd? I would take a knee."

Cherie looked momentarily overcome. "Brenda, I know you are a good woman, and your heart is in the right place. Please be patient with me."

"Of course. I love you!"

The timer on the stove pinged. "Our dinner is ready," said Cherie, getting up. "Let's eat so we can get to dessert." She gave Brenda a sly look.

6

"Hello!" called Lucy's voice. "Anyone home?"

"Out here! On the deck!" Liz called back. She was threading the line through the hole in the reel, and it was finicky work, so she didn't want to get up.

Lucy came out to the deck from the porch. "Your garage door was open," she explained. "I hope you don't mind that I let myself in."

"You're always welcome here, Lovely Lucy." Liz finally got the line through the hole.

Lucy bent to kiss Liz on the top of the head. "What are you doing?"

"Putting new line on my saltwater reels. The salt degrades them after a while, and they break at exactly the wrong moment." Liz tied a one-handed surgical knot.

"That's pretty cool," said Lucy, watching.

"Before surgical staples, knot tying was as important to surgeons as to Boy Scouts."

"Show me that again." Lucy sat down next to Liz on the bench.

Liz deftly looped and tied another knot.

"That's amazing," said Lucy, fascinated. Her green eyes carefully studied Liz's face. Whenever Lucy gave her that particular look, Liz squirmed because she suspected Lucy was analyzing her. "Do you miss surgery, Liz?" she asked in a sympathetic voice.

Liz put down the spool of fishing line and thought about it. "Sometimes. I don't miss the routine procedures, like lumpectomies. They get pretty boring after a while, especially if you specialize like I did. But every once in a blue moon, you get something really interesting or challenging. I certainly don't miss being an administrator. I hated that."

"But you run your practice."

"That's different because I call all the shots. I don't have a top-heavy administration breathing down my neck. It's my little business. I grew up in a small business, you know."

"Your parents' corporate design company in New York."

"That's why I have a soft spot in my heart for small businesses. I enjoy running one, even filing the government forms and the accounting."

"Liz, that's just weird."

"I know. I'm a Virgo. What can I say?" Liz mounted the reel on the rod. She stuck a pencil through the hole in the spool of fishing line. "Here. Make yourself useful. Hold the pencil by the ends and maintain some tension while I wind on the line." Liz began to crank the handle of the reel and the line came spinning on. "That's good," Liz encouraged. "Maintain the tension or we'll have fishing line all over the place." Liz cranked faster and soon all the line was transferred to the reel. "Thank you."

"Glad to be useful."

Liz glanced at the porch door. "What are you doing here?"

"Looking for Maggie. We were going to go over the hymns for Sunday worship."

"She's not here. She's in Webhanet talking to Tony about a virtual season at the Playhouse."

"Is that possible?"

Liz raised her shoulders. "I have no idea. What do I know about the theater?"

"A lot from what I've heard. Maggie told me you were the stage manager when you were in college."

"That was only to be around Maggie. In those days, she had a starring role in every production. When she wasn't going to class or sleeping, she was at a rehearsal."

"Such a shame she never realized her dream of being an actress."

Liz put down the reel she'd been lubricating with petroleum jelly. "Most aspiring actresses and singers never make it." Liz gave Lucy a probing look. "You did, but you gave it up."

"You know it wasn't my idea. Alex was very powerful at the Met. He pushed to get Kathleen Battle fired. Said he didn't like some uppity, black woman acting like a prima donna."

"But she was a prima donna. Why shouldn't she act like one? He sounds like a horrible man, but he's dead now. Prostate cancer that metastasizes to the liver is an ugly way to die."

"I never wished any suffering on him."

"Still. Karma is a bitch. A lot of men, who abused women, are getting theirs." Liz glanced away from her work to engage Lucy's eyes. "Will you ever tell Emily about her father and what he did to you?"

Lucy sighed. "What good would it do to know she's the product of a rape? If she asks or finds out somehow, I won't lie to her."

Liz mounted the second reel and poked the pencil through the spool of fishing line. "Here. You did such a good job the first time." She threaded the line through the hole and tied another surgeon's knot.

"Will you teach me how to do that?"

"Why? You thinking of taking up surgery now?" asked Liz, winding on the line.

"No, I just like to learn new things. Maybe you can take me fishing sometime. You know, with Brenda and Sam."

Liz eyed Lucy to size up the seriousness of her intent. Fishing with Brenda and Sam was usually an excuse to drink beer and be rowdy, which didn't seem like an activity that would appeal to Lucy. Next to Maggie, Lucy was the most feminine woman she knew, always fully made-up, toenails painted, and, when she wasn't in clericals, wearing a pretty dress.

"I'm going out fishing now," said Liz. "Want to come?"

"Really?" asked Lucy, clapping her hands like an excited child.

"We probably won't be back until after dinner. You should let Erika know."

"She's completely absorbed in that paper she's writing, but I'll call her, of course. She can give Emily some dinner."

Liz looked over Lucy's outfit. She was wearing a short-sleeved clerical blouse, a black skirt, and black pumps. "You're not really dressed for fishing."

"I keep shorts and a T-shirt and some sandals in the car for spontaneous visits to the beach."

"That'll do. You can change in the downstairs bathroom while I call Maggie to tell her we're heading out."

When Lucy returned a few minutes later, she no longer looked like the rector of St. Margaret's. In cotton shorts, an oversized T-shirt and rafting sandals, she could be any other middle-aged woman. Not quite. No matter what Lucy wore, she was drop-dead gorgeous. She noticed Liz admiring her and raised an auburn brow.

"Liz..."

"Sorry. Can't help it."

Lucy followed the direction of Liz's gaze.

"I know my legs are still really white."

"I'm glad you're staying out of the sun after I took that lesion off your back. Redheads burn really easily. I have sunscreen on the boat." Liz tightened the screw in the reel and got up. "When I told Maggie I was taking you fishing, she laughed."

"I bet she did. Erika laughed too. But I like to buck people's expectations."

"I've noticed." Liz handed Lucy the fishing poles. "Here. Can you manage these? I want to lock up the house. You can go down the deck stairs."

Liz met Lucy in the driveway. She stowed the fishing poles in the bed of the truck. "Hold on. I want to get some beer out of the fridge in the garage. Will you drink beer?"

Lucy wrinkled up her nose. "If I have to."

"I have some of those little screw-off wine bottles. I'll put some in the cooler for you."

Liz put an assortment of craft beer in a small cooler and added a four-pack of mini wine bottles. Maggie had once said, "You always cater to Lucy." It had been an off-handed remark, but it had hit home, because it was true.

When Liz climbed into her truck, Lucy was already strapped in, ready to go.

"You don't get seasick, do you?" Liz asked, starting the engine.

Lucy gave her an impatient look. "You really think I'm a wuss, don't you?"

"No, way! You're Mother Lucy, superhero!"

Lucy seemed to like that remark. She smiled radiantly.

Liz stopped at the clam shack on the way to the harbor, where she bought lobster rolls, slaw, and chips. At the dock, she hopped out to buy some frozen mackerel from the bait shop. She handed Lucy the cooler to carry.

"You put the bait in with our sandwiches?"

Liz rolled her eyes. "Why does everyone ask me that question? It's just fish. You eat fish, don't you?"

Lucy wrinkled her nose in disgust.

"Okay, Lucy," said Liz, stopping, which forced Lucy to stop too. "If you're going fishing with me, you're going to have to put up with a little yuck. Can you do that?"

"Of course. I'm tougher than I look."

They walked down the ramp to the berth where Liz kept her boat. With the mooring line, Liz pulled the boat closer to the dock, so Lucy could grab the rails of the ladder. Once she was aboard, Liz handed up the cooler and the rods.

"It's so peaceful here at this time of the night," Lucy observed.

"That's why I fish."

"Not to catch fish?"

"I don't mind catching fish, but that's not why I fish. It's to be out on the water, to feel the waves rocking the boat. I can take in the vastness of the ocean and think."

"Meditation."

"Something like that."

Liz started the engine and put the poles in the holders at the back of the boat. "Find a seat. I'm going to take us out," she said, casting off the mooring lines and looping them over the piers. She let the engine idle for a few minutes to warm up, then she carefully navigated out of the harbor.

Once they were in open water, she opened up the throttle. She saw the childlike pleasure on Lucy's face and smiled.

Liz navigated to a place where she knew the current would take them slowly back to shore and turned off the engine. She cut up one of the frozen mackerel into chunks and baited their hooks. "This doesn't really count as fishing," she said. "There's no technique to trolling. Not like lake or stream fishing. The blue pole's yours, by the way." Liz nodded in its direction and wiped the bloody fish guts off her hands with a paper towel. She rinsed them in a bucket of water and squirted on some hand sanitizer before she flipped open a beer. "Beer?" she asked, offering it.

"I'll taste yours."

Lucy wrinkled up her nose, and Liz laughed. She handed Lucy one of the miniature bottles of chardonnay. "Not the best wine, but it's not beer." Liz sat down beside Lucy. "I needed this tonight," she said. "Our asshole-in-chief said people aren't wearing masks because they don't like him. Can you believe it?"

"Yes, unfortunately, I can."

"We're just trying to keep people safe and healthy, and they're turning masks into a political football!"

Lucy reached over and patted Liz's thigh. "Stop thinking about it. Remember you came out here to relax. Take some deep breaths and enjoy the smell of the sea air. It's good for you." Lucy gave her one of those radiant smiles that compelled a smile in return. "You're always taking care of everyone else, Liz. You need to take care of yourself too. We need you."

Liz emitted a long, wistful sigh. "I know. I can't sleep at night."

"Another one. We're going to have to start a club."

"Just don't invite Olivia Enright. I don't want to see her face at three o'clock in the morning."

"I don't know…She's an attractive woman. Not bad to look at."

"You're not supposed to be looking."

"I have eyes, Liz. I can't help it. Didn't you say the same thing earlier?" Lucy turned in her seat. "Did you see the message I posted to you in the secure portal?"

"Yes, I already wrote her script for Alprazolam."

"There's a lot going on there," said Lucy.

Liz knew she was being deliberately vague. One thing Lucy took seriously was professional confidence. "I figured as much."

"I convinced her to sign on for another four sessions."

Liz raised her brows. "Good for you. But you can seduce anyone to do anything for you."

"I don't really try. They just do."

"You're naturally seductive. It helps to be beautiful."

"I don't know. I found it a deficit from time to time. When I was an opera singer, I wanted people to appreciate my voice, not just my face. Same with being a priest."

"But being gorgeous doesn't hurt."

Lucy looked doubtful. "Sometimes, I wish I looked like everyone else."

"I don't. I love to look at you and see your big smile. It makes my heart happy."

Lucy's green eyes searched hers. Liz took Lucy's face in her hands and placed a soft kiss on her lips. When there was no protest, she kissed her again. This time Lucy's mouth became soft and open, so Liz tentatively explored it with her tongue. As the kiss grew more intense, she felt small hands on her shoulders, gently pushing her back.

"Stop, Liz," Lucy whispered, but the misty look of desire in her eyes conflicted with her words. "We can't do this."

"You don't really want me to stop. You want me. I could feel it in your kiss."

"Yes. I do want you." Lucy sighed and turned away. "Maybe it was a bad idea to come out here alone with you."

"There's a comfy bed in the cabin below," said Liz. "Who would ever know?"

"I would know." Lucy's voice sounded sad. "Oh, Liz, I love you, but we're not going to make love, and you know it. Hold me. I need to feel your strength." Liz put her arms around her and held her tight. "When you hold me, I can feel your physical strength, but I can also feel your moral strength. I know you'll always do the right thing. I count on you. You're my swan knight. Remember?"

"So romantic," said Liz in a cynical voice. "But I want you. I can't deny it."

"At this moment, I want you too, but we're both married to other people, and I take my marriage vows seriously."

"Do you love Erika?"

"Absolutely. Do you love Maggie?"

"I do, but that doesn't mean I'm not attracted to you." Liz let Lucy go and reached for her beer. "I married Maggie because she needed reassurance. Maybe that wasn't the best reason."

"You told me you married her because you love her."

"Yes, that too." Liz sat forward and rested her elbows on her knees. "Forgive me for making an ass of myself."

"You're not an ass, Liz. Sexual attraction is complicated." Lucy rubbed Liz's back between the shoulder blades. "Maybe because I'm so passionate, I find Erika's cool personality attractive. She's so smart. Like you. I always wanted to be that smart."

"You're no slouch in the brains department, Lucy."

"Yes, but I'm not a genius like you or Erika. I'm surrounded with geniuses. My daughter. My father-in-law. Sometimes, I'm jealous because I can't go to those lofty intellectual places where all of you go."

"What does that say about you? History is full of women attracted to poor, misunderstood geniuses."

Lucy laughed. "You're not poor, Liz. And you're not misunderstood. I see exactly who you are. You want people to think you're the strong, silent type, but underneath, you're burning with passion, and not just sexual passion…a passion for medicine, for helping people, for social justice. That's what I find so attractive about you."

"Not many people know that about me. Don't spread it around."

Lucy tapped her finger against her lips. "Not a word." She reached for

Liz's hand and gave it a little squeeze. "Now, my dear, beautiful, loving friend, stop putting the moves on me and let's just enjoy being out here on the water. Please?"

Reluctantly, Liz nodded. "Would you like a lobster roll?"

Lucy's warm smile let Liz know she'd already been forgiven.

"Sure. Thanks."

❈❈❈

When they returned to Liz's house two hours later, Liz hauled two stripers out of the back of the truck. "Nice catch," Liz said as she hosed off Lucy's with water from the front spigot. "I'll clean it for you tomorrow and bring over the fillets."

"I hate to ask, but…"

"You'd rather I keep them in the freezer."

"For now. We don't have the room."

"Or you and your gang can come for dinner, and I'll grill it for you."

"I like that idea even better." Lucy pointedly landed a kiss on her cheek. "Maybe no more mouth kissing for a while," she said with a firm look.

"You smell like fish."

"So do you."

"Say hi to Erika and Emily," Liz called after Lucy as she headed to her car.

"To Maggie too!"

Liz hosed off the other fish. They were both a good size. She'd gutted and beheaded them on the boat to get them into the cooler. Even so, it was a tight fit in the refrigerator.

She opened the door to the house. "Catch anything?" Maggie called to her from the living room.

"We each got a good size striper. I invited them over for grilled fish tomorrow." Liz stood in the doorway and blew Maggie a kiss. "I need a shower. I smell like fish."

"I know. I can smell you from here."

Liz trudged up the stairs. She still refused to take the elevator to the third floor, even when she was tired. She took her time in the shower. Because her profession demanded so much cleanliness, she enjoyed being filthy once in a while, but after fishing, she liked to give herself a thorough wash. She shampooed her hair. Then she decided her legs felt a little bristly, so she shaved them.

She dried herself with her favorite bath towel and walked naked into the bedroom.

"Maggie! What are you doing here?" Liz was startled to see her wife, reading in bed. She was even more surprised to see her wearing one of her sexiest nightgowns. Nowadays, their encounters were less spontaneous. When they were under stress, as they were now, they made dates for sex.

Liz opened a drawer and took out a T-shirt.

"Leave that. You won't need it," said Maggie, putting her iPad on her night table. She motioned with a beckoning finger.

Liz wasn't about to refuse that invitation. She bounced on to the bed.

"This is a nice surprise."

"Well, you've been out for hours with Lucy, so I expect you're all horny by now."

Liz felt a quick, cold dread in the pit of her stomach. "Don't be silly," she protested, but she could hear the guilty tone in her voice. Maybe it was only her imagination because she felt guilty.

"I know you, Liz Stolz. You have a roving eye. Now, get over here, so I can remind you I'm your wife."

As always when they made love, Liz found the familiarity of Maggie's body comforting. She loved to caress and suck her soft breasts, thankful to still have them, despite the constant threat of the cancer recurring. She liked that Maggie enjoyed penetration and responded enthusiastically. The sex was always satisfying, so why would Liz even look at another woman?

Maggie caressed Liz's hair while she recovered from her orgasm. "Do you feel better now?" she asked.

"I always feel better after sex with you."

"I try to give you a long leash. You can look, but don't touch. My ex-husband played around…my ex-boyfriend…" The motion of Maggie's hand stopped.

Liz cringed, bracing for what might come next.

"If you cheat on me, Liz, it would break my heart."

7

As Erika headed to the bathroom, Lucy admired her naked buttocks. They were shaped like a perfect, inverted heart, tight and smooth for a woman of sixty-one. Lucy was almost tempted to hop out of bed and give that soft, white flesh a little pinch, but she felt languorous after morning sex and lay in bed gazing out the window instead.

The sex had been wonderful, both that morning and the night before. Erika always knew when to be aggressive or gentle, when the toys should come out of the drawer or when slow, natural sex was right. Erika's unerring perception of Lucy's needs and how to fulfill them left Lucy wondering why she had ever allowed another woman to kiss her.

Lucy finally decided to get up. She retrieved her nightgown from the floor, where it had landed during the night. She put on her bathrobe and fuzzy slippers, and headed downstairs for coffee. As she watched the dark liquid dribble into a cup, spitting and sputtering as it did, she wondered if she had done something to invite Liz's kiss. Her little flirtation with Liz had been fun up to now. No, it wasn't quite as innocent as everyone assumed. Not for Liz or for Lucy, but until last night they'd kept a tight rein on it. Guilt wasn't something Lucy gave much attention, but as soon as Erika had come to bed, Lucy had seduced her, hoping to blot out the scene on the boat with hot, sensual sex. It worked, briefly, but the memory of Liz's kiss wasn't gone, just momentarily forgotten.

Lucy had been attracted to Liz from the minute they'd met. After Lucy's first Christmas carol service at St. Margaret's, a tall, distinguished woman had come up to her and introduced herself. Lucy had instantly perceived her charisma, despite her casual manner and off-centered grin. Then, out of the blue, she'd invited Lucy to dinner.

That night, Lucy had seen Liz's warm, generous nature and her kindness to guests. She'd observed the dynamics between Liz and her pretty wife, how they gently teased one another but fit together perfectly. As an experienced marriage counselor, Lucy recognized the little dominance dance. Maggie liked to think she was in charge, but she always turned to the tall, gray-haired woman for guidance. Liz let Maggie think she ran the show, but she had the last word on anything of consequence.

In the after-dinner conversation, Lucy had learned that Liz was every bit as brilliant as Erika, just quieter about it. She didn't need to impress anyone with intellectual pyrotechnics. People instantly sensed that below the calm steadiness, Liz was a powerhouse—smart, accomplished, and a natural leader.

Lucy tried to remember when their flirtation began. She had felt Liz's eyes on her that first night at dinner, but then Erika, who had been practically falling over herself to get her attention, had distracted her. Erika's interest had taken her by surprise because it had been years since a woman had looked at her that way. No one ever guessed about Lucy. She always had to "come out." To find herself suddenly in a group of gay women, right in her own town, had been exciting. Obviously, they found her a curiosity, partly because of the collar she wore, but also because she had once been an opera star.

After dinner, it was Erika who'd occupied her attention. Lucy found herself lost in her pale eyes, the palest blue she'd ever seen, almost transparent. Watching from across the room, Liz's eyes were equally compelling. Passion burned in them like a blue flame. At the end of the evening, Liz had embraced her in a full-body hug. Feeling the soft breasts against her had caused a surprising jolt of arousal.

"Good morning, Mom," said a sleepy voice. Lucy jumped, and the memories instantly evaporated. She turned around to see Emily standing behind her. Her daughter had just gone through a growth spurt. Now, she was almost a head taller than her petite mother. She got her height and blue eyes from her father, but in every other way she resembled Lucy. As she bent to give her mother a kiss, her arms slipped around her waist. Emily's embrace was welcome after the spell of self-doubt. Lucy hugged her tightly, lingering a little to inhale the scent of her daughter's red hair.

"I love you, honey," Lucy whispered into her ear.

"Love you too, Mom."

Lucy gave her a tight squeeze and finally let her go. "What's on your agenda today?"

"I'm going to read on the beach for a while."

"Make sure you put on sunscreen." The precancerous mole Liz had removed from Lucy's back had given her a real scare. Now, she was more vigilant than ever. "Redheads like us are at higher risk for skin cancer, so we have to be careful."

"Mom…" Emily rolled her eyes. "I know all that."

"Never mind. Just do it for me. Please."

"Okay," said Emily, drawing out the word. "Now, can I get to the coffee maker, *please*?"

"Of course."

Lucy turned to add cream to her coffee and felt someone encircle her waist from behind.

"Good morning, luscious woman."

Lucy sensed a hand moving into her robe and gave it a light slap. "Someone's up early." Lucy turned to see Erika staring at Emily in surprise.

"Well, well, what have we here? Good morning, my dear. To what do we owe the pleasure?"

"The sun comes up so early now."

"That's why you must draw the shades. We're in the wrong time zone you know."

"Yes, I read about that. Why don't we get into the right time zone?"

"Because then we would be out of sync with the rest of the country, and that just won't do apparently." Erika filled a pod with coffee.

Lucy sat down beside her daughter at the kitchen table, but Emily's eyes were on her book. "What are you reading, honey?" Lucy asked.

"Susskind's book on quantum mechanics."

"Is it good?"

Emily shrugged and glanced at Erika. "For what it is, I suppose."

"I didn't enjoy it either," said Erika. "Although my father rather liked it."

Lucy despaired of ever understanding what her brainiac daughter and wife seemed to discuss so easily. She knew it was irrational, but it always made her feel so inferior. She couldn't understand a word, so she tuned them out while she sipped her coffee.

"Doesn't really sound like beach reading," she said, frowning.

"Anything you read on the beach is beach reading," replied Emily.

"Technically, yes," agreed Erika, sitting down at the table. "I think your mother means you should read something just for fun."

"This is fun. I mean, you can't really take it seriously. But I promised Stefan I would read it and give him my opinion, so I've got to finish it."

"Always good to keep your word," said Lucy, which earned her a dirty look. She was glad when Erika changed the subject.

"And what do you have on your plate this morning, Lovely Lucy?"

"My usual Monday morning counseling sessions."

Erika turned her pale eyes on her. "I'm not sure I like the idea of your seeing people in your office."

"I insist on keeping distance." Erika looked unconvinced, so Lucy added. "It helps me to see my clients' body language, the expressions on their faces. Well, even if it's only their eyes…with the masks."

Erika pursed her lips, which is how Lucy knew she wanted to say more but was holding back to avoid scolding her in front of Emily.

Lucy finished her coffee and put her cup in the dishwasher. "Speaking of agendas, I need to get a move on."

❈❈❈

Lucy glanced at the clock on her desk. Cherie had ten minutes left in her session. She'd been ranting nonstop about police violence. Lucy attempted to steer the conversation back to her personal feelings, but Cherie was stuck on her political outrage. Lucy found herself zoning out while she listened to the diatribe and tried to focus. Then Cherie asked her a question that forced her to pay attention.

"Are you going to wear your collar when you come to the BLM demonstration?"

"Well, yes, and my diversity stole."

"So how come you can wear your priest's uniform, but Brenda can't wear hers?"

Lucy faced the challenge in Cherie's eyes with one of her own. "That's asking a lot of Brenda, don't you think?"

"Why? She stood with all those police chiefs up in Portland."

"That was an official function, a gathering of the Maine Police Chiefs Association. Participating in a demonstration isn't the same."

"I don't get it. How is your collar different from her police uniform?"

"I'm ordained. Being a priest isn't just my job, it's who I am. Being Hobbs' police chief is Brenda's job, one I assume she wants to keep."

"Wearing her uniform would send a powerful message."

"It would, but I agree with her. It's not appropriate. It's one thing to go as private citizen, Brenda Harrison. Quite another to go as Chief Harrison of the Hobbs PD."

"Whose side are you on?"

"I'm on your side, Cherie. Stop making it about us and them. You may be part black, and we may be white, but we are all the same under the skin. As a medical professional with a science background, you know that even better than I do."

"Yes, and we only differ from chimps by one-point-two percent." Cherie grinned, and Lucy was glad to see some humor.

"Very funny."

Cherie sighed. "I'm trying."

"And so is Brenda. I think you're letting your politics get in the way of your personal relationships."

"The personal is political."

"Nice meme. Save it for Facebook or put it on a poster for Saturday's march, but leave it outside."

Cherie looked surprised. "I can't believe you said that. That's so harsh."

"I'm sorry it came across that way. Look. I completely understand your outrage over the political situation. Personally, I'm furious. Some nights I can't even watch the news. But you're channeling all your personal anger into this rather than dealing with it. And you're still making Brenda your target. Why? Brenda loves you."

At that, Cherie began to sob. She ripped open the packet of tissues on the table next to her. The ubiquitous tissue box found in every therapist's office had been replaced by individual packets for safety. Lucy sighed. She hadn't meant to be so hard on Cherie, but she knew that letting out the tears would be good for her.

After Cherie left, Lucy took a few minutes to catch up on the parish finances. Three and a half months of keeping the church closed had certainly depressed donations. Fortunately, Tom Simmons, the assistant rector, and Lucy had income from other sources, and it was summer, so they didn't have to pay the heating bill.

Lucy had asked Jodi to set up a Tithe.ly account on the parish website for online giving, but many of her parishioners were still out of work. They could barely feed their families. She couldn't expect them to squeeze out money for their church.

Suddenly remembering the cartoons from her childhood that showed moths flying out of an empty purse, Lucy cringed as she opened the revenue account. Her eyes scanned down the rows. An anonymous, single donation for twenty-five thousand dollars instantly jumped out. Lucy's mouth gaped at the sheer enormity of the sum.

She desperately hoped the donor wasn't Liz. She'd confessed to Liz how bad things were, and she wouldn't put it past her friend to throw an overly generous donation into the virtual collection plate. Lucy knew Hobbs Family Practice was struggling too. No, Lucy reasoned, it probably wasn't Liz. But then who?

There was a knock on the door, and it opened. "Mother Lucy, Olivia Enright is here to see you." She stepped back and the elegant woman came into the room. To Lucy's surprise, she was wearing a mask. It was a clever scarf that matched her outfit and could be pulled up to form a face covering.

"Thank you for wearing a mask," said Lucy.

Olivia nodded. "I've been listening to your sermons on the church Facebook page. You make a compelling argument for 'do unto others.'"

"I'm happy to know someone actually listens to my sermons. Thanks for telling me." Lucy gestured to the chair. "Have a seat."

"You're quite a remarkable woman, Mother Lucy. I'm so glad I found you."

8

Sam pulled the loops of her N95 dust mask over her ears and went to fetch the sledgehammer and a roll of plastic sheeting from the back of her truck. She found it hard to believe the Enright job had gone from initial consultation to demolition in just two weeks. The permit had been issued the same day she'd applied, partly because the planning office wasn't backed up like it was during the pre-pandemic boom. Besides, there wasn't much to approve in an interior renovation with no structural changes and minimal relocation of services.

Everything was on order and due for delivery in a week. In the end, Olivia had chosen the soaking tub in white. She took Sam's suggestions about coordinating fixtures without further discussion. Sam supposed that a successful hedge fund manager, who oversaw the investment of millions of dollars, would need to be decisive.

Sam was mentally planning the day's work while she waited for Olivia to open the front door. She did a double take when the door opened. Olivia was wearing a mask, but not just any mask. The beautiful fabric picked up the colors in her outfit.

"Good morning," said Olivia brightly. She glanced at the sledgehammer. "I see you're ready to knock down my house."

Sam laughed at the exaggeration. "I'm just breaking through the wall in your closet."

"Breaking through the wall in my closet," repeated Olivia, tilting her head to one side. "Now, that's an interesting metaphor."

Spatial rather than verbal subtleties usually made more sense to Sam, but she didn't miss the implication.

"Come in, dear," said Olivia. "That hammer looks heavy."

"It is, a little. If you don't mind, I'll leave it in the foyer while I get my other tools."

"All right. I'll leave the door unlocked. You know the way upstairs."

"I do. Thanks."

Olivia tilted her head again as if trying to put Sam in the right perspective. "You're quite sure of yourself, Samantha, aren't you?"

Sam tried to figure out what confidence had to do with knowing how to get to a place she had been before. The conversation was getting a little too weird, so Sam just shrugged and headed out to her truck.

Sam hated the prep work for a demolition, but she always did it meticulously because it meant less cleanup after the job. She brought in a roll of rosin paper and rolled it down the carpeted stairs, tucking it in carefully and securing the edges with masking tape as she went. In the bedroom, she taped a floor-to-ceiling sheet of plastic to keep the dust on the other side. Finally, she was ready to get to work. Knocking down the drywall in the bathroom only took a few minutes. She zipped out the screws with her drill. Instead of throwing the studs into the demolition dumpster at the transfer station, she always gave them to Liz to cut up for kindling.

Sam stuffed some disposable ear plugs into her ears and plugged in her recip saw. As she cut out the studs, she could visualize how this space would come together. She removed the closet hardware and trim before scoring the drywall on the bedroom side for removal. She hated it when people tried to patch the drywall instead, leaving witness lines everywhere. Sam preferred to create a smooth surface because it was more pleasing to the eye.

She carried the two-by lumber out to her truck with the idea that she'd drop it off at Liz's on her way home. When she got back upstairs, she was surprised to see Olivia sitting on the bed.

"Hey," said Sam.

"I just came up to see how far along you are," Olivia explained. "You're so quick." The way she said it sounded slightly suggestive, but her face was all innocence.

"This is a pretty easy job because the house is relatively new. In older homes, you never know what you'll find."

Sam had researched the provenance of the house in the town records when she'd pulled the permit. She'd discovered that it had been built by

Jason Enright. A quick Google search had confirmed that Jason was Olivia's son. There was a string of hits to the search, but Sam was in a hurry and not about to sit in the records office reading them.

"Samantha, I was wondering if you would like to join me for lunch. I broiled an enormous piece of salmon last night, so I made a salad from the leftovers."

"You don't have to feed me," said Sam, trying to deflect her. She never liked to get too friendly with clients in case there was trouble with the job.

"I don't mind giving you some lunch. I'd like to get to know you better."

"We'd have to sit at least six feet apart," said Sam, still trying to come up with excuses, but it had been hours since breakfast, and the salmon salad sounded good.

"I think we can manage that." Olivia smiled, evidently perceiving that she'd already persuaded Sam to join her. "Come out to the deck after you've had a chance to wash up."

As Sam washed in the bathroom sink, she imagined Olivia standing there to brush her teeth. No matter how hard Sam tried to picture Olivia with mussy hair and bleary eyes, she just couldn't. There was a well-lit vanity table in the powder room off the bathroom. Sam assumed that's where Olivia did her hair and put on makeup. Olivia always looked so carefully groomed, like she was ready for a photo shoot. Sam, who was overjoyed to leave professional attire behind, found Olivia's eternal perfection a little intimidating.

Sam washed the drywall dust off her face and arms. She shook it out of her hair. Her clothes were dusty too, but there was nothing she could do about that. She headed down the stairs, careful to avoid slipping on the rosin paper. She should remind Olivia to be careful too.

She went through the dining room to the enormous deck on the ocean side of the house. Olivia was waiting for her. She looked cool and relaxed in a polo shirt and capris. Her sandaled feet revealed the red toenails, which made Sam shiver a little.

"Have a seat," said Olivia, gesturing with her elegant hand. "It's more than six feet, so you'll be safe there." Sam's eyes measured the distance at seven feet. Plus, they were outside, so at less risk. The table was beautifully set with real china and cloth napkins. A bowl of delicious-looking salmon salad and a basket of fresh rolls sat in the center. There was also a fruit salad. Everything looked like it should be in a food magazine. "Help yourself," urged Olivia. "If you want me to step away while you serve yourself, I will."

"I think that's overkill, don't you?" said Sam, getting up with her plate.

"I want you to know I care about your safety."

"What changed your mind about the mask?" Sam asked as she put salmon salad on her plate.

"Reverend Bartlett has some compelling sermons on the church website. She explains that wearing a mask is a way of loving your neighbor as yourself."

"Yes, Lucy always has something to say."

"Not idle preaching though. She does have something to say."

Sam laughed. "Sounds like she's made another convert."

"Not quite yet. We'll see."

"Are you a churchgoer, Samantha?"

"Not for years, but sometimes I go to support Lucy. Out of friendship."

"I understand."

Sam pushed the bowl of salad in Olivia's direction. "Your lunch looks delicious. Like something out of *Martha Stewart Living*."

"She's a friend, actually. I used to have a house in Connecticut, but we go back to her days on the Street."

"I hear she's not the nicest person."

Olivia shrugged. "People probably say that about me too. You have to be tough to survive in the financial world."

"Greed is good?"

"I'm not that bad," said Olivia dismissively. "Not even close." She took off her mask now that Sam was seated, but she waited to pick up her fork until Sam did. Then she spent a long moment studying Sam. "It's nice to see you without a mask. You're very attractive." Women didn't usually say that kind of thing to one another, so Sam's antennae went up.

She deflected the compliment by saying, "I'm sure I look great covered with drywall dust."

"Reminds me of when we used to powder our hair to age us for the school play." Olivia's eyes continued their scrutiny of Sam's looks. "The white hair is giving me an interesting preview of what you might look like as you age."

Sam wondered why her future appearance would even interest her. Then she wanted to kick herself under the table. *The woman is coming on to me!* That left Sam confused because she was usually the one to make the first move.

Sam brushed off the thought and focused on her hunger. The salmon salad tasted even better than it looked. "Wow," she said, "that's amazing. You're a good cook."

"I love to cook. It's something of a hobby of mine."

"I guess I didn't expect you to be interested in something so…" Sam searched for a tactful word, but came up blank.

"Domestic?" Olivia supplied. She shook her head. "People are always making assumptions. So unfair."

"Yes, it would be better to get to know someone before making judgments."

"I agree, which is why I invited you to lunch."

"So that you can vet your assumptions?" asked Sam with a grin.

"No, so I can get to know you better." Olivia delicately dabbed her lips with her napkin. "What else do you assume about me?"

Sam hurried to swallow a mouthful of food, but it stuck in her throat. She tried to wash it down with a quick drink of water.

"I'm sorry. I'm putting you on the spot." Olivia turned her attention to her plate. Sam was glad for the break from her intense gaze. "I know that people in this town talk about me."

"What makes you say that?"

"Things get back to me through mutual acquaintances."

Obviously, they moved in different circles. Sam couldn't imagine that they had any mutual acquaintances.

"I wouldn't take it personally," Sam said casually. "It's a small town. Our winters are long. People need something to talk about."

"So, they do talk about me. What have you heard, Samantha?"

"Olivia, you're my client. I don't really want to have this conversation, if you don't mind."

"I understand. Enjoy your lunch. Let's talk about something else. What do you do for fun?"

"I draw—pen and ink mostly. I like to hike and fish with my friends. I do woodcarving and build furniture."

"You build furniture? Now, that's an interesting hobby for a woman."

"It goes with the architecture and design background."

"Of course."

"It's pretty common these days. Lots of women are into woodworking. Liz Stolz has been building furniture for years."

"Really?" asked Olivia, looking surprised.

"You can see how it fits. Surgery is all about spatial relationships. And the tools. Surgeons are the biggest tool junkies."

"How interesting."

"But Liz mostly builds period furniture—fussy, high-end pieces. I build from my own designs."

"Maybe you can build me that armoire for the bedroom."

"That's a lot of work and would be outrageously expensive. Why don't we see if we can find something in the antique shops first? Victorian furniture isn't really my style."

"You said yourself it doesn't have to be period-perfect. Any style would do." Sam realized she'd better watch what she said. Olivia didn't forget a thing.

To divert the conversation away from building an armoire, she asked her hostess to explain hedge funds and discovered how much Olivia liked to talk about her work. What she said was fascinating. Sam was so engrossed she didn't realize she had finished her salad and ended up scraping the bottom of her plate looking for more.

"I guess you liked it," said Olivia with a little smile.

"I did. It was delicious."

"There's more."

"Thank you," said Sam, "but I need to get back to work. I don't want to leave a big mess for the plumber."

"When is he coming?"

"The day after tomorrow."

"Will you be here too?"

"Yes, I want to make sure he understands the plan."

"Good. If you come a little early, I'll make you breakfast."

Sam frowned and wondered how Cruella had suddenly become Mrs. Potts, but she was touched by the invitation. "You don't need to make me breakfast. I usually just pick up coffee and a breakfast sandwich at Awakened Brews."

"But I want to make you breakfast. Please?"

"Well, all right. Jack usually shows up around eight-thirty. I'll be here at eight. Okay?"

Olivia smiled warmly. "Perfect. I look forward to it."

Sam replaced her mask and got up from the table. "I need to finish cleaning up, but I won't be long."

"Take as long as you need."

Sam went back upstairs. She scored the drywall so she could fold it like accordion bellows to carry downstairs. It took four trips, but she got it all down. She threw the small pieces into a contractor bag and swept up the dust into it.

"I'm heading out," she called into the house.

A moment later, Olivia appeared from a large room.

"Thank you for lunch," Sam said.

"Don't forget. I expect you for breakfast on Thursday."

"I'll be here."

Sam was thinking of Olivia's invitation as she drove home. Her client certainly was going out of her way to be nice. What a contrast to their first meeting. Sam told herself not to read too much into it.

At home, Sam closed the garage door behind her truck and stripped in the garage. Her dusty clothes went straight into the washing machine. She set it up with detergent but didn't turn it on, so that she'd have enough water for a shower. The well didn't have enough pressure for both at the same time.

She washed her hair and let the hot water stream over her face. Her skin always felt gritty after drywall demolition and she wanted to get rid of all the gypsum dust. It sucked moisture out of her skin and left it feeling dry and scratchy. She toweled her hair and smeared some moisturizer on her face and arms. While she did, she took in her naked body in the mirror. It sagged here and there. She was getting a little beer belly from drinking with Liz too often, but mostly it was a good body for a woman almost sixty. All the physical activity on her job certainly helped. She felt the muscles in her arms. They were a little sore from swinging the sledgehammer, but her biceps were still firm. They didn't sag into "bat wings," as her mother called them.

Sam pulled on a T-shirt and stepped into a pair of lounge pants, then headed downstairs to get a drink. She sat down at the kitchen island with her beer and opened her laptop. She entered "Jason Enright" into the Google search bar and clicked open an article from *The Wall Street Journal*. As she read, her eyes widened. She put down her beer to concentrate. The article reported that Olivia's son had been caught in insider trading worth millions. His death from a gunshot to the head was ruled a suicide. He was only thirty-four years old.

Sam whistled through her teeth. "Holy Shit," she whispered aloud as she continued to read the scandalous details.

9

Liz barely had time to glance at her schedule before her PA was knocking on her open door.

"Can you take a look at the lesion on Mr. Quinn's back? I'm not really sure."

Liz looked up into Cherie's perplexed face. "Do you think it suspicious enough to biopsy?"

"Yes."

"Trust your gut. Biopsy it."

"Right," agreed Cherie and disappeared.

Liz clawed at her forehead with her fingertips. The headache had settled in the center of her forehead and wouldn't budge. Liz was highly allergic to pollen. The cool weather was causing the tree bloom to last longer than usual. Everything, everywhere, was covered with neon-green, fine dust.

Liz opened her laptop and navigated to the schedule screen. Her morning was completely booked. When she scanned down to the afternoon appointments, her headache instantly got worse. Lucy Bartlett was scheduled for her annual physical.

Shit. Just what I need today! Liz threw back her head and stared at the acoustical tiles on the ceiling, wondering how to deal with Lucy. They hadn't spoken since the dinner party after their fishing trip. The conversation that evening had been pleasant, if subdued, but the tension between Liz and Lucy had been palpable.

Liz had felt Maggie's eyes on her through dinner. As an actress and theater director, Maggie was adept at reading body language, so Liz had made a special effort to appear relaxed and casual. A few times, Lucy's green eyes had met Liz's with a worried look. Lucy wasn't the type to wallow in guilt. Any concern on her part was for Liz and her emotional state. Liz had tried to defuse Lucy's anxiety with a smile, but the muscles in her face had strained to hold it.

Liz went down the hall to look for Cathy Pelletier, finding her partner in an exam room with a pediatric patient. Cathy's hand was poised to give an injection. The boy shot Liz an imploring look that seemed to say, "Please! Rescue me!" While he was distracted, Cathy deftly landed the syringe.

"What's up, Liz?" asked Cathy, taping a Band-Aid over the injection wound.

"Can you stop by when you're free?"

"Sure. Be there in a minute."

Liz returned to her office and stared out the window at the sumac trees behind the staff parking lot. Liz had thought about ripping them out until she'd read that monarch butterflies especially liked them.

The overgrown mess behind the parking lot was the least of Liz's worries. Patients were still afraid to come into the office. Telehealth was catching on, but most of the practice's patients were older and not tech-savvy enough to use it properly. The revenue loss during the shutdown might be permanent. For the second time in a month, Liz had to move her personal money into the business account to make payroll. If all that weren't enough, in a few hours, Lucy Bartlett would show up for a physical.

Cathy knocked on Liz's open door. "Now good?"

Liz waved her in. She studied her partner as she sat down.

Cathy had a pleasant, open face with high cheekbones that hinted at her Native-American heritage. Since her daughters had become teenagers, Cathy always looked harried. Before the pandemic, the poor woman had been driving them all over the state to sports games and practices. Now, the stress was homeschooling. After a full day in the office, Cathy had to deal with homework and the new Common Core math that no one could figure out, not even the teachers.

"Do you need something, Liz?" Cathy said, managing a smile, despite her obvious fatigue.

"Would you mind doing a pelvic exam for me this afternoon?"

There was a flicker of curiosity in Cathy's dark eyes. "Something special going on with this case?"

Liz unconsciously flinched. The words hit too close to the truth. Fortunately, this wasn't the first time Liz had asked Cathy to step in for a pelvic exam.

"No, but you did a residency in gynecology, so you're an expert." Cathy's eyes narrowed. *She's not buying it,* Liz thought. She smiled, trying to charm her.

"Liz, you don't give yourself enough credit. You've become a really good family doc. You need to stop worrying so much. Even the kids love you."

In the past, Liz would have given Cathy a sharp look for insubordination, but she no longer felt the same need to dominate everyone. Once the flash of irritation subsided, she realized that Cathy was giving her a compliment.

"Thank you," she murmured. "Will you do it for me?"

"Sure. Just give me a heads up before you start the physical. Anything I should be aware of?"

"The notes are in the file. A history of vaginal atrophy that's mostly been remedied by more activity."

"Hormone replacement?"

"Just phytoestrogens in the lubricant I recommended. Minimal."

Cathy looked pleasantly surprised. "Natural medicine? That doesn't sound like you."

"The more natural, the better, where vaginas are concerned."

"Liz, you never cease to amaze me." Cathy looked pensive. "Liz, you really should do the exam yourself. It's good for your relationship with the patient, but you already know that."

"I do, but you're more experienced. That's good for the patient too."

"I'll take a look at the file." Cathy still appeared skeptical when she got up to leave. "Call me when you need me."

That settled, Liz forgot about Lucy's physical while she saw her morning patients. Her headache even began to feel better. She treated herself to a lobster roll for lunch, which she ate near the old lobster traps in the back of the parking lot.

When she came back from Down the Hatch, Liz found her patient sitting on the bench outside the office. Instead of her clericals, Lucy was wearing a pretty, green sundress that complimented her red hair. Her beauty took Liz's breath away.

"Hello, Lucy."

She looked up and gave Liz a radiant smile. "They told me to wait out here until you got back," she explained, closing her book.

"We don't want people sitting together in the waiting room and spreading the virus." Liz waved to her. "Come in."

She led Lucy past the check-in desk. "I found her," Liz mumbled to Ginny as she passed.

"She's all checked in," the practice manger called after her. "She did it online."

"What a good patient you are," Liz said, gesturing into her office. Lucy took one of the visitors' chairs, and Liz closed the door. As she sat down behind her desk, she could feel Lucy's eyes taking her in, making a therapist's quick assessment. Liz felt momentarily self-conscious and looked down at her outfit. She was wearing her usual summer uniform—khaki high-performance cargo shorts and rafting sandals, but since the office had reopened, she always wore scrub tops because she could throw them into the washing machine in the office basement.

Liz could see the slightest pucker between Lucy's auburn brows. "Where have you been, Liz?" she asked gently.

"What do you mean?"

"You haven't come by in over two weeks. Erika keeps asking if you're mad at her."

Liz couldn't bear the tender concern in Lucy's sympathetic gaze, so she stared at the clock above the door.

"What's wrong, Liz? Are you still upset about what happened on the boat?"

Liz rubbed the sore spot in the center of her forehead. "That should never have happened."

"But it did happen. We need to accept it and move on."

"Easier said than done. Maggie knew right away."

"I'm not surprised. She's very intuitive. And people can read you like a book."

"What about Erika?"

Lucy chuckled. "You know Erika…always up in the clouds with her dead philosopher friends."

"Lucky you."

"Yes, I guess so, but sometimes I have to knock on her head to make her pay attention."

Liz took a deep breath to work up the courage for what she was about to say. "I've asked Cathy to come in for your pelvic exam, and I think you should switch to her as your primary." Liz had been looking at a point over Lucy's red hair as she spoke. Now, she dared to peek at Lucy's face. It was a mask of self-control, but Liz could feel her displeasure.

"Why?" Lucy finally asked.

"My patient load is getting too much for me to handle."

Lucy's green eyes blazed with open anger. "Don't lie to me, Liz. I expect more from you."

The vehemence of Lucy's response made Liz sit up straight. "All right, I'll tell you the truth. I feel strange being your doctor…now that it's out in the open."

"Liz, it's always been out in the open! Everyone knows we flirt with one another."

"But I never thought you took me seriously."

"I always took you seriously, but I never had any intention of acting on it. Before we went fishing, I never thought you did either."

"I didn't. It was an impulse, a spur of the moment thing. I kiss you on the lips all the time, but you never responded before. Of course, if you had gone along with it, I would have happily fucked you."

"That's it? Just a fuck?"

The hurt on Lucy's face stung and shamed Liz into saying, "I'm sorry. I should have said, I would have made love to you, because I do love you."

"I love you too, Liz. But we're not going to be lovers while we're married to other people. I love Erika and would never hurt her. Maggie is my best friend. I would never hurt her either. Do you know how many lives would be ripped apart if we gave in to our attraction?"

Staring at her desk, Liz nodded.

"We need to be more careful and not get into situations like on the boat. We can't help who we're attracted to. All we can control is our actions."

"Sounds like Erika has converted you to her soft determinist position."

Lucy made a face. "Her what?"

"You can do what you want, but you can't want what you want, so free will is an illusion."

"You explain it a lot more simply. When she gets into it, she can go on for hours."

"Goes with being a philosophy professor. Pontificating is in the job description."

"Never mind that." Lucy sighed. "Liz, I don't want another doctor. We've been attracted to one another since the day we met. That didn't stop you from taking me as a patient. Why can't you go on being as professional as you've always been?" When Liz didn't answer right away, Lucy asked, "Liz, what do you see when you examine me?"

"A patient."

"Exactly. And that's what I expect." She gave Liz a firm look to emphasize the message. "Something else is going on. I can feel it. Are things okay between you and Maggie? How's your love life?"

"I'm supposed to be asking the questions. It's your exam."

"Doesn't matter. What's your answer?"

"I admit that some of the steam has gone out of our sex life. She's been on Tamoxifen for years. It suppresses estrogen, and that can affect libido."

Lucy looked thoughtful. "Maybe you need to get more creative."

"I don't have time to be creative. There's so much going on!"

"Such as?"

"My mother isn't doing well. She fell again, but her problems are more than physical. Cognitively, she's declining. I haven't been able to get down there with the quarantine."

"That's sad, but you've been expecting her to fail for some time. What else?"

"The practice is having a hard time financially."

Lucy's eyes softened with sympathy. "I know what you mean. Our collections are non-existent. We're trying to get people to give online to keep us afloat, but you know how it is. Out of sight, out of mind."

There was a knock on the door. "Come in," Liz sang out.

Cathy stuck her head in. "Oh, hello, Mother Lucy." She smiled warmly, then glanced at Liz. "Let me know when you need me."

Liz shook her head. "Don't worry, Dr. Pelletier. I've got this. I can do the pelvic exam. I'm sure you're busy with other things."

Cathy looked puzzled for a moment. "Oh, okay. Nice to see you, Mother Lucy," she said and closed the door.

❋❋❋

As Liz sat through the chamber of commerce meeting, she thought about her conversation with Lucy. She hoped Lucy's clients appreciated her skill. With just a few well aimed questions, Lucy had managed to make Liz feel completely comfortable doing the exam. There was no more talk about Lucy changing doctors. Of course, that only made Liz love Lucy all the more, but at least, the cloud over their friendship looked less stormy.

Liz half-listened to Olivia Enright go on about her opposition to using the police to enforce the governor's mask requirement. As president of the group, Liz could have asked Olivia to cede the floor, but her argument wasn't unreasonable. She suggested they should increase the public service signs around town and use persuasion rather than force.

Liz gazed around to gauge how the others were receiving Olivia's message. They all sat safely spaced on the enormous deck of the Dockside restaurant, where they held their monthly meetings. The distance between them meant everyone had to raise their voices to be heard, which was particularly annoying after the day's non-stop headache. Fortunately, Olivia's voice was carefully modulated. Obviously, she was used to addressing large groups.

Sometimes, everything about Olivia irritated Liz: her arch tone, her perfect appearance, and the expensive clothes she wore, even in informal settings. She seemed determined to flaunt her wealth and completely unaware that it put people off.

Olivia's politics annoyed Liz most of all. Selectmen weren't identified by their party affiliation like other elected officials, but everyone knew that Olivia was a prominent member of the Hobbs Republican Committee. Liz didn't hold that against her *per se*. Liz, herself, had been a Republican, long, long ago, in a galaxy far away, but she wondered why such an apparently intelligent woman remained in a party increasingly hostile to women.

Olivia had plenty of allies on the chamber of commerce, mostly small businesspeople whose livelihood depended on the revenue from summer tourism. Some of their businesses were literally dying under the governor's restrictions. A few restaurants had already closed for good.

Finally, Olivia stopped speaking. Liz breathed a sigh of relief and asked for a motion to adjourn. Through the entire meeting, she'd been imagining the pleasure of enjoying a cold beer on her own deck. As she collected her papers into her messenger bag, she noticed Olivia at her elbow.

"Liz, I wonder if you would join me for a drink and a bite to eat?"

"Thank you, Olivia, but I've already eaten."

"Please. I think you'll agree this is important."

Liz sighed. "Okay."

"Do you want to stay here or go somewhere else?" Olivia asked. Liz was surprised that the bossy woman was giving her a choice.

"I'm tired, so I wouldn't mind staying here."

"Good. Let's get a table inside. It's getting a little chilly out here."

As they sat at opposite ends of a table meant for six, Liz glanced around at the sparse dinner crowd. No matter how much the locals tried to make up for the lost summer business, it was impossible. The year-round residents numbered less than ten thousand. In the summer months, the population of Hobbs swelled to four times that size.

"My heart breaks for these small businesses," Olivia said, speaking Liz's thoughts aloud. "The fourteen-day quarantine is killing them."

"Unfortunately, it's for people's safety and can't be helped. We just have to go out of our way to support the shops and restaurants."

Wearing a tie-dye, rainbow-burst mask, the waitress appeared. Liz remembered her pledge to support local business, so she ordered some appetizers along with her beer. Olivia ordered dinner and a glass of chardonnay.

While they sipped their drinks, there was an extended silence. Liz raised her glass in Olivia's direction. "Go on. You have the floor."

"As you know, my claim to being a chamber of commerce member is my financial consulting firm."

"Do you have many clients?"

"Unfortunately, no. Only three."

"Three is better than none."

Olivia chuckled. "Certainly. I was wondering if you might be interested in my services."

For a moment, Liz couldn't speak, incensed that Olivia had detained her after a long day to make a sales pitch. Liz reined in her temper and glanced around to make sure they couldn't be overheard. "Thanks, but I manage my own portfolio as well as my wife's."

"And I'm sure you've done very well for yourself. You're a smart woman."

Liz despised flattery, especially from people she didn't like, but she made an attempt to sound civil. "I've done all right, thank you."

"But I bet as soon as the market started to recover you fled to cash."

Olivia's accurate assessment took Liz by surprise, but she managed to control her face. "I'm at the age when I can't wait around for the markets to come back," she said in a slightly defensive tone.

"A good point, but I bet your portfolio is too conservative, and you're not leveraging your cash."

"I've paid hefty management fees before. They're a waste of money."

"Don't worry about fees. There would be no charge for my services."

Liz narrowed her eyes. "Why would you do that?"

"Because you need my help. You'll bankrupt yourself before you lay off your employees, even when you know you should."

Liz wondered how Olivia could know so much about her financial life. All of her business and personal files were carefully stored in an encrypted cloud.

"That's a lucky guess. You have no way of knowing anything about my investment strategy."

"No, but I know you. You're one of those people who would literally give the shirt off your back. I've read about how small medical offices are facing severe losses from the pandemic. You're a careful and cautious investor, Liz, but you could make more money with only slightly more risk. You may be a talented amateur, but I'm a professional."

"You've spent a lot of time trying to figure me out."

"That's why I'm so good at investment. Careful research."

Their food arrived. Liz bit into a popper still too hot from the deep fryer. She cursed her burned tongue and tried to cool it off with some beer. When she could finally speak, she asked, "Why would you help me? What's in it for you?"

"Our town needs a good family practice, and you have unique expertise that has value to me. Also, I hope we can become allies instead of adversaries. I'm tired of being shunned by the people in this town."

"Why do you think people shun you?"

"I don't know. I've done everything I know how to help this town. I've gotten involved in every civic club. I'm generous to all the local charities. I go out of my way to volunteer for town events."

"Yes, I've seen you do that."

"But you do the same and everyone loves you."

"My approach is a little different. I wait for people to ask my opinion instead of acting like I know it all. I don't argue every debate like it's a duel to the death."

"Is that what you think I do?"

"Since you asked, yes."

As Olivia raised her chin in challenge, Liz silently commended her surgeon for doing excellent facial work. She had no jowls and the skin at her throat was tight and smooth.

"I didn't realize I came on so strong. It's what I'm used to from Wall Street. It's pretty cutthroat in New York."

"I'm a New Yorker too, but that doesn't mean I have to be an asshole."

Olivia's eyes widened in surprise. "Are you saying I'm an asshole?"

Liz smiled to soften the insult. "I used to think I had to dominate people to get their respect. That turned out to be exactly the wrong approach. Eventually, I learned to model leadership and that works much better."

Olivia glanced away as if she needed relief from the sight of her dining companion. Finally, she looked back at Liz. "That was hard to hear, but thank you for your honesty and your advice."

Liz shrugged. "Don't mention it. Hope it helps."

"Will you let me help you with your finances?"

Liz let Olivia wait for her reply. Finally, she said, "I know when I'm in over my head. Thank you. I'd appreciate some advice."

10

Brenda's trained eye took in the people around her. She noted the position of the Portland police and their neutral expressions as they watched the demonstrators assemble. She knew they were surveying the crowd, sizing up people for potential threats, exactly as she was. Brenda noted there were as many older folks as young people in the crowd and surmised that at least some of them were old-school, social-justice warriors. Despite the racial theme of the march, the demonstrators were overwhelmingly white.

Out of the corner of her eye, Brenda saw a young man behaving oddly and focused her eyes on him. He was pale and slight, seemingly posing little danger to anyone. She observed him a little longer and made the casual assessment of autism or mental deficiency.

"What are you looking at?" Cherie asked, breaking Brenda's concentration.

Brenda turned and smiled. "Just checking out the crowd to see who's who and what's what."

"I thought you were here as a private citizen, not a cop."

"I am, but I can't help it. Cops develop an instinct to scan for threats." She nodded in the direction of the young man she suspected of being on the spectrum. "See that guy over there? His behavior might easily set off negative police action in the heat of the moment. Hopefully, the officers here have him pegged as handicapped and will leave him alone."

Cherie's eyes turned in his direction. "Why wouldn't they leave him alone?"

"His behavior makes him stick out. If there's a confrontation, he may act in ways they don't expect. That's hard to deal with when you're doing crowd control."

"You're saying the police expect everyone to act the same, their version of normal?"

Brenda took a deep breath to ratchet down her impulse to snap back an answer. "No, Cherie, that's not what I said. You're very edgy. Are you sorry I came?"

Cherie studied her with a frown. "I'm worried you only came to support me."

"Sometime, you need to take a look at the training videos I made for the NYPD. I was for black lives matter before it was even a slogan."

"But you won't carry a sign."

"I can't be seen carrying a protest sign. We talked about this. Do we need to have another fight?" Brenda was becoming increasingly irritated. She loved Cherie so much, but when it came to this subject, it always ended in an argument.

"Hello, ladies," said a cheery voice behind them. Brenda turned and saw Lucy Bartlett and Maggie Fitzgerald. Maggie was carrying a hand-lettered Black Lives Matter sign. Lucy was wearing a clerical collar and a rainbow stole that spoke louder than any sign.

"I'd give you hugs, but we're modeling social distancing," said Maggie through her gingham mask.

"We understand," Cherie replied. "Where's Liz?"

"She's down in New York visiting her mother. The governor finally relaxed the quarantine on New York, so Liz headed right down. It's the first time she's seen her mother since February."

Cherie's eyes were full of sympathy. "I understand her worry. When they start failing like that, it doesn't get better. It's just a matter of time."

Listening to Cherie, Brenda was reminded of her lover's compassion and generous concern. She wondered why, despite her kindness to others, Cherie was still prickly with her. Would she ever get over her sad history with the police?

Brenda felt Lucy's eyes on the side of her face. "How are things here?" she asked gently. Lucy's ability to sense emotional conflict was better than a fish sonar seeking a school of blues.

Brenda tried to convey her gratitude with her eyes. "This is a tough place for me to be."

"I know," said Lucy, touching Brenda's arm. "Stay strong, Brenda. Cherie needs you here."

Brenda gazed into Lucy's eyes and felt such love emanating from them. "I know. Thank you for your support."

"Always." The green eyes smiled.

"Hey." Brenda turned to see Sam McKinnon. She was wearing one of Maggie's gingham masks too. A couple more of them, and they'd have the beginnings of a patchwork quilt.

Lucy glanced at her watch. "They'll be getting started soon. How about a prayer?" Brenda wasn't much for public displays of piety, but she bowed her head along with the others.

"Dear God," Lucy prayed, "You said, 'Blessed are those who hunger and thirst for righteousness.' Bless us as we march to support our black sisters and brothers. Help us to remember that we come to protest violence, not spread it. May this demonstration be peaceful, so that people will be open to our message. Through Christ, our Lord, Amen."

There was a chorus of Amens.

"Where's Liz?" Sam asked, looking around.

"Went to see her mother in New York," Maggie explained. "This is the first opportunity she's had in months."

"Things any better there?" Sam asked.

Maggie shrugged. "I don't really know. You know how Liz is. She's pretty closed mouthed about her family problems."

"Even to you?" Lucy asked with a look of concern.

"Even to me."

Brenda watched Lucy's eyes narrow slightly as she made careful note of what Maggie had said. *That woman never misses a trick*, thought Brenda.

There was a booming bass scratch as the public address system switched on. An overly loud female voice announced: "Welcome to our Black Lives Matter march. It's so good to see all of you turn out in solidarity with people of color. Before we begin our march, we will hear from a few speakers."

Brenda tuned out the speeches while her eyes continued to scan the crowd for potential disturbances. The handicapped man was acting out again. An older woman, possibly his mother, was trying to calm him. Brenda tried to short circuit the critical thought forming in her mind, but it asserted itself anyway. *What was she thinking to bring him to an event like this?*

The scuttlebutt on how this day could go had been shared on the secret Maine Cops Facebook group. Everyone in the departments was edgy. Some of the comments were insensitive, if not downright racist. Except for the Somalian refugees around Portland and the seasonal workers from the islands, there were hardly any black people in the state. The Maine cops, except for those "from away," just didn't know what to think about race. Cops like Brenda, who'd worked in big cities, had a completely different perspective.

"And now we'll hear from the Reverend Lucille Bartlett, rector of St. Margaret's by the Sea Episcopal Church in Hobbs," the loudspeaker blared.

Brenda, who hadn't even noticed Lucy slip away, glanced up at the podium. The sun shone brightly on Lucy's red hair and the rainbow stole she wore, giving her an almost otherworldly glow of color.

"When I was asked to speak today," Lucy began, "I thought about writing a speech, but then I decided to let Matthew's Gospel do the heavy lifting:

'Blessed are they who hunger and thirst for righteousness,
for they shall be satisfied.
Blessed are the merciful,
for they shall obtain mercy.
Blessed are the pure of heart,
for they shall see God.
Blessed are the peacemakers,
for they shall be called children of God.
Blessed are they who are persecuted for the sake of righteousness,
for theirs is the kingdom of heaven.'

Lucy gazed around, engaging the faces of people in the crowd. Brenda envied Lucy's ease in front of an audience. Despite years of public speaking, Brenda still hated it, but, as chief, it was an important part of her job.

"As we join this protest against police violence," Lucy continued, "let us hunger and thirst for righteousness. Let us yearn for it with all our hearts, but let us also remember the peacemakers. Technically, police officers are 'peacekeepers.' I hope that, with our encouragement, they can also be peacemakers. Acts of racial violence are deplorable and should be condemned in every case, but let's not paint all police officers with the same brush. Many are good, decent individuals who long for justice as much as we do. And it's a funny thing. When we have high expectations for people, they often rise to the occasion. I have high expectations for our Portland police and for police officers all over this nation. Let us pray for their safety and for the safety of all people of color. May God bless you."

Brenda nodded in approval. Somehow Lucy always knew the right thing to say. She could nudge the most recalcitrant conscience without scolding. She overcame belligerence with unconditional love. In Lucy's presence, Brenda could almost imagine becoming a believer again.

When Lucy returned, Brenda put her arm around her. "Thank you for remembering we're people too."

"Of course, I remember you're people," said Lucy, squeezing Brenda's waist. "Very good people, mostly."

"Hey, Brenda," said Cherie, pulling at her arm. "We all love Lucy, but you're too close. Come over here where I can keep an eye on you." Brenda heard an odd note in Cherie's voice and hoped it wasn't jealousy.

"You don't think I meant anything by that hug?"

"No, of course not," said Cherie. "You were just too close. I know it's hard to remember to keep our distance, especially with our friends."

"But I've had the virus, and so have you. We can't still be catchy, can we?"

Cherie shrugged. "Who knows? And you'd never forgive yourself if you made Lucy sick. Neither would Erika."

"Now that you mention it, where is Erika?"

"Lucy said demonstrations are just not Erika's thing, but I can tell she's disappointed."

"Actually, I would have been surprised if Liz came. She's not the demonstration type. Of course, neither am I."

"I know." Cherie gave Brenda's arm a little squeeze. "Thank you for coming. Sorry I was crabby."

The lines were forming for the march. Brenda deliberately positioned herself on the outer flank in case there were any incidents. She ended up directly behind the handicapped man, who turned and stared at her briefly before facing forward. He had a completely flat affect, so it was hard to gauge his emotional state.

The march began to move. People chanted: "Black Lives Matter! Black Lives Matter!" A block later, the chant began to alternate with "Defund! Defund! Spend our Money Better!"

Brenda refused to join in. That was her budget they were talking about, her department—officers who had families, who'd read children's books on the website during the pandemic. That was the money that paid for the junior police who patrolled the beaches on bicycles, the 911 staff and dispatchers, and dog food for the K9.

Cherie gave her a light punch on the arm. "Well? What's wrong with you?"

"No, I'm not chanting that slogan. It's wrong."

Cherie glared at her, but the sound of shouting up ahead drew their attention. The handicapped man Brenda had been watching was shrieking at a policeman. He was right up in the officer's face, practically spitting at him, shouting, "Pig! Pig! Pig!" Brenda hadn't heard that expression in years. Brenda guessed he'd learned it from an elderly relative.

To his credit, the officer continued to stand at attention and ignored the screaming. That is, until the man began banging on his riot shield with his protest sign.

Instantly, officers flanked the policeman under attack and closed ranks on the assailant. Brenda broke away from the march to see what was happening. Two officers were shoving the man. Another shot pepper spray in his face. Blinded, the handicapped man howled in pain.

"What are you doing?" Brenda demanded as the policemen continued to shove the man.

"Stay out of this," growled one of them. "Go back to your march."

"No. Can't you see he's handicapped?" Brenda yanked her badge out of her pocket and held it up. "Your boss won't be happy with your actions. Now back off!"

The officers stared at the badge. There was a standoff for a tense moment. Scowling at Brenda, they returned to their positions on the curb.

Brenda turned around to see Cherie beaming at her with pride. Beside her was a gaggle of news reporters and a TV camera from Channel Eight News.

11

Sam lined up her tableware on her plate and wiped her mouth. "Delicious." Olivia's lunch of grilled tuna had indeed been superb as were all the meals Sam had eaten in her house. On workdays, Sam found herself looking forward to Olivia's lunches and would certainly miss them when the job was finished. "Thank you for lunch…again," she said, leaning on the table to get up.

"Sit down, Samantha. I want to talk to you about something."

"Okay," said Sam uncertainly. "What's up?"

"I saw you on TV at the Black Lives Matter demonstration."

Sam frowned. "Yes…what about it?"

"I was surprised to see you and your friends there. Mother Lucy in particular."

"Why?" asked Sam, not sure she liked where this conversation was going. "Lucy's very committed to social justice."

Olivia pursed her lips and made a little face. "Is that what you call it?"

"What do you call it?"

"Liberal causes."

"There's nothing wrong with being liberal, you know. Conservatives made it a dirty word, but some of the best ideas started as liberal causes."

"Name one."

"Weekends."

Olivia sighed and glanced away. Obviously, she couldn't think of any arguments against that one.

"I was disappointed to see you there. I thought you had more sense."

Under the table, Sam's hands involuntarily tightened into fists. "It's not about sense," Sam said in an even voice. "It's about fairness. I don't know why that would disappoint you."

"Your business is mostly in southern Maine. The customers who can afford your high-end renovations don't necessarily agree with your politics. You don't want to offend them by putting it front and center."

"It's not like I post my party affiliation on my website. I do good work. If people like what I do, they recommend me. If not, they don't."

"But if people see you on TV, carrying a protest sign, they might not recommend you."

"I don't really care," said Sam, getting up.

Olivia gazed at her with patient eyes. "Sit down, Samantha. I'm not criticizing you. I'm trying to give you some friendly advice."

"Doesn't sound friendly to me." Sam was still trying to hold her temper, but she knew her eyes were blazing. Meanwhile, Olivia continued to gaze at her calmly.

"Please sit down. I want to ask you something."

Sam reluctantly sat down. "What do you want to know?" she asked with forced patience.

"Is Chief Harrison one of your friends?"

"How is that any of your business?"

"It's not my business, but I'd like to know."

"Yes, Brenda is my friend. I've known her for years."

"What kind of person is she?"

"If you're asking if she's a good person, she's one of the best. She'd do anything for anyone. She's brave and tough as well as kind. She used to be a New York cop."

"Yes, I know. I've been looking into her background."

The idea that Olivia was poking into Brenda's past put Sam on edge. "Why?"

"Well, I'm the council member in charge of the police and fire departments. I like to know my people."

"Your people?" repeated Sam in a challenging tone. "The departments belong to the people of Hobbs, not you."

Olivia rolled her eyes. "You know what I mean. I like to know who I'm managing."

"Isn't that above and beyond the call of duty?" asked Sam suspiciously. Maybe Olivia was a homophobe in addition to being racist. Most people in

Hobbs knew Brenda was gay, but she tried to keep it quiet because of her law enforcement role. Sam didn't understand why anyone still needed to be in the closet until Brenda explained that her authority with homophobic, young men could be undermined by coming out.

"Context is important when dealing with personnel issues," Olivia continued. "I find it helpful to know who I'm dealing with. Besides, it's an old habit from being in finance and equity trading. There, research is essential to making good decisions."

The meter on Sam's patience had run out. By now, she figured she had nothing to lose by insisting Olivia get to the point. "What's your issue with Brenda?"

"It's not my issue. The other council members want to censure her for showing her badge at the demonstration."

"Why?" Sam threw her napkin on the table in disgust. "She was defending a handicapped man. I saw the whole thing."

"She was using her authority as Hobbs Police Chief at a political demonstration. She has no jurisdiction in Portland."

"What are you, a lawyer now?"

"No, but I did study law briefly before I went for my MBA. Besides, that's such a basic thing. She should have known better."

"You weren't there. It got testy. The Portland police were agitated after people started banging on street signs and overturning trash containers. They moved in quickly to push the demonstrators back."

"Their job is to protect property."

Sam bit her lip to keep from saying what she thought. *Your type is always more worried about property than people's lives.* "Like I said, you weren't there. The police were nervous. They were pushing people around. They moved on this autistic man like he was a real threat. If Brenda hadn't asserted her authority, they might have taken her in for interfering in an arrest."

"Is that what she told you?"

"Yes."

"It probably would have been better for all of you not to have been there in the first place."

"But we were. We want to support Black Lives Matter."

"An ironic twist for Chief Harrison."

"You don't know anything about Brenda."

"Oh, but I do. I know that she created the sensitivity training programs for the NYPD. They're still in use even though she's been gone for over a decade. Race relations is one of her hobby horses."

Sam didn't like that last comment. "You certainly do your homework. What else do you know about her?" asked Sam, reasoning that if she could find out more, at least, she could give Brenda a heads up.

"Enough to know that it's not as simple as censuring her. That's where you come in."

"Me? What do I have to do with it?"

Olivia peered directly into Sam's eyes. "Can't you guess?"

Sam shook her head. "No, I'm sometimes dense where social cues are involved."

"That's all right. Most people up here are. But what I'm asking is pretty simple. Take your friend aside and advise her to stay away from political demonstrations."

"You're kidding me."

"I'm afraid, I'm not. If it happens again, I don't know if I can hold off the others on the council."

Sam couldn't keep herself from making a face. "Yes, I'm sure your Republican friends don't believe in giving second chances."

Olivia sighed. "You're so quick to judge. People in both parties are being unreasonable at the moment."

"Don't tell me that you're a moderate."

Olivia looked thoughtful. "I suppose in comparison to what most Republicans think today, I am. I've always been a Republican, because I believe in working hard and being able to keep the fruits of your labor. I'm a fiscal conservative, but I also believe in environmental protection and a social safety net."

"Did you vote for Trump?"

There was a long silence. "Yes, but only because I couldn't stomach Clinton."

"Do you regret it now?"

"Yes, I do. But let's not get too deeply into this topic. I'm keeping you from your work, but first, I need to know if you'll help me."

"Brenda has the right to express her opinions."

"Of course, and I believe in free speech, but being on the TV news and the subject of headlines blaring 'the battle of the cops' is not doing your friend any favors. It's unprofessional and bad publicity for the town. Even you have to agree it looked bad. The media twists everything."

Sam was not about to debate this topic, so she got up. "If there's an opportunity, I'll pass along your message."

"Thank you."

"You're welcome…I think." Sam put on her mask and picked up her plate to bring it into the kitchen.

As she passed, she felt Olivia's eyes following her. "Remember that I'm counting on your discretion. More bad publicity could do irreparable harm to Chief Harrison's career."

Sam nodded and headed out. The conversation had infuriated her. She tried to calm herself by focusing on her task. Laying the high-performance underlayment was a quick and easy project. The only part of tile work she hated was mixing the mortar. It was messy and hard on her tools. Over the years, she'd burned out plenty of drill motors.

When she picked up the bag of dry mortar, it flexed the wrong way and covered Sam's arms, face, and hair with fine dust. Good thing she'd been wearing a mask, or she'd be breathing those fine particles that could wreak havoc on lung tissue.

When the mortar was the right consistency, Sam hauled the five-gallon bucket up to the bathroom and strapped on her knee pads. She troweled out the thinset with a practiced stroke, effortlessly forming perfect ridges.

The job was going so well she'd be done early if the marble for the walls came on time. Despite her quarrel with Olivia, Sam was surprised to feel an odd sadness at the thought. They didn't move in the same circles. After Sam finished the bathroom, she probably wouldn't be seeing Olivia again.

As she worked, Sam thought about their conversation. From Brenda's complaints about Olivia at the town council meetings, Sam had already guessed they were on opposite ends of the political spectrum. Now, she was beginning to realize it wasn't as simple as belonging to a party.

In less than an hour, Sam was done. She took her bucket outside to rinse it before the mortar set up. She wished she could hose herself off too. She always kept a tarp in her truck to cover the seats when a job got messy, but maybe Olivia would let her use her shower.

When Sam came around the house, she noticed that Olivia's Lexus was gone from the driveway. She'd left without saying a word. It pleased Sam that her client trusted her enough to leave her working alone in the house.

Sam glanced at her filthy pants and the haze of dust on her arms. She always kept a change of clothes and a towel in a duffle bag in case the job was really messy. She decided that Olivia probably wouldn't notice if she took a quick shower. After all, the bathroom was already a mess.

While the water heated up, Sam stripped, leaving her dusty clothes on the floor. After she stepped into the enormous shower, she helped herself to the grapefruit-scented body wash in the shower recess. The salon shampoo smelled like coconut. Grateful to be clean, she rinsed off all the foam, cutting some away from her eyes. She shut off the steaming water. When she turned around, she saw Olivia staring at her through the glass door. Sam tried to cover her crotch and breasts with her arms.

Olivia left. Shaking with embarrassment, Sam snatched her towel from her duffle bag, and hastily dried herself. She jumped into her underpants and cargo shorts. Her skin felt too damp to struggle into a bra, so she pulled a T-shirt over her head. She toweled her hair, ran her fingers through it quickly, and hurried out to the bedroom.

Olivia was hugging herself. "I'm so sorry!" she said in a flustered tone. "I had no idea. I heard the water running in the shower and came up to see why."

"I would have asked permission, but you were gone. I didn't think you'd mind."

"I don't mind. Of course, I don't mind, but please forgive me for barging in on you like that."

"It's your house. Don't apologize. I was intruding. I'm the one who should be sorry."

Olivia relaxed and smiled broadly. "Actually, I'm not sorry. I enjoyed the view. Your body is beautiful."

Sam opened her mouth to speak, but suddenly, she didn't know what to say.

12

Liz sat down at her desk and took off her mask. The elastic ties irritated her skin. She remembered the red marks on her face after a long day of surgery. She'd thought she'd left all that behind. Now, everyone was wearing a mask, or at least, they should be.

She opened her laptop to check the schedule. Her last appointment of the day was Olivia Enright. Liz dialed Ginny at the front desk. "Why is Ms. Enright coming in?"

"She wants a COVID test."

"Did you tell her we don't do that here?"

"I did, but she says Southern Med won't give her a test without a script from her primary."

"For God's sake! Why do they keep changing the rules down there?" Liz complained, despite knowing the answer. There was still a shortage of tests. She glanced at her watch. She had ten minutes before Olivia's appointment. Maybe they could do this by Telehealth. "Is she here already?"

"Just called from the parking lot."

"Okay. When she comes in, send her down."

Reluctantly, Liz put on her mask again. A few minutes later, Olivia was standing in her doorway, and Liz motioned for her to enter.

"Hello, Liz," said Olivia, taking one of the visitors' chairs. "Nice to see you."

"You too, Olivia, but we could have done this remotely. No need for you to come all the way up here."

"Really, it's just up the street, and I prefer to see you in person. All this virtual business is getting on my nerves."

"I know what you mean, but I hear you want a COVID test. Why? Do you have any symptoms?" In fact, Olivia looked healthy. She had good color. The whites of her eyes were clear. Her makeup looked professional, and every hair was in place. How could anyone look so perfect? It was almost surreal.

Liz found herself wondering how much time it took Olivia to get herself together in the morning. Despite Maggie's years of experience putting on stage makeup, she never achieved such perfection. Charmingly, there was always a stray lock of hair or a little mascara smudge, despite the magnifying mirror Liz had installed when Maggie began to have trouble seeing details.

"No, I don't have any symptoms," said Olivia. "That's not why I'm interested in the test. I want to spend more time with someone, and she seems to take your advice about social distancing very seriously."

"I'm glad. I wish all my patients took it seriously."

"One of your friends," said Olivia with a canny smile.

"Sam?"

Olivia nodded.

"Is she still working on your bathroom?"

"She is, but she's almost done. She promised we would look for an armoire to replace the closet she demolished to install the new tub. I want to be able to accompany her and have a bite afterward in a restaurant…like a civilized person."

"The COVID test is a snapshot. If you want to guarantee that you're virus-free, you'll have to quarantine until you get the results. Could take a week or more."

"I understand, Dr. Stolz."

"I thought we were on a first name basis."

"We are, but at the moment, you look so doctor-like, your title seems more appropriate." Olivia grinned mischievously. Playfulness wasn't something Liz would have expected from Olivia, so she was surprised.

"Everyone calls me Liz. Except the kids. They call me Dr. Liz."

"I like that about you—your veneer of informality. You like to downplay your success and influence, yet that only enhances it."

Liz ignored the remark to keep the conversation on track. "There's a shortage of tests. You're taking one away from someone who might need it."

"*I* need it. If I have the virus, I want to protect Samantha."

"Samantha?" Liz laughed. "She lets you get away with calling her that?"

"So far."

"Well, good for you. Even I wouldn't dare call her that, and I've known her for twenty years."

"How do you know her?"

"We belonged to the same woodworking club."

"Yes, she said you build furniture. Such interesting ladies I meet up here in Maine."

"Ladies," Liz repeated with a slight tone of contempt. "Doesn't that date us?"

"There's nothing wrong with being a lady," said Olivia. "You and Samantha were raised properly. You went to girls prep schools. I'm sure that had some influence."

Liz's eyes narrowed. "How do you know that?"

"I always research people I want to know better. Given Samantha's rough and ready appearance, I wouldn't have expected her to be a trust fund baby with such an impressive pedigree. You have quite a background yourself. Your parents were wealthy and quite philanthropic."

"But I'm not a trust fund baby like Sam. I've worked for everything I have. I even put myself through medical school."

Olivia raised her chin and smiled. "Yes, you have the confidence of a self-made woman."

Liz was skeptical of the compliment. She didn't know why, but she still didn't entirely trust the woman. "Let me write your script so you can get out of here."

"I'm in no hurry. I'm enjoying our conversation. I don't see many people these days."

Liz glanced at the clock above the door. She'd hoped to get some weeding done in her herb bed that afternoon, but she sensed that Olivia needed to talk.

"The pandemic is isolating people," Liz said. "Can you call friends or message them online? That might help."

"I have plenty of acquaintances, but not many friends."

"Well, what can you do about that?"

"I was hoping you could help me."

Liz instantly felt anxious. "How so?"

"It seems you're the hub of a group of women who go to our church."

"Go to our church?" Liz repeated. "Except when my wife sings, I don't go to church. I'm an atheist."

Olivia dropped her chin and gave Liz an intent look from under her brows.

"Oh! *That* church! Yes, I do know some gay women in town. Why is that of interest to you?"

Another intent look.

"I see," Liz said slowly. "You're gay."

Olivia offered an exaggerated nod. "I was hoping for an introduction to your little club."

"It's not a club, Olivia." Liz shifted uncomfortably in her chair. "This isn't why you're cultivating my friendship and offering help with my finances?"

"No, no. That's totally sincere. You have great credentials. The town needs a solid family practice, and I need you as my doctor."

It was on the tip of Liz's tongue to say, "It's all about you, isn't it?" Instead, she opened her desk drawer and took out a prescription pad. With a few quick strokes of her pen, she wrote the order for a COVID test and pushed it across her desk.

Olivia scanned the paper. "Now I know you're a good doctor. Your handwriting is illegible." She stood. "Thank you, Liz. Think about what I said, please. And I'd like to get together soon to go over your finances. It would be good to get things in order soon. The economy is still uncertain."

"If your COVID test comes back negative, which I expect it will, I'll invite you over for dinner. You can meet my wife."

"The amazingly talented Maggie Fitzgerald."

"Are you a fan?"

"Have been from years ago. Plus, like you, I'm a big patron of the Playhouse."

"Then you'll enjoy meeting Maggie. She's on the board."

"Yes, I know. I'm thinking about applying for membership, especially since I have all this time on my hands." Olivia's nod almost seemed like a little bow. She was being playful again. "Thank you, Dr. Stolz. You've been very helpful."

After she left, Liz shut down her computer for the day. As she showered, she thought about their conversation. Olivia was obviously used to getting her way, but so was Liz, probably why her patient hadn't pushed harder.

Liz tried to imagine how Olivia would fit in with her friends. They were all so down to earth. "Authentic," Lucy would call them, even Erika, who always had her head in the clouds, and Maggie, who was always "on" as an actress. It seemed unlikely Olivia would be comfortable with them, but it might be entertaining to watch.

❖❖❖

After sitting in an air-conditioned office all day, Liz was shocked to step into a wall of warm, sticky air. She thought about going down to the boat to have a beer, but she really wanted company. Ordinarily, she'd drive down to the island to see Erika, but she was still keeping her distance from Lucy, so that didn't seem like a good plan. Liz decided to stop at Sam's place instead.

After Liz started her truck, she pressed the button on her steering wheel to call Maggie.

"I think I'll stop over at Sam's for a beer. What time is dinner?"

"I'm making white chili in the slow cooker. Dinner can be anytime you want it to be. I can feed Alina and the kids, and you and I can eat whenever you get here."

"You are the best wife ever!"

"I'm your only wife. Remember that." It was intended to be humorous, but Liz got the message and felt a little chill. Strange how people could sense things without having them obviously confirmed. "Don't be too late," Maggie added. "I could use some help with the kids."

Liz almost never turned on the air conditioner in the truck. Her trips around town were short, and it never seemed worth the extra gas. Tonight, the humidity defeated even her tolerance for heat. Rain was in the forecast. Maybe it would clear the heaviness out of the air. Liz knew it would be even stickier by the pond at Sam's and wondered whether she had some low-Deet insect wipes in the glove box.

She found Sam on the back deck watering her tomatoes. She was barefoot, wearing cargo shorts and a sleeveless shirt. To avoid startling her as she approached, Liz called out, "Hey, Sam. Tomatoes are looking good."

"Thank you. The chipmunks keep eating the green ones. I might have to start popping them with my CO_2 gun. Hate doing that, but they don't even eat them. They take two bites, decide they're sour, and leave 'em."

"They do that in my garden too," said Liz. "I plant extra to share, but sometimes I'm tempted to shoot them too."

Sam shut off the spigot. "What brings you over here?"

Liz shrugged. "No reason in particular. How is your bathroom job going?"

"Really well. I think I'll be finished early. Just waiting for the tub to be delivered. Then Jack can come over and install the plumbing, and I'm done."

"That was fast."

"It was a simple job. She let me take the closet space she wasn't using. I put the tub in there. But now I have to help her find an armoire."

Liz noted that the two stories jived. Truthfulness was a trait she valued. She chalked one up for Olivia.

"I have some crawlers. Want to cast a few?"

"Sure, why not?"

Sam brought out the fishing poles and a paper carton with a plastic lid. "I still love fishing with live bait. Reminds me of being a kid. In the summer, I walked down to the pond every day to catch sunfish with worms. But then, I dug them myself instead of buying them out of the cooler in a convenience store."

"Nothing like fresh-dug worms," agreed Liz, rousing her own childhood memories of pond fishing.

"Those little worms straight out of the ground certainly had more life than these guys." Sam shook the container and snapped off the plastic lid to show Liz. Yes, the nightcrawlers did look sluggish.

"Probably just cold from your fridge. They'll wake up once they're hooked."

"I'll get us some beer," offered Sam. Liz watched her head into the house. Sam's back and arms were muscular from the gym and construction work. She had a lanky body and a graceful walk. Her patrician features gave her face refinement. By anyone's standards, Sam was an attractive woman. Liz often wondered why someone hadn't snapped her up by now.

When Sam had first talked about moving to Maine, Liz had encouraged her to go to some Meetups, but her suggestion was met with reluctance. Sam's relationships never lasted more than a few years. There were long spells when she dated but had no one special. "I'm not sure I want a partner at this point in my life," she'd finally said when Liz had suggested a dance at the gay bar in Webhanet. "I like living alone."

"What about sex?" Liz had asked.

"I can always find sex if I want it."

After that, Liz didn't push. Although Sam called her an honorary big sister, Liz respected Sam's right to find her own way.

Liz dug a lethargic nightcrawler out of the dirt. As soon as she began to thread it on the hook, the fat worm writhed like it was possessed. She leaned over and washed her hands in the pond water, making sparkling ripples that reflected the late afternoon sunlight.

Sam returned with a small cooler and sat down beside Liz on the dock. She opened two beers and handed one to Liz.

"The mosquitos aren't too bad tonight," Sam observed. "Too much breeze, I guess."

Liz took a slug of beer and cast her line. It landed with a plop near the floating dock. Not satisfied with that position, she quickly reeled in. The gears squealed softly as she did.

"What do you think of Olivia Enright?" Liz asked, casting out, this time landing in a more favorable spot. "I mean, now that you've been working for her for a couple of weeks."

"Why do you ask?"

Liz shrugged. "Just curious."

Sam looked thoughtful for a moment. "She scares the shit out of me."

"Really? Why? Is she too demanding? I thought you said the job was going well."

"It has nothing to do with the job. She just looks so perfect all the time. She reminds me of my mother's friends when I was growing up," said Sam. "They would get together for bridge or cocktail parties. When I came into the room, they would stare at me like I was Grendl."

Liz laughed. "Why?"

"I was a tomboy. I always dressed down. They were always dressed to the nines."

"They made you feel uncomfortable?"

"They would look me up and down with their eyebrows raised. I could feel their judgment as surely as if they had spoken it out loud, but they just stared at me, not saying a word. In those moments, I wished the earth would open up and swallow me."

Sam expertly cast out into the pond.

"Those Junior Leaguers were all so fake," grumbled Liz. "Country club drunks, pickled most of the time. If not booze, they popped pills and smoked like chimneys. For all their fussing over their looks, they looked like old hags before their time." Liz reeled in. She pulled up her hook and found it bare. "The fish are hungry." She speared another writhing worm on her hook.

"My mother was just like the others," said Sam. "She was always trying to get me to 'fix myself up.'"

"So was mine. I suppose I should be grateful. She taught me how to look professional, how to 'dress the part,' as she called it. But I still hate wearing grown-up clothes."

"Me too. That's why I'm glad I'm just a humble bathroom renovator now."

"Not quite," said Liz, turning to her with a raised brow.

Sam grinned. "We're both frauds, but do we care?"

"Nah, not me," said Liz, casting out again.

"I think Olivia Enright is growing on me," said Sam.

"Me too."

"She's a great cook," Sam said. "She makes me delicious lunches. She made me poached salmon, grilled tuna, chicken piccata…almost as good as yours, but not quite."

"The way to your renovator's heart is through her stomach. Maybe she likes you."

Sam's eyes grew wide. "You think?"

Liz nodded. "But I'd be careful if I were you."

13

Lucy waited while Cherie tried to regain her composure. She was rapidly going through the packet of tissues. While Cherie tried to mop up the ruined mascara, Lucy wondered if there were more tissues in the bottom drawer. Jodi was usually pretty good about replenishing the supply, but with the stress the pandemic was causing, they'd been going through tissue packs like crazy.

Pandemic or no, if a client was truly willing to face their demons, they eventually reached a point in their therapy where the floodgates opened. Cherie had been a therapist herself, so the milestone came earlier for her than most. The rallies and violent protests on the news every night provided stimulation to dislodge the bad memories of the night when Cherie's sister was shot to death by a trooper.

Cherie had relived those awful moments many times during her therapy sessions. Each time more of the fear and pain were dredged up, and Cherie wept harder. This time she was weeping like her soul was leaking out along with the tears. The unspent grief over her sister's death was commingled with mourning the death of her father and her guilt over Brenda's career troubles. Cherie admitted that sometimes it was really hard to keep herself together. Externally, Lucy always maintained her professional demeanor, but her heart ached for Cherie.

"Brenda only came to the march to support me," Cherie said in a mournful voice.

"She came to the march because she wanted to be there. You didn't force her to go. She went on her own."

"I did lay on the guilt pretty heavily."

"It doesn't matter. Brenda is a grown woman who makes her own decisions. Don't you agree?"

"Of course, I agree!" insisted Cherie. The vehemence of her response was undercut by the mascara smudge under her eye. Lucy tried not to stare at it.

She was grateful to be able to see the range of facial expressions that helped her interpret a client's reactions. Liz had reluctantly agreed to relax the mask rule. Lucy's fair skin was sensitive, and she'd been getting a rash where the mask touched her face. Showing Liz the angry, red outline was enough to get her to rethink her position. They'd moved back the tape delineating the safety zone and put Lucy's desk closer to the window.

"If Brenda hadn't come to the demonstration, she wouldn't be in this mess. And why couldn't that hateful woman tell her herself? Why did she send Sam to do her dirty work?"

Lucy sighed. She'd asked herself the same question, but after thinking about it, she understood. Using Sam as the messenger kept the communication completely off the record. Unfortunately, Sam, for all her virtues, was a blunt instrument and had awkwardly revealed her source.

"Look at it this way. Brenda got away with it this time. Now, she needs to be more careful. There are probably people on the council who would love an excuse to fire her."

"Have you heard that?" asked Cherie with apprehension.

"Not directly, but Liz tells me some people in town don't like the idea of a female police chief."

"That's crazy. Brenda is a great chief. The town loves her."

"There's still plenty of sexism in our culture. People get ideas in their minds and it's hard to dislodge them."

Brenda wasn't the only one being talked about behind her back. Lucy knew that some of her conservative parishioners still griped about having a lesbian rector.

"Cherie, I think you need to let Brenda handle the fallout from the march her way. I want to hear how this episode has impacted your relationship. Are things better or worse because of it?"

"A little of both. Brenda is stressed about her job. That makes her distracted, sometimes cranky. It's harder to get her interested in sex because she can't relax."

"Don't let her get away with that. Be sensitive but don't take excuses for avoiding intimacy."

Cherie momentarily forgot her problems and grinned. "Is that the way you handle it? Take no prisoners?"

Lucy mimed exaggerated thought. "I don't know. Taking prisoners could be interesting. Haven't tried that yet."

"Lucy! Sometimes, the things you say really shock me."

"I doubt it. But before we get into that, tell me how your relationship is better."

Cherie thought for a moment. "I can see how devoted Brenda is to me. She's willing to take risks to support me. She really does care about racism."

"You sound surprised."

"No. I could always sense Brenda is a good person, even when the uniform kept me away." Cherie grinned. "Speaking of the uniform, I did it!"

Now it was Lucy's turn to make big eyes. "No! You didn't!"

Cherie nodded conclusively to confirm it.

"And how did that go?"

Cherie's little grin turned into a full smile. "Worked like a charm!"

After that, Cherie changed the subject to her concerns about her patient load. People were still afraid to come into a doctor's office. Cherie worried that Liz would cut her hours and her salary. Although Lucy knew that Liz would do everything possible before she stopped paying her staff, she was worried too. If donations didn't pick up soon, they might need to cut Jodi's hours. Lucy and Tom had already stopped drawing a salary from the parish. Tom had volunteered to mow the lawn around the church to save on landscaping costs. The stop-gap measures might help St. Margaret's in the short term, but they would hurt people who were already under economic pressure.

After Cherie left, Lucy checked the Tithe.ly receipts. She was shocked to see another anonymous, twenty-five-thousand-dollar donation. Who was this mystery donor? Hearing Cherie's concerns about her wages confirmed Lucy's assumption that it wasn't Liz, but then who?

Lucy bowed her head and murmured a quick prayer of thanksgiving for the donor's generosity. When she opened her eyes, she saw Jodi standing in her doorway. "Sorry to disturb you Mother Lucy, but Olivia Enright is here to see you."

When Olivia sat down, Lucy could instantly tell from her eyes that her client needed more sleep.

"Do you mind if I take off my mask?" asked Olivia. "I just tested negative for COVID, so I'm not a risk." She glanced around the room. "I see you've rearranged a bit."

"We've put the chairs farther apart, so we don't need masks."

"Good idea."

While Olivia took off her mask and put it into her bag, Lucy gave her a critical once over. "How are you? Is the Alprazolam helping you relax?"

"I only take it when I'm desperate for sleep. I don't want to become dependent. I'd hate that."

"How are you sleeping?"

"Not well."

"I can see that."

Olivia compressed her lips. "That bad?"

"Only to the practiced eye. To anyone else, you probably look fine."

She smiled wanly. "That's good to know. I never slept very much. The world financial markets never sleep. I had alerts set for when the major markets opened. Sometimes instant intelligence can make all the difference."

"Surely, it's not worth your health."

"When you're as invested as I was in my business, you don't think about that."

Lucy gave Olivia a critical look. "Was your business the most important thing in your life?"

Olivia nodded solemnly. "Yes, I'm afraid it was."

"More important than your family?"

Olivia stared at her lap. "I'd like to say no, but that wouldn't be the truth. In the beginning, when Jason was born, I became one of those obsessive mothers and tried to micromanage his development. What do they call them now? A helicopter mom. I treated raising my son like managing my fund, something to be monitored constantly, tweaked, sometimes by force."

"I'm hearing some regret."

"Oh, of course! Don't you regret giving away your child for adoption?"

Lucy had to force herself not to show how much the question upset her. "I do regret it, although at the time, it was the best I could do. I wasn't ready to give up my career to raise a child."

Olivia frowned and gave her a penetrating look. "But your career ended anyway."

"Once you're blackballed at the Met, it's the end."

"So much harder for us women, isn't it?" said Olivia in a sympathetic voice. "No matter what they say, we can't have it all. It's our job to bear and raise the children. Nothing can change that."

"Were you involved with a man at the time you gave birth to Jason?"

"I was married to my ex-husband."

"Did he help with parenting?"

"Michael Enright didn't care about anything but himself and the almighty dollar. We divorced by the time Jason was ten. Being a father wasn't for Michael. Nothing that required emotion was for him."

Sounds like you were a perfect match, Lucy thought, then mentally pinched herself for being so judgmental.

"When did you discover you were attracted to women?"

"In college."

"But you married a man."

"It's what women did in those days. Don't you remember?"

Lucy nodded. "It's what they do now too."

"It's not the same. When I first started in finance, there were few women in positions of importance. Most were tokens and had to have the right pedigree to be valuable for the corporate image. You proved your stability with marriage. Men as well as women. It made you seem more reliable."

"So, love had nothing to do with it?"

"Don't be naïve, Mother Lucy."

Lucy tried to moderate her irritation by forcing herself to assume a kind look. It took a moment, but it worked. Eventually, she felt less hostile toward her client.

"You portray yourself as being tough. Is that who you are?"

"I have my moments…like everyone."

"Moments when you're not using other people?"

Olivia showed real anger for the first time. "Everyone uses other people. We might tell ourselves nice stories about why we do it, invent benign justifications, but ultimately all relationships are self-serving. Otherwise, we wouldn't stick around. The investment has to be worth the return."

"What about your feelings?"

Olivia gave her a canny look. "I bet you're thinking I'm a cold fish who has no feelings."

"You have no idea what I'm thinking."

"Yes, but I'm good at reading faces and body language. You don't like me. You think I'm heartless. Well, I've got news for you. I'm not."

"But you work very hard at projecting that image. It's defensive, isn't it?"

"Of course. I don't want people to take advantage of me."

"I'm your therapist, not someone negotiating a business deal with you."

"True. And so far, you've put up with a lot from me. Why?"

"Because I offered to help you. And you agreed to allow it."

"Why would you do that? What's in it for you? Do you think you'll make another convert? Another parishioner willing to pay the tithe?"

"Not everything is about money. I try to reflect God's love in everything I do."

"As a priest."

"Yes, as a priest, but also in counseling. I don't talk about religion in sessions unless someone brings it up. But my motivation is the same either way."

"But you don't like me."

"Love, in the Christian sense, is not about liking someone. In fact, love is especially important when someone is unlikable or has different views. Is it important that I like you?"

Olivia struggled to answer. "Yes," she finally admitted.

Lucy heard the pain in Olivia's voice and decided not to lecture her on professional objectivity. Instead, she smiled warmly to comfort her. "Why don't we get to know one another and we'll see?"

Olivia's control returned. Lucy felt herself being carefully scrutinized. She willed herself to relax as those shrewd eyes studied her.

"You're very good at what you do, Mother Lucy. This town is lucky to have you."

"Thank you."

"Next time we meet, I'd like to talk about my son."

"Why not today?"

"I've never spoken about it before to anyone. I need to think about what I want to say."

"We only have two sessions left."

"I know. I always save the best for last."

14

Liz watched Maggie prepare a tray of appetizers for Olivia's visit. Maggie's food presentation was always so artful. Tonight she had arranged the raw vegetables around the dip to make a color wheel of the brightly colored peppers, carrots, purple cauliflower, and green vegetables. While she went about her kitchen tasks, she was uncharacteristically quiet, which made Liz worry because Maggie always had something to say.

"Maggie," said Liz, hugging her from behind, "are you angry because I invited Olivia?"

"I wish you had asked me before you did. I'm not sure how I feel about that woman, especially after she used Sam in that way."

Liz tightened her embrace and leaned her chin on Maggie's shoulder. "I know. I'm not sure either," she whispered into Maggie's ear. "Trust me on this. Please."

Maggie sighed and turned around. "Sometimes it's hard, Liz. You're so generous, and for a person who takes such pride in being fierce, you're incredibly trusting."

"I'm really not. My Spidey sense tells me Olivia's more needy than ferocious. She's covering up something really big."

"Since when did you become so intuitive? You're like a brick when I try to tell you something."

"Thanks," said Liz, making a face.

Maggie touched her cheek. "I'm sorry. That wasn't nice. It's just that you don't always hear what I say."

"You don't always hear what I say either. It's like you tune out the wavelength of my voice."

"You have selective hearing too."

"Does every couple stop listening?" Maggie's hazel eyes searched hers. "I want you to hear me," she said, shaking Liz's shoulders. "I treasure our conversations. They're more intimate than sex. Try to listen more carefully? Please."

"Okay, I'll try." Liz mumbled and moved away.

Apart from Maggie's professed hostility toward Olivia, Liz was anxious about how this evening would go. Maggie and Olivia were both actresses in their own way, so they'd probably be smooth and buttoned down as they tried to impress one another. Liz was already planning to tune out during that part of the conversation. She was done with one-upmanship and impressing people. *Been there. Done that*, she thought as she opened a bottle of red wine to breathe.

Maggie returned from the porch. She gave Liz a half hug around the waist. "I'm sorry, honey. I should be more welcoming to your friends."

"She's not my friend yet. She offered to give me financial advice, and I took her up on it."

Maggie stood back to look at Liz's face. "I know what a big concession that was for you. You think you're quite the investor."

"Yes, but I'm smart enough to know when I can learn from someone even smarter."

"I love that about you, Liz. You're an arrogant person, who knows when to be humble. Well, maybe not humble, but at least not as arrogant as you could be."

"Arrogance comes with the territory when you're a surgeon. It's part of the training."

"You're kidding."

"Yes." Liz grinned.

"Smart ass." Maggie grabbed an olive from the hors d'oeuvres tray and popped it into her mouth. She offered one to Liz, who opened her mouth.

As Liz chewed the olive, the doorbell rang.

"Go on," said Maggie, nudging her. "Let Godzilla in."

Liz laughed and headed to the front door. She opened it to find Olivia standing there with a bouquet of roses and a bottle of wine.

"Beware of geeks bearing gifts."

"Hah! Good pun. Come in," said Liz, taking the wine and the flowers. "Are these from your garden?"

"They are."

"Beautiful and so fragrant! Floribunda?"

"Yes. The variety is 'Sheila's Perfume.' Are you a gardener, Liz?"

"I am."

"Of course, you are," said Olivia. "You're quite the Renaissance woman, aren't you?"

Liz continued to smile despite her loathing for flattery. "Come in and meet my wife," she said and led Olivia through the kitchen.

"Your house is very clever. You built up, not out."

"Yes, Sam McKinnon designed the renovation."

"Did she?" Olivia looked impressed. "Can you see the ocean from upstairs?"

"Yes, from the third floor, but I'm high enough here to be out of the flood plain, so I have a usable basement."

"You don't really believe in all that global warming nonsense, do you?"

"I do believe in it, and I eat as much lobster as I can because when the Gulf of Maine warms too much, they'll be gone."

Olivia looked pensive. "Hadn't thought of that. It would be catastrophic for our economy."

Liz put the roses in a vase. She left the gift bag containing the wine bottle on the island.

"Come out to the porch and meet my wife."

Maggie's eyes remained focused on Olivia's face, but Liz knew her wife was surreptitiously inspecting their guest from head to toe and wasn't necessarily impressed.

"Maggie Fitzgerald! What a pleasure to meet you," said Olivia with overstated enthusiasm. "I've been a fan since *Les Mis*. I *never* miss a single one of your appearances at the Playhouse. We're so lucky to have such wonderful local talent!"

The slight narrowing of Maggie's eyes indicated she didn't really buy the exaggerated praise, but she graciously extended her hand. "Liz tells me you're interested in being on the board of the Playhouse. We could use someone with your knack for finance. We artists are usually at sea where money is concerned."

"I'd be happy to lend a hand."

"Wine, Olivia?" asked Liz, poised to pour red wine into a glass.

"Why not open the wine I brought? It's very good."

"All right," said Liz. "I'll get it." She grabbed the gift bag from the kitchen island and a corkscrew. "Let's see what we've got here." When Liz saw the papal tiara and crossed keys molded into the wine bottle, she took a deep breath. "Châteauneuf du Pape." She forced a smile and glanced at Maggie.

Olivia apparently perceived their discomfort. "Don't you like the pope's wine?"

"Maggie finds it too dry," Liz said quickly, "but it's fine for me."

"I'm sorry, Maggie. I didn't know."

"Of course, you couldn't, but I'm sure Liz will help you drink it. She's probably missed that wine. It was her ex's favorite."

Olivia's hand flew to her mouth. "Oh, no! A double faux pas!"

"Let me open your wine, so it can breathe," said Liz, peeling off the metal foil. "Will you slum with us and have a couple of sips of this California pinot while it does?"

"Of course," said Olivia. Liz gestured to a seat and Olivia sat down. While Liz uncorked the wine, she noticed Maggie winding a strand of long, gray hair into a ringlet around her finger, an unconscious habit reserved for uncomfortable moments. Liz refilled her glass in the hopes that alcohol would put her more at ease. She poured a glass of wine for Olivia.

"Thank you, Liz." She raised the glass in Maggie's direction. "Thanks for the invitation."

Liz was pleased to see Olivia smile after she sipped the wine. "Like it?"

"It's wonderful. Smooth. Great nose."

"You can find it most places for fifteen dollars or less. A real find." Liz handed her the bottle.

"I'll have to remember that."

"Olivia, how long have you been living in Hobbs?" Maggie asked.

"I moved up here from New York the summer before last. I hoped that being by the ocean would improve my mood."

"Did it?"

"Yes and no. The house has a lot of memories. My son built it. When he passed, I inherited it because he didn't want it to go to his ex-wife. But it's a beautiful house, and I'm enjoying the ocean views."

"It must be wonderful to be right on the beach," Maggie said.

"I don't know why I didn't spend more time here. I was always invited. But my life and my business were in New York. I still haven't decided what to do with my condo. I probably should have sold it when the economy was booming, and the prices were high."

Obviously, Olivia liked to talk about herself. Liz poured herself a glass of wine and sat down next to Maggie.

"I've been renting out my apartment in the Village," Maggie said. "I make a little income on it, but I only kept it because I always thought I would go back to Broadway. Then I became so involved in teaching and the theater here in Maine, it just never happened."

"Do you miss New York?" Olivia asked.

"Sometimes. I miss the energy. Of course, I miss the theater and eateries. But we have some fine restaurants in Maine."

"So, I've discovered. Too bad so many of them are suffering during the pandemic."

"The good ones will survive, I think."

Maggie and their guest seemed to be getting along well enough that Liz felt comfortable excusing herself so that she could get dinner going. She put up the rice and turned on the grill. As she speared the lamb kabobs onto skewers, she wondered how the conversation on the porch was going, but she trusted Maggie to carry the ball.

Olivia was originally from Syracuse, so at dinner, she and Maggie shared stories about growing up there.

"I'm from upstate too," Liz interjected.

Maggie pursed her lips. "Liz, Westchester is not upstate."

"To people who live there, it is."

Olivia and Maggie laughed in unison, and Liz saw, to her surprise, they were not only getting along, but a bond had formed between them. *So far, so good*, thought Liz as she cleared the table.

When Liz returned to the porch, Maggie said, "Liz, why don't you get your meeting with Olivia going while I clean up the kitchen? We can have dessert later."

Liz glanced at Olivia.

"I could use a break after that wonderful meal. Liz, I must certainly add chef to your impressive list of talents."

Liz felt uncomfortable with the compliment, but she smiled. "Let's go into my office, where I have my financial records."

"Lead the way."

When Olivia stepped into Liz's office, she gazed around curiously. "Are all these awards and plaques yours?"

"Yes," said Liz, sitting down behind the desk.

"Very impressive."

Liz shrugged. "My ex put them up when she was considering moving up here with me."

"Dr. Carson?"

"Yes," said Liz with a little frown. "How did you know?"

"We have friends in common. George Stevens from NYU."

The name explained why Olivia's facial work looked so natural. Stevens was an outstanding plastic surgeon.

"I worked with him when I was visiting professor at NYU."

"I know. He speaks highly of you."

"I thought he retired."

Olivia confirmed it with a nod. "Unfortunately, but we stay in touch." She gazed at Liz expectantly.

"Are you looking for a recommendation?"

Olivia pulled her chin into her shoulder with mock horror. "Do I look like I need one?"

Liz shook her head. "No, you look great. George does nice work." Liz opened her laptop to indicate that she'd rather move away from this topic and get down to business. Olivia got the hint. She opened her bag and took out a notebook computer.

"I'm sending you an invitation to share my screen," said Olivia. She shifted seamlessly into a polished review of Liz's finances, complete with graphs, spreadsheets, and bullet points. Liz scribbled some notes on a pad as she did.

"So, to summarize," said Olivia, "you're too conservatively invested and I would advise you to take a little more risk. On the next screen, I've recommended some funds and stocks to consider."

Liz glanced at the screen. "I see you like the Enright fund."

Olivia grinned mischievously. "I think I should, don't you? But don't worry. It's not self-serving. I've divested. The new manager is good. I'll introduce you if you like."

"Let's see," said Liz cautiously.

"I also recommend placing a large bet on Abbott labs. I see you like supporting local companies. Their new rapid COVID test looks promising."

Liz had read about the test in the medical news and had already considered buying stock. "Good idea."

"The next part of the plan concerns your business." Olivia gestured toward Liz's laptop. "Go on. Open the invitation I just sent."

Liz did and listened carefully as Olivia laid out an in-depth business plan in a sophisticated Power Point presentation.

"To summarize, you should use the tax advantages of your LLC instead of bearing the entire burden yourself. You can transfer money, pay your people, and get significant tax relief. I'm surprised your accountant never recommended it before. I'm sure this isn't the first time you've had to put money into the business."

"No, it's not. But never this much."

"I'm a CPA," Olivia said casually. "I'd be happy to look over your books."

Liz gazed at Olivia intently. "I still don't get why you're doing this."

"I told you. This town needs a doctor like you."

"I get the civic duty part," said Liz, "but what's in it for you?"

Olivia smiled mysteriously. "You'll see."

15

"And tonight, I will take my first bath in my new bathtub," said Olivia, reaching across the table to tap Sam's glass. "Congratulations, Samantha McKinnon, on a job well done."

"Thank you, but it was a pretty basic upgrade."

"Don't be modest. The bathroom looks beautiful. You made it seem like it should have always been that way."

"Well, that's how it should have been. I know it was a custom house, but they don't usually let you get away with no tubs. People need them for young children."

"I'm sure my son paid off the right person. His kids were past the bathtub stage when he built the house. But *you* solved the one problem I've always had with that house."

"You should see what I can do when I have a real challenge."

"Actually, I'd like that."

Sam wasn't sure how to respond. As much as she'd enjoyed the lunches and found Olivia attractive in an icy, upper-crust way, she'd planned to cash her client's check and move on. That is, after they found an armoire to replace the demolished closet. They had spent the morning looking for it, but after a tour of the best used-furniture dealers, they'd come up empty-handed.

Olivia lined up her tableware on the plate at the nine and three o'clock position. Sam recognized the code from her prep-school etiquette class and agreed with the message. The meal of seared scallops had been perfection.

"I'm impressed that you got a COVID test, so that we could go out together," said Olivia.

"It's hard to social distance and shop for furniture."

"How did you manage to get tested? I had to jump through hoops."

"Liz took care of it."

Olivia's perfectly arched brows rose slightly. "Really? She made me go down to Southern Med, where I had to wait in line for hours."

"You got the real test. I got the quickie Liz uses for her staff. They get tested every day. Unfortunately, it's not as accurate as the real test."

"You mean, you could be a danger?"

Sam laughed. "Some people say so."

"Hmm. You don't look very dangerous," Olivia leaned on her hand. "Tell me more."

"When I was a design architect, I was always getting into trouble, shooting my mouth off when I should have kept it shut. Lost quite a few commissions that way. I'm not one of those architects who think you should build something ugly just because someone else is paying for it."

"Obviously, you got enough commissions to win awards."

"I did, but not because of my tact or charm."

"No, because you are truly gifted."

Sam suddenly felt hot and took a sip of water. "You're embarrassing me with all the compliments."

"I'm only speaking the truth. Always take a compliment when it's sincere."

That sounded too much like something Sam's mother might say. She could feel herself squirm in her chair, but she made an effort to smile pleasantly.

"You deserve the accolades from what I understand. Your designs were innovative."

"In underlying structure, yes, but in externals, I borrowed heavily from the mid-century moderns. That is, the twentieth century, of course."

"All art is derivative, Samantha. The idea is to improve on the good things of the past."

As Olivia spoke, Sam found herself focusing on the movements of her lips. She particularly liked the color of the lipstick Olivia was wearing today, a slightly coral pink. Nowadays, you didn't often see that color. It was a little retro, but the shade suited Olivia's coloring perfectly. Sam studied the woman's bone structure. She had high cheekbones, a good chin, a high forehead, and a patrician nose. As Sam looked into the blue eyes, she saw the yellow flecks in them for the first time. They receded as Olivia's pupils widened.

"Samantha? Did you hear what I said?"

In fact, Sam hadn't heard a word. "No, I'm sorry. I must have been zoning out." She grinned. "I like the color of your lipstick. You don't see corals very often."

"I can't wear true pinks. They turn blue on my complexion." Olivia smiled. "You would know about color, wouldn't you? Why don't you wear makeup?"

"I wore it for years when I worked in an office. I had to because I did C-suite presentations. As you know, corporate board members expect a certain 'look.' Now, I don't wear it because no one cares how I look."

As Olivia leaned forward, her bracelets slid down her forearms and clinked gently. "Are you one of those women trying to make a statement? I loathed those old-fashioned, hard-line feminists. Burn my bra? Never!"

Sam chuckled. "I don't doubt it. You look like you appreciate a good foundation."

"In clothing, buildings, and relationships."

"That's quite a span. Clothing to relationships."

"I told you I'd like to get to know you better. Don't you remember?"

Sam remembered, but then, she'd been so annoyed by Olivia, she'd brushed it aside. "And here I thought you were just feeding the help."

"I was, but I also wanted to get to know you." Olivia's blue eyes peered into hers until Sam was nearly mesmerized. "You fascinate me, Samantha. You have this sensitive, artistic side, and yet, you'd rather swing a sledgehammer."

"I'd rather set tile. Not the same. Sometimes, I need the sledgehammer to achieve my other goals."

"I see," said Olivia. "But you look so confident with a hammer in your hands. So in control!" The way Olivia said it made it sound like a sexual innuendo.

"Are you coming on to me, Olivia?"

Olivia laughed aloud. "Do you think I'd bother being so subtle?"

"No, probably not."

Olivia carefully refolded the napkin and looked around for the waitress. "If we can't find an armoire this afternoon, will you build one for me?"

Sam hadn't bargained on that question, so she took a moment to think. "I'd rather find a used armoire, or even one I could modify to suit your purposes. It will be a lot cheaper, and it's greener to reuse things."

"That's right. You're LEED certified. You would say that. But if it came to it, *would* you build it for me?"

"I usually don't build big pieces."

"You've designed and built high rises, but you don't build large furniture?"

"Maybe that's why my woodworking is smaller, built with delicate pieces of figured wood. I want each piece to be a jewel. Plus, my shop isn't set up for big casework. If I built an armoire, I'd ask Liz to help me. She's built some big pieces, and she has the machinery for it."

"Now, that's an interesting idea…a piece of furniture custom built by my doctor and my architect."

"Don't get your hopes up. My plan is to find a used armoire. That was our deal."

"So it was," said Olivia, opening her bag. "We should be going." Sam fished in her knapsack for her wallet. Olivia showed her palm. "No, I've got this. It's a celebration."

"I just got paid," said Sam, pulling out Olivia's check.

"So, you did. Now, put that away. And your wallet."

Olivia inserted her credit card into the slot of the folder and set it on end to get the waitress's attention. "I apologize if my interest offended you."

Sam thought for a moment. "It doesn't offend me, but I don't usually respond well to women who come on too strong."

"Because you're butch?"

Sam shook her head. "I don't believe in playing roles, and I feel that foreplay should be mutual. Too much aggression turns me off."

"I'll remember that."

"Good," said Sam.

"But you're not opposed to getting to know one another?"

Sam thought about the question. "No, but I wonder if that's possible. You're so busy putting on a show for everyone, it's hard to see anything but the performance."

Olivia blinked and sat back, but otherwise Sam had no way of knowing how her words had landed. She could see that they'd had some effect. Olivia looked pensive. "How could I make a better impression?"

"Researching people feels invasive. You could try listening instead of talking. You can learn a lot when you listen. Instead of interviewing people, you could let them volunteer information."

"I always felt that asking questions is a way of showing interest."

"I bet you learned that in some sales training course."

"Yes, as a matter of fact."

Sam barked out a laugh. "My first firm sent me for sales training. I was great at selling designs but stunk at the small talk that goes along with business deals."

"Obviously, you learned something. You were a success."

"But not by charming clients. I got there by doing great designs that won contracts. I didn't sleep my way to the top."

"You think I did?"

"Let's just say you married the right guy, who helped you get where you are."

"But you're a self-made woman."

"No, I had the privilege of growing up in a wealthy family, going to good schools, getting a great education."

"You went to Princeton, if I remember."

"Here we go again with the interviewing."

"I'm sorry. You were telling me something."

"I was, if you'd only give me the chance. I was about to tell you about my advantages. My father knew the head of my first architecture firm. That got me an interview, but it was my portfolio that got me the job."

"Would you have been hired if you didn't have connections?"

"Maybe. Affirmative action wasn't a dirty word then, but it tainted the careers of a lot of women."

"Not your Hobbs friends."

"No, they're the real deal. That's why we're not impressed by pretentious people who flaunt their wealth."

"Like me?"

Sam shrugged.

"Now that you have your check, you think you can say whatever you want."

Sam shook her head. "No, you could stop the check, and I wouldn't put it past you."

The intense eyes peered directly into Sam's. "You don't think much of me, do you?"

"I don't know you well enough to think anything."

"Maybe we can change that. Come for dinner, so we can get to know one another better. You'll see. I'm not what you think."

Sam swirled the last of the wine in her glass as she considered the invitation. "Let's see how the afternoon goes, and I'll let you know."

16

Brenda watched Tom and Jeff set down the recliner in the living room. Tom arched his back and rubbed his flanks. "Now I know I'm old!"

Jeff snickered. "You're a year younger than I am. You're just out of shape."

"I'm sorry, Tom," said Cherie, approaching. "I knew we should have gotten professional movers. I hope you didn't hurt your back. Let me see."

Brenda's heart swelled as she observed her partner's concern for Tom. Being a physician's assistant fit Cherie's personality perfectly. She was so naturally kind.

Tom waved Cherie off. "It's all right. Just a twinge. It wasn't that heavy. I'm exaggerating for effect."

"Cherie, you know how gay men are," Jeff called from across the room. "Exaggeration is our signature trait."

"Oh, stop," said Tom. "That's a stereotype!"

"Not completely. Look at you, moaning and groaning!"

Liz and Sam came in with boxes. "Standing around again?" scolded Liz. "Come on, you loafers. We're almost done. Get to work!" She glanced at Cherie. "These go upstairs to your room?"

"Yes, thanks, Liz." Cherie touched Tom's shoulder. "Are you sure you're okay?"

"Of course. I just want to get out of here and take off this blank, blank mask. It's so hot."

"I know," said Cherie in a soothing voice, "but we all thank you for the consideration."

Brenda moved the chair into a better position, so people could pass around it. Cherie stood beside her and frowned. "It doesn't really fit with the rest of the furniture, does it? And it makes the room crowded."

"That's what happens when a couple moves in together. Mismatched stuff and too much of everything."

Cherie's eyes searched hers. "Are you sure it's okay here? We can still ask the guys to bring it up to my room. It will fit. I measured the space."

"It was your Dad's, so it belongs in a place of honor." Brenda reached around Cherie and pulled her close. "When you sit in it, you'll feel Jean-Paul hugging you. He'll be with us in your new home."

Cherie turned into Brenda's arms. "I'm sorry I've been so difficult," she said, her voice breaking. "I could have moved in when you asked and been here all along."

Brenda kissed the top of her head. "It's okay. I know you needed time. It's been a lot to deal with…being sick, your Dad's death, the demonstrations triggering all the bad memories. I get it." A sob alerted Brenda to the fact that Cherie was actively weeping, so she strengthened her embrace. "Oh, sweetie, don't cry," said Brenda, stroking Cherie's back.

"I'm sorry. This grief thing doesn't always go like I expect. One minute, I'm just fine. Then, I'm crying all over the place!"

Brenda held Cherie in her arms, gently rocking her, while people went in and out bringing boxes up to the second floor. No one paid any attention to the couple, as if following the unspoken campground rule—never look into another camper's tent.

Finally, Tom's pastoral instincts overcame his respect for their privacy. "Cherie, is there anything I can do?"

Cherie wiped her tears with the back of her hand. "No, Tom. I'm okay. The grief thing. You know how it is."

"Don't try to manage it. Just go with the flow." He sighed and gave her a long, sympathetic look. "I wish I could give you a hug."

"I know. Me too."

Tom touched the front of his mask and raised his hand. "Kisses and hugs to you both. Blessings."

"Thanks, Tom," said Cherie. "You too."

After Tom headed out the door, Brenda rubbed Cherie's shoulder. "Are you okay? It's a big deal to move in with your girlfriend."

"I know, but I'm ready."

"You're sure?"

"I'd better be. My landlord already has a new tenant. If I don't live here, I'm homeless!"

"Someone would take you in. Probably Liz. She always takes in strays."

"I heard my name. Are you talking about me again?" Brenda looked up and saw Liz standing in the doorway.

Brenda gave Cherie's shoulders a quick hug and let her go.

"Sorry to interrupt your foreplay," said Liz, "but I wanted to ask if you're coming over for Thirsty Thursday this afternoon."

"Of course, we are," said Cherie. "I want to see everyone."

"Maggie invited Tony and Freddie. Stefan says he adores women, but he's desperate to see more people who can grow a beard."

"We love Tony and Freddie," said Cherie.

"And I'm bringing a surprise guest."

"Who?" asked Brenda.

"If I tell you, it won't be a surprise." Liz winked. "Later, girlies." She closed the door.

Cherie pulled Brenda close. "Hug me. I need hugs!"

"I can think of other ways to get close," Brenda whispered near her ear.

Cherie shook her head. "No, just hugs right now."

"Okay." Brenda held her and leisurely stroked her blond hair. It smelled pleasantly of the rinse she used to tame the tight waves, a vestige of her black heritage. "I love you, and I'm so glad you're here." Brenda kissed the top of her head.

"Me too," murmured Cherie into her shoulder.

Brenda liked the feel of Cherie in her arms. She closed her eyes and thanked the universe that they were together, that they had survived the coronavirus, and that Cherie had agreed to move in with her.

Brenda was enjoying the pleasure of Cherie's soft breasts against her when she felt gentle fingers caressing her nipple. Cherie looked up with a grin. "I think I changed my mind about going to bed."

"Okay. Let's go." On the way to the stairs, Brenda locked the front door.

"Just in case someone forgot something and wants to come back. I don't want any interruptions."

❊❊❊

When they awoke, two hours had passed. Brenda jumped up. "Cherie! We need to get dressed. It's almost five!"

"We should shower first, or everyone will know what we've been up to."

"So what? They do it too. Let's get dressed and go."

They were only a few minutes late. As soon as they arrived, Liz waved to them. "Step right up for your free COVID test! Step right up!" called Liz in her best imitation of a carnival barker. She blocked Cherie's progress with her arm. "Not you, Cherie. You had one this afternoon."

"What's this?" asked Brenda, looking over the test analyzer.

"The governor made Abbott's instant test available to doctors' offices at cost, so, with the help of a friend, I bought a couple thousand test kits. I got the idea of using our Thirsty Thursday's gang and the town services as our control group. I'll test everyone once a week and keep track." Liz approached with the long probe. "Put your head back."

"I already had the virus."

"Doesn't mean you can't get it again. Studies show immunity falls off rapidly. Not a good sign for vaccine development." Liz withdrew the probe and deposited Brenda's sample into the machine. "So far, everyone in this group is in the clear."

"Does that mean we can hug and kiss?" asked Lucy, watching.

"Yes, I guess so," said Liz. "Just don't go overboard. No tongue kissing, please."

Lucy had on a low-cut T-shirt, making it difficult for Brenda to avoid admiring her cleavage.

"You don't know how hard it's been for us huggers," Lucy said. "It's excruciating!"

"Don't I give you enough hugs?" asked Erika, feigning concern.

"Yes, but I want more. No one can ever have enough hugs!"

Maggie opened the screen door from the porch. "Liz your other guest has arrived."

Brenda noted that despite her cheerful tone, Maggie didn't look happy.

"Excuse me," said Liz. She glanced at Brenda. "Your test results will be available in a few minutes. You're in the danger zone until then. Sit over there." Liz gestured to chairs on the other side of the deck.

Brenda helped herself to a beer from the cooler in the center of the deck. She flipped off the cap with an opener. Liz only bought craft beers, and Brenda had hurt her fingers trying to twist off the caps. She took a quick sip and noticed that the group had suddenly gotten quiet. Everyone was staring at the door from the porch. Brenda turned around to see why.

Olivia Enright stood in the doorway. She was smiling her practiced smile and looked perfect in every way. Her outfit had obviously been planned to suit the casual gathering, but there was nothing casual about the selection of the color-coordinated Bermuda shorts and nautical, striped top. She wore classic sandals and her toenails were painted a subtle shade of deep rose. Her put-together appearance exuded two things: class and money.

"Hello, everyone," she said to the silent group. "So nice to see everyone."

Liz's frown revealed her disappointment at the chilly reception the group was giving her guest. "I think you all know Olivia Enright. I want you to know that our testing program is being underwritten by the Enright Foundation."

Brenda glanced around at the other guests. No one seemed impressed by this news. Everyone stared stone-faced at the newcomer. The tension was palpable.

Lucy jumped up and took Olivia's hand. "Let's get you a drink. I just opened a bottle of pinot grigio. Would you like to try it?" Lucy shot one of her solar flare smiles around the group, and reluctantly, the others smiled in return.

Liz checked the testing machine. "Looks like you're in the clear, Brenda. You can join the group."

Brenda approached to speak confidentially. "You brought *that* woman to our gathering? What were you thinking?"

"She's trying, Brenda," Liz whispered. "Let's give her a chance."

Brenda screwed up her face. "Liz, she wanted to fire me!"

"No, the others wanted to fire you. She stuck up for you."

"How do you know?"

"I have my spies on the council."

"Yeah, right," said Brenda.

"I do," Liz protested. "You're one of them. How else would I know what's going on in town?"

Brenda deliberately lowered her shoulders and tried to look calm. "It's hard enough to listen to her go on in the council meetings. Now I have to socialize with her?" Brenda glowered in Olivia's direction.

"That's your choice, Brenda. Just be nice. She's trying to make friends with people like us."

"People like us? You mean, she's *gay*!" Brenda realized her voice was too loud and lowered it.

Liz glanced at Olivia. "You wouldn't know from looking at her, but that's what she says."

"I don't understand how any gay woman can belong to that backward party."

"Tut tut. Let's leave the politics out of it. This is a social gathering."

Brenda let out a long stream of air. "Okay. I can be civil."

"Good. I know you can."

After Brenda found a seat beside Cherie, Olivia looked in her direction. She quickly wound down her conversation with Lucy and approached. Brenda realized she intended to take the empty chair beside her.

"Just what I need," muttered Brenda under her breath. She pasted a smile on her face. "Hello, Ms. Enright," she said pleasantly as Olivia sat down. "It's really generous of you to sponsor the testing."

"The Enright Foundation supports medical research. This benefits a local company and the town too." Olivia offered her hand. "Please call me Olivia."

Brenda eyed the extended hand before she took it.

"Do you mind if I call you, Brenda?"

"That's fine."

"I'm so glad to see you looking so well after your illness," said Olivia with a practiced smile. Her teeth were too perfect to be natural.

"It was quite an experience," admitted Brenda. "I never felt so sick in my life."

"It's a terrible illness. I hope there's a vaccine soon." She lowered her voice. "I'm sorry the council was so hard on you after the demonstration."

"I hear that you stuck up for me. I just wish you had the guts to tell me to my face."

Olivia leaned closer to speak confidentially. "I thought a word to the wise would be sufficient."

"It was unfair to Sam to use her like that."

Olivia stared at her wine glass. "I realize that now."

Brenda was surprised that Olivia wasn't digging in her heels like she did in council meetings. "Next time you want to tell me something, tell me yourself."

"Brenda, you are an excellent police chief," said Olivia in a patient voice. "This town needs you. Don't throw away your career for your politics."

"It's more than that." Brenda glanced at Cherie.

"Don't do it to impress your friends either." Olivia studied her carefully before she spoke. "There are other ways to promote causes. I've watched the news clips of your speech at the Maine Chiefs' summit, several times, in fact. You were showing leadership in a volatile situation. You are well spoken, attractive, very telegenic. Instead of marching, you should do more appearances talking about the compassionate side of policing."

"That was a photo op. It was good publicity for Hobbs."

"It was, just like flashing your badge at the demonstration was bad publicity. When you're a high-profile person, everything you do in public is noticed."

"I had no choice. It was a tense situation. Without my badge, I was just another middle-aged woman yelling at the police. I could have been arrested. That would have been even worse publicity for the town. Once the Portland cops saw the badge, they backed down right away."

Olivia compressed her lips and nodded. "Unfortunately, men often disregard women unless they see tangible symbols of power. I understand, but I'm only one of two women on the council. I tried to explain why you needed to use your badge. Unfortunately, my plea for understanding fell on deaf ears."

"I'm not surprised, but thanks for sticking up for me," said Brenda in a flat voice.

"Look. We have to work together. Let's try to make it as pleasant as possible." Olivia paused for a response. When there was none, she added, "It would be easier if it were a mutual effort."

"I can promise I'll always be professional."

"I'm hoping I can count on your support. I'm thinking of running for town manager."

Anger flashed through Brenda. Was this grand overture nothing but politics? "I never take sides in political campaigns," she snapped.

"Of course not. A public official endorsing a candidate is inappropriate. However, on a personal level, I would rather you not be against me."

"You know, Olivia, for someone who just suggested I leave my politics at home, you really should follow your own advice."

Lucy came over. Evidently, she'd been watching the tense exchange. "Olivia, I'd like you to meet my wife, Erika." Lucy reached out her hand.

Olivia smiled, looking relieved to be rescued. "Yes, Mother Lucy. That would be lovely. Please introduce us."

Brenda glared at Olivia's back as she walked away.

17

At the other end of the table, Olivia saluted Sam with her wine glass. "I'm so glad we can finally get together for dinner."

Sam picked up her glass. "Thank you for inviting me." She took a sip of wine. It was excellent, a dry chardonnay. "You're always cooking for me. I should return the favor."

"I didn't know you can cook," said Olivia, picking up her fork.

"I can. I'm not a fancy cook like Maggie Fitzgerald. She went to La Varenne in France, so she's the real deal, but I can put together a decent meal when I set my mind to it."

"Then invite me and show off your culinary skills."

"Next week?"

"Name the day. The only evening I'm not free is Wednesday. I have a Rotary meeting."

"Friday, then."

"Perfect."

Sam put a forkful of coq au vin in her mouth and smiled. Everything Olivia prepared was delicious, even something as simple as a classic stew. The presentation always looked like it belonged in a cooking magazine. As she ate, Sam wondered if inviting Olivia to dinner had been too impulsive. Sam wasn't a fancy cook like Olivia. Maybe she would be disappointed.

Olivia interrupted Sam's thoughts by asking, "Have you convinced Dr. Stolz to help you build my armoire?"

"I haven't asked her yet."

Olivia didn't try to hide her disappointment. "You said you would ask her, Samantha."

"Olivia, why can't you call me Sam like everyone else? Only my mother still calls me Samantha."

"I've never been a fan of nicknames, and I told you why. You're far too attractive to be called by a man's name. What a silly lesbian thing, calling women by men's names."

Sam didn't know which annoyance to address first: the fact that it was disrespectful to disregard her wishes or the put down of lesbians.

"I like being called Sam. Samantha sounds so formal."

"But you use it professionally. It's on your business card. Does it really bother you that much?"

Sam thought about it. In a way, she liked that Olivia had a special name for her. The formality was oddly intimate. "Let me think about it."

"You are a beautiful woman. I love the warmth in your eyes, the way they reflect the candlelight. When you smile, they glow. I envy you that you don't have a single gray hair. It's not right!"

Sam laughed. "Oh, there are a few." Sam bowed her head and pointed to the part in her hair, as if Olivia could see the few grays from the other side of the table.

Olivia wasn't paying attention anyway. She was busy giving Sam admiring looks. "You look very pretty tonight. That outfit suits you."

Sam had rifled through her closet to find something dressy enough for a dinner date, finally settling on a peach-colored, linen blouse and white capris. Although she usually just ran a brush through her short hair, she'd taken time to blow it dry and style it. She'd even put on some makeup and jewelry. She was pleased that Olivia had noticed the effort she'd made. Of course, there was little Olivia didn't notice.

"So, when are you going to ask your friend to help you with my armoire?" Olivia asked, reaching for the salad.

"When I see her again. It's not something I'd ask Liz on the phone. She can be hard to read."

"That's because she's a doctor. They practice that deadpan look, so they don't alarm their patients when they have bad news."

Sam already knew that about her friend, but she tried to look attentive. "How did you get Liz to bring you to Thirsty Thursday?"

"I bribed her with some financial advice."

"Usually, Liz isn't that easily manipulated."

"She wanted the foundation to fund the test kits."

"Still not buying it. She must see some value in you."

Olivia cocked a shoulder. "Well, of course, she sees value. I have value, if anyone would take the time to see it!"

"You can't blame them. You work so hard at being a pain in the ass."

"Samantha!" Olivia made a face. "Maybe I don't want to accept your dinner invitation. Why should I be insulted?"

"You're not serious."

"No." Olivia smiled. "I'm not serious. I want to see your house on the pond. I hear it's quite the showplace."

"I put a lot of work into it. So, you will come?"

"Of course. I like to keep you guessing. That's why you keep coming back. Even when you thought you didn't like me. You just can't figure me out."

"I can't," Sam admitted, "but I keep trying."

"See? My strategy works." Olivia exhaled a big sigh and put down her fork. "I'm really not as complicated as you think. I've just learned that the best defense is a good offense. Sounds trite, but it's true. And I've learned not to lead with my vulnerabilities. Too many women do that in business and fail. To survive on the Street, you need to be tough."

"But there are vulnerabilities. What are they?" asked Sam, trying not to sound too curious.

"Oh, let's see." Olivia gazed around as if trying to remember. "Let's just say I've had my share of disappointments. I'm as damaged as any other woman our age."

"You keep up a good front, but to have a relationship, you have to let down that front."

"Yes, a very scary thought. It would only be worth the risk if I thought it would pay off."

"Do you see everything as a business transaction?"

"Many things, but not everything." Olivia gestured to the dishes at the center of the table. "Have you had enough or would you like more?"

"Thank you, no. It was delicious."

Olivia pushed her chair back from the table and got up. "It's a nice evening. Let's have dessert on the deck."

Sam got up to help Olivia clear the table. Despite knowing they were free of the virus, the old habit of social distancing was hard to break. Sam had to remind herself to approach without hesitation. She leaned against the counter while Olivia rinsed the dinner dishes.

"For some reason, I expected you to have someone for your household chores," Sam said.

"I do have a cleaner once a week, but I'm pretty neat, so she doesn't have much to do. I like to cook, so I don't need someone for that. When my son was young, we had a nanny and a housekeeper, but now that it's just me…" Olivia looked up. "You assumed that I'm incompetent around the house."

"No, I bet you're as competent at housekeeping as everything else. I just thought you'd find household chores…" Sam struggled to come up with words that didn't sound insulting.

"…beneath me?"

"Well, yes, but I wasn't going to be quite that blunt."

Olivia's forehead wrinkled in a frown. "Everyone is always assuming things about me."

"Because that's what you project. Old money, patrician family, upper crust…"

Olivia shook her head. "And they couldn't be more wrong. I grew up on the wrong side of the tracks. My father was a mechanic, who drank too much, and my mother tried to make ends meet by working as a check-out girl at the supermarket."

"What?" Sam blurted out before she could stop herself.

"Surprised, aren't you?"

"Very."

Olivia carefully folded the dish towel and set it on the stand. "More wine before dessert?"

"I think I might need alcohol for this."

Olivia uncorked the wine and refilled their glasses. "Come out on the deck, and I'll tell you more."

They settled into Adirondack chairs, carefully positioned for the best view of the ocean. "Such a nice evening," Olivia said and sipped her wine.

"It is, but you were going to tell me your story."

Olivia turned in her direction. "I'm trying to decide if it's worth the risk."

"Olivia, anything you tell me stays between us. I'm an honorable person."

"I bet you are, Samantha McKinnon. I'm sure your patrician family raised you right." Olivia smiled indulgently. "My upbringing was quite different. I was born Magda Olivia Szymanski, one of five. I haven't seen any of them for years. One of my brothers died of alcoholism, another had a heart attack before he was fifty. My sister spent time in jail for drugs."

"What about your parents?"

"They're long dead."

"I couldn't wait to get out of Syracuse and studied like a demon because I knew education was my ticket. I won a full scholarship to Barnard College. During the summers, I worked on Wall Street as a page to pay the rent. I met people who helped me get into law school. When that didn't turn out to be the right thing, I applied for and got a full scholarship to Harvard Business School. That's where I met my future husband.

"Michael Enright had a seat on the stock exchange before he even graduated. He came from old money. I went to work in his firm. We married a year later. Not long after, I became pregnant. I was a stay-at-home mom until Jason went to school. Then I came back to the Street with a vengeance. I was bored out of my mind being a mommy and couldn't wait to get back to work." Olivia glanced at Sam. "How are you taking this?"

"No way in particular," said Sam, "I'm just listening. Go on."

"By the time Jason was ten, I knew that Michael was playing around. In fairness to him, our sex life wasn't great. I got involved with one of the other brokers…a woman. I'd known that I preferred women since college, but to realize my ambitions, marriage was very important. Plus, it gave me a nice, WASP name."

Sam had been listening so intently, she realized she'd forgotten to drink her wine. She took a sip for fortification. "That's pretty calculating."

"You know how it is to be a successful woman. You need to strategize to achieve your goals. You always need to know how to answer the question, 'Where do you see yourself in five years?'"

"Actually, my career took off because I had a powerful woman as my mentor."

"Cynthia Hickson."

"Yes."

"I read about her when I was researching your background. Lucky you. You found the right person to advance your career, and you had the talent to make good on your promise. All I had was hard work. No one worked harder than I did. I researched corporate reports and futures like a maniac. People thought I was just lucky. The fact is, luck had nothing to do with it. I worked for everything I have."

"You mentioned disappointments."

Olivia nodded. "My greatest disappointment is my son. I poured my heart and soul into the Enright Fund. It was my legacy to him, but he wasn't willing to do the work. He'd rather cut corners and do dirty deals. Then he killed himself rather than face the consequences."

Sam could see that Olivia's face was ashen. "I'm sorry," Sam said softly and reached for her hand, but Olivia put hers in her lap rather than take it.

"I don't want your pity."

"It's not pity, Olivia. It's empathy. I don't have kids, and I can't imagine the pain of losing a child, but I'm sure it must have been awful."

"It was," said Olivia, and her voice caught. "Jason was a difficult child, but in my own way, I loved him."

"I'm sure he knew that."

"Yes? I'm not so sure. I wasn't the best mother. I know that."

"Still, losing a child must be devastating."

"His death was the last straw. Everything…all my dreams…gone in an instant." Olivia snapped her fingers for emphasis.

"It's hard to give up a dream. It's not the same, but when I realized I was never going to be a top-drawer architect, I told myself it was because my designs were out of fashion, which they were. The real reason is female architects never make it to the top."

"A sad commentary on our society."

"Realizing I'd hit the glass ceiling was depressing. It took a while for me to face facts. I began to mentor other women, and for a while, that was enough until it wasn't. About that time, Liz talked me into coming up here, and I saw my opportunity to do something I really loved."

"Tile installations?"

"Yes, I know it sounds crazy, but I really enjoy it. I even went to Italy to study ancient mosaics. When I get into something, I really get into it."

"I like that about you. You're so passionate about your work, but you've found a creative and satisfying second act. I still can't figure out what mine will be."

"You will," said Sam in an encouraging voice.

Olivia turned and smiled. "That's another thing I love about you, Samantha, your optimism."

"When you design buildings, you have to be optimistic. You have to imagine something into being that never existed before. But I'm also optimistic that a woman with your determination will find her way."

"You're not disappointed, now that you know I came from nothing? That I'm just a Polka from the wrong side of the tracks?"

"No, why?"

"You come from old money."

"My parents taught me never to look down on anyone."

"They raised you well," agreed Olivia. "Because I've always had to pretend to be something better, I'm always envious of people who were born there."

"Maybe you should let more people know who you really are. Maybe they'd like you more."

"Are you going to tell your friends, now that you know?"

"Of course not. That's no one's business, and it's your story to tell."

Olivia turned her face to the ocean. "Your friends are all so accomplished, a former Metropolitan Opera star, a chief of surgery at Yale, a Broadway star…"

"They might be super achievers, but they're just regular people. You know, Olivia, when you get to our age, you don't have to be what you do anymore. You can just be a person. It's one of the best things about retirement. It's not about leaving work behind. Most of us still work our asses off. It's about leaving behind that ambition to keep trying to be something bigger and better. Instead, it's okay to just *be*."

"Interesting point of view," said Olivia. "I'll have to think about that."

"Good," said Sam. "And I've thought about what we talked about earlier. You may call me Samantha, if you like."

That brought an instant smile to Olivia's lips. "Thank you. I consider it an honor."

18

Today, Lucy really needed the ten-minute break between clients. She'd spent most of the session listening to Cherie rehash her guilt over getting Brenda in trouble with the town council. She endured her diatribe about what a horrible person Olivia Enright was. Between Lucy's jobs as rector and therapist, she sometimes wondered if she alone kept Hobbs from tearing itself apart.

Lucy instantly chastised herself for the self-centered thought and murmured a little prayer for patience and humility. While she was in that mental space, she allowed herself a few moments of meditation to re-center herself. She couldn't quite put a finger on why she was so on edge today, but she suspected it had something to do with Maggie's invitation to do yoga together.

Apart from Thirsty Thursdays, she'd hardly seen Maggie. Lucy knew she should have found the time for a cup of coffee with the woman she called her best friend. Of course, it had less to do with being busy than her uneasiness in Maggie's presence. Since Liz had kissed her on the boat, she'd found it hard to face her friend. Lucy pictured Maggie in her mind and sent her a silent blessing.

"Mother Lucy," said Jodi, knocking on the open door, "sorry to interrupt, but Olivia Enright is here."

Lucy nodded and Jodi moved away, so Olivia could enter. She pulled the loops of the mask away from her ears.

"It's so nice to know you're safe and I don't have to wear this thing with you."

"It will be interesting to see how Liz's experiment turns out. The social bubble idea would be great if it works."

Lucy made a quick assessment of Olivia's posture and body language. She seemed more relaxed today. Maybe there had been a positive development.

"You don't find it difficult to have me as a client, now that you know me socially?" asked Olivia, putting away her mask.

"If that were the case, I'd have to close up shop. It's a small town. I'm the rector of the church. I know most people in Hobbs one way or the other." Lucy studied Olivia cautiously. "Are *you* uncomfortable knowing me socially?"

"No, not at all. I loved meeting your wife, the professor, who seems delightful, and seeing you with your friends. A nice group of women. Stimulating conversation."

"Always," said Lucy. "But tell me how your week has gone."

"Actually, it's been good. I finally had the opportunity to have dinner with a woman I find interesting."

"Really? That sounds positive."

"You know her, of course. Samantha McKinnon."

Oh dear, thought Lucy, and instantly scolded herself for judging the situation. She could think of stranger couples than Olivia and Sam.

"Tell me more." Lucy folded her hands in her lap and sat back to indicate that she was ready to listen.

"There's not much to say yet. We had a pleasant time and talked. I told her how I worked my way up to where I am now. She listened sympathetically. I feel her kindness when she listens. The way I do when I come here."

"Sam is a good person, and you couldn't have a more loyal friend."

"That's what I like about this town. Old-fashioned values like kindness and loyalty are important."

"Too bad they're not important everywhere. The world would be a better place."

"I agree."

"Okay. Last time, you told me you wanted to talk about your son." Lucy's practiced eyes saw Olivia almost imperceptibly flinch at the mention. There was a quick, anxious look on her face before it returned to its usual composure.

"Yes, I did."

"Are you ready to talk about that subject?"

"No, but it's something I need to do."

"Go on. I'm listening."

Olivia smiled. "I love to watch you listen. It's as if you listen with your whole body, with every cell. Everyone should listen as well as you do."

"Most of my job, as a priest and as a therapist, is listening. Practice makes perfect they say. But we're here to talk about you, not me."

Olivia took a deep breath. "You know the bare bones of the story already. My son was caught at insider trading, but he committed suicide before he could be arrested."

"Yes, you told me."

"There's more to the story."

"There usually is."

"I need to back up a little. You see, I wasn't the best mother. Yes, I was very attentive when he was young, not because of maternal instinct, but out of a great desire to excel as a parent. My husband was wrapped up in his business, so he was mostly absent. I was more or less a single mother. Jason wasn't the easiest child to raise. He was a colicky baby and pushed me away. I was determined to breastfeed him, but he wasn't interested. I took it as a personal insult. My boobs just weren't good enough for him." Despite the angry tone, Olivia looked sad.

"New mothers are often nervous, which can make breastfeeding difficult."

"Except the other women in my circle were successful. They were all talking about their breast pumps and bragging about their output."

"I'm sure the peer pressure didn't help."

"I'm very competitive, so it drove me crazy. If you recall, breastfeeding was the big thing then. It was good for the baby. Good for the mother. It made your uterus go back to normal. Et cetera. Jason just wasn't interested. I felt like such a failure."

Lucy found herself thinking about Emily. Would her child have accepted her breasts? Lucy tried to imagine the feeling of her daughter nursing from her body. Olivia looked at her curiously as if she'd perceived that Lucy had retreated into her own thoughts.

"The rejection must have been painful," Lucy said, trying to refocus.

Olivia's eyes were suddenly bright with tears. She nodded instead of speaking. Lucy had to decide whether to press the issue. It was a wound close to the heart. *Better to save it for another session*, Lucy decided.

"Did you have disciplinary issues with your son?"

"Of course, I did. I ultimately decided to send him to a strict boarding school in the hopes of straightening him out. That made me feel like an even bigger failure. There I was, directing a staff of over a hundred, yet I couldn't make my own son listen to me."

"Did he respond to your husband?"

"He was out of the picture at that point. I was living with a woman."

"Is that when the discipline problems began?"

"No, it was all along. From the moment Jason could sit up, he resisted any efforts to bring him into line. But the boarding school did help…a little. He came back with reasonably good manners and was attentive to what I said, even if he still did what he wanted."

"Adolescent boys sometimes develop what we call, 'mother-deafness' and need to hear a male voice in order to respond. They need more structure than girls. That's why military training is often good for troubled boys. Don't get me wrong. I'm against war and militarism, but discipline can be a good thing."

"He managed to get through high school. He went to Columbia, my alma mater. I pushed him hard to get good grades. I pushed him until I realized it was backfiring. So I retreated. Then things were better. He fell off the dean's list, but he seemed happier and graduated with a respectable B."

"So far, so good."

"I took him into the business right after graduation. We didn't even bother with B-school. It's a waste of time anyway, although it was very much the thing to do when I was coming up. He did well. People seemed to like him, and things were going along just fine. He married a nice girl from a well-to-do family. Then his marriage broke up, and all hell broke loose."

"Why did the marriage break up?"

Olivia looked directly into Lucy's eyes as she spoke. "His wife accused him of molesting their daughters."

"Oh, no!"

"Oh, yes," confirmed Olivia, leaning forward. "I couldn't believe it. Or I should say, I *wouldn't* believe it. I told her she was a lying bitch and took his side."

"Understandable. You're his mother."

"Well, yes, but I didn't believe it because I had never seen any sign of it."

"There were never any complaints? Younger students in school? That kind of thing?"

Olivia shook her head.

"He wasn't molested as a child?"

"Not that I know of, but we weren't that close after he went to boarding school, so maybe he wouldn't tell me if he was."

"So, you had no reason to suspect he might be a pedophile. Maybe the accusations weren't true, but it probably wasn't the best way to respond to your daughter-in-law. Did you, at least, hear her out?"

"I'm afraid not. I cut off all communication, and that's how it stayed. Then the insider trading story broke in the financial papers, and we were so busy doing damage control, we didn't have time for that kind of personal nonsense."

"I hope for the sake of your grandchildren, the accusation against their father isn't true."

"So do I, but when my son's computer was seized for the insider trading investigation, they found kiddie porn on it."

Lucy clenched her jaw to avoid exclaiming what she felt.

"It just breaks my heart to think my son may have done such a thing to his own daughters. I could kill him, but he's already dead. I think the real reason he killed himself was the discovery of the kiddie porn. He was a tough businessman. I think he would have fought the insider trading charge and weathered the scandal. The discovery of his dirty secret is what did him in."

"That didn't come out in the public story?"

"No, thank God. Through my lawyers, I bribed some people in the DA's office to bury it. Even my daughter-in-law doesn't know about the computer porn. At least, I don't think she does."

"Maybe you should let her know. It would confirm her worst fears, but more importantly, she could get help for her daughters." Lucy heaved out a sigh of frustration. She heard so many horror stories in her practice, but the ones involving children just broke her. "Telling the mother is the right thing to do."

"I know, but I worry it will just make matters worse. Besides, she's not speaking to me."

"If your granddaughters are adolescents, getting them help now could go a long way toward preventing more problems in the future."

"Yes, yes, I know I should say something, but it was hard enough telling you." Olivia gave her a sly look. "Maybe you could give me absolution and make it all better."

"I can give you absolution, but this is a sin of omission, not commission. Absolution won't make it all better. You really should to tell your daughter-in-law the truth, so the healing can begin."

Olivia looked contrite. "Unfortunately, I realize that."

"What will you do?"

"I don't know. I'll get back to you on that."

❀❀❀

After that heavy conversation, Lucy was looking forward to her yoga date with Maggie. An hour of stretching was sure to help her relax. They went upstairs to the enormous bedroom on the third floor to lay out their mats. From there, they had a view of the ocean that could aid in meditation. Lucy could feel the tension and anxiety flowing out of her like water as they went through the positions.

"Thank you, Maggie. That was just what I needed," said Lucy, rolling up her mat.

"Thank you for coming over. "It's more fun to do yoga with a partner. How about a glass of iced tea?"

"Sounds wonderful." They headed down to the kitchen.

"I've missed you," said Maggie handing her a glass. "I've wondered why you haven't been around lately."

"Now that I'm back to a nearly normal schedule, I'm really swamped. I meet with my groups on Zoom. I see my counseling clients in my office. Tom's been doing the hospital visits, so at least I don't have that."

Maggie took a step closer. "Are you sure?"

"Sure that I'm busy? Oh, my word, yes!" Fortunately, that was no lie.

Maggie's eyes probed hers. "Lucy, is there something you haven't told me?"

Lucy had a sinking feeling. She knew where this conversation was heading, but she wasn't about to betray Liz by blurting out a confession.

"What do you mean?" she asked coyly.

Maggie's eyes clouded with sadness. "I keep having these fits of anxiety. At first, I didn't know why, but now I think I do. I've had this kind of anxiety before."

"I'm so sorry, Maggie. Is there something I can do?"

"Yes, you can tell me the truth."

"What do you mean?"

"Is there something going on between you and Liz? Something more than your usual flirtation?"

Lucy felt the heat creeping up her neck into her face. She tried to control the expression on her face because she couldn't control her color.

Maggie continued to look her right in the eye. "Lucy, I can see in your eyes that you want to tell me something. I hope you will. You say you're my friend."

Lucy had to look away because she couldn't bear the intensity of Maggie's gaze a moment longer.

"I know Liz is a player," Maggie continued. "I think it's in her genes, but I would hate to find out you were cheating with my wife."

Lucy shook her head. "I would never."

"Has Liz ever made a pass at you?"

Lucy felt slightly nauseous. She didn't want to hurt Maggie, but she couldn't bring herself to lie. She stared at her feet. "She kissed me when we went out on the boat."

"She kissed you, or she *kissed* you?"

"It was a tongue kiss," admitted Lucy, trying not to squirm.

"And what did you do?" asked Maggie with unearthly calm.

"I pushed her away and told her we were not going to hurt our spouses by doing anything we'd be sorry for."

Maggie exhaled slowly. "Thank you for telling me the truth." When Lucy looked up, she saw tears in Maggie's eyes. "I knew it! I just felt it. The suspicion is worse than having it confirmed."

"I'm so sorry, Maggie." Lucy wanted to hug her but knew that an embrace from her would likely be rejected. Lucy would be the last person Maggie wanted to comfort her. "It's not what you think. It was completely impulsive. We stopped before it went any further."

"But you responded at first."

"I did," Lucy admitted. "Your wife is very attractive."

"Yes, and she knows it." Maggie reached over and patted Lucy's arm. "At least one of you has some integrity."

"I'm sorry, Maggie. It won't happen again."

"You better believe it won't happen again!"

19

Liz was reviewing the next day's cases with Cherie when her phone began to vibrate. Liz picked it up and saw Lucy's ring photo with her trademark red hair and incandescent smile.

"Would you excuse me, Cherie? I need to take this."

"I think we're done here," Cherie said, inserting her stylus into her tablet case. "I'll come back later if I have any questions." She went out and closed the door behind her.

Liz smiled as she swiped across the phone screen. "Lucy! What's up?"

"I hope I'm not interrupting anything important."

"I was meeting with Cherie, but we were winding down."

"Are you sure?"

"Lucy, you are the only person besides Maggie and my mother whose call I'll always take. What's going on?"

"I wanted to give you advance warning. Maggie knows what happened on the boat."

Incredulous, Liz got up and stood at the window. "You told her? Why?"

"Because she asked."

Liz closed her eyes and thought of Maggie's face, that anxious expression she sometimes had when she thought no one was looking. She tried to be so brave about the cancer, so patient when Liz was late at work, or a family gathering was interrupted. She smiled when Lucy and Liz flirted, but she wasn't amused. She was frightened.

"How much did you tell her?" Liz asked.

"The facts. I told her you kissed me. I responded, then broke it off."

Liz whistled through her teeth. "Shit!"

"Exactly. But I wanted you to know before you got home."

"Thank you for the heads up." Liz pulled her duffle bag out of the closet. "What did she say when you told her?"

"At least one of us has integrity."

"Ouch."

"I'm sorry, Liz. She's my best friend. I couldn't lie to her."

"No, I get it. Thanks, Lucy. You did the right thing. I appreciate the call," said Liz, heading down to the shower.

"I love you, Liz. Good luck."

"I love you too, Lucy," said Liz, turning on the shower. "Don't worry. I'll handle it." She ended the call and threw her phone into her duffle bag on top of her clothes. She pulled the scrubs top over her head and wiggled out of her shorts and underwear. She still preferred to shower in the morning, but since the pandemic had started, she'd switched to showering after work to prevent carrying the virus home on her clothes or hair.

From her days as a surgeon, Liz was used to taking quick showers. She could be done, including a hair wash, in less than two minutes. Being a Virgo, she'd even timed it. She was equally quick at dressing. A quick blow-dry, and she was ready to walk out the door. She unlocked the cabinet where she kept her gun purse and headed down the hall. Cherie was doing paperwork in the staff lounge.

"You okay for tomorrow morning?" Liz called from the doorway.

Cherie nodded. "Yes, I think I have it under control."

"Call me if you need me."

Cherie raised a thumb. "Yes, boss!"

As Liz started the engine of her truck, she wondered whether she should go directly home. She knew that one way or the other she was heading into a firestorm. However, delaying her arrival might give Maggie some time to absorb the information and calm down. She wanted advice on the best way to handle it, but the two people she counted on, namely Lucy and Erika, weren't in a position to offer it. Sam was also an option. It just seemed strange to ask for her advice. For years, Liz had been Sam's sounding board through the ups and downs in her many relationships. Maybe the time had finally come for Sam to return the favor.

Liz tapped open the Bluetooth. "Call Sam," she ordered Siri.

"Samuel Dimmenstein, MD?"

"No!"

"Samson Arteri, MD?"

"No. Samantha McKinnon!" corrected Liz impatiently. Siri finally figured it out and called the right number.

"Hey," said Sam when she answered.

"Hey, yourself. What are you doing?"

"Cleaning the house. I'm having company for dinner tomorrow."

"Really? Who?"

"Wouldn't you like to know?" Sam laughed softly. "No, I'll tell you, but don't tell anyone else. I'm having Olivia Enright over for dinner."

"Aha! The plot thickens," said Liz, backing out of her assigned parking space. "You interested in her?"

"Maybe. We're just getting started."

"Uh huh. Doesn't sound like you. The Sam I used to know would have bedded her by now. What's wrong with you?"

Sam laughed. "Older and wiser, I guess."

Liz saw a break in the afternoon traffic and pulled onto Beach Road. "Mind if I come over for a few minutes?"

"Sure. In fact, I have a new brew you might like."

"Be there in ten. Just pulled out of the parking lot."

As she drove to Sam's place, Liz imagined the scene between Lucy and Maggie. She'd instantly forgiven Lucy for revealing the truth. Lucy never lied because she'd been lied to by so many—her agent, her attorney, and the man she'd trusted to help her during the mess at the end of her opera career. In reward for her trust, he'd raped her.

But Liz wondered why Maggie had asked Lucy instead of asking her directly. Obviously, Maggie had suspected something that night. Why hadn't she just asked? As Liz thought more about it, she realized the answer was simple. It would have hurt too much to hear the truth from Liz.

Liz beeped the horn before she got out of the truck. Sam came around the side of the house. "I'm back on the dock," she said, pointing in that direction.

The bounce of the dock always made Liz step carefully, but the sight of the pond, its surface as smooth as glass, calmed her. It reflected the deep blue sky and the clouds like a mirror. Soon they each had a beer in hand and were cooling their bare feet in the pond.

"I need advice," said Liz.

"You're asking *me* for advice?" said Sam with a little laugh. "I never thought I'd see the day. What happened?"

"I'll tell you the short version." Liz was good at giving the short version from having to summarize medical cases. Maggie, who liked blow by blow descriptions, sometimes had to yank the details out of her.

"Lucy showed up one night when I was getting ready to go out fishing," Liz began. "She invited herself to come along, so I let her. When we were out there, I kissed her. She kissed me back but cut it off really fast. Maggie figured it out when I got home but didn't ask. She asked Lucy, who told her the truth."

"Of course, she did. Lucy would never lie to save her own ass," said Sam. "So, what are you going to do about it?"

"Throw myself on my sword and beg for forgiveness. What else can I do? It was stupid."

"Liz, everyone knows you have the worst crush on Lucy. It's almost a joke. Why did you have to push it?"

"I don't know. Everything is so out of whack with this pandemic. Even me, I guess."

"Well, unless you want to blow up your marriage, you better make peace with Maggie. It wouldn't hurt to dial it back with Lucy for a while."

"I have. I've been avoiding her."

"But you have to work together on so many things. Just stop flirting with her so much. You're giving yourself permission to come on to her."

Liz sighed. "It's more than just flirting."

"Everyone falls in love with Lucy. But you're a big girl, Liz. Can't you just admire her from afar?"

"I wish, but I want that woman in the worst possible way."

"I was afraid you'd say that." Liz could feel Sam's eyes boring into the side of her face. "You have to stop, Liz. Maggie isn't Jenny. She's not going to look the other way."

"I know."

They sat looking out at the water and sipping their beer.

"What do you think of the IPA?" asked Sam.

"It's good. Not too bitter. Hoppy but not gassy. Good."

"Do you want to leave Maggie?"

"I would never leave Maggie. I love Maggie."

"Then stop thinking about Lucy so much."

"Easier said, than done." Liz stared into the dark water. She could see a few fish swimming by and thought about fishing, a fleeting distraction from the mess.

Her cell phone wailed—Maggie's ring tone.

"Guess who?" said Liz, pulling her phone out of her bag.

"You want me to leave while you talk to her?" Sam asked.

Liz shook her head.

"Where are you?" Maggie demanded in a calm, but stern tone. Liz could feel the weight of her anger in the silence that followed.

"I'm sitting on Sam's dock having a beer," replied Liz, trying to sound light and friendly.

"Come home." It was an order.

"Okay," said Liz. "I'll be there soon."

The call ended abruptly, no response, no goodbye.

"Have to go?" Sam asked, studying Liz's expression.

"After I finish my beer."

Sam's eyebrows rose.

"No one tells me what to do," Liz said. "Not even my wife."

They finished their beer in silence. Sam walked Liz to her truck. She patted her friend's shoulder. "Good luck, pal." She waited while Liz backed up the truck and waved as she pulled away.

When Liz got home, she parked the truck in the driveway and sat there for a few minutes, trying to work up the courage to face her wife. Finally, she noticed Maggie standing at the screen door of the front porch. Reluctantly, Liz got out of the truck.

Maggie held the door open for her. She let Liz give her a kiss but put up her hands when Liz tried to hug her.

"I'm not in the mood for a hug right now."

"Maggie…I'm sorry."

"I'm sure you are, now that I've found out what you've been up to."

"It was only once."

"Once is one time too many." Maggie turned and headed down the hall. "Come on. Dinner is ready. We're eating out on the porch."

Liz went out to the porch to find a beautifully prepared table and a tasty meal of eggplant parmesan, toasted garlic bread, and salad. They had discussed clearing out the freezer before the next harvest, so the eggplant was from last year, but Maggie had obviously made an effort to make an impressive presentation, complete with a tablecloth and cloth napkins. Liz wondered why, given her anger.

Maggie came in with a bottle of wine. "Go on. Sit down."

"Where's Stefan?" asked Liz.

"I told him I needed a dinner alone with you, and he understood. He ate earlier. He's in his room now, listening to music. He really likes those new headphones you gave him."

Maggie sat down and arranged her napkin on her lap. "I'm sorry it's from the freezer, but I took it out two days ago and thought we should eat it."

"No apologies needed. Your eggplant parmesan is the best I've ever tasted. I always enjoy it." Liz picked up her fork.

Maggie attempted a smile, but Liz saw a sadness in her hazel eyes that yanked at her heart. "Enjoy your dinner," said Maggie quietly. "We'll talk later."

Maggie eventually broke the silence by telling Liz about some mischief Katrina, their eldest grandchild, had gotten into. Liz did the usual recap of her day, bringing home news about the town. The conversation sounded like any other night.

Liz cleared the table. While Maggie was putting away the leftovers, Liz tried to give her a little hug from behind, but her wife moved away. "Not yet. Let's talk first."

After the kitchen was tidy, Maggie poured herself a glass of wine and one for Liz. "Let's sit out on the porch," she said, handing Liz a glass.

They sat in silence for a few minutes until Liz said, "I'm sorry it happened, and I'm sorry you found out that way."

"I wish you had told me. I gave you an opening that night."

"I know, but you offered sex, and I never turn down sex." Liz grinned, but then regretted it.

With an impassive expression, Maggie gazed at her. "Don't I give you enough sex? I know your sex drive is stronger than mine. I try to be interested even when I'm really not. Sometimes, I have to force myself."

"The Tamoxifen doesn't help. It suppresses estrogen."

"Is it about sex?"

Liz thought about it and shook her head. "No."

"I know you have a roving eye, Liz. And I know you've been in love with Lucy since the day you met. I've tried to look the other way when you flirt with her. I've always thought it was harmless until now." Maggie gave her an extended, searching look. "Do you want a divorce?"

"No, I don't want a divorce," Liz replied instantly. "Besides, Lucy is married to my best friend, and I'm not going to break up someone's marriage."

"Really? Is that because of our marriage or their marriage?"

"Our marriage."

Maggie looked frustrated. "Then why did you kiss her?"

"I don't know," Liz admitted honestly. "I've wanted to for a long time, so I did."

Maggie chewed on her lower lip. It was an old habit that Liz recognized from their college days. Maggie was trying to keep herself from crying. The only thing that prevented Liz from scooping her up to comfort her was the fear that she'd be pushed away.

"I don't want you to blame Lucy," said Liz. "I initiated it. She stopped me."

"What if she hadn't stopped you? Would you have had sex with her?"

"Honestly, I don't know." Liz glanced cautiously at Maggie. "I'm sure that's not what you want to hear."

Maggie shook her head. "Liz, if you intend to be unfaithful, I want to end this marriage. I've been cheated on before, and I won't go through it again. Do you understand?"

"I understand."

"And you'd better figure out how you'll handle it the next time you're alone with Lucy and you want to kiss her. I expect you to stop yourself, not wait for her to stop you. You're damn lucky she did. I know she really cares for you. I'm sure this hasn't done your friendship any good."

"No, it hasn't," said Liz, remembering her anxiety on the day of Lucy's physical.

Maggie exhaled slowly. "I'm going to sleep in one of the guest rooms tonight. Maybe for a few nights. It's not a punishment. I just need to be away from you for a while. Do you understand?"

Liz nodded.

"I'm going upstairs to get my book and my night things. I'll see you tomorrow.'"

Liz felt a lump form in her throat as she watched Maggie walk away.

Hoping for a better state of mind, Liz headed to the media room, where she poured herself a glass of single-malt scotch and turned on the enormous TV. She had a backlog of super-hero movies in her Netflix queue. Usually she saved them for nights when her wife was babysitting her granddaughters in Scarborough or had rehearsals. Maggie had made it very clear that she wasn't a fan of action films, especially because Liz liked to listen to them loud enough to cause temporary deafness.

Liz flipped through the offerings in her watchlist, but nothing appealed to her. She turned off the TV and switched on the stereo. None of the music she usually relied on to calm her worked. She considered knocking on Stefan's door and asking him to play chess, but it was late for him. The truth was, the only company she really wanted was Maggie's. As Liz sipped her whiskey, she realized she was seeing a preview of life without her wife, and it was desolate.

Liz finished her drink and brought the glass into the kitchen. As she was rinsing it out, she wondered if Maggie would talk to her if she knocked on her door.

Maggie had chosen the seashore room, one of the largest and most comfortable guest rooms on the second floor.

"Liz, I told you I need some space," came the answer through the door when Liz knocked.

"Please, Maggie, I just want to talk to you."

"All right, but just for a minute."

Liz tried the knob and found the door locked. She snatched her hand back as if she'd touched a hot stove. Maggie had never locked the door against her. A moment later, the door opened. Maggie stood there in one of her sexiest nightgowns, low-cut and sheer around the bodice. Her pale nipples showed through the lace.

"What do you want, Liz?"

"Can I come in?"

"No, I need my privacy right now. I need some time to think."

Liz grinned. "Expecting company? That's a pretty sexy nightgown."

"It's not for you. Not everything is about you, Liz."

Liz tried to hold the smile, but it faded by degrees. "I didn't think so."

"Sometimes I wear a sexy nightgown to remind myself that, despite being what most people consider old, I'm still attractive. What you did with Lucy was a big blow to my ego. It really hurt. Can you understand that?"

Liz inhaled slowly. "Yes, and I'm sorry it hurt you. I didn't do it to hurt you. I love you."

"I know you do, or I wouldn't still be here. You're not the easiest person to live with. You give everyone else attention. Sometimes you forget to give it to me."

"I love you," Liz repeated.

"I know." She reached out and gave Liz's hand a little squeeze. "Now, go to bed and give me some peace. Good night."

With tears in her eyes, Liz stared at the closed door before heading upstairs.

20

Lucy tried to focus on what Emily was saying. Her daughter was effervescent with joy because the paper she had written with Stefan Bultmann had been accepted by the American Mathematical Society. The editor, also the chairman of the Math department at Yale, had offered Emily a full scholarship and advanced status. If things went according to plan, she could join the PhD program within a year.

Erika came in from the kitchen where she was making what smelled like a tasty dinner. She sat down at the table with them. "Of course, my father will make sure they take care of all your expenses. They want you, my dear, in the worst possible way."

"I'm so glad I took those classes at Colby and the AP classes at the high school. They're accepting *all* my credits."

"Of course, they are," said Erika, patting her arm. "No disrespect to your hard work, but that's a mere formality. They'll grant you an undergraduate degree as a matter of course."

"Emily, are you really sure you want to be a mathematician?" asked Lucy anxiously. A part of her still hoped her multi-talented daughter would become a musician.

"No, I'm not sure, Mom, but Yale also has a great music school."

Lucy took her daughter's hands in hers. "I'm so, so proud of you!"

Erika glanced at Lucy's empty wine glass. "Thirsty tonight? That wine disappeared rather fast." While Emily had been speaking, Lucy had been distracted, wondering how things were going between Liz and Maggie. At the same time, she was trying to show her daughter all the enthusiasm her big news deserved. "Difficult day?" Erika asked, reaching for her hand.

Lucy nodded sadly.

"Why don't I refill your glass? We can sit on the back deck, and you can tell me about it."

Lucy glanced at Emily to see if she minded the interruption, but she saw that her daughter was happily tapping on her phone, probably sharing her news with her friends.

"Emily, pet," said Lucy, needing to touch her on the arm to get her attention. "I'm going out to the deck with Erika. Do you mind?"

"No, Mom. That's chill. I'm going up to my room for a while." She got up, and moments later, Lucy could hear her daughter's feet running up the stairs.

Lucy glanced at Erika for sympathy.

"Don't take it personally. You're only her mother. At this age, everyone else is more important." Erika picked up Lucy's glass. "I'll get you a refill."

Lucy felt abandoned, and now that she was alone, her anxiety returned to the forefront of her mind. She was actually shaking. The view of the salt marsh always calmed her, so she went out to the deck. The tide was in, and the calm water reflected the brilliant blue of the sky. Ducks floated on the river. A heron alighted to fish.

"Lovely evening," said Erika, coming out with a tray bearing a wine chiller and their glasses. "I brought the bottle. From the looks of you, you'll need your glass replenished frequently. It must have been quite a day." Erika reached over and took Lucy's hand. "A difficult counseling session?"

"Yes, that too."

Erika's eyes were full of curiosity but kind, as always. Lucy had been instantly attracted to Erika's quick mind, although she could do without her sharp tongue. But it was Erika's gentle caring, especially during difficult moments, that had made Lucy fall in love with her.

"Tell me what's on your mind, love," Erika urged gently.

Lucy had kept the incident on the boat to herself because she didn't want to hurt Erika unnecessarily, but now that Maggie knew, it was only fair that Erika know too. The last thing Lucy wanted was for her wife to find out from another source.

"Lucy, you're thinking so loudly I can hear the gears in your brain turning. In fact, there's smoke coming out of your ears." Erika smiled so subtly that it could only be seen in her pale eyes.

"I'm sorry, Erika. I just don't know how to say it."

"Then, love, just come out with it. Nothing you say shocks me anymore."

"But I don't want to hurt you."

Erika frowned slightly. "Oh dear, Lucy. What have you done?"

"Remember the night Liz took me out fishing?"

"Yes," said Erika slowly.

"She kissed me, and I kissed her back."

"And…?"

"That's it."

Erika laughed. "Is that all?"

Lucy blinked. That wasn't the response she'd expected. "Aren't you mad?"

"Yes, I may be mad, as you Americans say, but I'm not angry…nor even surprised."

"You're not?"

"No."

"If you did something like that, I'd be furious!"

"Yes, Lucy, but I'm not *you*." Erika studied her over the rim of her wine glass. "You forget that we approach sex very differently. This is my first monogamous relationship. All the others were completely open."

"Yes, but I thought you loved me. That I'm your first, true love."

"You are, my dear, but getting married was your idea. You made it abundantly clear that we couldn't continue the relationship unless we did. It was very important to you, so I went along with it."

A maelstrom of emotions vied for Lucy's attention. Was she hurt? Shocked? Angry? Had she been deceived? Only her training kept her from screaming in pain. Shaking, she took a sip of wine and turned her attention to the salt marsh.

"I'm sorry, Lucy. I'm sure you didn't want to hear those words. At heart, you're such a romantic."

"Does that mean you don't care if I'm faithful?"

"No, not at all. I do care. Of course, I care. I would prefer to be your only sexual partner."

"You prefer...?"

"But I can understand your attraction to Liz. There was a time I was attracted to her myself, but once was enough for me."

"Once what? *You slept together?*"

"Yes, about forty years ago," replied Erika in her rational philosopher's voice. "Why? Is that a problem?"

Lucy made exaggerated big eyes to emphasize how obvious the answer was.

Erika chuckled. "Now, you're wondering why I never told you. I don't know. It was the eighties, when everyone was fucking everyone. Liz wasn't my type, but she's an excellent lover. You might learn a few things from her. Not that you really need any instruction." Erika wiggled her eyebrows suggestively.

"You want me to *sleep with her*?" asked Lucy shrilly. By now, all of her training had flown out the window.

"Actually, I'd rather you didn't," said Erika quietly. "Knowing you, you'd probably fall in love with her."

Hot tears sprang to Lucy's eyes. "I can't believe I'm hearing this!"

Erika patted the air downward. "You might wish to lower your voice. I'm certain you don't want Emily to hear this conversation.

Lucy sat up straight. No, she certainly didn't want Emily to hear. Fortunately, her daughter usually had her ears plugged with ear buds, but Erika was right. They should keep their voices down.

Erika turned her face and gave her a fish-eyed stare. "You're not pleased with me, I can tell."

"I expected a different response."

"Do you want me to make a fuss and be angry? I am a little angry. I know Liz can be very aggressive at times, but you went along with it. Did you want her to kiss you? More to the point, would you like to have sex with her?"

"No!"

Erika gave her a hard look. "Lucy, be honest. You're intrigued by Liz. She's dashing compared to me."

"No!"

"And your little flirtation has been going on forever. I'm only surprised it's taken you this long to act on it."

Lucy couldn't stand to hear another word. She jumped up. "I'm going up to change. This black blouse is too hot in the sun."

"I told you to buy some of those pastel-colored clerical blouses for the summer, but you wouldn't listen," Erika scolded in a mild voice.

Lucy shook her head. They'd just had a conversation about cheating, and her wife was saying, 'I told you so,' over clerical blouses!

As Lucy passed, Erika caught her hand to stop her. "If it makes you feel any better, I forgive you for kissing Liz, but you probably don't want to do it again. For your sake, as well as mine."

Once Lucy was out of Erika's sight, she allowed the tears to flow. They streamed down her cheeks as she marched up the stairs. She didn't bother to wipe them, even when they dropped on her black blouse, where she knew they'd leave little white stains. She didn't care. The conversation had left her numb.

Until now, she hadn't known how casually Erika took her wedding vows. Erika didn't share Lucy's religious beliefs but had agreed to marry her because of them. Had that been a good enough reason?

Lucy's mind was a jumble of thoughts. Flashing lights, like the test signal on old TVs, were blocking her vision. She undressed to her lace bra and panties and lay down on the bed. She hoped that closing her eyes and shutting out the light would make the optical migraine pass.

As her mind began to drift into unconsciousness, Lucy remembered the day she stood before Tom Simmons and proclaimed her wedding vows. Dressed in a beautiful, white gown, her blond hair brilliant in the October sun, Erika looked like an angel. Lucy thought her heart would burst from all the love she felt for her.

Lucy awoke to motion on the bed. She felt a warm hand on her arm and soft breasts against her back.

"Lovely Lucy," Erika whispered into her ear, "I'm ever so sorry if I disappointed you."

"It's all right," Lucy murmured in a sleepy voice.

Erika nibbled gently at her ear lobe. "I don't believe you. Remember, I know you too well." Soft fingers began to gently caress her between her legs. "Let me remind you why you married me."

Lucy wanted to say, "It wasn't because of sex," but she was so distracted by what Erika was doing, she couldn't speak. And if it wasn't because of sex, why was tongue kissing Liz such a big problem? Lucy forgot the question as Erika eased down her panties and continued stroking her.

Erika kissed the back of her neck with warm lips. "Your skin is salty," she said. Lucy could hear the smile in her voice. A thumb slipped inside her while another finger caressed her outside. Lucy kicked away her panties with her foot and pulled up her legs to welcome Erika's probing fingers. "You are so luscious, my beautiful woman," Erika whispered into her ear. "How would you like to come?"

"This way."

Lucy loved to be taken from behind, sometimes gently, sometimes forcefully. Erika was alternating inside and outside, which helped Lucy stay focused instead of falling into a stupor. The orgasm built slowly but when it came, it was powerful and Lucy was a little stunned. After she caught her breath, she turned into Erika's arms.

"I want you too," she said, reaching between Erika's legs.

"That will have to wait. Dinner is almost ready. I only came up to wake you, but you looked so inviting, I couldn't pass up the opportunity." Erika kissed her. "You always come fast, so I knew we could be quick."

Lucy pouted. "Too quick?"

Erika chuckled and raised Lucy's hand to her lips. "You make up for it in quantity. Come on, love. Get up now."

When Lucy sat up, her insides still tingled from Erika's touch. "I love you," she said.

"I know. Please don't be angry because I didn't make more of a fuss. It's not my way, you know."

"I do, but sometimes, I wish you'd be a little more possessive."

"All right, then," said Erika, pulling Lucy close. "I'm glad you didn't give in to Liz. I rather like having you all to myself."

21

Sam felt like a savage stabbing the lobster with a sharp knife through its back. She quickly dismembered it with a few deft cuts, cracked the shell, and threw the pieces into the pan.

"You do that very well," Olivia observed. "You have that killer instinct."

"Not really. I can't bear to throw the poor creature into the pan alive." Sam rinsed off the knife and set it aside. "I learned that stabbing trick from steaming lobsters. Saves me from listening to them thrashing around while the heat builds up in the pot."

"Where did you get this recipe?" Olivia picked up the piece of paper on which it was printed. "*The New York Times*. No surprise there. I pegged you as a *Times* reader."

"They don't have recipes in *The Wall Street Journal*, do they?" asked Sam, half serious.

"Occasionally. More women are reading it nowadays."

"That's sexist. Men cook too."

"We're both full of assumptions tonight. You assumed I read *The Journal* because it's conservative."

"No, I assumed you read it because you were a Wall Street trader."

Olivia dropped her chin and gazed at Sam through her eyebrows. "And you would be correct, but I also read it because its political slant is conservative." She studied the paper. "This recipe calls for shrimp."

"I know, but the only wild-caught shrimp we can get is from the Gulf. Our shrimp harvest has been cut down to nothing because of overfishing and the warming. The lobster men have been screwed by the trade war. They need our support, so I'm substituting."

"Clever girl."

Sam bristled at being called a girl. After all, she was almost sixty and hadn't been a girl for more than four decades. Getting used to the vocabulary and thinking of a "conservative" woman wouldn't be easy, but she didn't want to correct Olivia all the time.

"You're certainly competent in the kitchen," observed Olivia as Sam sliced the kernels off the corn cobs. "I'm impressed."

"I think if you're going to do something, you might as well be competent." Sam tossed the corn into the pan and unloaded a strainer of cherry tomatoes on top of it.

Olivia sniffed appreciatively. "Smells delicious."

"Garlic. The secret to every great recipe."

"I'm glad we're both eating it." Olivia's lips curved into a sly smile.

"Now that we don't have to maintain social distancing, garlic breath could be a concern."

"I wasn't thinking of breathing, except maybe heavily."

Sam turned and stared. Olivia's bold statements still took her by surprise. "Are you planning something more than dinner?"

Olivia rolled her eyes and affected an innocent look.

"Don't you think we're getting a little ahead of ourselves?"

Olivia shrugged. "We've been spending a lot of time together. That's where we're heading, isn't it?"

"We hardly know each other."

"You probably know more about me than most people ever will. Isn't sex a way to get to know someone?"

Sam stirred the contents of the skillet and took the rice off the burner. "Don't get me wrong, Olivia. I've had lots of casual sex in my day, but I think I'm a little past that now."

"Am I being too forward?"

Sam stared at her. "Yes, a little. I'm not used to that from the women I date."

"Maybe you've never dated a woman like me. I believe in saying what I want."

"I've noticed. Excuse me," Sam nudged Olivia gently with her hip. "I need to get into the oven."

Olivia stepped aside and folded her arms on her chest. "I'm being too aggressive, and you don't like that. Apologies for my bad habits."

"You're forgiven."

Sam put on oven mitts and took out the plates that had been warming in the oven. She scooped out rice into each and spooned the lobster scampi over it. On top, she arranged a sprig of bright-green, fresh basil.

"I hope this is good," Sam said, carrying the plates to the table. "I haven't made it before."

"You're brave to cook a new recipe for a guest."

"I don't get fancy for myself, so if it's something more exotic than grilled fish or meat, it's probably for a guest. I don't mind taking risks." She sat down. "Please," she said gesturing to Olivia's plate. "I gave you some paper napkins because this looks like it will be messy."

"There is something so primal about eating with your hands." Olivia extracted the pink meat from the claw with her hands but cut it with a knife and fork. "Delicious!" she proclaimed. "Plenty of garlic."

"That's pretty much what scampi is. Garlic with seafood on the side."

"Yes, I guess you're right." Olivia closed her eyes as she savored a bite. "The garlic is potent. Good thing we took kissing off the table."

"We did?" asked Sam, dipping some bread in the infused olive oil. "When did we decide that?"

"But I thought…"

"Olivia, you plan too much. Why not let things develop?"

Olivia wrinkled up her nose. "I've never found that effective."

"You really need to be in control, don't you? What are you afraid will happen if you're not?"

Olivia ran her hand over the tabletop. "This is beautiful. Did you make it?"

"Yes, I did, but you just changed the subject."

Olivia nodded. "I didn't like the previous one."

"Olivia, it takes one to know one. I'm a control freak too. I had to learn to dial it back because being an architect means giving up control to the people who execute your plans. Where relationships are concerned, I like to have my say."

"You're butch, I can see that."

Sam shook her head. "No. It's not that simple. I can take as well as give."

"Well, how would you characterize me?" Olivia asked. "Am I femme?"

"People are still into roles?" Sam looked down the table and tried to make an objective evaluation. "You've got the feminine appearance down pat. Gestures. The walk. Perfect hair, makeup, nail polish. Very sexy, by the way. I love nail polish on women."

Olivia waved at her, showing off her red nails. "If you love it, why don't you wear it?"

"Doesn't go with trowels and thinset. Not that I'd wear it anyway. I only agreed to wear it once…for my sister's wedding, and only because all the women in the bridal party were having their nails done."

"Tell me what else turns you on. Do you like negligee? Lace underwear?"

"Yes. All of the above."

"Now we're getting somewhere," said Olivia, reaching for the salad.

"Not really. We're talking about sex. There's more to a relationship than sex."

"Most certainly. But it's a good place to start."

"Maybe it's a good place to end…after there's a relationship."

Olivia narrowed her eyes. "I never expected you to be so deep."

"What were you looking for? A quick fuck?"

"No, certainly more than that."

"What, Olivia? Companionship? A long-term relationship? Marriage?"

"All three would be nice."

That answer surprised Sam. She stopped eating and sat back. "Why me?"

"Well, let's see." Olivia counted off Sam's virtues on her fingers. "You're beautiful. Smart. Competent. Wise. Interesting. Kind. Talented. Accomplished. Honest. *Double on the honesty.*" She gestured toward her plate. "And you can cook!"

"Is that how you choose a partner? Make a list like that and check off the boxes?"

"No, first I have to feel attraction. There has to be chemistry. With you, it was nearly instant. Tall. Muscular. After I saw you in the shower that day, I fantasized about joining you, running my hands up and down your soapy body, caressing your breasts, touching you between your legs, slipping my fingers inside you." Olivia smiled. "Then I imagined what you would do to me, and I was sold!" Olivia smiled almost primly.

Sam was so surprised and aroused that all she could do was clear her throat and smile in return.

"I've shocked you," said Olivia, looking proud of herself.

"No, but I wasn't expecting that."

"Good. I like to use the element of surprise. Did you find it erotic?"

"I did."

"But not inspiring."

"I find other things more inspiring."

"Such as?"

"When you shared your story of your humble beginnings."

Olivia covered the lower part of her face with her hand. "My pathetic story of deception? Maybe I shouldn't have shared that. Now, you think I'm a fraud."

Sam shook her head. "No. I admire you for setting a goal and working so hard to achieve it. I was moved by what you told me, that you trusted me enough to share it."

"I do trust you, Samantha. My instincts tell me you are completely trustworthy."

"It must have been really hard to cut your family off."

Olivia sighed and stared at her plate. "I miss my mother. I often think about her, how I ran away to New York and just left her there with those needy, snotty things at her apron strings. She worked hard too. In fact, she worked like a dog to keep the family going. Sometimes I wonder what dreams she had…before we weighed her down."

"Being a mother is a big sacrifice. Probably why I never wanted to be one. I know I'm too selfish. Plus, I could never deal with a man. They just don't interest me."

"Not me either, but it was how you played the game in those days."

Sam smiled what she hoped was a reassuring smile. "Thank you for trusting me with your story."

Olivia put down her fork and tapped her chest with her fist. "See? That's what I love about you. You say these things that just go right to the heart."

"Give me some space, Olivia, and I'll come to you. I have lots to share too."

Olivia touched her fingers to her lips and sent a kiss in Sam's direction.

"Let me just clear the table. I made a rustic peach tart. Erika gave me the recipe."

"You're trying all these new things for me."

"Yes, new things for new beginnings." Sam smiled in Olivia's direction. "We can sit out on the dock and watch the moon rise."

"Won't the mosquitos eat us alive?"

"That's why I have lemongrass in those planters."

Olivia pitched in with clean up, rinsing the dishes and putting them in the dishwasher, while Sam packed the leftovers. Sam cut sections of tart and made a pot of tea. They took the tray to the end of the dock, so they could put their feet in the water.

"I love it here," said Olivia. "It's so simple and perfect!"

Sam reached over and gently stroked her thigh. "Thanks for saying that. I love it here too. When Liz suggested I move to Maine permanently, I wasn't so sure, but it was the best thing I ever did."

"Oh, look at that. The moon is coming up over the trees. It's so beautiful!" Olivia pointed and Sam followed the direction of her finger. "The man in the moon!"

Sam smiled at Olivia's childlike delight and found herself admiring her perfect profile. She turned Olivia's chin and lightly touched her lips to hers.

When Sam drew back, Olivia's eyes were wide, and she looked surprisingly young in the moonlight. Sam smiled and kissed her again. She caressed her lips with her tongue until they opened, surprised that Olivia seemed tentative, almost shy. That made Sam want to scoop her up in her arms. Instead she eased her down on the dock. Her exploration of Olivia's mouth was gentle. She kissed the soft skin along her neck. She could feel Olivia's breath catch as Sam ran her hand down her arm. She finally dared to reach for her breast when Olivia abruptly sat up, almost banging heads in the process.

"I don't want to miss the moonrise," she said.

Puzzled, Sam sat up too. Could it be that this woman, who was so aggressive in proposing sex, was shy? It made no sense, but instead of pushing, Sam put her arm around Olivia while they watched the moon come up.

❅❅❅

Sam came back from the bathroom and picked up her phone to see the time—a few minutes past three, her usual time to get up and pee. She tried to remember when she could still sleep through the night. It was probably a decade ago or more.

She saw that she had Facebook notices but knew she shouldn't open her page because the light would keep her awake. Against her better judgment, she decided to see who might be on Messenger. Often, Liz was awake at the same time and they chatted online for a few minutes. She was surprised to see Olivia's name in the column of active users. Olivia had announced that she didn't believe in social media and had only joined Facebook because the isolation of the pandemic had gotten to her.

Sam knew if she tapped to open a chat, it would be harder to go back to sleep. That's what usually happened when she allowed herself to become engaged online, instead of using the advantage of being half-asleep.

For a long moment, her finger was poised over the screen.

Hi, she finally typed.

Samantha! What are you doing awake?

Got up to pee.

Funny. Me too.

It was obvious that Olivia wasn't a big chat user. She used punctuation.

I probably should go back to sleep, Sam typed. *Just wanted to say hello.*

I appreciate it. Kind of a rough night.

Everything okay there?

A bit anxious.

Why? Because of tonight?

No. I get panic attacks.

Now, Sam was fully awake.

Want me to come over and sit with you?

The little gray bubble that meant Olivia was typing started to move, then stopped. Nothing happened for a long time. Then a message came through.

You are so sweet. I'm fine. Took my medication. Should be able to sleep soon.

Okay.

You are such a dear for offering! Thank you!

Welcome. Sleep well.

Sam scrolled through the emoticons for a heart. She considered a red one, but sent a purple one instead.

22

Liz's regular patients knew she had no office hours on Mondays, but that never stopped them from calling. They knew that Cherie would take care of any emergencies.

Because Liz wasn't supposed to be in the office, she tried to sneak past the front desk. Ginny looked up and caught her. "Liz!" she called after her. Liz stopped in her tracks and waited.

"I bet you think you're funny," said Ginny, cornering her. "What are you doing here on your day off? Again!"

"Forgot my duffle bag. It's full of dirty clothes. Ellie's coming today to clean and do the laundry."

"I'm sure she's glad to get back to work and make some money. The shutdown must have really hurt her."

When Liz smiled sheepishly, Ginny frowned. She'd been Liz's practice manager long enough to practically read her mind. "You were paying her during the shutdown, weren't you? Even though she wasn't cleaning your house." Ginny's freckled forehead wrinkled into a frown. "Liz, I know you're generous, but you have to think of yourself too."

"Think of it as creative socialism." Liz tried to mollify her with a big grin.

Ginny wasn't taken in. "It's your money. At least, more people are coming into the office now, especially since we can offer them a test."

"I'm getting some good financial advice. Things are looking up, aren't they?"

Ginny gave her a firm look, but she nodded. "Yes. We're able to make payroll and keep up with the bills." She raised her crossed fingers.

"But you didn't stop me in the hall to talk about our finances. What's going on?"

"Olivia Enright said she really needs to see you...*today*."

"Did you ask if she can see Cherie instead?"

"Of course. She says she needs to see *you* and only *you*."

Oh, no. Not this crap again! thought Liz, glancing at her watch. She'd promised to take the kids out on the boat, so Maggie could go to a rehearsal. The governor had finally raised the limit on gatherings to fifty. Tony, the artistic director of the Webhanet Playhouse, had come up with the idea of live performances on the terrace, where the chairs could be spaced far enough for safety. They were lucky to have the space and facilities to sponsor outdoor performances. The pandemic had forced summer stock theaters to cancel their seasons, and the revenue loss was killing them.

"Okay, Ginny. I'll give Ms. Enright a call." Liz tapped Olivia's number on the way to her office. When the call opened on the other end, she asked, "Why didn't you call my cell? You have the number."

"I know, but this is a medical issue. I thought I should go through your office."

"Thanks. I appreciate it." Liz closed her office door and sat down behind her desk. "What's the matter? Are you sick?"

There was a long pause on the other end. "Not exactly."

"So, why do you have to see me? Today's my day off."

"Yes, I know. Your receptionist told me. Please. Can you just give me a little bit of your time today? My anxiety is through the roof."

"Call Lucy. You're still seeing her, aren't you?"

"Yes, but she can't help me with this."

Liz rolled her eyes. "How about Telehealth?"

"No, I need to see *you*. I want you to examine my breasts."

Unfortunately, Liz was used to dealing with panicky women who'd discovered a breast lump. She always made a special effort to sound steady and calm for them. Liz glanced at her watch. "Can you come now?"

"Yes, I can be there in five minutes."

"Okay. See you then."

Liz tapped off the call and drummed her fingers on the desk. She called Maggie to explain that she would be a little late picking up the kids. Maggie sounded annoyed but, after living with a family doctor for six years, she was used to delayed departures.

"I'll make it up to you," Liz assured her. "I'll cook dinner tonight."

"All right," Maggie grumbled, "but please don't let me down. I have to be in Webhanet by one o'clock."

"Don't worry. I'll be there."

While she waited for Olivia, Liz read the top stories on *Bloomberg*. Olivia had predicted the shifts in the bond markets that were only now being reported in the financial news. She had suggested rearranging Liz's investments accordingly. When Liz logged into her brokerage account, she could see the positive impact of Olivia's strategy.

The button lit on the desk phone. Liz tapped it. "Ms. Enright is here for you, Doctor," said Connie, the head assistant.

Liz glanced at the time on the top of her computer screen. It had taken Olivia less than five minutes to get there.

"Give her a gown for a breast exam." Liz took a white coat from the hook on the back of the door and checked the pocket for a stethoscope. On her way out, she grabbed a surgical mask from the box on the cabinet.

"Thanks so much for letting me come in on such short notice," Olivia said as Liz closed the door to the exam room.

"You're welcome. Lie down." Liz brushed aside the paper gown and gave Olivia's breasts a quick visual inspection. Her practiced eyes instantly noticed the faint scars.

"You've had work done," she said as she palpated Olivia's breasts. She closed her eyes, so her fingertips could "see" and found the edge of the implant.

"You found them," said Olivia as Liz defined the edge of the implant in the other breast.

"Almost undetectable for an implant above the pectorals. Someone did very nice work. Stevens?"

"Yes. I've been very lucky in my plastic surgeons. This is my fourth set of implants."

Liz closed the gown. "You can sit up now." Liz took a seat on the nearby stool. "You really should tell me about these things when I take a medical history, not when you feel like it."

"I know," said Olivia in an apologetic tone. "I'm sorry. I intended to tell you when I came in for a physical next month."

Liz rolled back the stool and pulled a keyboard, mounted on a retractable arm, toward her. She typed in some notes about the implants in Olivia's file.

"When was this work done?"

"Two years ago, October."

Liz made a note in the file. "And the others?"

"Oh, let's see." Olivia rubbed her forehead with her fingertips, as if pressure could help her think. "The first surgery was over twenty-five years ago. I starved myself to fit into size-six suits, which made me almost completely flat chested. Then, it was one complication after another. Infections. Scarring making one breast bigger than the other and hard as a rock. I had brain fog from the silicone reaction."

"Do you mind if I take notes while we talk?"

"No, of course not."

Liz tried not to frown while Olivia recounted the sad history of her breast surgeries. While Liz understood the need for reconstruction after breast cancer, she didn't have a high opinion of cosmetic breast augmentation. Scar tissue always formed, eventually requiring implant replacement. The silicone leaked out. Many women lost sensitivity in their breasts.

By the time Olivia finished her story, she looked near tears. Liz gave her arm a reassuring pat.

"Your breasts seem perfectly fine. No lumps that I can feel. Did you have a specific concern today?"

"Could you feel the scar tissue? Last time it made my breasts so hard."

"No, they feel natural. I can feel the capsules, of course, because I know what I'm looking for. Stevens does good work. He matched the implants very well to your body type. Cosmetically, it's a great result. How's the sensation in your nipples?"

"Pretty good. Although it's been years since I've had completely natural breasts. How would I know?"

"You would know." Liz typed in a few more notes. "Everything looks fine. Why was this suddenly an emergency?"

Olivia stared at the floor.

Liz bent down to look into her face. "Well?"

"I'm starting a new relationship."

Liz quickly put the pieces together. "You're afraid your partner will have a negative reaction to the implants?"

With a sad look, Olivia nodded. "Would someone be able to guess about the implants?"

"You mean during sex? Maybe, but I doubt it. They feel almost completely natural. I only know because I'm a breast surgeon, and I've felt lots of breasts."

"I bet." Olivia managed a little smile.

"Believe me, in a clinical setting, feeling breasts isn't as much fun as it sounds." Liz crossed her arms on her chest. "Olivia, I know you like to keep things close to the vest, but why don't you just tell your partner before you have sex?"

"But it's so unromantic, stopping foreplay to say, I have to tell you something."

"So, tell her ahead of time or wait for her to ask about the scars. They're well hidden, but you can see them." Liz pushed the keyboard back to the wall. "Why don't you ask Lucy how to handle it? She's very good on conversations about sex."

"That's a good idea. Maybe I will."

Liz reached out her hand. "I know we're not supposed to shake hands, but you were just tested."

Olivia took Liz's outstretched hand. "Actually, I could use a hug."

Liz tried to moderate her surprise, but she put her arms around Olivia.

"You don't know what a nightmare this implant thing has been," Olivia murmured into Liz's shoulder.

"I can imagine, but don't worry. I'll keep an eye on it. Convenient to have a breast specialist as your PC. Now I know why you want me to stick around."

Olivia finally released her. "Exactly."

"I'll be involved in the practice for a few more years. My wife won't like that, but she puts up with it. And speaking of my wife, I've got to go. It's my turn to mind the grandkids." Liz headed to the sink to wash her hands.

"You're so lucky to have a relationship with your grandchildren."

"Another story I can't wait to hear, but it will have to wait until next time. You can get dressed. No charge for this visit."

"Oh, yes! It's business, and as your financial advisor, I say take the money and run! The practice needs it."

"Thanks. Good luck telling your partner." Liz headed to the door.

"One last question."

"Yes?" Liz stepped back into the room.

"If Samantha asks you to help build an armoire for me, would you help her? I'm only asking because she seems afraid to ask you herself."

Liz laughed. "I don't know why everyone is so afraid of me, but if Sam asks, and I have time, I'll help if I can."

"You are a good friend, Liz Stolz."

"I try."

23

Carats by the Bay was known to the locals as the best jeweler in town. Julia, the owner, had a special knack for taking heirloom jewelry and refashioning it into something meaningful in the present. Brenda had entrusted her with a pair of diamond earrings that had once belonged to her mother. Together, she and Julia had looked at dozens of solitaires to use as a centerpiece for a very special ring.

"It's just beautiful," said Brenda, admiring it in the light from the window.

Julia wiped down a jeweler's loupe with an antiseptic towelette. She pointed to her eye to give Brenda the idea.

"You'll see how clear the older stones are," Julia explained as Brenda put on the loupe. "They are high quality. By today's standards, they'd be rated at the top of the scale for color and clarity."

"You did an absolutely amazing job," said Brenda, putting the loupe down on the counter.

Julia put another ring in a tiny, plastic bag. "Did she miss her ring while it was gone?"

"No, she doesn't usually wear it because of her job. She has to wash her hands all the time. But I know it fits because I've seen her wear it when we go out."

"Always good to have a ring that fits to size a new one." Julia handed Brenda the plastic bag. "Have you chosen a place to pop the question?"

"I've reserved a table overlooking the ocean in the tent at Dockside. The weather is supposed to be nice tonight. We can watch the sun set over the harbor."

Julia smiled. "Sounds so romantic. I hope she says yes."

"Oh, God! Me too! But if she doesn't say yes the first time, I'll keep trying."

"You go, girl!" Julia raised a fist in encouragement.

Brenda put the ring box and the plastic bag containing the ring she'd filched from Cherie's jewelry box into the pouch on her service belt. They barely fit alongside her wallet, car keys, and a tube of lipstick. She'd resisted getting a pouch the next size up because she didn't want the temptation to carry around a lot of junk.

Behind her, the bell over the door tinkled. A man and a woman came into the shop. Brenda knew almost everyone in town, but she didn't know these two. She guessed they were tourists from the way they were dressed, and their wide-eyed stare as they gazed around. Funny how easy it was to tell the summer people from the townies.

"Thanks for trusting us with such an important commission, Chief," said Julia, looking around Brenda to wave at the people who'd just come in. "Good luck tonight."

"Thanks. I might need it. I don't think she has any idea this is coming."

Brenda picked up her hat from the counter and put it on. As she headed to the door, Brenda could feel the eyes of the tourists follow her. Maybe she should have worn her civvies when she picked up the ring. Whenever she popped into a local store, even to pick up some groceries on her way home after duty, everyone stared. As Brenda got into her squad car, she decided that people noticing her presence was probably a good thing, especially if it made them think twice about wrongdoing.

Brenda dropped off the squad car and picked up her truck from the department parking lot. When she got home, she stowed her service weapon and accepted a quick kiss from Cherie before heading upstairs.

"I thought you'd changed your mind about going out," Cherie called up the stairs after her.

"I'm not that late," Brenda called back. She stopped at the landing to admire Cherie, who was wearing an off-the-shoulder top that accentuated her good figure. She'd put up her hair in an interesting braided style. Although her biracial heritage made her always look slightly tan, she got more color when she was in the sun. Her cheeks were rosy, and her skin was a warm brown that contrasted beautifully with her blond hair and blue-green eyes. Her unique coloring never failed to turn heads. "Damn. Aren't you just gorgeous!" said Brenda with heartfelt admiration.

"Get moving, girlfriend. I want to be able to return the compliment."

Brenda slipped off her blouse and gratefully took off the bullet-proof vest. She'd been wearing it more often since the protests against the police. She hated to wear it in the summer, and usually only put it on when she knew she might be backing up the patrol officers. She rifled through her closet to find the see-through linen top she'd imagined wearing for this dinner date. Combined with black pants, heeled sandals, and a low-cut tank top, it would be casual but special enough for the occasion.

While Brenda was refreshing her makeup, Cherie wandered into the bathroom. "I came up to see what's taking you so long." She leaned over the sink to look at Brenda even though she could see her reflection in the mirror.

"Oh my! You're going all out tonight. I like that dark lipstick. Very sexy."

Brenda blotted it with a tissue. "Glad you think so."

"We'd better get going soon, or I might want to keep you here and have my way with you."

"You can do that later. We have to go. I made reservations."

Cherie put her arm around Brenda's waist and bumped her hip against hers. "We don't have to do anything we don't want to."

"But you made all that effort to look nice."

Cherie put her hands on her hips in mock indignation. "You're not supposed to say a woman made an effort for you! You're just supposed to compliment the results."

"Guess I missed that lesson," said Brenda with a chuckle. She went out to the bedroom to put on her sandals. "You ready?"

Cherie agreed to take her car, but as usual, she let Brenda drive, saying it gave her a chance to take in the scenery she usually missed when she was the driver. On the way, Cherie rested her hand on Brenda's thigh. Brenda always enjoyed those sweet, new-lover gestures. She hoped that, after they'd been married for years, they'd still exchange small tokens of affection. Brenda's first wife, Marcia, had never missed an opportunity for a quick caress or a little kiss.

Brenda sometimes felt guilty that her status as the town police chief entitled her to special service at restaurants, but she never turned it down. The hostess escorted them to the best table in the tent. The weather was clear, so the sides of the tent were open, offering a perfect view of the harbor. Limited indoor dining was now allowed, but many people were still choosing to eat outside, and not just for health reasons. Restaurant owners were saying the practice might become a permanent feature, one of the few good things to come out of the pandemic.

"I'm going to order champagne," said Brenda. "Okay with you?"

Cherie looked surprised. "Sure. What's the occasion? Did you get a raise?"

Brenda sighed and shook her head. "There won't be any raises this year. The town is struggling as it is."

"Okay. I like champagne, but why do I feel that you're up to something?"

"Because maybe I am." Brenda smiled slyly.

The waiter brought the champagne and opened the bottle with a perfect pop.

"I might be jumping the gun here," said Brenda as she watched him pour the champagne.

Cherie made a little face. "Guns again. Do you have yours?"

"I have a .38 special in my handbag."

Cherie closed her eyes and shook her head.

"I'm sorry, honey, but I feel naked without a sidearm."

"It's okay," said Cherie, opening her eyes. "I've mostly gotten over my gun thing. Unfortunately, it's the price of living with a cop."

Brenda raised her glass. "Then let's drink to your progress."

"Okay, but first, I want to know, what's the big occasion? I knew you were up to something when you said you'd like me to dress up a little for our date."

Brenda took a deep breath. Should she ask her now or hold it until after dinner? It didn't take more than a few seconds to decide. Since she'd picked up the ring, she'd been conscious of its presence, as if it were sending her telepathic signals. She glanced shyly at Cherie.

"Come on, girl," Cherie demanded. "Spill it!"

Brenda opened her purse and put the ring box on the table.

Cherie's eyes grew wide. "Is this what I think it is?"

"I don't know. What do you think it is?"

Cherie stared at the box. "Don't you think it's too soon?"

"On whose timetable?"

"We've only just moved in together. Shouldn't we see if we get along?"

"Have we had any problems so far?"

Cherie thought for a moment. "Apart from my own issues about the police violence, no, I don't think so."

Brenda reached out and nudged the box a little closer to Cherie. "Come on. Aren't you curious?"

Cherie gave Brenda a brief pleading look. "Yes, but I'm afraid, too."

The idea that this special moment was causing Cherie anxiety gave Brenda a little twist of pain. "Why?"

"It's all so perfect now. I don't want it to stop."

"That's why I want you to marry me, so it will never stop." Brenda pushed the box closer. "Please look at it. I had it specially made for you." Brenda took the plastic bag with the other ring out of her bag and set it next to the box.

"I've been going crazy looking for that thing! I thought I left it in the office."

"I borrowed it," said Brenda with a guilty look. "I couldn't tell you because it was a surprise." Brenda finally picked up the box and put it in Cherie's hand. "Please just look at it. At least, tell me if you like it."

Cherie opened the box with a smile and her eyes shut. When she opened them, she made the kind of face someone makes at a cute kitten or an adorable baby. She pressed her lips together and waved her hand in front of her throat. It was obvious she was overcome. "It's beautiful," she choked out. "Of course, it's beautiful."

"The small diamonds came from a pair of earrings my mother left to me. The big stone is new."

"Something old, something new…" said Cherie repeating the old rhyme.

"You look sad," said Brenda, worried.

Cherie, still overcome, shook her head. Finally, she managed to say, "No, I'm happy, so happy! But I'm sad because my father always wanted to throw a big wedding for me. When he realized I was never going to marry a man, he kind of gave up. After he met you, he started to talk about it again."

"You never told me."

"I didn't want to give you any ideas until I was sure about you."

"Your dad will be with us when we tie the knot," Brenda said, reaching across the table. "Please put it on. I want to see how it looks."

"I haven't said 'yes' yet."

Brenda felt a pang of anxiety. "You will marry me, won't you?"

"Of course, I'll marry you!"

Brenda sat back and let her breath out slowly. She hadn't realized she'd been holding it while waiting for Cherie's answer. "Thank God! You had me going for a minute."

"But can we wait until we can have a big wedding and invite all our friends? I still have some family in Louisiana. Aunts and cousins…"

"We can wait, but not too long." Brenda gave her a firm look. "I want to make sure I catch you before you get away." Brenda moved her chair closer, so she could put the ring on Cherie's finger. It fit perfectly. "Like it?"

Cherie held up her hand to admire it. "It's beautiful."

"Not too fancy."

"No, it's perfect." Cherie leaned forward and gave Brenda a quick kiss.

"That's all?" asked Brenda.

"We're in public. And everyone knows you're the police chief."

"Okay, but you need to do better when we get home."

Cherie reached under the table and caressed Brenda's thigh. "Don't you worry, girl. I've got you covered."

24

The repetitive sound of the waves as the tide came in was mesmerizing. The waves had their own rhythm, two short, one long. The long wave pushed the water up the beach. Sam had never noticed the pattern until Lucy had pointed it out and explained that it was like timing in music.

"You're so quiet over there," said Olivia. "What are you thinking about?"

"The syncopation of the waves. If you pay attention, you can hear it. Two short. One long. Lucy told me about it. And the pattern changes, like in music. Listen and you'll hear it."

Olivia reached out her hand and Sam took it. "You're a complicated woman, Samantha. I never realized."

"You always seem surprised to find out things about me."

"I tend to pigeonhole people into their resumes. That's why I was better at managing at a high level. When it came to working one-on-one or doing staff development, I was a disaster. I never gave people a chance to explore and grow."

"That's a shame."

"It was, because I lost many good people."

"When did you realize this?"

"Last winter. When I was all alone up here and had nothing to do but think."

"Sometimes isolation is good for that."

Olivia squeezed Sam's hand, then let it go. "Those long, dark months were difficult for me. When the days finally got longer, the pandemic set in, and I felt even more alone. I wish I had known you and your friends then."

"We were all here, shut up in our houses, self-isolating. Not Liz. She likes to say she takes in strays. She had Lucy and Erika living with them, and Erika's dad, and Maggie's daughter and grandchildren. I was on my own."

"How did you spend the time?"

"I worked on my house. I did some carvings. I've always wanted to learn woodcarving. I got pretty good at it."

"Sounds like you found productive ways to entertain yourself."

"I don't mind being alone. I like my own company."

"Good for you. You're lucky you do." Olivia raised her wine glass to her lips and took a delicate sip. "I hope you don't mind, but I asked your friend to help you build my armoire."

Surprised, Sam turned in her seat. "When did you see Liz?"

"I had an appointment with her today."

"Are you sick?"

"No, no. I just wanted her perspective on something." Olivia finished her wine and replenished her glass. "I've had some work done. Cosmetic work."

"Liz doesn't do that kind of surgery."

"I know, but she's an expert on breasts."

Sam felt uneasy. "What are you trying to say?"

"The work I've had done wasn't just on my face."

"Implants and a tummy tuck."

Olivia looked surprised. "How did you guess?"

"It's almost a cliché, isn't it?"

Olivia studied her carefully. "Does it bother you?"

"No. If that's what you need to feel good about yourself, it's your business."

Olivia faced forward and looked thoughtfully at the moon high above the ocean. "I was afraid you'd say that."

"Don't read into it," said Sam, a little on edge. "You look great."

"But you don't approve."

Now, Sam was becoming impatient. "I didn't say that, Olivia. It's your issue, not mine. Don't stick it on me." Sam finished her wine in a gulp and got up. "I don't want to have a fight about nothing. Maybe I should go."

"Samantha, please sit down," said Olivia in a calm voice that conflicted with the anxious look on her face.

Reluctantly, Sam sat down.

"I felt I should tell you in case we decide to have sex. I didn't want you to discover the implants in bed."

"You're afraid I'd reject you for having implants? You think I'm *that* shallow?"

Olivia shook her head. "I feel like I've botched this royally. I hope you don't find me abhorrent."

"Abhorrent? Now, there's a twenty-dollar word."

"I learned it when I took a course to improve my vocabulary. My husband thought it would make me sound more educated."

"But you are educated. You went to Barnard and Harvard B-school."

"Yes, but people's vocabulary and speech patterns are formed when they're young…by their families and schools. I also took classes in elocution to get rid of my upstate New York twang."

"So, your accent is fake too?" Sam blurted out.

Olivia looked pained. "I tried to better myself. What's wrong with that?"

"Nothing. I'm sorry. I didn't mean to sound so mean."

"Thank you for the apology, but why are you hanging around with someone you think is fake?"

"I admit I find the phony front difficult. Sometimes, it's hard to get past it."

Olivia sighed and turned her face to the sea. "Many people were attracted to me because of the image I project…and my money. None of that means anything to you, does it?"

"Not really. I grew up with money. My trust fund meant I never had to work, but I built a career because that's what my parents encouraged me to do. Now, living simply and being easy on the environment mean much more to me than money and success."

Olivia turned and gave her a careful inspection. "I think that's why I'm drawn to you. You know who you are. You're completely genuine. Artifice means nothing to you. I'm encouraged to think you might learn to like who I really am…instead of what I appear to be."

Sam realized that Olivia was clumsily revealing herself. It was probably brand new to her. She'd spent so long concealing her true self, this getting-to-know-you phase of a new relationship must be excruciating. Sam felt guilty about jumping down her throat.

"How could you have relationships with people only interested in your image and money?"

"The easy answer is, I didn't. I mean they weren't really relationships. They were associations of convenience. My marriage is a case in point."

Sam frowned sympathetically. "I'm sorry," she murmured.

"Why are you sorry? It's my own fault. I chose it."

"I'm sorry I'm so harsh and judgmental. I'm not usually this way. You bring it out in me."

Olivia rolled her eyes. "Oh, great."

"You're everything I was brought up to despise. Nouveau Riche. Pretentious. Manufactured class as thin as tissue paper…"

"Anything else you'd like to add while you're being so hurtful?"

"No, I guess I've said enough. Maybe I should go before I can never get my foot out of my mouth."

Olivia sat up and reached out for her hand. "Don't you see anything worthwhile in me?"

Olivia looked so vulnerable at that moment, Sam wanted to hug her, but after saying such harsh words, she wasn't sure it would be welcome.

"Well?" Olivia prompted. "Do you?"

"I see a lot worthwhile. You're trying to do good for the community. You don't just sit around sipping martinis like my mother and her country club friends. You're actually involved. You're obviously very smart. I like having my mind stimulated, and you provide lots to think about. I don't mind that you're beautiful. And I find you a challenge. I'm really curious to know what's under that façade of yours."

"What if you don't like what you find?"

Sam shrugged. "No harm. No foul."

"Did you have more in mind than a fishing expedition?"

"I like fishing," Sam replied with a quick grin, "but I also don't mind catching something."

Olivia raised her chin and regarded Sam through her eyelashes. "You think you're very clever, don't you?"

"No. I try, but humor isn't really my thing. My timing is always off."

"You're doing pretty well tonight." Olivia glanced at their empty wine glasses. She picked up the bottle and found that empty too. "We've run out of wine. Would you like to go in?"

Sam got up. "I really should go."

Olivia got up too. "Will you, at least, let me give you a kiss goodbye?" She took a step forward and drew Sam into a soft kiss. "Thank you for coming tonight."

"Thank *you*. I thoroughly enjoyed it."

"I wish you wouldn't go. What I mean is, I wish you would stay."

Sam put her arm around Olivia's waist and pulled her close. "That was your plan all along, right?"

Olivia affected an innocent look but said, "Guilty as charged."

Sam liked the feel of Olivia's body pressing against hers. "All right. Let's go in. Let's see if you can seduce me."

"I was hoping you'd seduce *me*." Olivia gently nipped Sam's ear with her teeth, then blew into it.

Sam staggered for a moment, hanging on to Olivia to keep her balance. She felt faint when Olivia molded her body around hers.

"I thought you wanted *me* to seduce *you*," Sam managed to say.

"That's the oldest trick in the book…when a woman holds all the cards, she tries to convince her partner to play them," Olivia whispered into her ear. Her warm breath tickled. She nipped Sam's ear again. "Come inside and I'll take care of you."

"Can we have another glass of wine before bed? I'm a little nervous. I haven't done this in a while."

"Of course," said Olivia, giving her a sweet kiss. "I completely understand. It's been a while for me too." She ran her hands along Sam's shoulders and down her arms. "I love your strength. I loved watching your muscles flex when you were swinging that sledgehammer. It made me crazy. That's when I decided I had to have you."

Sam chuckled softly. "You like women with tool belts, do you?"

Olivia gripped Sam's arms. "I like strong women who take what they want."

"Forget the wine. Let's go upstairs."

Olivia smiled. "I knew you'd see it my way."

The deliberation they took in bringing in everything from the deck and locking up the house belied their impatience. They held hands as they went up the stairs. When they walked into Olivia's bedroom, Sam gazed around. "I remember this place."

Olivia said, "I remember you in my shower." She began to unbutton Sam's camp blouse. She shrugged it off her shoulders and ran her hands along her arms. "So beautiful." She gave each of Sam's breasts a little kiss above her bra. "Very nice." She nudged Sam in the direction of the bed. "Now, sit down and relax." Sam's head was swimming at the thought of following Olivia's instructions in bed.

Sam's mouth gaped a little as she watched Olivia open her blouse and let it drop. She was wearing the sexiest black-lace bra she had ever seen. "Nice underwear."

"Just for you," said Olivia and blew her a kiss. She slowly pulled down her capris to reveal matching lace panties.

Sam was so turned on by the sight of the sexy underwear, she forgot to think about how perfect it was. Olivia sat beside Sam and took her face in her hands.

"You like what you see. I can tell."

"Where sex is concerned, I'm an open book."

"I like that about you. Everything is open," said Olivia, easing her down on the bed. "Come on. Let's get rid of these," she said, tugging on Sam's shorts.

"I thought I was supposed to seduce you."

"You are. I'm just helping a little."

Olivia pulled off Sam's underwear along with the shorts. She lightly ran her hand over her pubic hair, then nudged her over on the bed. She reached behind Sam and unhooked her bra. "Serviceable underwear."

"I like cotton when it's hot."

"So practical."

Olivia positioned herself on Sam's hips. She unhooked the front open closure of her bra so that her breasts were free.

"Oh my God," breathed Sam. "You're gorgeous."

"With a little help from my friends."

"Do those gorgeous breasts have feeling?" asked Sam.

Olivia looked pained. "Why do you ask?"

"I dated a breast cancer survivor whose breasts were reconstructed. She lost sensation in her nipples, but she liked me to touch them."

"I have sensation in mine, if you'd like to touch them."

Sam closed her eyes and reached out to caress those perfect breasts. The skin was so soft and warm, each breast was exactly the right size to fill her hand. She gently squeezed the nipples. She opened her eyes and saw the pleasure on Olivia's face, but when she tried to sit up so that she could kiss them, Olivia held her down by the shoulders.

That wouldn't do, so Sam rolled Olivia off her hips and onto her back. She kissed and sucked the beautiful breasts while Olivia moaned. The nipples were tight and pert, and she couldn't get enough of them. Meanwhile, she gently pulled down the lace panties.

"Yes!" Olivia whispered into her ear as Sam caressed her. She opened her legs and Sam found her way in. Olivia put her arms around Sam's neck and pulled her closer. "Yes, please!"

25

When Lucy approached the turn for the summer chapel and saw the Episcopal flag flying below the stars and stripes, she felt like a girl on the first day of school. The bishop's permission to open the summer chapel had come as a surprise. Of course, it made perfect sense now that the governor had allowed restaurants to reopen for outdoor dining. Why not an outdoor church?

Too bad the order hadn't come before Pentecost, when Lucy could have donned the magnificent red vestments to celebrate the Eucharist on the birthday of the church. Some of the vestments at St. Mary's by the Sea went back to the 1950s, gifts of moneyed summer parishioners. Many were embroidered with real gold, and the work in them was splendid.

From her background in the opera, Lucy had mixed feelings about wearing ornate vestments to lead the liturgy. She loved the rituals of the Church and the comforting effect they had on her congregation. Another part of her saw the vestments as a costume in another form of theater. Today, none of that mattered. Lucy couldn't wait to put on real vestments, stand at a real altar, and see real people in the congregation.

Lucy spied the warden's car in front of the chapel. The new warden had been a blessing. The elderly man she'd succeeded would have been an impediment rather than a facilitator during the pandemic. Lucy had prayed for his replacement by a younger and more able person, and in Abbie Roberts, her prayers had been answered. Abbie was a retired tech executive and her expertise had helped St. Margaret's make the transition from live to virtual services during the shutdown. She efficiently managed the parish's business, enabling Lucy to focus on spiritual matters.

After parking the car, Lucy put on the clear-plastic, M99 mask Liz had given her. When Lucy had tried it on, she'd panicked just like on her first scuba dive, but cleverly concealed, filtered vents allowed her to breathe normally. It muffled sound, but Lucy had learned to project her voice so it could be heard in an enormous opera house like the Met. The benefit of the clear mask was people could see her entire face.

"Your smile is what people come to see," Liz had explained when she'd presented it. "Your smile makes your parishioners feel happy and whole, so let them see it." The insight surprised Lucy. She wouldn't have expected Liz to be so sensitive to the nuances of ministry.

Lucy entered the church through the side door and saw Abbie busily loading the cart used to transport the communion elements and sacred vessels to the outdoor, stone altar.

"Good morning, Mother Lucy." As many times as Lucy had asked the warden to dispense with her title, Abbie insisted on formality. "Our verger is a little late this morning, so I thought I'd pitch in."

"Thank you, but you shouldn't have to do everything."

"Neither should you." Abbie straightened. "Wow. Cool mask. Is it effective?"

"It's rated above medical grade according to Dr. Stolz. She got it for me."

"Very smart." Abbie nodded her approval. "Dr. Stolz is always looking out for you."

The remark, innocently intended, caused Lucy's cheeks to color. She wondered how many in the community had noticed the special attention Liz gave her.

Abbie, apparently unaware of Lucy's discomfort, had gone back to her task of loading the items on the cart. "We're following guidelines. We've got plenty of hand sanitizer. You'll need to use it before you distribute communion. I sanitized all the vessels."

Lucy glanced at the cart. "It's all so extreme. We've always been careful. I always scrub my hands before the Eucharist, but who would think we'd have to be so worried about simple things like door handles?"

"I know. This pandemic has given me a whole new perspective on cleanliness."

Lucy scrutinized the stocky, blond woman. Abbie looked tired. She had retired a few years earlier, and now, she was the primary caretaker for her elderly mother. Maybe the warden's role was too much for her, but Abbie was the kind of person who needed to be busy. The only time she ever sat still was in a pew, and then, she fidgeted.

Abbie glanced up. "Here's Jim." The verger entered the chapel. Over her mask, Abbie gave him a disapproving look.

"Sorry to be late," he said, but he didn't look sorry. "I'll take over from here." He glanced at Lucy. "Good morning, Mother Lucy. Cool mask."

Lucy wanted to avoid having to explain the technical details again, so she greeted Jim and headed to the robing room.

Because it was a warm morning, Lucy had worn a collared bib under her suit. She pulled the white alb over her head. It was her ordination alb, which she saved for special occasions such as this. She kissed the cross on the white stole, a gift from Susan, the woman who had inspired Lucy to become a priest. Susan's love had brought her back from that dark place after the rape. Susan's love had taught her that God loved her, and that love was the most important thing of all. As Lucy cinched the cord around her waist, she silently blessed the woman to whom she owed so much.

Lucy checked her laptop to see if there were any last minute reservations to approve. Before she'd left the rectory, the number had been close to the maximum of fifty. She navigated to the parish website. There were six people waiting for the five remaining seats. Lucy had a pang of indecision. She could call her wife and ask her not to come. Erika was unwavering in her agnosticism, and only came to church to support Lucy. The same was true of Liz, although she also came to listen to Maggie sing.

Lucy decided that whatever her friends' reasons, they had as much right to attend worship as anyone. Before she opened the page to approve the requests, she decided to deal with them on a first-come, first-serve basis.

Her finger was poised to tap through the requests when she came to one from Olivia Enright. *Well, that's different.* Lucy shrugged and approved it. The next request, made within seconds of the first, was from

Sam McKinnon. *Hmm*, thought Lucy, as she flipped through the remaining requests. As she approved them, Lucy knew she'd have to call Erika and ask her not to come. No, that meant Emily wouldn't have a ride to church. She'd have to ask Liz instead. Lucy let her breath out slowly, hoping Liz wouldn't think it had something to do with the incident on the boat.

Liz's cell phone rang on the other end. Lucy tapped her foot while it did, then became conscious of it and stopped.

"What's up, Lucy?" Liz asked when she answered. As usual, there was no greeting. "We're almost there. Did you need something?"

"I'm sorry, Liz, but I'm one over the reservation limit."

"Lucy! Are you telling me *not* to come to church? You're always trying to convert me, and now, you *don't* want me to come?" Lucy could hear the smile in Liz's voice and unconsciously smiled back.

"Liz, I'm only asking you because I know you're an atheist and only come for Maggie and me."

"Who cares why I come?"

"I care, if it means someone else can't."

"Too bad. I'm coming anyway."

"Liz! It's against the law."

"So what? You think Brenda's going to arrest me at church?"

Lucy closed her eyes and took a deep breath. She should have anticipated this. Liz enjoyed breaking rules.

"Lucy, someone's bound not to show up, and the fifty-person limit is completely arbitrary. It has no medical basis."

Maggie, who'd been listening in the whole time on the Bluetooth speaker, chimed in. "Don't bother arguing with her, Lucy. You know how she is."

"All right, but if there's any trouble, I'm sending them to you."

"It would be an honor to defend you, Lucy. Remember, I am your pledged knight." It was meant as a joke, but Lucy had no doubt that Liz would be there if she ever needed her.

"All right," said Lucy. "See you in a few minutes. Liz, you may have to stand in the back."

"Doesn't matter. As long as I can admire you from afar."

"Stop it. I have to go." As Lucy clicked off the call, she wondered what Maggie thought of that little exchange. Obviously, Liz hadn't learned her lesson and was back to her old flirtatious ways.

From the window of the robing room, Lucy watched the congregation arriving. The ushers had been instructed to make sure people sat six feet apart and handed out the bulletin with the service and hymns printed inside. Common hymnals were forbidden because they might spread disease.

Lucy chose a modern chasuble. As much as she admired the beautiful work in the antique vestments, the gold brocade made them heavy. Because they had been made for male priests, some were too long for her. Now that Pentecost and the Easter season had passed, the liturgical color was green. As Lucy slipped the garment over her head, she wondered where the time had gone. It was as if it had vanished, sucked into a black hole while they were in lockdown. She put on the clear mask, anxious again about being able to breathe, but, after taking a few deep breaths, she was fine.

She went out to join the procession, pleased that everyone was honoring the social distancing requirements. The congregation had settled down, appropriately spaced. There were exceptions for families or people living in the same house.

Lucy waved to Maggie to begin the entrance hymn. Maggie was on her own because they didn't want to give up available places by inviting the whole choir, so Lucy helped Maggie keep the congregation on key. She modulated her voice to avoid drowning out Maggie or drawing too much attention to herself.

As she passed, Lucy noticed Olivia and Sam sitting together. Lucy tried not to be obvious about watching them while she stood in front of the altar to sing the remainder of the hymn. They were holding hands, which told Lucy all she needed to know. She reminded herself that it wasn't her place to judge.

At the altar, Lucy took off her mask because it was allowed. She crossed herself and began the collect for Trinity Sunday. At the conclusion, she gazed around, smiling and nodding to acknowledge her regular parishioners.

"Welcome back! I hope you're as happy to be back as I am! I feel like we've been wandering in the desert of the internet, but I thank God we had a way to worship when we couldn't meet in person. It's so good to see everyone. I wish I could hug every one of you! But I can't. Neither can you at the kiss of peace. No handshakes either. Please, for the sake of continuing our common worship, observe the safety guidelines."

Lucy saw Emily and Erika sitting together at the end of an aisle. As always, Erika was glowing with pride. Standing in the back was Liz with her arms crossed and her little smirk. Lucy shook her head and focused on Mrs. McPherson in the front row.

Some of the changes to the usual order of the rite were easy; others made Lucy anxious. The readers read from printed papers. Only Lucy read from the common Lectionary. She didn't share the broken host and consumed all of the consecrated wine, which, on an empty stomach, gave her a surprising jolt, more physical than spiritual. She replaced her mask and used hand sanitizer before coming into the aisle to distribute communion. Tom gave out communion from the side aisle. They'd practiced putting the host in the communicant's hands without touching their skin. The ushers directed traffic so that the communicants remained six feet apart.

Erika and Emily came up to receive. Followed by Liz, who gave Lucy a wink over her mask as she took the host. *What does she think she's doing?* Lucy wondered as she waited for the next communicant. *Isn't she already in enough trouble?*

The social-distanced fellowship that followed was welcome, even if it felt odd. This was the first time in four months that Lucy had seen most of her parishioners. As two chairs in Lucy's circle became vacant, Olivia and Sam appropriated them.

Lucy felt her smile freeze.

"What an inspiring sermon, Mother Lucy," gushed Olivia.

"How nice to see you here, Olivia," Lucy said as sincerely as she could.

"Sam talked me into coming this morning." Olivia smiled sweetly in Sam's direction.

"Nice to see you too, Sam. I know you're not one of my regulars."

"It was really Olivia's idea."

Oh dear, thought Lucy, realizing her instincts were right. They were involved sexually. Lucy mentally pinched herself to stop the judgment forming in her mind. Try as she might, she just couldn't warm up to Olivia. Lucy was fond of Sam and didn't want to see her get hurt.

Out of the corner of her eye, Lucy saw Liz approaching.

"I'm sorry to interrupt, but I have to go in a few minutes," said Liz, bending to speak near Lucy's ear. "I wonder if I could have a word with you."

"Excuse us, please, ladies," Lucy said, relieved to have the excuse to leave. "Meet me in the robing room," Lucy said to Liz. "I have to pick up my things."

Lucy carefully hung up the chasuble with the others in the closet. She pulled the alb over her head. When she turned around, she saw Liz standing in the doorway and motioned to her to come in.

"You shouldn't stay long. I don't want you to get in more trouble than you are," Lucy said, reaching up to give Liz a hug. "How are things at home? More or less back to normal?"

"Not exactly. We're not talking about it."

"That's not good. You should talk about it. Maybe some counseling would help." Lucy opened the buttons of her cassock.

"Ordinarily, I'd go to you."

"For obvious reasons, I'm not available. Talk to Tom. He's great at couples' counseling." Lucy carefully hung her cassock in the closet.

"Forget it. I'm not going to air my problems in front of Tom. We go back too long."

"He's a priest, Liz. He can look past your friendship."

"You know the priest thing doesn't mean a whole lot to me."

"You need to convince Maggie the incident was impulsive and won't happen again," said Lucy as she slipped her arms into a black jacket. "She's insecure about you. I've known that since I met you. I could kick myself for getting involved in our little flirtation. It only makes her uncomfortable."

"There's some history. When Maggie and I first got back together, I was still involved with my ex."

"Ugh!"

"Yes."

Lucy slipped her laptop and the white stole from Susan into her bag. "Did you have something specific you wanted to talk to me about?"

"No, I just wanted to look at you. I miss you."

"I miss you too," Lucy gave Liz's shoulder a little squeeze. "We should get out of here before someone finds us alone together." When Lucy turned, she saw Liz's wife standing in the doorway.

Maggie stared at them for a moment. Without a word, she left.

"Liz, go," said Lucy, pushing her. "Take Maggie home. Explain that we were just talking."

Liz gave Lucy a quick, anxious glance and headed out.

Lucy's eyes stung. *What a mess!* She missed Liz too. She missed their easy companionship, the silly banter, but most of all, her calm and strength. In stressful situations, Liz had always been her rock. She also missed Maggie's friendship. They'd barely talked since their yoga date.

Abbie came in. "Are you all right, Mother Lucy? You look upset."

Lucy forced a smile. "I'm fine, Abbie. I thought I'd spend a few minutes in the chapel before I leave. Don't worry. I'll lock up."

Abbie studied Lucy with concern. "Okay. Thanks." At the door, she added, "It was wonderful to have a real Eucharist after all these months."

"Yes, it was." Lucy managed another smile. "Thank you for arranging everything...as always."

"It's a pleasure to work with you, Mother Lucy."

Lucy listened to Abbie's footsteps fade away as she locked up the robing room. Once she saw Abbie head to the parking lot, Lucy went into the chapel. Kneeling in the first pew, she leaned her forehead against her clasped hands and tried to focus.

Her moral theology professor had spent most of the semester on what he called the "social commandments." Stealing and lying were pretty simple, but then came adultery and coveting your neighbor's wife. At first, Lucy resented the focus on sexual sins, but as the course went on, she began to understand why the professor had emphasized them. The smallest social unit was a committed, sexual relationship. When its boundaries were violated, all kinds of havoc could ensue. Families could be ripped apart. Reputations destroyed. Communities left in upheaval. In her therapy practice, Lucy had seen this play out over and over again.

Erika, who had a special interest in social ethics, had a different point of view. She agreed that social norms had value but saw rules about sexual relations as the patriarchy's way of controlling women. Sometimes, Lucy's head hurt when Erika went on about this subject. It was all so easy for her. So tidy. She totally missed the human mess that resulted from violating the rules.

Lucy cleared her mind and begged for enlightenment. She was so deeply into her meditation that she jumped when someone tapped her shoulder.

"Lucy, dear, I'm sorry to disturb your prayers. I just wanted to tell you we're leaving," Erika said. "Emily wants to go to the beach."

"Tell her to put on sunscreen," said Lucy, getting to her feet.

"I will." Erika frowned in concern. "What's wrong, love? You look distressed."

"Maggie is still upset with Liz about that kiss."

Erika rolled her eyes. "Oh, for Pete's sake! Maggie needs to grow up!"

"Erika," chided Lucy gently. "Be kind."

"I'm not being unkind. If she continues to fuss about this, she will only push Liz away." Erika bent to kiss her. "I'm going now. I'll see you at home."

As Lucy watched Erika walk toward the door, her heart ached over the human mess a single, impulsive kiss had caused.

26

Liz was almost glad to be back at work. Although Maggie hadn't moved out of the bedroom this time, she was sparing in her words, and her tone was chilly. Liz was running out of patience. She was willing to do some penance for kissing Lucy, but Maggie's cold shoulder treatment was really getting on her nerves. She and Lucy hadn't done anything wrong. They were just talking.

Thinking about the episode put Liz in a foul mood. She scowled at the computer screen as she reviewed the day's schedule and gave herself a little lecture. It was going to be a heavy day. She couldn't afford the luxury of being irritable.

Out of the corner of her eye, she saw her phone screen flash with a text message. She picked it up when she saw it was from Lucy.

How are you?

Okay.

Did you argue?

Not exactly. She's barely talking to me.

After a pause, Lucy wrote: *Don't argue. Speak quietly. Listen carefully. Whatever you do, don't get defensive. Let her calm down.*

Liz texted back. *Is that your advice as a shrink?*

LOL. No. That's my advice as a woman.

Liz smiled and pressed Lucy's number. "Yours is the only advice I would trust."

"Do you ever say hello when you call?"

"Not unless I have to."

"You're so bad."

"What are you doing?"

"Waiting for my next client."

"Me too."

"She's here. Have to go, Liz."

"Okay."

Liz stared at her phone as Lucy's smiling image vanished. The conversation had been completely innocent, but Liz felt guilty. Why? There was nothing wrong with talking to Lucy. They worked together. Sometimes they *had* to talk.

Confusion roiled her emotions. She loved Maggie, and she loved Lucy. No, she *adored* Lucy and everything about her—her exquisite voice, her beauty, her wise advice, and her natural warmth. Lucy was sexy just taking a breath. Liz would never admit it, but she also loved Lucy for trying to convert her. "God loves you, Liz. How can you resist?" The tug of war was exciting. It was the ultimate seduction.

Liz tried to put herself in Maggie's place. How would she react if Maggie had tongue kissed someone? She had to admit she wouldn't like it, especially not if that someone was male. All the bad memories of their college days came flooding back. Liz could feel the fury rising in her like heartburn after eating a triple-meat pizza.

For distraction, Liz navigated to *MedPageToday*. She frowned when she saw yet another article about COVID's multiple organ involvement. By now, it was obvious the coronavirus caused more than pneumatic pathology. Autopsy reports on victims were finally being published. They found extensive damage in the lungs, but COVID affected nearly every organ in the body. Most worrisome of all was the permanent lung, heart, or kidney damage. Even people with mild cases were still suffering from symptoms long after recovery.

Liz thought of her two favorite COVID patients—Brenda and Cherie. Both seemed perfectly healthy after getting over the disease. Apart from a slight fever, Cherie had been completely asymptomatic, but Brenda had suffered a full-blown case, including the characteristic shortness of breath and high fever. So far, neither had complained about any long-term symptoms.

Liz called Cherie's desk phone in the staff room.

"Hi, Liz. What's up?" Cherie asked when she picked up.

"Can you come back here for a minute?"

Cherie appeared in a matter of seconds. Liz always appreciated her responsiveness.

"Have you been following the literature on COVID-19 long-term effects?"

Cherie's eyes widened. "Yes, I've been reading every article I can find."

"Are you worried?"

"I feel fine."

"How's your kidney function?"

"Perfect. I ran some labs."

"When you have a chance, you should have Cathy listen to your chest. I wouldn't mind if you scheduled an MRI."

Cherie's eyes were suddenly bright with concern. "Is this one of your little research projects, Liz, or are you really worried?"

"Both. If you were my patient, I'd insist on examining you. Would you mind if I do?"

"Now?" Cherie asked, surprised.

"Sure. I'll use that portable ultrasound," said Liz, brightening at the thought.

"You just want to play with your new toy. All right. I'll meet you in an exam room. I'll text you when I'm ready."

While Liz waited, she reread the article on the autopsy results and searched the database for more information, disappointed to find there were only a few studies with small samples. She sat staring at the headline on the screen. If the organ damage caused by the coronavirus was permanent, there could be long term consequences for public and individual health. She thought of Brenda, who was athletic and otherwise healthy. At fifty-two, she still had some of the best years of her police career ahead of her.

Liz reminded herself not to jump to conclusions. The science was slowly working its way through the data, but there was still so much they didn't know about this disease. The study reported a high percentage of patients with heart damage, but it was too soon to tell if the effects were permanent.

When her phone vibrated, Liz glanced at the screen. Cherie had sent a text that she was ready. Liz grabbed her stethoscope and headed down the hall. Out of habit, she rapped on the exam room door before she opened it.

"I suppose we should have waited for your regular doc to do this."

Cherie chuckled. "Cathy's off today, and I know you, Liz. When you're on a mission, nothing can stop you."

"Thanks for indulging me."

Liz carefully listened to Cherie's heart and lungs with her stethoscope, closing her eyes so that she could hear better. She was relieved that everything sounded perfectly normal.

"Hmm," said Liz. "Lucky you. You sound fine. Now let's try our new gadget. No one seems eager to play with it but me."

"I've used it a few times for bladder and gastro issues," Cherie said as Liz unwound the leads. "I heard Jim saying he really likes it."

"I'll do a little poll at our next staff meeting to see who's been using it."

"You don't need to. The machine keeps a record of everyone who logs in."

Liz snapped her fingers. "I forgot about that."

"That's why you need me. I'm your backup in case you miss something."

"You're right. That's why I keep you." Liz squirted some gel on Cherie's chest.

"Yikes! That stuff is cold."

"Sorry about that." Liz positioned the probe. "Let's see what's going on." To Liz's relief, the image showed nothing abnormal. She yanked some paper towels out of the dispenser and wiped off some of the gel. She pressed a handful of towels into Cherie's hands. "You're fine. You can sit up."

"Thanks for your interest, Liz. Another boss wouldn't care."

"Another boss wouldn't poke her nose into your business like I do. I'll meet you in my office."

While she waited for Cherie, Liz searched for articles on the long-term side effects of SARS. She'd recalled reading that some of the so-called "permanent" damage had eventually resolved itself. Google returned a few hits with twelve-year studies. She was in the middle of reading a lengthy article when Cherie returned. Liz bookmarked the page.

"Thank you for insisting on an exam," Cherie said, leaning against the wall. "It's a relief to know I'm okay."

"I think your mild case prevented you from long-term damage. Some experts think differently, but I'm guessing more severe cases will have more problems."

In the look they exchanged, they each knew what the other was thinking.

"We could wait until we know more," said Liz. "Why alarm Brenda before we have more facts?"

"I think she'd like to know as soon as possible. I would."

"Can you get her to come in for an appointment?"

"I'll set it up. Would you mind doing the exam?"

"Of course not. Brenda is my patient. But we need to keep this between us. She's already on thin ice with the town council. We don't want to give them another reason to question her fitness."

Cherie nodded. When she compressed her lips and wouldn't make eye contact, Liz realized how upset she was.

"Are you okay?" asked Liz, getting up.

Cherie shook her head.

"May I give you a hug?"

Cherie nodded and Liz gathered her up. "Oh, Cherie. I'm sorry you have to face something so difficult right after your engagement. Have I congratulated you, by the way?"

"No, but I didn't expect it. It's not your thing."

"Maybe not, but congratulations anyway."

"Thanks, Liz. As bosses go, you're not so bad."

※※※

Liz had three physicals that afternoon. By then, her brain was numb. The conversation with Cherie about long-term COVID effects had depressed her, and the last thing she wanted to face was Maggie's icy disapproval. Even so, she texted Maggie out of courtesy.

I'm going to hang out on the boat for a while.

I'll put your dinner in the refrigerator.

Liz sent a red heart. There was no response. Usually, when she said she would hang out on the boat, Maggie at least texted back: *Have a good time.* Now, there was nothing.

Liz decided she could use some company. She called Erika. "I had a bad day. Want to join me on the boat for drinks?"

"Oh, I'm sorry, Liz. I'm preparing for a PBS interview with John Yang. I need to catch up on the latest political news, which is nearly impossible. Every day there's some new antic from that horrible man. Maybe Lucy can make it." Liz waited while Erika conveyed the invitation. "Lucy says she may join you after supper. She wants to spend some time with Emily. Then, if she's up to it, she'll come over."

Liz lowered her voice. "Are you sure you trust me to be alone with your wife?"

"Oh, Liz, you're a fool sometimes, but you're not an idiot." Now, Erika spoke softly. "I hear things are rather tense at your house."

"It's not the friendliest place at the moment."

"Liz, when will you learn? Why can't you remember not to shit where you eat?"

Liz had to stifle a laugh. It was always funny to hear Erika use American expressions. Her German-inflected-British accent made them sound ridiculous.

"Are you mad at me?"

"No, and I hope you're not disappointed. I think Lucy might be…a bit."

"Acting more jealous would probably solve that."

"I'll try, but jealousy is not in my nature. Even if it were, I needed to block it during all those years with Jeanine."

"Yes, she was a piece of work. Okay. I'll see you another time. Good luck with your interview prep."

After ending the call, Liz wondered if entertaining Lucy alone was a good idea, but she was looking forward to it. As she passed the IGA on the way to the harbor, she stopped in to buy a bottle of white wine for Lucy.

Liz set up a sling chair on the back deck and watched the sky change in the west. She sipped her beer and listened to music through her earbuds, choosing recordings of Lucy singing Wagner. Tiny Lucy made an unlikely Wagnerian, but her voice was incredibly powerful for her size.

Liz was completely absorbed in the music when she felt a gentle touch on her shoulder. When she looked up, Lucy gave her a light kiss on the lips.

Liz pulled out the earbuds. "Hi, Lucy. I was just thinking about you."

"What are you listening to?" Lucy picked up Liz's phone. "Not me again! No wonder Maggie thinks you're obsessed."

"I'm not obsessed. I just love your voice," protested Liz, yanking back her phone. "I got some wine for you. I'll go below and get it."

Liz brought up the bottle of wine and a special, no-tip, plastic wine glass as well as a beer for herself. She set up another sling chair. They sat in companionable silence as they watched the fading sunset.

"Thanks for coming tonight. I'm feeling a bit lonely."

Lucy reached over and gently stroked her arm. "Maggie's still not speaking to you?"

Liz shook her head.

"I'll talk to her. She's punishing you for nothing."

"She's really sensitive to infidelity. All her important relationships ended that way."

"I know," said Lucy with a thoughtful look. "She told me. I wonder what that says about her. Is she attracted to cheaters? Does she push people away?"

"She's sure pushing me away."

"She knows you're a player."

"But I'm not really. I've been faithful to her for over six years. That's a record for me."

"You weren't faithful to Jenny?"

Liz coughed up a chuckle. "Are you kidding me? If you think I'm a player, you should get to know Jenny."

"No, thanks. We have nothing in common…except you."

Liz gazed at Lucy. The humidity had made her red hair fetchingly bushy. Soft wisps poked out everywhere. Liz's eyes traveled down from Lucy's classic profile to her breasts. She watched them rise and fall with her breaths.

Without looking at her directly, Lucy raised an auburn brow. "Stop staring at my boobs."

"Just appreciating the view."

Lucy turned and gave her one of those evaluating, "shrink" looks. "Liz, we have to talk about this attraction."

"All right," said Liz, drawing out the words.

"You don't sound very enthusiastic."

"Why should I be? I know what you're going to say because you've said it all before. We can't act on the attraction because we're married to other people."

"Well, that's true, but that's not what I was going to say. You know that I love you, right?"

"I know. As a good Christian and a priest, you love everyone."

"I try to love everyone. I don't always succeed. It's hard to love the current occupant of the White House. But you know about the three kinds of love because you've studied philosophy. With you, all three kinds come into play. I also find you sexually attractive."

"I feel the same. That's why it's so damn frustrating!"

"You'd be even more frustrated if we consummated our love but couldn't continue a sexual relationship."

"Yes, that would be hard."

"Look. Let's put all the other reasons why we can't be lovers aside. Let's talk about the one, important reason."

Liz slouched down in her seat, sure she wasn't going to like this. "What's that?"

"I love you too much for sex. Sex would ruin what I feel for you. And it would ruin what you feel for me. Our love is too big for sex."

"Oh, what bullshit!"

"No. You are pledged to me. You are my knight, and I am your lady. Our love is perfect."

"Don't tell me you're going to lecture me on the courtly love tradition."

"No, because you already know all about it. And you also know that the longing for the beloved is far more exciting than sex. Once you get what you want, it's downhill from there. That's why opera heroines *have to* die."

Liz gave her a skeptical look. "They have to die because operas are grand tragedies."

"Liz, trust me. I know something about this. When I was an opera singer and people met me offstage, they were often disappointed. They expected something different. They were shocked that I was so petite. Or so down to earth. Or used profanity. They wanted me to be the goddess they imagined from hearing me on the stage. Finding out I'm just a woman was a tremendous let down."

"Spoken like a true diva." Liz saluted her with her beer bottle. "I'm very aware that you're a woman, a woman like no other. That's why I want you so much."

Lucy put her wine glass down and got up. She put her hands on Liz's face and squeezed her cheeks. "Liz! You are so dense sometimes!"

"I am not dense. I'm a contrarian." Liz put her arms around Lucy's hips and pulled her close. Through the light fabric, she could feel Lucy's pubic bone against her cheek. *So near, and yet so far!*

Lucy gently stroked her hair. "Liz, you're torturing yourself…and me. Let me go."

Liz released her.

"You look miserable. What can I do to make you feel better?"

"Other than sex? I don't know. Maybe you could sing for me. A little sublimation never hurts."

Lucy glanced around. "Here? In the harbor?"

Liz shrugged. "There's no one else around. It would be no worse than blasting a radio."

"All right. What would you like me to sing?"

"The *Liebestod*."

Lucy's mouth opened a little. "You want me to sing the *Liebestod* on the deck of a boat, in the middle of the harbor, with no warm up?"

Liz grinned. "Yes."

Lucy took out her phone, Liz guessed, to look for the accompaniment. She gave Liz a dirty look. "After this, *never ever* doubt that I love you." She sang a few scales, then switched on the accompaniment.

Liz was tempted to close her eyes at hearing the familiar sound of Lucy's magnificent soprano, but she focused on her face. When she sang, Lucy always entered into the spirit of the music. Singing words that barely disguised the sexual message of the aria, she looked like she was making love.

Finally, Liz gave in to the exquisite music. She felt tears forming in her closed eyes, but she didn't try to stop them. She allowed them to roll down her cheeks and land with a warm splash on her bare thighs. At the crescendo, Liz thought her heart would break. The aria wound down to its sublime conclusion. The tears dried on her face as the last notes faded away.

Liz opened her eyes. Lucy was gazing at her with a look of perfect love, almost like when she was offering communion. It was so overwhelming that Liz had to make a smart remark to break the spell.

"Better than an orgasm," she said with a quick grin.

Lucy didn't smile. "Yes, it is. And that's how much I love you. Don't *ever* forget it!"

27

Sam stumbled into Olivia's kitchen to make coffee. She really needed a caffeine jolt after staying up late to watch the election returns. The pandemic had prevented traditional, election-night watch parties. Instead, people in the campaigns were meeting on Zoom. After her opponent had conceded around midnight, Olivia, the new town manager-elect, had thanked her supporters and signed off.

Sam had never imagined herself campaigning for anyone from the other party, but once Sam had learned more about her new lover's policies, she'd even worked the phone bank. Like Sam, Olivia believed in increasing the minimum acreage for building new homes, expanding wetlands protection, and confining commercial development to downtown. On women's reproductive rights, they were solidly aligned. They disagreed on who should pay for health care and raising the minimum wage, but now that they had a special connection, maybe Sam could sway her.

Sam grumbled when she opened the canister and saw whole coffee beans. At least, she could brew a pot of coffee here, not like that single-serve thing Liz had in her kitchen. Sam found the coffee grinder. She hoped the loud, pulsing noise wouldn't wake the woman she had left sleeping upstairs.

Olivia had looked exhausted when they'd headed to bed, yet she'd insisted on a celebratory round of love making. Sam felt a twinge in her crotch at the thought. Olivia could flip from being high femme one moment to a powerful aggressor the next. At first, Sam was startled, but now, she went with the flow because the sex was absolutely amazing.

"How sweet of you to make coffee," said a voice behind her. "But you are a dear, aren't you?" Sam turned around to see Olivia, face made-up, hair combed, and wearing a designer robe over her sexy nightgown. "Good morning, my darling girl," said Olivia, raising her face for a kiss.

"Thanks for the compliment, but I'm almost sixty."

"Doesn't matter. You're only as old as you think you are."

Sam leaned down to kiss her. Olivia's lips opened, so Sam explored her mouth, which tasted clean and minty. Sam was glad she'd brushed her teeth before coming downstairs.

When the kiss ended, Olivia smiled. "What a nice way to wake up." She gave Sam's shoulders a little squeeze. "What would you like for breakfast?" Olivia opened the refrigerator. "No bacon. Eggs and ham?"

"I don't usually eat right after I wake up. And I can't stay long. I promised I'd go fishing with Liz and Brenda."

Olivia left the refrigerator door open as she stared at Sam. "I'd hoped we could take a walk on the Marginal Way."

The refrigerator door ping was getting annoying, so Sam went over and closed it. "I'm sorry. I meant to tell you we were going fishing, but you were so busy with the campaign, we barely had time to talk."

Olivia covered her upper lip with the lower in a little-girl pout. "Abandoning me for your friends already?" Then, she smiled brightly. "Maybe I could come along!"

Sam took a deep breath before saying, "I don't think so. It's our thing. We fish and drink beer."

Olivia scowled as she opened the refrigerator to take out the cream. "Sounds like something guys would do."

"Not necessarily. We like to fish, and we enjoy one another's company."

"And you think I'd be horning in on your little butch thing."

The pucker between Sam's brows grew deeper. "No. Why are you pushing roles on us?"

"I think differences make life interesting."

"They do."

"But you think I'm too prissy to go out fishing with you. I have news for you. I enjoy fishing."

"It wasn't planned, and honestly, Olivia, I don't know what their reaction would be."

Olivia headed to the cabinet to get a cream pitcher. "They still don't like me."

"It's not about *liking* you. It's just that people move in circles based on their interests. Lucy and Maggie hang together because they're both singers. Liz and Erika like to talk philosophy and drink scotch. You can't expect to join in just because you and I are having sex."

"Usually when someone has a new lover, she *wants* to spend time with her," said Olivia, filling the cream pitcher. "I was hoping you'd spend today with me."

Sam felt a nudge of guilt. "Maybe we can do something tomorrow."

"It's supposed to rain."

"We could go up Route 1 and look for that armoire."

"I thought you were going to build one."

"Only if we can't find one you like."

Olivia made another pouty face, then smiled. "All right. We can have breakfast at that cute place in Kennebunk." She took two cups from the cabinet. "You will spend the night, won't you?"

As much as she enjoyed the sex, Sam was feeling a little claustrophobic. "Aren't you sick of me by now?"

"Not possible," said Olivia, giving her a kiss on her way to the coffee maker. She filled two cups and brought them to the table. "I'll make you dinner when you come back from fishing."

Sam gazed out the window at the ocean as she thought about Olivia's invitation. She considered making excuses, then decided to be honest. "Thanks, Olivia, but I want to be home tonight. I need to water my plants and do a few other things. I'll pick you up in the morning."

Olivia's eyes went cold. Sam tried to decide if she was angry or hurt.

"I understand," Olivia said in a neutral voice. She offered a plastic smile. "Your coffee is very good, by the way."

❈❈❈

Sam was late getting to the boat. She'd felt guilty about turning Olivia down, so she'd allowed herself to be seduced into going back to bed. By the time she'd taken a quick shower, dressed, and picked up her fishing gear from her garage, she was almost twenty minutes late.

She'd called Liz from the road. Fortunately, Liz seemed to be in a mellow mood. "Whenever you get here. Brenda and I are hanging out… talking about you and your girlfriend, of course. Not really. We don't care that you've gone over to the dark side."

"Ha ha, very funny. I'll see you in a few."

Sam found them sitting on the back deck, drinking beer.

"Well, look who finally decided to show up," said Brenda, grinning. She saluted Sam with her beer bottle.

"Couldn't tear herself away from her new girlfriend," Liz said. "Hope it was worth it."

Sam felt herself blush. It had been worth it. Very much so.

"You guys ready?" asked Liz, starting the engine. The deck began to vibrate, so Sam quickly found a seat.

"Is Olivia happy about winning the election?" asked Brenda, raising her voice to be heard over the engine.

"Yes, I think so."

"I didn't think much of the last town manager, but I'm really worried about this one."

"She's not as bad as you think," said Liz.

"No? She tried to get me fired."

"She did not!" Sam protested. "The board was after you. She called them off. Give the woman a break."

"You're sleeping with her. You're prejudiced."

"Probably, but I've talked to her about her policies. She's not like those other crazies."

"Did you vote for her?" asked Brenda, leaning forward to look Sam directly in the eye.

"I'm not saying."

"You did, didn't you? Traitor."

Liz, who was busy at the helm, didn't turn around. "I voted for her, so I guess I'm a traitor too. I think she'll be good for the town. She's smart, and she gets things done."

"Well, you used to be one of them," said Sam.

"Decades ago, but yes, I was a Republican."

Brenda took a long pull on her beer. "We'll need to watch what we say, Liz. Now that Sam's sleeping with one of them."

"Don't pick on her, Brenda. Sam's the sensitive type. Right, Sam?" Liz glanced over her shoulder and grinned. "Is she good in bed at least?"

"Wouldn't you like to know?"

"Yeah, I would."

"Fantastic."

"Good for you. You've needed a good lay. I wish you many more."

As she listened to their banter, Sam wondered if Olivia had been right about her fishing buddies. They did sound like a bunch of guys. Maybe not as raunchy as guys, but pretty bad. *So what?* thought Sam. *We're not hurting anyone.*

***

Spending the afternoon on the water was exactly what Sam needed. She felt herself relaxing. The silly conversations with her friends made her chuckle. Sometimes, she laughed until she ached. She caught a nice-sized blue, and by that time, the sun and the wind off the water had made her sleepy.

"Hey, Liz, do you mind if I go below and take a little nap?"

"Hell no. Go right ahead."

As Sam was dozing off, she heard her phone ping. She blinked to focus on the screen and saw a text from Olivia.

Sorry I said those things about your friends.

LOL. Turns out you were right.

If you change your mind about company, I picked up some beautiful lamb chops at the butcher. I could come over and cook them for you.

Sam felt a tug at her heart when she realized that Olivia wasn't being pushy. She was lonely. Sam stared at the ship-lapped ceiling above her as she thought about how to respond.

We're still out on the water. I'll call when we get back.

OK.

Sam sighed. She punched up the pillow and rolled over on her side. As she was drifting off to sleep, she wondered what she had gotten herself into.

Sam awoke to someone shaking her arm.

"It's almost five," said Liz. "We're heading back. I thought you'd want me to wake you, so you don't get sea sick while I take us in."

Sam sat up and shook her head to clear it.

"Hard night?" asked Liz with an off-center grin.

"She's not what you'd expect."

"Oh, I'm sure."

Sam pulled on her sandals. "Do you think it's safe to be involved with her?"

"Safe? In what sense? Medically? Legally? You're letting her fuck you and you're asking me now?" Another lopsided grin.

"Seriously."

"Seriously, my instincts say yes. She's trying hard to get us to like her, but she keeps stepping in it because we play by different rules. But she's a smart woman. She'll figure it out…eventually." Liz thumped Sam on the back. "You like her, don't you? This isn't just a fling."

"I don't know what it is yet."

"That's okay. You have time to figure it out. Just don't move into that big Victorian until you do."

"Nah. I'm not giving up my little house by the pond after I spent all that time and money fixing it up."

"Maybe you can flip for where you're going to live. I'll give you my lucky quarter." Liz patted Sam's knee. "Come up while I take us in."

After Liz went up to the deck, Sam picked up her phone and texted Olivia.

Heading in now.
Have you thought about dinner?
I love lamb chops.
See you at your house in about half an hour.

28

Lucy watched Maggie supervise the youth group as they loaded food boxes. The diocese had networked with the state's largest food pantry to facilitate distribution through the parishes.

Lucy loved to see Maggie working with young people. She sometimes envied her friend's easy way with adolescents, especially when Emily frustrated her. Now that the novelty of reuniting with her birth mother had worn off, the difficult moments with Emily were more frequent. Maggie had been the first to offer sympathy. She'd warned Lucy that it was never going to be easy to mother a child who had shown up in her life as a sixteen-year-old. All the happy memories of Emily's babyhood, the early critical bonding of mother and child were absent. Maggie knew what that meant. She'd adopted her daughters as toddlers from a neglectful Romanian orphanage. Lucy suddenly found her thoughts turning to Olivia Enright, who bore the twin burdens of her son's crimes and his suicide. No, motherhood wasn't easy, and coming up short was inevitable.

Maggie had noticed Lucy's attention and looked up with a frown. She quickly refocused her eyes on the box she was packing. Lucy continued to watch, hoping Maggie would approach. Apart from discussing the music for Sunday worship, they'd barely spoken since their yoga date. After discovering Liz and Lucy in the chapel, Maggie wouldn't even look at her.

Finally, Lucy marched up to the packing table. "Maggie, I'd like to talk to you."

Maggie's hazel eyes over the colorful mask looked surprised at first, then anxious. "Give me a minute, Lucy. Let me just get these kids organized to take the boxes out to the truck."

Lucy clearly heard the reluctance in her voice. "Don't worry," she said, reaching for Maggie's hand. "We'll find our way."

Maggie's eyes filled, and she looked away.

"I'll meet you in my office."

Maggie nodded her agreement.

Lucy checked her messages while she waited. There was one from Liz regarding a patient she'd sent for evaluation. While Lucy was reading Liz's text, Maggie came in. Lucy's face reddened. She quickly locked the screen and put down the phone.

"Sorry. I should have knocked," said Maggie, apparently perceiving Lucy's discomfort.

"I get so many texts. Sometimes I think I should get a separate phone for church business."

"That would make you even crazier." Maggie took a seat in one of the visitor's chairs. "How have you been, Lucy?" she asked in a cautious tone.

"Good. Glad to be back to live worship at the summer chapel."

"Me too. I never realized how much I missed seeing live human beings until this crazy thing. I missed communion. Funny. I left the Church for so many years and never missed it, but now that I've come back...."

Lucy nodded, understanding what she was trying to say.

"How are *you*, Maggie?"

Maggie heaved out a big sigh. "Not sure." She frowned suspiciously. "You're not trying to counsel me, are you?"

Lucy smiled and shook her head. "No. I just missed my friend and wanted to talk to her."

"Lucy, you're entirely too good." Maggie swallowed loudly enough to be heard. "It makes it really hard to stay mad at you." She tore open the packet of tissues on the table next to her and blew her nose. "Allergies," she explained.

"I have them too. Terrible this year."

The commiseration apparently undermined Maggie's last defense. She began to cry openly. Lucy got up and rubbed her back to soothe her.

"I'm sorry," Maggie mumbled between blowing her nose. "I've been such a mess."

"I understand. This situation has been stressful for you. It brings back bad memories."

"It's not only my husband cheating. That was bad enough. It ripped our family apart. Tom, well, he was an idiot. I don't expect men to be faithful, but I thought Liz really loved me."

"Liz does love you, Maggie," Lucy reminded her gently. She wondered if telling Maggie the truth had been the right thing to do, but hiding it would only have led to more distrust, more lies. The suspicion would have eaten at Maggie until she doubted her intuition and sense of reality. This was exactly the reason why infidelity was so dangerous. It made everyone involved question all their assumptions about themselves and the people around them. The social fabric of their lives was more fragile than anyone imagined.

"We had an argument the other night, and I said I always knew she was a player, but I tried to look the other way. She said I should talk with all the men I fucked while we were together in college. She knows I didn't *fuck* anyone but the man I married."

Maggie's use of the expletive shocked Lucy a little. Her friend was notorious for hating bad language. "Hurts that deep have a way of sticking around long after we think we're over them."

Maggie gave Lucy a skeptical look. "You *are* counseling me, aren't you?"

"No, we're talking as friends."

Maggie's expression abruptly changed. "My friend who kissed my wife?"

"See what I mean about deep hurts? Yes, I let her kiss me. But we've talked about this. It was an impulsive thing. Don't you believe me?"

"You're a priest, so I guess I have to believe you."

"My collar has nothing to do with this. I don't lie, especially not to the people I love."

"Then why didn't you tell me right away?"

"You think I should have run to you and confessed?"

"If you're really my friend, yes!"

"That would have only hurt you and made you angry." Lucy huffed out a sigh. "Maggie, you're being such a hard case today. What's wrong?"

"I think I've screwed things up with Liz, and I don't know how to fix it."

"What do you mean?"

Maggie mopped her face with a tissue. Her mascara had run, but Lucy tried not to focus on it.

"I'm still seething. I want to punish her. When I see her, I want to scream at her and call her names. Then I miss her and want everything to go back to the way it was before. But it can never be the same. Never again!"

"No, she betrayed your trust."

"She did, but now, I'm pushing her farther and farther away. She spends every night down at the boat instead of coming home. In my mind, she's meeting you and screwing you in that comfy cabin of hers."

"Well, I know she goes to the boat because she often invites me and Erika."

"And do you go?"

"Occasionally. Usually, I'm too tired."

Maggie's eyes grew wide. "Alone?"

"Just once. We sat and talked. She asked me to sing for her."

"I bet she did," Maggie said in a contemptuous tone. She abruptly got up. "I should go. Those kids will have made a mess of things by now."

"Please stay. We're not finished talking. You have more to say. I can sense it."

"I'm not sure I can talk to you. I'm not ready to forgive you yet."

"Forgiveness is part of healing. I deeply regret accepting Liz's kiss. I hope that someday you can forgive me."

Maggie threw up her hands. "Oh, Lucy, it's not you! It's Liz! I know she's crazy about you."

"But that doesn't mean she doesn't love you, or she loves me more. We can't help who we're attracted to. The only thing we can do is control our behavior."

"Tell that to Liz."

"She knows."

Maggie flopped into the chair and looked miserable. "I really miss her."

"Of course, you do." Lucy pulled the other visitors' chair closer and sat down beside her. "You don't have to miss her. You can reach out to her."

Maggie shook her head. "She'll think I'm up to something."

Lucy sat forward a little to see Maggie's face. "Is the standoff better?"

"No, Lucy, of course not!" she said impatiently. "What do you suggest?"

"Invite her out on a date."

"That will certainly catch her off guard. She's always doing the inviting."

"See? Maybe you've gotten into a rut. Call her right now and invite her out. Start with a drink and then stay for dinner. Go on. I'll leave, so you can phone her."

"I already planned dinner."

"Forget that, Maggie. Make it tomorrow. This is more important."

"She could make an effort too."

"Yes, she could, but if you wait around for it to happen, things won't get better. They might even get worse."

Maggie opened her bag and took out a mirror. "Oh, God. I look like hell."

"You can fix your makeup in the bathroom down the hall. The light is good. I've had to use it myself a few times."

"Thank you," said Maggie, getting up. She clamped Lucy into a tight hug. "I love you, Lucy."

"I love you too, Maggie."

While Maggie was repairing her makeup, Lucy saw that Erika had left a text message.

Can I interest you in going out to dinner tonight?

Lucy smiled and thought, *great minds.* She called Erika. "What about Emily? Shouldn't we include her?"

"She's not interested. She ordered an extra-large pizza at four PM and gorged, leaving one piece."

"She's going to get a tummy if she keeps eating like that."

"She's a child and still growing. I ate like a horse when I was her age."

"I'm glad one of us knows something about kids." Lucy opened a video chat. When Erika's face came on, Lucy said, "I love you." She pressed her fingers to her lips and touched the screen.

"You are wicked…kissing me in your office." Erika winked. "So, about my dinner invitation…?"

"Sounds great. As soon as I say goodbye to Maggie. She's fixing her makeup. I made her cry."

"You're good at that," Erika said. "Is she there for counseling?"

"No, I kind of…sort of…forced an intervention. She wasn't talking to me. I couldn't stand it anymore." Lucy heard footsteps in the hall. "Yes, to dinner. I'll see you at home in a few minutes. Love you. Kisses."

Maggie knocked on the open door this time, and Lucy waved her in.

"Thanks for making me talk to you," said Maggie. "I feel much better."

"I'm so glad." Lucy got up. "Hugs?" She reached out her arms and Maggie fell into them. "I'm going to give you some advice," Lucy said. "Don't argue with Liz. Don't accuse. Listen. Smile. Remember. You're a great actress. This isn't going to be easy, but you can do it. Now, go get her!"

Lucy took Maggie's arm as she walked her out. "Between us girls, I'm sure a little inspiration in the bedroom wouldn't be a bad idea."

Maggie stopped and stared at her. "And you know this *how*?"

For a moment, the question put Lucy off balance. She scrambled to think of something to say. "My wife likes surprises. Maybe Liz would too." She tugged Maggie forward. "Don't worry. It was just a guess."

When Maggie nodded, Lucy breathed a sigh of relief. Everything was so sensitive right now. Words meant casually could be easily taken the wrong way.

After Maggie left, Lucy returned to her office to fetch her bag. As soon as she got into her car, she took off her collar and unbuttoned a few buttons. If she could get away with taking off her bra, she would have done that too. That had been the one good thing about the shutdown.

"Hello, Love," said Erika, giving Lucy a kiss as she came through the door. "Are you going to change?"

"Oh, yes!"

Lucy put on a snug T-shirt dress and put up her hair. She exchanged her ballerina flats for sandals. Before she went downstairs, she poked her head into Emily's room.

"Want to come to dinner with us, honey?"

Emily rolled over and pulled her earbuds out of her ears. "No, Mom. I'm listening to a live broadcast of the Field Medals awards."

"Sure?"

"Sure."

Lucy came into the room to give her daughter a kiss. "Love you, sweetie pie. See you later."

Erika's smile when Lucy descended the stairs was priceless. "Thank you for accepting my invitation," said Erika. "We needed a date night." Lucy liked the comforting feel of Erika's hand at her back as they headed out to the car. The gesture implied a proprietary attitude toward Lucy, despite Erika's casual response to the kiss. Maybe she cared more than she let on.

Lucy enjoyed people watching in Webhanet as they headed down the Post Road, but she was surprised when Erika pulled into Nathan's parking lot.

"Erika! We're not dressed for this place!"

"Tent dining is more informal. Don't worry. You look lovely, as always. Besides, we can't go to Dockside. Liz told me they're going there. Apparently, a big summit meeting…at your instigation."

"You know about that already?"

"Liz and I talk."

"I'm glad the kiss hasn't affected your friendship."

"We've known each other too long for something so ridiculous to come between us." Erika pulled into a parking spot. "Are you certain this place will do?"

"It's very expensive. Are you buying?"

"Yes. I asked for the date, and I'm still making a decent salary. You can buy next time."

"It's all our money."

"I know, but it sounds good." Erika winked conspiratorially.

After the hostess seated them in the tent, Erika glanced at the wine list and ordered a bottle of chardonnay. When the waiter departed with their order, she reached across the table for Lucy's hand. "Thank you for your intervention with Maggie. Liz was very excited to be invited to dinner. You are so clever."

"They have to start talking to one another. Otherwise, their relationship is over."

Erika gazed at her with no discernible expression. It frustrated Lucy that she could easily interpret the feelings of others but found it hard to read her own wife. "Do you regret your role in this?" Erika finally asked.

"Of course, I do. I love them. Both of them."

Erika shook her head. "Liz has always been a naughty girl. Jenny always looked the other way because she was worse." Erika leaned forward and rested her chin on her hand. "You could have slept with Liz to satisfy your curiosity. You must be curious. You've only had one female lover before me."

"That would be adultery."

"You know that argument means nothing to me."

"Yes, but it means something to me."

"Talk to me as a woman, not a priest. Would you like to sleep with Liz?"

Lucy had to dig deep for the answer. "If it hurt no one, wasn't breaking God's commandment and my marriage vows? Yes, probably."

Lucy tried to interpret Erika's dispassionate expression. Her pale eyes regarded her coolly. "Why do you find her so attractive?"

"Her passion is like mine. As a doctor, she works so hard to control her feelings. She keeps them all bottled up. That's exactly why they overflow. I know what that's like, but I have music as an outlet."

"It's not only her medical training. It's ethnic. Behind the discipline is that dark, brooding romanticism."

"Wagner."

"Among other things." Erika regarded Lucy with a long, reflective look. "Why are you attracted to me if you love passion so much?"

"You haven't figured that out yet?"

Erika narrowed her eyes. "Maybe. Let's see if I'm right."

"Your rationality intrigues me. It beckons, like a lighthouse on a stormy night. I want to cling to the light, but also to find its dark side. Seducing you is a challenge, but when I do, it's so satisfying."

Under the table, Lucy slipped off her sandal and ran her foot up Erika's bare leg.

Erika's eyes held hers with a steady gaze. "Lucy, people might see."

"Who cares?"

"You're a priest."

"I'm not wearing a collar. We're in another town." Lucy raised her foot a little higher. "And you're my wife."

"I adore you."

29

Liz caressed Maggie's thigh and planted a soft kiss on her naked buttock. Maggie rolled over and groaned. "Let me sleep, Liz. You kept me up last night."

Liz grinned and kissed the soft, pale flesh again, ignoring the stretch marks and slackness. Despite its flaws, Maggie's body was dear to her.

"I want more," Liz whispered into Maggie's ear only to be swatted away like an annoying mosquito.

"Not now. Get dressed or you'll be late for work. I'll give you more tonight, *if* you behave yourself."

"Promise?"

"Yes, I promise. Now, go!"

Liz decided that after such an active night, she should bathe before going to work. She hummed in the shower, but she'd have to wipe that stupid grin off her face, or everyone would know that she'd "gotten some."

When they'd arrived home from Dockside, lovemaking was inevitable. Maggie knew exactly how to seduce Liz. She had an unerring sense of the rhythms of her wife's body. As exciting as a new lover might be, making love with someone who needed no instruction to get it right the first time was even better. The little hiatus had added pent-up desire to the mix and made the encounter all the more special.

Liz blew her hair dry and ran a brush through it. Then she added some gel and messed it up again to tease up the grunge waves. She dressed quickly, carrying her sandals to avoid waking Maggie.

"No, you don't!" called Maggie from the bed. "Come back here and give me a kiss." She sat up when Liz came to the bedside and put her arms around her neck. "I love you. Have a good day." She gave Liz a sweet kiss on the lips.

"Tonight. You promised."

"I know. I keep my promises."

Liz hummed an air from *La Traviata* as she ran down the stairs. She was still humming as she drove to Hobbs Family Practice.

The melody abruptly stopped when Liz walked into her office and found Cherie and Brenda sitting there.

"Jeeze," said Liz, glancing at her watch. "I'm so sorry. I forgot you were coming in early."

"It's okay. We haven't been here long."

Liz gave them a quick once-over to gauge their mood. Brenda seemed her usual, calm self. Cherie looked anxious, so Liz surmised her PA hadn't already peeked at the test data.

"Sorry to be late. Give me a moment," said Liz, flipping open her laptop. Usually, she reviewed her patients' labs before they sat in her office. She quickly scanned the column of numbers, willing her face to stay neutral when her eyes landed on the results for heart enzymes and the CRP test for inflammation. Both showed elevated levels.

Liz glanced at Brenda, who looked like she should be featured in an article on staying healthy in your fifties. She was tan. Her cheeks were pink. Her blue eyes were bright and clear.

"How are you feeling, Brenda?"

"I feel fine."

Cherie elbowed her fiancée. "Tell her the truth. She's your doctor."

Brenda stared at her hands. "I get tired faster. Sometimes, I'm short of breath."

"Any other symptoms? Heart palpitations? Feel like your heart is racing?"

"No," said Brenda. "Except the other night. I woke up Cherie."

Liz peered at Cherie. "And…?"

Cherie's warm complexion was suddenly pale. "Her heart was racing. I thought it was alcohol-induced tachycardia because she'd had too much wine. It calmed down after a while."

Liz forced herself not to frown, but she did allow herself a thoughtful, "Hmm." She lowered the laptop cover and sat back in her chair.

"Well, don't keep us in suspense!" said Cherie.

Liz nodded in Cherie's direction, but she looked Brenda in the eye. "Your blood work shows some inflammation, which isn't surprising after a serious infection. The same for your heart enzymes, but elevated levels also can indicate a heart event."

"A heart event," Brenda repeated. "What does that mean? A heart attack?"

Cherie reached for Brenda's hand.

"Not necessarily," said Liz in the quiet, even tone she used to explain medical issues to patients. "We know the virus can affect the heart, but we don't know enough yet to say whether the effects are long term. This virus affects many organs, and different people have very different responses. Just in case, I'd like to listen to your heart and use our portable ultrasound to see what's going on. Okay?"

"Whatever you say, Liz. You're the doctor."

"Cherie, would you mind helping Brenda get ready for the exam?" Liz opened her laptop. "I want to take a deeper dive into her labs." Cherie didn't answer at first, so Liz tore herself away from the test results to see why. "If it's a problem, Cherie, I can call Connie."

"No, I can do it," said Cherie, looking uncertain. Of course, she understood the implications of the elevated enzymes and inflammation and was upset.

"Never mind," said Liz. "I'll ask Connie to help. Just show Brenda where the exam room is. I'll be there in a minute."

The lab results indicated that Brenda's cholesterol levels and blood sugar were low. Her thyroid was normal. Everything else was within the normal range. Brenda could be a poster girl for a healthy woman in her fifties.

Liz knocked on the exam room door as usual. Cherie, who was holding Brenda's hand, let it go and moved out of the way.

Brenda's lungs sounded perfectly clear, but the blood movement through the valves in her heart sounded sluggish. The ultrasound confirmed some vague anomalies. Brenda's heart wasn't pumping as strongly as it should.

When Liz turned off the machine and looked up, Cherie's face was pale. As a PA, Cherie could see the reason for concern, but she was doing an admirable job of holding herself together. Liz patted her shoulder to reassure her and headed to the dispenser to yank out a few towels. She handed them to Brenda, so she could wipe off the ultrasound gel.

"Get dressed. Then come into my office and we'll talk."

Cherie followed Liz to the door. "Can I talk to you while Brenda gets dressed?"

Liz motioned to her to follow. Once they were behind closed doors, Cherie's eyes revealed the depth of her worry. "How serious is this?"

"The ultrasound didn't reveal any obvious damage, but it's a cheap, little portable. I'm going to send her down to Southern Med for better imaging. I want to refer her to a cardiologist in Boston. Think she'll go?"

"You better believe it. I'll make her go."

Liz chuckled. "Leveraging your new status, I see. Good for you. Brenda needs you now." Liz sat down behind her desk to send a text to Alyson Gagnon, head of the radiology department at Southern Med.

"Brenda will be devastated if there's something seriously wrong," said Cherie, hugging herself.

"Calm down. You need to be really cool-headed about this. We both have to model professionalism. Knowing Brenda, she's already figured out something is wrong, and she's beside herself."

"She kept asking me the other night, when her heart was racing, if she was having a heart attack."

There was a knock at the door. Cherie opened it, and Brenda slipped into the office. She took one of the visitors' chairs.

"Liz, you're my friend," Brenda said sternly. "I expect you to tell me the truth."

"I always do, but the fact is, I don't know very much. Your lungs sound fine. I heard some minor heart anomalies when I listened to your chest and saw some things I don't like on the ultrasound. It could be a residual effect from the virus. We're seeing strange symptoms show up in COVID patients long after they've recovered."

Liz watched her friend's face carefully as she spoke, but decades of police work had taught Brenda the value of deadpanning in difficult situations.

"I'm sending you down to Southern Med for better imaging. I just wrote the script. If you're lucky I'll get a call back while you're here. I have an in with radiology there."

"You mean, Alyson?" asked Brenda.

Liz turned to Cherie to explain. "Alyson is an ex of mine. Now she's department head."

"Is my heart damaged?" Brenda asked, leaning forward to look directly into Liz's eyes.

"I don't know, Brenda. All I can say is, it's not performing normally right now."

"If I have a bad heart, I could lose my job."

"We don't know if you have a bad heart. There is something going on, but it might not be permanent. SARS had heart effects too, but in many patients, they weren't permanent."

"I could lose my job," Brenda repeated.

"Let's not go there. One thing at a time. I'm referring you to a cardiologist in Boston. Cherie's going to go with you. Right, Cherie?"

"Of course."

"I'll cover for you with your patients."

Cherie's look of gratitude was instant. "That's so kind, Liz."

Liz shrugged. "That's what we do up here. We look out for each other."

Liz could see that Brenda was still distracted. "Brenda, are you okay?"

"Yes, I'm fine." Her voice was a bit gruff and defensive, which told Liz she was really upset. She studied her friend, wondering how to reassure her, when her cell phone vibrated on the desk.

"Hey, Al, thanks for getting back so fast." Alyson told Liz she had cleared the way for Brenda's MRI. "You can do it in an hour? That's great." She glanced at Cherie, who nodded. "Yes, they'll be there."

"I guess it pays to have friends in high places," Brenda murmured when Liz hung up.

"Never mind that. With the summer traffic, you should head right down there. Cherie, here, take my parking pass." Liz opened her desk drawer and handed it to her. "I'll call you as soon as I hear something from the cardiologist's office. Since you're getting all the imaging done today, they should get you in for an appointment pretty fast."

"Why do I have to go all the way down to Boston?" Brenda asked.

"Because I trust this guy, and I'm sure he's up on all the latest COVID information." Liz got up to open the door. "Only the best for my friends."

"Don't believe that," said Cherie. "She pulls strings for all her patients."

Brenda turned to Liz with a forlorn look.

Liz held Brenda by the shoulders and looked straight into her eyes. "It will be all right. Let's be optimistic, okay?"

"Sure," said Brenda, but her tone wasn't convincing.

30

Brenda sat with her feet up on the wicker hassock. She watched the chipmunk brazenly eat the ripe tomato hanging from the potted plant on the deck. Ordinarily, she'd get up and shoo the damn thing away, or she'd shoot it with rubber pellets, but she continued to stare at it as it savaged the tomato.

As Brenda sipped her coffee, she thought about how the last few days had completely changed her life. First, there was the echocardiogram and MRI at Southern Med. Then she'd run on a treadmill with wires hanging off her chest, feeling like a gerbil in a caged wheel. Finally, she'd met with Dr. Wheeler at Mass General in Boston for the verdict.

He struck Brenda as a sharp, young guy, but he smiled too much. She never trusted people who smile when they tell you bad news. "A fifty-five percent ejection fraction is still in the normal range," he'd said. "It's right on the bottom, but it's normal."

"Does that mean I'm still fit for duty?"

"Does your job entail strenuous activity?"

"I'm a cop. Sometimes pursuit is necessary."

He stared at her with a puzzled look and a little frown.

"That means running really fast," said Brenda, explaining the obvious.

"I wouldn't do that for a while. At least not, until we get this under control."

"Does that mean I can't do my job?"

"You're the chief. Can't you assign yourself to desk duty for now?"

Brenda cringed at the idea that she'd been bargaining with the man. That was one of the stages of grief, wasn't it? Brenda remembered that from the bereavement counseling after Marcia had died.

Cherie had explained that sudden big losses could cause grief like when a loved one died. Brenda's loss of her health felt like a death. The healthy Brenda, who used to run marathons and had twice competed in triathlons, was dead. The Brenda, who'd survived COVID, was a heart patient, an invalid.

Cherie came to the door of the screen porch. "Sweetheart, would you like another cup of coffee? It's decaf, like the doctor ordered."

Brenda shook her head. She hated decaf coffee. Cherie told her it was her imagination, but to Brenda, it tasted flat.

"What are your plans for the day?" Cherie asked, coming out on the deck to sit down next to Brenda.

"I don't have any."

"Would you like to come with me for a walk on the beach?"

"No, thanks."

"Would you like me to leave you alone?"

"Yes."

Cherie got up and kissed Brenda on the top of her head. "When your meds kick in, you'll feel better."

"I don't feel bad now. It's just the idea of it. I was healthy, now I'm not."

Cherie hugged Brenda's shoulders. "You're still healthy. It's not life threatening. The damage might heal. It did for many SARS patients."

"What if it doesn't?"

"Then we treat it." Cherie gave her another little squeeze. "We caught it early. Be positive."

Brenda patted Cherie's arm. "I'll try."

"If you come into the kitchen, I'll make you a cheese omelette."

"I'm not hungry."

Cherie came around to face her. "Brenda, what can I do to help you feel better?"

Brenda shook her head. "You can't." She finished her coffee and got up. "I feel sleepy. I think I'll go back to bed and take a little nap."

She saw the anxiety like a shadow in Cherie's eyes. "Okay," she said, "but you've been sleeping a lot lately."

"I'm tired."

Cherie pursed her lips and nodded. She reached up to give Brenda a kiss. "Enjoy your nap."

※※※

When Brenda awoke, she heard voices. She went to the window and looked out. Cherie and Liz were sitting on the deck, speaking softly. She couldn't hear what Cherie was saying, but Liz's voice carried. Brenda understood from the audible snatches that Cherie had called Liz. Cherie raised her eyes to the bedroom window as if she knew she was being watched, and Brenda stepped back.

She went into the bathroom to brush her teeth, then decided she needed a shower. She hadn't bathed in two days. She turned on the spigot to let the water heat up. As she waited, she brushed out her hair.

She stepped into the shower and let the hot water spray on her face. For the first time in days, she felt the sensation. Lately, she'd been so wrapped up in her thoughts, she had taken perfunctory showers and afterward, couldn't even remember doing it. Today, it felt different. Every nerve was close to the surface. Raw.

Without warning, tears sprang to her eyes. The next moment, she was sobbing. She leaned against the wall to steady herself. Finally, she sat on the shower floor and let the water beat on her back while she cried. When the tears stopped, as suddenly as they'd begun, Brenda got to her feet. She lathered and rinsed her hair. At least, she was clean, which would make Cherie happy. After she combed out her hair, Brenda pulled on a pair of shorts and a T-shirt and went downstairs.

"Hey," she said, coming out on the deck.

Liz looked up. "Hey, Brenda. I thought you were going to sleep all day."

"How long have you been here?"

Liz glanced at her watch. "Half an hour at least. Thought you might want to come out on the boat and drop a line. I hear the blues are running."

Brenda shook her head. "Thanks. I don't really feel like fishing today." She saw Cherie exchange a worried look with Liz.

Cherie got up. "I'll let you two talk. I have some reading to do."

"Work or pleasure?" asked Liz.

"Work."

"So dedicated," Liz said with a warm smile as Cherie passed on her way into the house. "Pay attention, Cherie, so you can tell me all about it on Monday."

"I will," Cherie said, smiling in return.

Brenda admired her as she passed. *Damn, what a beautiful woman she is!*

For a long moment, Brenda and Liz sat in silence. Finally, Liz nudged Brenda's foot with the toe of her rafting sandal. "You could offer me a beer."

"You know where the beer is."

"I do, but you could get me one. When you come to my house, I always get *you* a beer."

"What time is it?"

Liz glanced at her watch. "Three twenty-three. Miller Time."

Brenda huffed a sigh and hauled herself to her feet. "Only because it's you."

"Aren't you going to have one?"

"Can I?"

"Sure. Why not? But just one."

Brenda returned with two beers and the bottle opener in her pocket. She flipped off the cap of a bottle and handed it to Liz. "You didn't come over here to ask me to go fishing."

"I came over to talk. I figured we could talk on the boat. Being on the water is very calming."

"My problem is I'm too calm."

"Depressed and calm are not the same."

"Well, if you were my age and had to give up your career, would you be calm? I can't afford the mortgage on my pension from New York. I'll have to sell the house."

"Who said you have to give up your career?"

"I'm not fit for duty. You have to certify me every year. My physical is due soon."

Liz shrugged and took a slug of beer. "We might be able to get it under control by then."

"Liz, I have a heart condition!"

"I know. I'm your doctor."

"You can't lie. You know I'm not fit for duty."

"Let's see how it goes. In the meantime, just stay in your office and let the kids run after the bad guys. In your position, you should be doing that anyway. It's just vanity that makes you take backup. Am I right?"

Brenda glared at Liz. "You don't understand."

"I'm trying." Liz glanced at the house. "I wouldn't worry about the mortgage. Now, you have Cherie's salary to help."

"As long as you can afford to pay her."

"I can afford it," Liz said confidently. "The market's been going up. The patients are coming back. It's tick season. Every other case is a tick bite."

"I don't expect Cherie to pay the mortgage."

"Why not? You're getting married. That's what married people do. They support one another."

"Maybe."

That got Liz's attention. She rested her elbows on her knees, so she could see Brenda's face. "You're not having second thoughts about marrying her?"

"Things have changed."

"Things haven't changed. The only difference is you know about the heart damage. It was there when you proposed to her."

Brenda nodded reflectively. "Yes, I guess it was."

"Don't do that to Cherie. She really loves you. It was hard work to get over her fear of cops and see you as the great person you are. Don't throw all that effort away. It's disrespectful to her, to Lucy, and to me."

"Gee, thanks, Liz. Whose side are you on?"

"It's not about sides. I don't want to see my friend do something stupid because she's feeling sorry for herself."

"You never pull any punches, do you?"

Liz finished her beer in a few swallows. "Have I ever?"

"No. You always tell it like it is."

Liz got up. "Well, if you don't want to come fishing with me, that's fine. Thanks for the beer."

Brenda watched Liz head into the house. Part of her wanted to call her back, but she didn't know what to say except, "I'm sorry." But that seemed so hollow.

Cherie opened the door to the deck. "That was a short visit. Why don't you want to go fishing? You love fishing."

Brenda hunched forward and stared at the beer bottle in her hands. "I don't feel like doing anything."

Cherie came out and sat down next to her. "That doesn't sound like you. You never sit still."

"That was before."

"It would be good for you to go out with Liz," Cherie said. "I'm sure she didn't get far. Give her a call."

Brenda shook her head. "Not today."

"Did you argue?" asked Cherie in the controlled voice left over from her years of being a therapist.

"No. But you know Liz. She can be pretty direct. Like a sledgehammer."

"That's how surgeons are. Blunt. One of the things I like most about her." Cherie sighed. "I feel so helpless watching you like this. Please talk to me. I'm your fiancée now and one day, I'll be your wife. We're supposed to share our burdens."

"Well, maybe we should put our engagement on hold for a while." It was out of Brenda's mouth before she could stop it.

Cherie blinked as if she'd been slapped. "What?"

"I'm not saying we call it off. I just want to see what happens."

"What happens with what?"

"My heart."

Cherie's eyes began to glisten, and she pressed her lips together. "The heart that beats in your chest will be fine. The heart that says she loves me, I'm not so sure about."

"I do love you, Cherie. I love you so much, and I do want to marry you."

"Then why are you saying these hurtful things?"

"Because I'm scared."

"I know. Brenda, I'm scared too. I don't want anything to happen to you."

"I feel like a burden. You spent all those years taking care of your Dad. I don't want you thinking you have to take care of me."

Cherie looked directly into Brenda's eyes. "Maybe years from now, one of us might have to take care of the other, but not now."

"I don't want you staying with me because you agreed to marry me. Things have changed."

"Nothing's changed. You're still the same Brenda I fell in love with." Cherie patted her cheek. "Now, you have to eat something. Come into the kitchen. I'll make you an omelette." She kissed Brenda's forehead. "I love you."

31

Olivia pulled herself on to the dock. She pressed her hair back to squeeze out some of the moisture. "It's like a bathtub. So much warmer than the ocean."

"That's what people don't realize about Maine. The ocean isn't warm enough for swimming until summer's nearly over."

Olivia looked around. "You have so much privacy here. Are there any other houses on this pond?"

Sam nodded toward the opposite shore. "Just that place hidden in the trees, but they're hardly ever here—New Yorkers who bought it for a weekend house. They use it so seldom I wouldn't be surprised if it's on the market soon."

Olivia toweled her hair. "It's so secluded, we could swim naked."

"When Erika and Lucy come over, we often do."

Olivia mimed exaggerated shock. "You swim naked? With the vicar?"

"She's just a woman. A very hot woman, yes. She's actually sexier in a bikini than naked."

"You shouldn't be spreading these rumors about a priest. You could damage her reputation."

"What's wrong with skinny dipping in private?"

Olivia laughed. "Nothing, I suppose. What about your other friends? Do they swim naked too?"

Sam shrugged. "Sometimes. Why? Does that really shock you?"

"Well, they're all ladies of a certain age."

"That's why they don't care." Sam stood up and peeled off her tank top and shorts and jumped into the water. "Come on. Don't be shy. I've already seen it all."

"Yes, I guess you have." Olivia pulled down the straps of her suit and wiggled out of it. Being wet, it wasn't easy to pull off. She flung it back on the dock and slipped into the water. Sam swam toward her.

"Feels good, doesn't it?"

"We couldn't do this at my house."

Sam teasingly reached between Olivia's legs. "Nope. Too many nosy neighbors."

Facing one another, they treaded water. The cooler evening air was causing vapor to rise off the water in an eerie mist.

"Want to swim out to the floating dock?" asked Sam. "I'll race you."

"No contest. I was on my swim team in high school *and* college."

"Ready, set, go!" Sam shot off with Olivia in pursuit.

Olivia won easily. She pulled herself out of the water, dousing Sam in the process.

"Thanks!" complained Sam, hauling herself up. "You're so competitive, Olivia."

"Always was. From birth probably."

Sam looked up. "The moon is rising." She lay on her back. "The sky is beautiful tonight."

Olivia lay down beside her. "I'm always amazed at how many stars there are up here."

"It's the same number of stars. The lack of light pollution makes them more visible. We even have laws about that."

"I'd like to go up north and see the milky way and the Aurora."

"I'll take you," said Sam.

"Would you really?"

Sam rolled on her side to look at Olivia. "Yes. If you don't mind roughing it in my cabin. No running water or electricity."

"I'd have to think about that."

Olivia was gazing at her with a longing in her eyes that made Sam want to kiss her, so she reached out and pulled her face closer. Olivia's response was always so enthusiastic as if she'd been waiting a long time for that kiss.

Sam released her mouth. "You mind making love in the middle of the pond?"

"It sounds kind of exciting." Olivia teased Sam's nipple with her fingertip. The water had been warm, but still a bit chilly, so the nipple was puckered before she'd touched it. Sam caressed the inside of Olivia's thigh where the skin was especially soft. Sam already had her favorite spots on Olivia's body. One of them was the hollow at her throat. Sam liked to trace the collar bones in each direction and back again. She reached between Olivia's legs and found her hot and wet. After stroking her some more, she slipped inside her.

Olivia threaded her fingers through Sam's short hair and tightened the grip until it hurt a little. The slight pain was exciting, like when Olivia pinched her nipple too hard.

"I like your muscles," Olivia whispered into her ear. "I like when you take what you want." That was the cue to thrust harder. Olivia loved penetration. Nothing excited Sam more than being active and probing a woman's depth. When Olivia raised her legs, Sam became even more aroused. She had to focus because Olivia's orgasm was close. When she came outside to stroke her, she felt a hand come between her legs. To Sam's surprise, she began to come at the same moment that Olivia arched her back and moaned.

They lay panting as the moon rose overhead.

"I want to get a dildo so you can really fuck me," said Olivia. "Would you like that?"

Sam's clitoris twitched at the thought. Yes, she'd like that very much. "I have a strapon at the house. Want to swim back and give it a try? I might be a little out of practice. It's been a while since I've used it."

"I'm satisfied for the moment. Let's stay out here and watch the moon come up. We can do that later."

"Okay," said Sam, reaching for her hand.

Olivia turned her head and looked into Sam's eyes. "Do you think this relationship could ever turn into something?"

It took Sam a moment to decide what Olivia was asking. "I don't know. Maybe. We've only been together for a couple of weeks."

Olivia looked up at the moon. "It's beautiful here. If we got together, where would we live? Would you ever give up this place?"

"That would be hard," Sam admitted honestly. "I really love it here. I've got my workshop set up just right."

"Would you ever consider living in my house?"

"I'm not saying absolutely no. Just that I'd really need to think about it. Your house isn't really my style."

"Not mine either." Olivia sat up. "It's cold. It has no personality."

"I could tell right away an interior designer decorated it. It looks like an HGTV set."

"That's what my son wanted…that perfect look…like in a magazine." Olivia smacked her leg. "Mosquitos are coming out."

"We could swim back."

"No, let's stay a while. I like it out here." Olivia swung around and put her feet in the water. "My house is haunted."

"What? You're kidding, right? What makes you think so?"

"Things go bump in the night."

"It happens in all houses…settling…materials adjusting to changes in temperature and humidity…expanding…contracting."

"I know, but this is different. When Jason first separated from his wife, he brought the girls up here for weekends."

"That's nice."

"You don't understand. Jason was probably a pedophile."

"What?"

"Yes, I know. It's horrifying."

"You don't think…you don't think he molested his daughters?"

"That's what my daughter-in-law claims."

"Jesus Christ!" exclaimed Sam, sitting up. "That's terrible!"

"I don't have any proof, but when the Feds seized his laptop for the insider trading probe, they found kiddie porn on it. Lots of kiddie porn."

"Good God!"

"My daughter-in-law tried to tell me, but I wouldn't listen. I took his side. That's why she won't let me see my granddaughters. He left the house to me, so she wouldn't get it. Yes, the location is beautiful, but the gift was tainted."

"Oh, Olivia, I'm so sorry." Sam took her hand.

"Sometimes, I can't sleep, thinking of what he might have done to those sweet, little girls in that place."

"I'm so sorry, but where would you go if you sold it?"

"I don't know. Buy a condo. Something on higher ground now that the climate is warming, and we have so many storms."

"I thought Republicans don't believe in global warming."

"This one does."

"Could you live here?"

Olivia glanced at the house on the shore. "I wondered if I'd be welcome."

"It's a little early to hire a U-haul. Plus, I find it hard to imagine you being content in my little shack."

"Don't be modest, Samantha. You've done an amazing job with the place. It's adorable and beautifully finished inside and out. Of course, I wouldn't expect anything less from a prize-winning architect."

"But it's microscopic compared to your place."

"Believe me. It's palatial compared to where I grew up." Olivia smacked her leg again. "Bugs love me. I have the right blood."

"Let's swim back."

Sam dived into the water, and Olivia followed her. They swam to the shore with long, slow strokes. This time Olivia used the ladder to pull herself out of the water.

"That was both refreshing and stimulating. What a good idea," Olivia said, wrapping her towel around her torso and snatching up her bathing suit. "I can see why Reverend Bartlett is such a fan."

"You tell anyone about that, and you're dead."

"I am the soul of discretion."

"You'd better be."

"Are you serious about showing me your toys?"

"It's not like I have a whole collection. Just a few favorites." Sam pulled on her shorts and shirt over her wet body. They clung to every curve.

"Nice wet T-shirt look," Olivia said, looking Sam over from head to toe. "I approve."

"How about a glass of wine before bed?" asked Sam, as they came into the house. "But first, I could use a hot shower. It's getting a little chilly out here."

"Good idea."

"You can use the guest bathroom," said Sam, pointing down the hall.

"Why waste water?" said Olivia with a suggestive smile.

"That would be nice, but my bathroom is a lot smaller than yours."

As Sam showered, she remembered the sex on the floating dock. Her mind reluctantly left the pleasant sensations to focus on their conversation. She could understand why Olivia wouldn't want to live in the house where her grandchildren could have been molested. The idea of moving in together, there or in Sam's house, was mind boggling. Sam liked her privacy. The few times she lived with a partner had ended badly.

She rinsed the soap out of her hair and toweled herself. She put on shorts and a T-shirt but skipped the underwear. She didn't expect to be dressed long.

* * *

When Sam awoke, the combined heat in the bed felt alien. It had been a long time since she'd had a bed partner. She preferred to sleep alone. That's why she usually didn't invite women to spend the night, but for Olivia she'd made an exception.

Sam listened intently in the dark, hearing the far-off, plaintive warbling of a loon followed by the sound of sniffling. She moved closer to Olivia, whose back was toward her, and kissed her shoulder.

"Are you okay?" Sam asked gently.

"Yes," came the muffled reply.

The sound contradicted the message, so Sam came closer and spooned her, surprised to feel Olivia's skin so cool. She was trembling.

"Are you cold?"

"No."

"Why are you shaking?"

"Panic attack."

Sam tugged at Olivia's shoulder, trying to get her to turn around. "What are you afraid of? You're safe here with me. Nothing's going to harm you."

"It's not that simple."

"What can I do?"

"You're doing it."

"Do you have your medication?"

"At home. I didn't think to bring it. I didn't think you'd ask me to stay. You always leave afterwards."

"Do you want me to call Liz?"

"God, no!"

Sam pulled at Olivia's shoulder again. "Come on. Turn around. Let me hold you."

Finally, Olivia turned into Sam's arms.

"I could bring you home so you can get your meds."

"That's so kind, but not necessary. I've had worse attacks. Just hold me, please."

"Do you want to tell me what this is about?"

"No. I don't want you to think less of me."

"I won't think less of you," said Sam impatiently. "Of course not! Tell me why you're afraid. Maybe then you can fall back to sleep."

"Are you sure? I don't want to keep you awake."

"I'm sure, and I'm listening. Go ahead." Sam nudged her on her back and covered her with her body. "I'll warm you up while you do."

"You're nice and warm. Thank you."

"Okay. Now tell me what's going on."

"The sound of the waves lapping against the shore reminded me of something. It's a different sound from the ocean at night."

"Yes, it's much more peaceful and relaxing."

"Yes, but doesn't it make you want to get up and pee?"

Sam chuckled. "Sometimes."

"The sound reminds me of the time my father and his friend took me and my oldest brother fishing on a lake upstate."

"That sounds like a nice memory."

"It's not. My father and his friend drank a lot of beer. Dad passed out. Stan, my brother, and I ran around playing until Dad's friend made us get into our sleeping bags. He wanted us to go to sleep, but we were having fun and kept talking. So he said he would tell us a bedtime story."

Sam felt a little nudge of fear pushing her closer to Olivia as she began to realize where this story might be heading.

"The man, whose name I don't even remember, lay down between us. He stank of beer and body odor, but he did tell us a rambling version of 'Little Red Riding Hood.' After he finished, he continued to lie in the tent between us. Stan fell asleep, but I was still awake. I never slept well. Not even as a child."

"What happened next?"

"He stroked me gently at first, and I was mesmerized. It felt really good, and I didn't want it to stop. Then, he reached around to cover my mouth, so I wouldn't scream and wake the others and he put his fingers inside me. They were big, so it was painful."

Sam, who had barely breathed while Olivia told her story, finally allowed herself to take a deep breath.

"Oh, my God! I'm sorry, Olivia." Sam tightened her embrace. "No wonder you were so determined to get away from that family!"

"You're the first person I ever told about it. They say abuse is passed down in families. I wonder if…"

"Don't even think it," said Sam, stroking Olivia's hair. She kissed her forehead. "Go back to sleep. I'll hold you."

32

Lucy ate a few squares of super-dark chocolate. She rarely ate sweets during the day, but she had hit an energy low, and she still had another session. She hadn't slept well the night before. Erika had made a spicy Indian dish that gave Lucy indigestion and weird dreams. She had dreamt about her mother being in the hospital when she was dying from ovarian cancer. Apart from the night Alex had raped her, Lucy had never felt more powerless than when she watched her mother die. That's how she felt now. Powerless. The pandemic was so big and had affected every aspect of life. In the background was the crazy political situation, heating up even more as the election drew near. Lucy was an optimist by nature, but sometimes, even she felt dragged down by the sheer weight of it all.

The chocolate was bitterer than she expected, but somehow that made it more satisfying. It was brittle and Lucy had to bite it hard to break it. It didn't melt easily on the tongue like the candy bars Lucy remembered from childhood. Even though it was full of sugar, Lucy felt virtuous because dark chocolate was supposed to be good for the heart. So far, Liz had said her heart was fine, but a little insurance never hurt.

After a few minutes, the sugar high kicked in, and Lucy felt ready to deal with Olivia Enright. She still didn't know what to make of the woman. Now that Olivia was the town manager, would she try to throw her weight around more than usual? It was her bossiness that annoyed so many people. If she would just learn to be more of a team player, people might be more receptive to her leadership. Lucy had been trying to think of a gentle, charitable way to explain this to Olivia.

Lucy was tempted to eat more chocolate, but she carefully wrapped the remains of the chocolate bar and put it back in her desk. A sugar boost was one thing. Making a pig of herself was another. She gave the remaining chocolate one last, longing look before she closed the drawer.

The clock on her computer told her she had five minutes before Olivia arrived for her session. Lucy opened her laptop and navigated to the parish financial records. Cash flow had improved since they'd opened the summer chapel, but that would only last until the end of September. After that, who knew what would happen? The Catholic church in Hobbs was allowing in-person worship, but the Episcopal bishop wasn't convinced it was safe.

Lucy scanned the revenue column and was shocked to see yet another twenty-five-thousand-dollar Tithe.ly contribution. In her distraction, she didn't respond at first to the knock on her open door.

"Mother Lucy, Ms. Enright is here for you." When Lucy still didn't answer, Jodi prompted her. "Mother Lucy?"

Lucy finally looked up. "Send her in, Jodi," she said, closing her laptop.

Wearing an elegant mask that coordinated perfectly with her sea-green outfit, Olivia entered the room. After she sat down, she took off the mask and stowed it in her bag.

"Wonderful that we're part of Liz's testing project, and we don't have to worry."

Lucy smiled warmly. "Wonderful that you were so generous in funding it."

"The Enright Foundation is a national charity, but I've been looking to make more of a difference here in Hobbs. What's that old expression? Charity begins at home?"

Lucy suddenly connected the dots, feeling stupid for not having guessed before. "You're our anonymous donor."

Olivia smiled slyly. "I'll never tell."

Lucy sank down in her desk chair and stared at her. "Why would you do something like that?"

Olivia shrugged. "I'm an Episcopalian. Your church needs money. I have money. One plus one equals two. Simple, really."

"But that's over-the-top generosity."

"I assure you, Mother Lucy, I never do anything halfway."

Lucy sighed and shook her head. *What a puzzle you are!* "Why are you being so generous? Is it because you want us to like you?"

"If I were doing it for that reason, would I make my donations anonymously?"

"Olivia, I have to admit. You baffle me."

Olivia laughed merrily. "You're not the first person to say that." Her smile had warmth and affection. "I'm very impressed by you, Reverend Lucille Bartlett. I'm sure it's not easy running this parish, even for a woman of your talents. I want to support you in the one way I know how. I'm sorry if you think it's excessive. In the grand scheme of things, it's really not. At my level of income, donations have to be really big to make an impact on my taxes."

Lucy stared at her, seeing the irony in Olivia looking for tax deductions while many people in the parish were losing their jobs and going hungry.

"And if there's something you really need," Olivia continued, "an emergency repair or something like that, I hope you'll tell me."

"Fortunately, the summer chapel is funded by an endowment. Keeping St. Margaret's going is the challenge."

"Promise you'll let me know if I can help."

Olivia's blue eyes held her gaze, and Lucy perceived her offer was completely sincere.

"I will. Thank you."

"I'm sorry I haven't been more attentive to the church before now. It was the last thing on my mind."

"I understand. It's been a difficult time for you." Lucy gave her an encouraging smile. "But we're taking up your session with business. How has your week been?" Lucy settled back to indicate she was ready to listen.

"My new relationship is moving along. It's very satisfying."

"That sounds promising."

"I hope so."

Lucy waited for her to say more. When the pause in the conversation became unnatural, Lucy decided to take a new tack.

"How about the subject we were discussing last week?"

"My son?" Olivia sighed deeply. "I realized after we talked that I should contact my daughter-in-law. My attorney has sent her a letter."

"Have you considered calling her?"

Olivia shook her head. "She would never take my call."

"You're sure about that?"

"Quite sure. Our conversations have been nothing but acrimonious since the separation. She won't talk to me."

"How long has it been since you last spoke?"

"Almost three years."

"A long time."

"But maybe you should try calling her. Hearing a human voice is very different from getting a letter from an attorney."

"I agree," said Olivia, "but I don't see any alternative at this point."

"What will you say when she responds?"

"If she responds…" Olivia corrected mildly. "I will say that I'm sorry I shut her down when she tried to talk to me…that I realize I've been gaslighting her…that I'm willing to listen."

"Those are all good messages. She might respond positively."

"If she'll talk to me."

"Let's be optimistic. I'll pray she responds, and you should too. I'm sure you're excited about the possibility of seeing your granddaughters."

Olivia averted her eyes. "I'm a little afraid to face them…knowing what I know about their father."

"You don't know for certain that your son molested them."

"No, and I can't confront him about it, but the evidence is compelling. His suicide makes the case for his guilt stronger." Olivia looked pensive. "If only I had known. I would have made sure he got some help."

"Someone needs to want help."

As Lucy listened to Olivia berate herself for her failure as a mother, she thought of her own failings. So many women who came for counseling were full of guilt over their child rearing. Lucy encouraged self-forgiveness, but could she ever forgive herself? God had given her the gift of a second chance with Emily. Maybe this time she could get it right.

Lucy let the session run over because Olivia was her last client of the day, and this was her final session. Finally, she had to stop her.

Olivia glanced at her watch. "Do you charge overtime?"

With a smile, Lucy shook her head.

Olivia approached the desk and extended her hand. "Thank you, Mother Lucy. I hope your church appreciates what a gift you are. This is our last session according to our agreement."

"Yes. I hope you found our time together helpful."

"Immensely, which is why I'd like to continue seeing you. I realized there's much more to talk about. Would you consider taking me on as a regular client?"

"Sure," said Lucy, trying to moderate her surprise. "Tell Jodi on your way out to schedule more sessions."

"I will. I hope to see you at Thirsty Thursday."

After Olivia left, Lucy shut down her computer and collected her things into her bag. She was especially looking forward to her private prayer today. The thought of kneeling in her own church and spending time in God's presence had kept her going through the long hours of listening to other people's troubles. She needed to recharge her spiritual batteries after they'd been so thoroughly drained.

"Mother Lucy," said Jodi. "Chief Harrison is here. She wants to know if you have time to speak to her. I told her your office hours are over, but she said it was important."

Reluctantly, Lucy nodded. "Ask her to wait a few minutes, and I'll come out for her. You can go home, Jodi. I'll take care of it."

"Yes, Mother."

"And close the door please."

The door closed. With a sigh, Lucy put down her bag. She clasped her hands on her desk, closed her eyes, and bowed her head. "Dear God," she prayed. "Forgive the delay. I promise to rejoin our conversation after I speak to Brenda."

Then, as clearly as if someone stood in the room, she heard a distinctive, female voice say, "Don't worry, Lucy. I'll be here."

Lucy's eyes flew open. This had happened before, and she recognized the voice at once. It was the voice she'd heard asking her to become a priest.

Intellectually, Lucy knew it was an internal voice, something she heard only in her mind, but she always trusted what it said. She murmured a silent prayer of thanksgiving for the words of encouragement.

She found Brenda waiting outside on the visitors' bench, an old pew removed when the church was renovated.

"Lucy, I'm really sorry to take up your time," Brenda said, getting to her feet. "I know it's the end of your workday, and you must be tired. I wouldn't bother you if it wasn't really important."

Lucy reached up to put her arms around her. "Don't be silly. I always have time for a friend."

Brenda bent to accept the hug. "You and Liz. You always have time for everyone."

"That's our job. Now, come in and tell me what's going on."

Brenda followed her into the office. She looked surprised when Lucy pulled the other visitors' chair closer instead of sitting behind the desk.

Brenda leaned her elbows on her knees and rotated her hat in her hands. Lucy reached out and touched her shoulder. "What's wrong, Brenda?"

"I really hope you don't mind me barging in on you like this. I haven't been a faithful churchgoer."

"That doesn't matter. I'm always here for you." Lucy leaned forward so she could see Brenda's face. "Please tell me what's wrong. You look so upset."

Lucy could see how she was struggling to find the right words. Finally, she blurted out, "I'm resigning."

Instead of showing her surprise, Lucy forced her pleasant expression to freeze. "Why?" she asked in a soft voice.

Brenda continued to finger the brim of her hat and stared at the floor. "The coronavirus damaged my heart."

"Oh, Brenda. I'm so sorry. Is it serious?"

"It's pretty serious."

"What does Liz say?"

"She thinks I could get better…eventually. Sometimes, the damage heals, but in the meantime, I won't be at the top of my game."

"Can't you scale back your activities until you recover?"

"I'm the chief. I have to set a good example, including physical fitness."

Lucy tugged at Brenda's arm. "Look at me." When Brenda turned her face, Lucy saw that her eyes were filled with tears.

"I never wanted to be anything but a cop. Now, I don't think I can be… not with just half a heart. I'm not sure I could perform my duty."

"Oh, Brenda. You don't know that!"

"I don't, but if the moment came, and someone got hurt because of my problem, I could never forgive myself."

Lucy got up and pushed lightly on Brenda's shoulders to encourage her to sit up. "Brenda, you are an excellent police chief. The people of Hobbs love you. You can't let them down. We need you. Now, more than ever!"

"Liz will have to certify me fit for duty. I don't want her to lie."

"Liz would never lie about a medical matter. You know that."

"I know, but she's a good friend, and I don't want to put her in that position. And I need to be honest with the town about my health issues. Hiding them would be fraud."

Lucy sighed as she thought about what to say. Unfortunately, there were no easy answers. "You're sure about this?"

Brenda nodded.

"You know I'd never tell you to do anything illegal or against your conscience. So why have you come to me?"

"Because I needed to hear you say it's all right to do what I need to do."

"Oh, Brenda. Get up and let me give you a hug!" Brenda stood. She towered over Lucy, so she leaned down a little to allow Lucy to reach her arms around her neck. As she did, a sob escaped. "I never thought my career would end like this." As Lucy hugged her, she could feel her pain right through the bulletproof vest under her blouse. Brenda clung to her, and Lucy held her until the weeping stopped.

"Lucy, will you give me your blessing?" asked Brenda, finally letting her go.

"Of course."

Brenda bowed her blond head, and Lucy placed her hands lightly on it. She murmured the traditional blessing, then made a cross on Brenda's forehead with her thumb. "May God bless you and keep you and always hold you safely in Her arms." She laid a gentle hand on Brenda's cheek.

"Thank you," murmured Brenda. "Thank you for letting me tell you what I have to do and not judging me."

After Brenda left, tears came to Lucy's eyes. This virus had stolen so much from everyone—the lives of loved ones, the freedom to travel, the ability to connect with others in public places, the shared Eucharist. Now, it was stealing the health of people who had so many years of productive life ahead of them.

Lucy's need for the solace of prayer was now even greater than before. She picked up her bag and slung the strap over her shoulder. After she locked up the rectory, she headed across the quadrangle to the church.

As she approached, she admired the beautiful, old building. This was her church, once a vibrant parish full of engaged, generous people. Now, they were locked out of worship in God's house.

Lucy entered through the side door and knelt in the first pew. She bowed her head as she always did during prayer. Tears flowed into her clasped hands. A sob escaped. She allowed herself some time to spend her sorrow before trying to calm herself. Feeling more steady, she opened herself to feel God's presence. She prayed for all her intentions, but especially for Olivia, her daughter-in-law, and grandchildren. She asked God to help Maggie and Liz find their way and prayed that Brenda had made the right decision.

Her ears became aware of footsteps behind her. A pew creaked as someone sat down. Lucy had waited all day for this opportunity to pray. Whoever had entered the church would have to be patient.

Finally, she crossed herself and sat in the pew to bring her mind back to the ordinary world and center herself.

Whoever had slipped into the church approached. "Lucy?" asked a familiar voice. "I hope I'm not disturbing you."

Lucy looked up into Liz's earnest face. "You're not disturbing me. I've finished my prayers." Lucy slid over in the pew to make space for Liz to sit down.

"What are you doing here?" Lucy asked.

"I was on my way home and I saw your car outside the rectory. I wanted to ask about that patient I sent. When the rectory was locked, I figured you were here."

"You're so bad, coming alone."

"I never even thought about it until…."

"You know what I hate most? I could always go to you when I was unsure or frightened, and you'd be there…solid as a rock."

"I'm still here. Nothing's changed. I'm always here for you."

Lucy turned and engaged the intense, blue eyes. She thought again of a blue flame, like the pilot light in an old-fashioned stove. "My knight," said Lucy, patting Liz's thigh. "Hold me. I need to feel your strength. Everything is so overwhelming today."

Liz put her arm around her and pulled her close. Lucy leaned into her with a sigh.

33

Brenda had to wait outside in a socially distanced line until she got a call from the town council admin. It annoyed her that even the chief of police had to set up an appointment on the town hall website like anyone else. She was reviewing her text messages when her service phone rang.

"Hi, Brenda. Ms. Enright is ready for you." *Ms. Enright? What kind of bullshit is that?* All of the Hobbs town employees were on a first-name basis. Brenda stuffed down her irritation. She needed to be in the right frame of mind to deal with Olivia. An attitude certainly wasn't going to help.

Despite Brenda's police uniform, some of the people in line gave her hostile looks when she passed them on the way into the building. Inside the door, a young man took her temperature with a temporal thermometer.

"You're good," he said, stepping aside. "Go on in."

Usually, when Brenda came to the town hall on business, she'd stop to chat with the women in the town clerk's or the tax collector's offices. From them, she found out what was going on in Hobbs before it even happened. She knew about the argument between the developer on Drake's Road and his contractors. She'd known the vice-principal was going to lose his job before it was even discussed in the school board meeting.

Now, socializing in the town hall was actively discouraged. Arrows made of colored tape on the floor indicated the direction of the one-way traffic inside.

Brenda took off her hat when she stood at the admin's desk. Protocol allowed female officers to retain their covers indoors, but Brenda always felt there should be one set of rules for everyone.

"Good morning, Brenda," said Lynette, the town council's admin.

"How are things going today?"

Lynette raised her shoulders. "The usual. Many of the summer people aren't following the mask requirements. Ms. Enright is thinking of putting up more signs on the beaches. Maybe even getting your people to enforce it."

That's different, thought Brenda. When the subject of wearing masks had first come up in a town council meeting, Olivia had been extremely vocal in her protests. She'd come a long way since then.

"Is she ready for me?"

"She is. Go right in." Lynette pointed down the hall toward the open door at the end.

On the way, Brenda reviewed the little speech she'd composed. She poked her head in the door. "Good morning, Olivia."

"Brenda!" Olivia smiled broadly. "Come in. Please! Have a seat."

Brenda tried to figure out whether Olivia's cheery friendliness was an act or sincere. The smile seemed warm enough, but what had changed? Olivia was screwing Sam, but sex alone wasn't enough to cause that kind of change in a person.

"I'm so glad you came," said Olivia. "I was going to call you, but I'm so new at the job and just learning the ropes."

The admission that Olivia wasn't completely competent was surprising, but it was the other message that got Brenda's attention. "You were going to call me? Am I in trouble again?"

Olivia laughed. "No, no. I wanted to continue the conversation we were having at Liz's gathering. I have an idea."

Now, Brenda was genuinely puzzled, but intrigued. "Which conversation?"

"The one about becoming a spokesperson for compassionate policing. I have a friend at Fox News. We used to be on a corporate board together. I sent her the video of your speech at the Maine chiefs' demonstration. She was very impressed."

"But Fox is right-wing."

Olivia gave her a tolerant smile. "Not always. Fox invites people with opposing views to preserve the illusion of following the fairness doctrine. They're interested in having you on a show."

"I can't even watch Fox News for five minutes. Why would I go on there?"

"Think, Brenda. Yes, it might be a conservative audience, but if you're only preaching to the choir, how many minds do you think you'll change?"

"None, I suppose. They're already convinced."

"Exactly. That's where you come in. If you appear on a show watched by the 'other side,'" Olivia drew imaginary quotation marks in the air, "you could sway opinions. You're intelligent and exceptionally well-spoken. You passionately believe in what you do, and you're an attractive blonde."

"What do my looks have to do with it?"

Olivia's eyes revealed her forced patience. "Just watch five minutes of Fox and you'll see. All the female personalities are pretty blondes. You look like what their audience expects, so they'll take you more seriously, and, because of the venue, they won't necessarily expect the message you've come to deliver."

Brenda thought about it for a moment and realized that Olivia's plan was brilliant. Here was an opportunity to talk about community policing, a subject dear to Brenda's heart.

"But there's one problem."

"What's that?"

"I came in today to resign."

The smile on Olivia's face instantly faded. Her mouth opened in surprise. "What?"

"I don't want to go into detail, but something has come up that makes it difficult for me to remain in the department." Brenda opened her service pouch and took out the sealed envelope containing her letter of resignation. She tried to hand it to Olivia, who wouldn't reach for it, so Brenda put the envelope on the desk.

There was a slight pucker between Olivia's brows, not really a frown, just a hint of concern. "That makes no sense, Brenda. The people of this town venerate you. Never mind that you're much too young for retirement."

"I've put in over ten years in the Hobbs PD, so I'm due a pension."

"Yes, but you're only in your fifties. You have many good years ahead of you." A trace of suspicion flickered in Olivia's eyes. "Did you get a better offer from another town?"

Brenda shook her head. "No, no. Nothing like that."

Now the pucker between Olivia's brows became a definite frown. "You're under contract until the end of next year."

"I'm very much aware of my contractual obligations."

"We could enforce them."

"Olivia, I've been involved in personnel matters for a long time. It's really hard to enforce an employment contract when it's the employee who wants out."

Olivia sat back in her chair and gazed at Brenda with what seemed like new respect. "Brenda, please be honest with me. You've been successful as our police chief. You've served Hobbs honorably for eleven years. The only blot on your record is that demonstration."

Brenda felt her shoulders tense. She willed herself to relax them. "If you think that's a blot on my record, that's a problem. I was exercising my constitutional right to peaceful assembly."

"Yes, of course. But the optics were bad. The 'War of the Cops' ran for days on local TV. It made the national news in some places."

"Good. People need to see that there are good cops. Cops who have a conscience. We're not all thugs. There were officers taking a knee at some protests. That's why I spoke at the chiefs' summit when it all got started."

"That speech was eloquent. You are a natural speaker."

"I actually hate it."

"Almost everyone does, even if they don't admit it." Olivia sighed and studied her. "Oh, Brenda, I had such plans for you." Her frustration was obvious, but she spoke in a warm voice. "I wish you would be honest with me. Maybe there's something we can do to work this out."

Brenda glanced away so Olivia wouldn't be able to read her conflicting emotions. "I wish it were something that could be 'worked out,' but it's not."

Olivia frowned sympathetically. "I'm sorry you feel you need to do this, whatever your reasons. Let me think about the best way to handle it. I'll let you know." She finally picked up the envelope and put it in her desk drawer.

"Keep me posted," said Brenda as she got up. "Thanks for your time, Olivia."

After she closed the door, Brenda stood in the hall to think. That hadn't gone the way she'd expected. Not at all. She thought Olivia hated her and would be eager to replace her with a hand-picked loyalist.

Lynette approached. "I'm sorry, Brenda, but you have to leave. You're holding up the line for the next customer."

"Of course," murmured Brenda, "sorry." She followed the one-way arrows taped on the floor to the exit.

❋❋❋

Brenda was glad for a busy day after her meeting because it distracted her from her dread of telling Cherie what she'd done. Cherie's last word on the subject had been, "You're a grown woman. Do what you think is best." The words echoed Mother Lucy's. She'd seen the same expression on their faces—doubt about the resignation and reluctant affirmation of her autonomy.

At least, Brenda could say the decision hadn't been made impulsively. She'd thought about it for a week.

While she was debating what to do, Brenda wished she could talk it over with someone who could really appreciate her situation. Resigning before retirement was something only another cop could truly understand. Unfortunately, she couldn't talk it over with the cops in her family. Her father was dead, shot in the line of duty, and she wasn't close to her two brothers who were cops. She only spoke to them on holidays and birthdays. Calling them out of the blue to ask for advice felt wrong.

Brenda had done some back-of-the-envelope accounting and figured out she could get by on her New York and Maine pensions. It would be tight. No vacations in Europe—not like they could go anywhere with the pandemic travel restrictions. She'd apply for disability. In the NYPD, going on long-term disability was fairly easy. Everyone knew which doctors had an "in" with the review board.

As always when she came home, Brenda hung up her hat on a peg, locked up her service pistol, and hung her service belt on its hook. She closed the closet and turned around to see Cherie standing behind her.

Cherie reached up to draw her down into a kiss. She instantly tensed and backed up to give Brenda a quick inspection.

"What's the matter, honey? Bad day?"

Brenda attempted a smile.

"That bad? Come in and tell me about it." Cherie reached for her hand and led her into the living room.

"I think I need a drink first."

"I'll get it for you. Red wine okay? I opened a bottle a few minutes ago."

"Perfect. Thanks," murmured Brenda. Her eyes followed Cherie's pert rear as she left the room. It was the first sexual spark Brenda had felt since she'd heard the cardiologist's diagnosis. Cherie had tried to interest her a few times, but Brenda just couldn't respond. Maybe now that she'd made a decision, things would be better in that department. Fortunately, the cardiologist had said sex was allowed.

Cherie returned. She handed Brenda a glass of wine and sat beside her. She tapped her glass to Brenda's. "Here's to a better night than your day. And maybe…" There was a suggestive twinkle in her eyes.

Brenda chuckled. "Maybe. Let's see." The taste of the wine was welcome. Brenda took a few more sips to savor it. Cherie knew about wine and always picked good ones.

Cherie nudged her. "Go on. I'm listening."

"Are you listening as a shrink or my friend?"

"I always listen to you as your friend, not a therapist. Sometimes my training shows, but that's probably a benefit. It means I don't judge you or see everything from my own point of view."

Brenda gazed into Cherie's eyes, wondering how she deserved a girlfriend, not just beautiful, but so smart!

As if she'd been reading Brenda's thoughts, Cherie leaned forward and kissed her. "Brenda, you obviously have something on your mind. Stop admiring me and *talk*."

Brenda took another slug of wine. "I handed in my resignation today."

"Oh, Brenda!" Cherie put down her wine glass. She took Brenda's and put it down too. "Why couldn't you wait?" She took Brenda's hands in hers.

"Wait for what? My heart will never be the same again."

"You don't know that!"

Brenda gave her a hard look. "You heard what Dr. Wheeler said. There's a *remote* chance it will heal."

Cherie squeezed her hands. "Brenda, it's not that remote. He's just being cautious so you don't get your hopes up too high. In the meanwhile, we can manage your symptoms with medication."

"But I'll never be the same again."

"Maybe not. Maybe you won't run marathons or climb Mt. Washington in the middle of winter. But your heart is not that damaged. You need to be more careful, but you can still live a healthy, active life."

"You don't understand."

"I do understand. I deal with lots of heart patients. If you think what you're going through is bad, you should see the runners or the body builders. They don't take the news well."

"I can understand. Who wants to admit that they're just a shell of what they used to be?"

"But you're not! You're still the wonderful Brenda I fell in love with. Look, we all develop health issues as we age. It's a natural process. Yes, you were dealt a bad hand with the coronavirus, but the outcome could have been worse. Much worse!"

"I tried so hard to take care of myself," said Brenda, practically weeping in frustration. "I did everything I was supposed to do. I ate right, worked out at the gym regularly."

Cherie put her arm around her. "I know, baby. And you've done a great job. Your good health is why you have the possibility of a full recovery."

"I'm glad one of us is optimistic."

Cherie reached for her wine. "Who did you resign to?"

"Olivia Enright. She's the town manager now."

"Oh, shit. I forgot about that."

"Yeah, I was worried too. But it wasn't as bad as I expected. I was sure she hated me, but she was almost…sympathetic."

Cherie's blond eyebrows rose. "Well, that's different. Did you tell her why you were resigning?"

"No."

"Good. That's no one's business."

"It will be obvious when I apply for disability."

Cherie narrowed her eyes. "You're not disabled enough to qualify. I doubt any doctor will certify you."

"They would in New York."

"Yes, I've heard there's plenty of crooked business in New York, but federal disability is hard to get. Sometimes, it takes lawyers and years of going to court. You should have seen what my father had to go through. Thank God for his veteran's pension." Cherie drummed her fingers on her thigh. "When is your resignation effective?"

"When they find my replacement."

"Good. That buys us some time." Brenda opened her mouth to speak, but Cherie cut her off. "Don't tell me I'm wrong. You're not being reasonable. Someone needs to talk some sense into you."

"I thought you weren't judgmental."

"Surprise, surprise. Sometimes I am. I'm human like everyone else." Cherie took a big gulp of wine. "What did Olivia say?"

"She'd think about it."

"Well, that's hopeful…sort of."

"You're angry," Brenda guessed, watching Cherie's face.

Cherie closed her eyes and shook her head. "No, Brenda. I'm disappointed."

"You don't want to be married to a disabled ex-cop."

"I don't want to be married to a person who doesn't see when she's hurting herself. But I take you as you come, and I love you no matter what." She gave Brenda a kiss. "Go change, girlfriend. Dinner will be ready in a little while."

34

Sam brought the last of the dinner dishes to the kitchen. She admired Olivia's efficiency in the kitchen. She'd washed and set aside most of the cooking utensils before they'd even sat down to eat.

Olivia finally turned off the water and closed the dishwasher. "Why don't we take our wine and go out to the deck?"

"Sounds like a plan. I'll get the glasses and meet you there."

"Good. I'll bring out the wine."

When Olivia sat down, Sam admired her profile. It was perfect. Sam knew it wasn't all natural, but she definitely approved of the result. She got up and nudged Olivia aside on the chaise lounge, so she could sit down.

"Yes?" asked Olivia with a curious smile.

"You just looked so beautiful I wanted to kiss you."

"I'm not saying no to that." Olivia sat up to receive the kiss.

"You've been quiet tonight," Sam said. "Don't you like your new job?"

"It has its drawbacks like all administrative jobs. I hate dealing with personnel issues."

"I know what you mean. I had to do it when I was the managing partner in an architecture office. When people come to personnel, it's never because they're happy."

"No," agreed Olivia, refilling her glass.

"Want to tell me about it?"

"I can't tell you because of privacy issues. You know that. Besides, it involves a friend of yours."

"So much for keeping it private. Who are we talking about?"

"Nope. Not telling."

"Well, give me a hint then."

"She runs a big department in town."

"Brenda?" asked Sam with surprise. "Not again!"

"It's not what you think. That business with the demonstration has blown over. No one in town talks about it anymore."

"So, you're going after Brenda about something else?"

"I'm not 'going after' Brenda," said Olivia impatiently.

"You never liked her." Sam got up and retreated to her own chaise lounge.

"That's not true. Yes, she annoyed me in the town council meetings. She was always so stubborn, but I never disliked her for it. I respected her opinions."

"Well, hell, Olivia, now that you've told me this much, you have to tell me the rest."

"No, I don't. It's a private matter for now. You'll know about it soon."

"Oh, for fuck's sake, Olivia!"

"Don't swear, Samantha. It's unbecoming a lady."

"In case you haven't figured it out yet, I'm not a lady."

"That's complete nonsense. You were raised to be a lady…unlike–"

"If I find out you're going after Brenda again, I'll be really angry."

Olivia heaved out a sigh of exasperation. "I'm not doing anything to Brenda. She offered her resignation today."

"What? You're kidding."

"No, I'm not. And it's confidential until it's announced, so I'll thank you to keep it to yourself."

"Did she say why she's resigning?"

Olivia shook her head. "She won't tell me."

"But you accepted her resignation?"

"I can't force someone to work for the town. Come on, Samantha, you've dealt with employee issues. You know that!"

"Why didn't you push her for the reason?"

"She doesn't need to give any reason." Olivia frowned. "I suspect she may have a better offer in another police department."

"No. That makes no sense. She loves this town. Hell. She's involved with Cherie, who's as settled here as Brenda. They're engaged!"

"They are?"

"For someone who prides herself on knowing everything, you sure don't know much." Sam knew she was being bitchy, but she was in such a temper she couldn't stop herself.

"Well, it's not as if I'm the confidante of the lesbian high society of Hobbs."

"Maybe if you were nicer to people, you would be!"

Olivia put her head back and raised her hands toward the sky. "God, give me strength!"

"Are you praying to the Republican God or the real God?"

"Samantha, please…"

Sam got up and threw down the rest of her wine. "Thanks for dinner," she said, heading into the house.

"Samantha!" Olivia called after her.

"I'll talk to you later."

❖❖❖

From her truck, Sam called Liz. "Can I come over?"

"Sure, but I'm not at home. The kids are there, and they're driving me crazy. They've been there all week. Even Stefan's had enough. He's decided to take his chances at the senior residence."

"He probably just needs his own space. Don't take it personally." Sam thought for a moment. "If you're not at home, where are you?"

"At the boat. Come down. I'll give you a beer."

Sam backed up the truck. It was a quick drive to the harbor. The parking lot was usually empty by dusk. She easily found a spot and headed down the ramp to the berth where Liz kept her boat. Sam pulled the mooring line to bring the boat closer to the dock, which alerted its owner to her presence.

"What say you, matey?" Liz called as Sam climbed the ladder.

"Avast! Permission to come aboard, Captain!"

"Forget it, Sam. You obviously flunked 'Talk Like a Pirate Day.'"

Sam stepped into the wheelhouse, where she found Liz seated in the captain's chair. Her bare feet were up on the instrument panel. Her ball cap was perched slightly off-center on her head. Sam flopped into the other chair.

"What's going on?" asked Liz, taking a beer out of the cooler and opening it for Sam.

"I had a fight with Olivia."

"Too early for that, Sam. Why didn't you just fuck and make up?"

"I thought the expression was 'kiss and make up.'"

"Why stop there?"

"Are you buzzed, Liz?"

"A little." Liz raised the beer bottle in her hand. "This is my last one." She took her feet off the dashboard and sat up. "What did you fight about?"

"Did you know Brenda was going to resign?"

Liz got up and smacked the railing with her open palm. "Shit! What *is wrong* with that woman?" Sam had no idea what was going on, and now, was afraid to ask. "Who told you?" Liz demanded in an irritated voice.

"Olivia."

"Did she tell you why?"

"No."

"That's good, because it would be a serious breach of confidentiality."

Sam blinked hard as she thought about that. "Olivia said she didn't know the reason, but I got the idea that she was holding off so that she could think about it."

"That's big of her," Liz said with contempt. She turned around and leaned against the railing. "That's not really fair. Olivia's doing the right thing by holding off."

"I kind of stormed out on her," Sam admitted. "You know I can be a hothead. I said some pretty mean things to her."

"Maybe you should call her and apologize."

"Do you always apologize to Maggie right away?"

Liz shrugged. "Most of the time. Sometimes I let her stew."

"Naughty, naughty."

"Send her a text. That way, she'll have time to think about her response."

"Good idea." Sam pulled out her phone and texted a quick apology.

Liz glanced at her beer bottle. "Hey, can you give me a ride home? I *am* buzzed."

"Sure, but how will you get back?"

"I'm off tomorrow morning. Maggie can give me a ride to the harbor. I'll take her and the kids for donuts at Congdon's. They'll love it."

Sam sent the message to Olivia and put her phone in her pocket. "What's the story with Brenda? Do you know?"

Liz shrugged.

"You *do* know. Tell me."

"Nope."

"So, it's medical."

"Didn't say that." Liz sat down and put her feet back on the dashboard.

"Shit. The town wouldn't be the same without Brenda as chief. We'd get tickets all the time."

"I know. But that's not why it wouldn't be the same. Brenda is a great chief. Her officers would follow her anywhere."

"Please tell me why she quit."

"I can't. Only Brenda can tell you…if she wants to."

"You're useless. I'm calling her." Sam found Brenda's number in her contacts and called.

"Hey," a sleepy voice answered. "Sam?"

"I'm sorry. Were you sleeping?"

"Just taking a little nap after supper. I was just so tired. It was a hard day."

"I'm sorry to disturb you. Go back to sleep."

"No, it's okay," said Brenda, sounding more alert. Sam sensed that she was now sitting up. She imagined her smoothing back her blond hair and rubbing her eyes. "Is everything okay?" Brenda asked.

"Yes, I'm really sorry to wake you up."

"It's all right," said Brenda in a kind voice. She yawned. "It's still early.

Cherie made a fantastic dinner, but the full belly put me right to sleep. I should get up, or I won't sleep tonight. What's going on?"

"I was wondering if you'd care to join me and Liz on her boat. I'm being rude and inviting you without her permission." She put the phone on speaker so Liz could join the conversation.

"You know you're always welcome," called Liz.

"Did you hear that?" Sam asked.

"Yes, I did. Hold on." There was a muffled sound indicating Brenda had covered the speaker. Sam wondered why someone as smart as Brenda hadn't figured out she could just tap the screen to mute the call.

"My girlfriend says I can come. I'll be over soon."

"Cherie's a doll," said Sam, ending the call.

"She sure knows how to manage Brenda. Smart woman. Good at her job too."

❖❖❖

Within ten minutes, Brenda was climbing up the ladder.

"Ahoy there, matey," called Liz.

"Are ye hearties ready to splice the mainbrace?"

"See?" said Liz. "Now there's someone who knows how to talk like a pirate! Give the woman a beer!" She took a beer out of the cooler and flipped off the cap. "Here, Sam. Give it to her."

"To the *tres amigas!*" Brenda proposed. They all clicked bottles.

"Maybe Brenda can drive me home," Liz said to Sam. "She goes past my house."

"Sure, I'll drive you. Better than having you picked up by one of my officers."

"*Your* officers?" challenged Liz. "I heard you resigned today."

"She's buzzed," Sam explained on her behalf.

"Not *that* buzzed," Liz protested. "What the hell do you think you're doing, Brenda?"

"How did you find out?"

"Sam squeezed it out of Olivia under duress," Liz said. "You'll be glad to know that your friend defended your honor."

Brenda gave Sam a long, thoughtful look. "I didn't have a choice–" she began to say.

"Bullshit!" Liz interjected. "You have a choice!"

"Liz, I'm not fit!"

Liz spun around in her seat. "Keep telling yourself that, and you'll believe it."

Brenda obviously ignored Liz to speak directly to Sam. "The virus damaged my heart."

"Oh, my God!" Sam exclaimed.

"Yes, exactly," Brenda agreed.

"Won't you get better?"

"She might, if she gives herself a chance. But nooooo," said Liz, shaking her head, "she had to go and resign." Liz gave Brenda a filthy look. "What is it, Brenda? Your pride hurting? Your ego?"

Brenda stared at her. "Liz, I'm going to forgive you for saying that because I know you've had too much beer."

Liz shrugged. "Don't forgive me. See if I care. I'm talking to you as your friend."

"Then support me as my friend!"

"I don't support my friends to do stupid things. You can do your job just fine. I can help you manage the symptoms until your heart function improves. You jumped the gun!"

Sam was beginning to regret getting into the middle of this, and sat back to get out of the line of fire. "I'm so sorry, Brenda," Sam murmured.

"It sucks, but as my fiancée reminded me today, it could be a lot worse."

"What if Olivia accepts your resignation?" Sam asked.

Brenda sighed. "Then I'm out of a job…I guess."

35

A little breeze blew through the pine trees in the backyard, making a soft whooshing sound. In the last few weeks, the angle of the light had changed. It was nearing five o'clock, but the sun was already low in the sky, another sign that fall was approaching. August always brought a few days of cool weather, and it had been chilly enough for a hoodie all week. After Liz turned on the propane and lit the mosquito traps, she decided to light the gas fire pit too.

By now, Thirsty Thursday had become a regular fixture in their lives. Liz wondered if it would survive the pandemic like the outdoor dining along Route 1. Life before the virus was a vague memory, a pleasant dream of a distant past. Yet it had been less than a year since Lucy had been rediscovered by her biological daughter, and Erika was contemplating a commitment for the first time in her life. Sam was coming up from New Haven on weekends to finish renovating her house on Jimson Pond. Olivia was tormenting the town council, and Brenda was still admiring Cherie from afar. So much had happened in such a short time, yet it seemed an eternity.

Liz sat down in a chair and stared into the fire. Maggie came out to the deck. When she saw Liz parked in front of the fire, she came over and began to massage her shoulders.

"Oh, that feels good!"

"You look like you need it. I recognize that pose—my brooding philosopher. What's the matter?"

"I was thinking about how much our lives have changed since last year. All the things that once seemed important, now seem trivial."

"It's all relative. And they weren't trivial."

"Remember when no one believed me about the coronavirus?"

"I remember," said Maggie, sitting down beside her. "But I believed you. I believe in you, Liz Stolz. I always have."

Liz beamed a smile at her. "Thank you. I need someone to believe in me, especially when I doubt myself."

"Which isn't often, my arrogant-surgeon friend, but I recognize it when you do." Maggie patted Liz's thigh. "We all need someone to believe in us. I need you to believe in me too."

"I do. And I love you."

"I know you do. Otherwise, we wouldn't still be together."

"And here they are!" Erika stepped onto the deck, followed by Lucy.

"Where's Stefan?" asked Liz, getting up to greet them.

"He's not coming tonight. He's so happy to be home with his books and things. Don't get me wrong, Liz. He's incredibly grateful for your hospitality, but he wanted to give you some privacy."

"What privacy?" asked Maggie, getting up. "Our house is always full of people."

"Which is why you can use the break," said Erika, bending to kiss her.

"Stefan needed to be with his own things," Lucy explained. "They remind him of his wife and his old friends."

"The artifacts of a long life well lived," mused Erika. She glanced at the fire pit. "Finally cool enough for a fire." She gave Liz a half hug around her waist. "I hope you don't mind, but Lucy asked Tom and Jeff to stay home too. She thought we could use a ladies' night for a change."

"Good idea," said Maggie. "I can really do without the testosterone. The juvenile behavior of the occupant of the White House has been getting on my nerves."

"I fear it will only get worse as the election approaches," observed Erika.

Maggie reached out her hand to Lucy. "Come sit by me."

Liz breathed a sigh of relief. Any animosity between the two friends had apparently faded. Hopefully, things could now get back to normal.

"Who else is coming?" asked Erika.

"I think Cherie and Brenda are coming." Liz glanced at her phone. "I haven't heard anything from Olivia, but Sam said she'll be here."

"I made two big trays of eggplant parmesan. I hope they show up."

"Don't worry, Maggie," said Lucy. "We'll gratefully take any leftovers. Emily loves your cooking, and I'll drop off some to Stefan."

"Hey," said a familiar voice. Liz turned around and saw Sam approaching.

"Nice touch," she said, gesturing toward the fire pit.

"It's chilly tonight. I thought we could use the heat." Liz glanced behind Sam. "Where's your girlfriend?"

"I don't know."

"Is she coming tonight?"

Sam looked chagrined. "We haven't spoken since we had words. Maybe she won't show up."

Lucy put her hand on Liz's arm. "Why don't you text Olivia and remind her that she's welcome?"

Liz made a little face, but she sent a quick text to Olivia. While her fingers were tapping out the message, she felt an enthusiastic thump on the shoulder and turned around to see Brenda with Cherie beside her.

"I thought you might not come after what I said the other night," said Liz.

"Are you kidding me? Haven't missed a single one of your Thirsty Thursdays. Why break my perfect record?"

"I need to turn on the oven. I'll be right back." Maggie got up and headed to the porch door.

"Thanks for having us," said Cherie, looking around. "Small group tonight."

"Lucy decided to ban testosterone. She thought we needed a ladies' night." Liz grinned in Lucy's direction. "She's not exactly a conventional priest. Maybe she's planning a naked ritual around the fire."

Lucy raised an auburn brow. "I'm sure you'd love that, Liz."

"You bet I would." Liz threw Lucy a kiss, but the green eyes flashed a warning and glanced toward the kitchen window. Liz instantly understood the message: no more flirting. They needed to play it cool for a while.

Maggie emerged from the porch with platters of snacks: raw veggies and dip, followed by shrimp and cocktail sauce. Liz opened some wine. As the sun went down, the air grew cooler. Everyone pulled their chairs closer to the fire.

"I have something to tell you," Brenda announced. The extended pause was obviously to make sure she had everyone's attention. "I think most of you know I put in my resignation."

Cherie stared into the fire. For the span of several moments, no one said a word.

"Brenda, I didn't know," said Erika. "I'm sure you have your reasons, but for the sake of the town, I'm very sorry to hear this news. You are a fine, ethical police officer at a time when we definitely need such people. If you don't mind, I would like to hear how you came to this decision."

Cherie turned to Brenda. "Go ahead. These are our friends. Tell them."

"You're probably the only one who doesn't know, Erika. When I had the virus in the spring, it damaged my heart."

"My God, I am so sorry!" exclaimed Erika with genuine sympathy. "You are so young. Is it serious?"

Brenda glanced at Liz. "My doctor thinks she can treat it, and I could recover."

"Forgive me, Brenda, but I don't understand," said Erika. "If your condition can be treated, why are you resigning?"

Cherie reached for Brenda's hand. "She thinks it's her duty."

"Your duty? Your doctor thinks you can perform your job. I would say your duty is to honor your contract."

"Thanks, Erika," said Liz. "She won't listen to me. She's been such a fitness freak her whole life, she thinks she should be able to do everything she did thirty years ago. There aren't many of us who can!"

"You can say that again," Erika said. "There are days when I am quite creaky. Granted, I have almost ten years on you, Brenda, but still."

Brenda hung her head. "Now that I've had time to think about it, I realize that resigning was impulsive. But it's too late now. I can't take it back."

"Is that so?" asked a voice behind them. As if connected by a string, they all turned in unison. A figure approached the fire. Her perfect features were accentuated by the dancing light.

"Good evening, ladies," said Olivia, taking the empty seat next to Sam, whom she studied cautiously. "Is it safe to sit here?"

"Of course," murmured Sam.

"Well, well," said Olivia looking around the circle. "Here we are again. I hadn't planned to come. I wasn't sure I'd be welcome. Thank you, Liz, for your text message."

"It was Lucy's idea."

"I should have known." Olivia glanced at Lucy. "At least, someone in this group knows how to show Christian charity."

Lucy's eyes narrowed. "Acting like a Christian usually works better than shaming people."

Olivia gave her a cool look. "Point well taken."

When the uncomfortable silence lasted a moment too long, Maggie said, "Olivia, I'm sorry we ate all the snacks before you got here. Can I get you some cheese and crackers? How about a glass of wine?"

"A glass of wine sounds wonderful. White, if you have it open, Maggie."

"I think we killed all the white wine, but there's more in the kitchen." Maggie got up and headed inside. Once again, the group was conspicuously silent.

"I know I'm not your favorite person," Olivia said, looking at the faces around the fire. "Despite my efforts to earn your friendship, you don't like me."

Cherie shifted in her chair. The wicker made a little creak of protest. "You can't force friendship on people. It's a two-way street."

"Yes, and it seems I've been the only one driving it."

"That's not fair," said Sam. "We've all been trying to give you a chance."

Olivia glared at her. "Yes, you especially. But as soon as one of your friends was threatened, you abandoned me and sided with her. And I've shared so much with you. Didn't that matter?"

Sam stared at her feet.

Olivia looked at each person in turn. "What do I need to do to join your little sorority? Why don't you trust me? Is it my politics? Am I trying too hard? What am I doing wrong? Please tell me."

"We're trying too," said Liz. "But with us, what you see is what you get. That's not always true of you."

"Leave it to Dr. Stolz to be the blunt instrument," said Olivia. "At least, I can always count on her to tell me the truth. And Mother Lucy, although she's more tactful. If not for the two of them, I wouldn't bother with any of you."

Sam looked at her sharply.

"Well, maybe you, Samantha. You offer some benefits I might not find otherwise."

"Olivia—" Brenda started to say.

"And you! You can't even trust me with your reason for resigning. I wanted to help you…to work it out. This town needs you, especially in these difficult times. You provide steady leadership. You're a powerful model of good policing. You could make a real difference, if only you'd step out of your comfort zone."

"Olivia, I think Brenda was trying to tell you something before you cut her off," said Lucy in a kind but firm tone. "You might want to stop talking now and listen."

"Good idea," said Olivia, sitting back.

Maggie came out with the wine. She looked around at her friends' grim expressions. "I step away for one minute, and you all look like someone died. What's going on?"

"Olivia decided to give us a piece of her mind," Liz volunteered.

"But I'm done now." Olivia got up to take the glass of wine from Maggie. "Brenda, what were you going to say? I'm sorry I interrupted you."

"I think I need a beer," Brenda said.

"I'll get it for you." Liz got up to rummage in the cooler.

Brenda gave Olivia a sheepish look. "I think I jumped the gun in handing in my resignation. I didn't really think it through."

Olivia opened her bag and took out an envelope. "See? I haven't even read it yet. It's still sealed. It's been sitting locked in my desk drawer since you gave it to me."

"Why?"

"Because I wanted to think about it. And this is what I think. I won't accept this," she said, waving the envelope, "unless you're honest and tell me the real reason you're resigning. I'm willing to help you through this. I'll do whatever is needed, but I need to know that you trust me."

Brenda looked over her shoulder. "Liz, can you tell her? You can explain the medical stuff better than I can."

Liz handed Brenda the beer and sat down. "Olivia, we're just learning about the long-term effects of the novel coronavirus. It doesn't just affect the lungs. In autopsies, they've found the virus in every major organ. In Brenda's case, it affected her heart and caused some damage. It may be permanent, but there's a good chance it could heal, and she would recover most, or even all, of her heart function."

"But can she do her job?" asked Olivia, her eyes never leaving Brenda's.

"I think so. She might be putting herself at risk running after perps and jumping fences like they do on TV, but Brenda tells me that's rare for the Hobbs PD. I'd probably advise desk duty until we get her meds sorted out. After that, she can go back to her regular duties."

"You're not saying this because the chief is your friend?" Olivia asked, still focused on Brenda's face.

Liz bristled, but she spoke in a calm voice. "No, of course not. I could lose my license for lying about her medical condition."

"Good. Now, did you hear what your doctor said, Brenda?"

"Yes, I heard her."

Holding Brenda's gaze, Olivia picked up the envelope resting in her lap and tossed it into the fire. "There. That's the end of it."

"You mean you won't accept my resignation?"

"No, and I don't want to hear about this subject again. No one, except the people sitting here," Olivia pointed around the circle, "knows anything about it, so I'll thank you all to keep this to yourselves."

They watched the envelope burn. The letter inside blackened and curled in the flames. Sparks rose in the darkening sky.

"Thank you," said Sam. In the firelight, her eyes were bright with tears. She tugged Olivia's arm to pull her closer.

"Don't get emotional, Samantha," Olivia warned. "It's good business. Brenda is an excellent police chief, and I don't want to waste the town's money suing her for breach of contract." Olivia's tone had an edge, but Liz perceived it was for effect.

"Sam's right," Lucy said. "Thank you for giving Brenda the benefit of the doubt. We're all grateful."

"Excuse me," said Brenda, getting up. Liz watched her head into the house and realized her tough friend was close to tears. Cherie jumped up to follow her.

Maggie opened the kitchen window and called out, "Dinner's almost ready."

Lucy nodded in Olivia's direction. "This could have been a disaster, but you did the right thing."

"Because it was the right thing."

"Well done," said Erika, getting up to shake Olivia's hand.

When Erika stepped aside, Sam pulled Olivia up into a hug and kissed her. The kiss became prolonged and passionate.

"Get a room," called Liz through cupped hands.

Erika and Lucy laughed. Sam and Olivia ended the kiss and looked charmingly embarrassed.

Out of the corner of her eye, Liz noticed Maggie signaling through the screen door. "I think my wife is trying to tell me we can eat." Liz got up and bowed theatrically as she gestured towards the door. "Dinner is served."

They all filed into the enclosed porch except Olivia, clearly hanging back to speak to Liz alone.

"Dr. Stolz, your healing goes well beyond your medical practice."

"Lucy always does the real work."

"Yes, but you set the wheels in motion."

"You noticed? It doesn't always turn out this well, but sometimes, it does." Liz offered her hand. "Welcome to Hobbs, Olivia. You're one of us now."

"Oh, I hope so!"

36

Brenda gazed around Liz's enormous media room. The handpicked audience included the captains and other senior officers of the Hobbs PD as well as the town council. The hosts had presented their guests with a lavish spread, including Liz's homemade popovers and blueberry muffins, and a traditional continental breakfast with cold meats, smoked fish, and cheese. There were Congdon's donuts and Brenda's favorite: breakfast pizza. Brenda had never seen breakfast pizza before she'd moved to Maine, but she always looked forward to it, especially topped with sausage, peppers, and onions. She could eat it every day.

Brenda was touched that so many people had come to watch her TV debut on *Fox and Friends Weekend*. The Enright Foundation testing program had ensured that everyone invited was safe. People were wearing masks to be sure, but seeing them together like this almost seemed like the days before the pandemic.

As Liz passed, Brenda grabbed her arm.

"Hey, thanks for all this. I can't believe all these people showed up for me."

"Believe it. You are the woman of the hour."

"Thanks for getting breakfast pizza. You know I love it."

"You should thank Olivia."

"How did she know to order double of my favorite?"

"I told her."

Brenda glanced across the room at Olivia, chatting with Paul Duvaney, the Hobbs fire chief. "I can't believe she even paid for a private jet to take me to New York and back."

Liz put her hand on Brenda's shoulder. "I told you she wasn't as bad as we all thought." She moved closer to speak confidentially. "Are you nervous?"

"Hell, yes, but not as nervous as when they were taping it."

"Did the tranquilizer help?"

"I didn't want to be dopey when they asked the questions, so I only took half."

"Next time, you probably won't need any. Good thing they give you the questions in advance. Did you memorize your answers?"

"Yes, and I practiced them with Cherie." Brenda gazed across the room to where her fiancée stood, chatting with Tom and Jeff.

"Yes, your girlfriend is good at working the crowd," Liz said, following Brenda's line of sight. "You know, Jeff was in the TV business. He has contacts too. You could be a star."

"Thanks, but I'm happy with my day job, now that I know I can do it."

Brenda noticed Maggie's daughter and the Channel Eight station manager talking to Erika.

"Alina said that if this goes well, her station manager wants to do a special segment on how we choose and train officers. I could get behind something like that. Maybe it will get us some new recruits."

"Maybe," Liz agreed.

"He thinks a less political message showing cops in a positive light will be even more effective than pushing politics down people's throats. You have to hand it to these media types. They sure know how to manipulate their audience."

"Nothing new. Goes back to the Greeks. They practiced oration in the public square," Liz said. "Have you seen the tape?"

"Just ten seconds of it. They put too much makeup on me. I wanted to do my own makeup the way Maggie taught me for the town council broadcasts, but they kept telling me to put on more blush."

"Probably wanted to make sure you looked 'feminine' enough for their audience."

"Do you think they knew I'm gay?" Brenda asked anxiously.

"Nah, you don't look especially gay."

Lucy approached and extended her hand to Brenda. "Congrats on your debut, Chief Harrison."

"Thank you, Lucy." Brenda scooped her up into a hug. "And thanks for the coaching."

"My pleasure. I suffer from stage fright myself from time to time."

Brenda stared at her. "I don't believe it."

"It's true, but I've learned to hide it well."

Olivia marched up to them. "Brenda, sit next to me, so you can say a few words after the broadcast. I'll introduce you and talk about our community outreach program. Then you can share a few words about your experience at Fox News or whatever you like. Nothing too political, please." She smiled and walked away.

"Bossy, as usual," Liz said under her breath once Olivia was out of earshot.

"Liz! That's how God made her!" Lucy gestured around the room. "Look at all the good she's doing. And, you can be pretty bossy, yourself."

"You can be too, but you flash that incandescent smile, and nobody notices."

Brenda noticed that Olivia was moving toward the front of the room. She waved in Brenda's direction. "I'm being summoned. Come down and sit with me," she said, putting her arms around Lucy and Liz.

"I think Cherie will want to sit with you," Lucy said, "but we'll be right behind you."

Lucy found Erika, and they took seats in the second row behind the leather sofa.

"I heard Olivia was thinking about switching parties," said Brenda as she and Liz headed to the front.

"She resigned from the town Republican committee, but she said she wants to work for change from within. She just gave a huge donation to the Lincoln Project. So did I."

"Do you trust them?"

Liz smiled cannily. "Not really."

As Brenda took a seat on the leather sofa, she noticed that behind the scenes, people were moving into position. Alina had gone up to the stage to manage the video feed. The enormous TV screen was descending. Brenda checked her watch. It was almost time.

Brenda motioned to Cherie to join her, but Cherie shook her head. She chose a seat next to Lucy and Erika in the second row. She leaned forward to speak in Brenda's ear. "Baby, this is *your* time to shine."

Olivia stood up and clapped her hands. "All right, people. Find a seat. The broadcast will begin soon." She glanced at Alina, who nodded her readiness. "Thank you, everyone, for coming this morning," said Olivia, making a smooth transition into her town-manager role. "Today, our very own Hobbs police chief, Brenda Harrison, makes her debut on national TV. I've only seen a short clip, but I hear that her performance was superb. Her answers were smart, articulate, and pertinent. Let's hear it for Chief Harrison and the Hobbs PD." She applauded, and everyone in the room joined in.

When Olivia sat down, Sam, who'd obviously been waiting for the speech to end, slipped into the row behind her. She patted Brenda's shoulder. "I'm sure it will be fantastic. Way to go, Chief." She reached her hand forward, and Brenda shook it. Sam then reached out her hand to Olivia. "Good job, Madam Town Manager." Sam smiled and whispered, "I'd kiss you, Olivia, but everyone's watching."

The enormous screen flashed on, and Brenda saw herself staring into the camera like a deer in the headlights. She remembered that moment of pure terror. She'd taken Lucy's advice on how to deal with the stage fright: "Pinch yourself. The pain will distract you."

The announcer set up the segment with a brief review of recent demonstrations against the police. He read the statistics of deaths at the hands of the police and police officers shot in the line of duty. The first question went to Brenda. "Chief Harrison, what do you think police departments should do when officers are accused of unnecessary force?"

"I think the most important thing is to investigate every incident thoroughly and transparently." There she was, speaking to millions of people, and yes, she was wearing too much blush.

Olivia reached over and took Brenda's hand. "You're doing beautifully," she whispered. "You make us so proud." She smiled warmly and returned her attention to the broadcast.

Also by Elena Graf

Hobbs Series

HIGH OCTOBER

Liz Stolz and Maggie Fitzgerald were college roommates until Maggie confessed their affair to her parents. When Maggie breaks her leg in a summer stock stage accident, she lands in Dr. Stolz's office. Is forty years too long to wait for the one you love?

THE MORE THE MERRIER

Maggie and Liz's plans of sitting by the fire, drinking mulled wine and watching old Christmas movies get scuttled by surprise visits from friends and family.

THIS IS MY BODY

Professor Erika Bultmann, a confirmed agnostic, is fascinated by Mother Lucy, the new rector of the Episcopal Church, especially when she discovers Lucille Bartlett was a rising opera star before mysteriously disappearing from the stage.

LOVE IN THE TIME OF CORONA

Police Chief Brenda Harrison shows an interest in Liz's biracial PA, but first Cherie needs to get past her loathing for all law enforcement since a state trooper shot and killed her sister.

THIRSTY THURSDAYS

Liz Stolz initiates Thirsty Thursdays, a weekly cocktail party on her deck, so her friends can socialize safely during the pandemic. Pretentious, overbearing Olivia Enright pursues Liz's friend, architect Sam McKinnon, and tries to push her way into the tight-knit group.

THE DARK WINTER

Erika hires Sam to build a sound-proof practice room for Lucy. Fortunately, the early Christmas gift is ready before tragedy strikes. As the women of Hobbs pull together to help a beloved friend deal with her loss, the dark winter brings tension and realignment in their small community.

SUMMER PEOPLE

Melissa Morgenstern, a high-profile lawyer from Boston, is spending the summer with her widowed mother. She's doing some trust work for Liz who introduces her to the attractive Courtney Barnes, Hobbs Elementary's new assistant principal. The arrival of Susan, Lucy's ex, complicates her deepening relationship with Liz.

STRANDS

Cherie hears her biological clock ticking and would like to start a family. When a shocking tragedy creates an opportunity for her and Brenda to become parents, their friends need to step up to make it happen.

THE RECTOR'S WEDDING

The sudden opportunity for Lucy to return to her singing career throws everything in her life into doubt—her vocation as a priest, her settled life in Hobbs, even her upcoming marriage to the woman she loves.

THE VANISHING BRIDGE

Rev. Susan Gedney tries to rebuild trust after her humiliating exit from Hobbs. Bobbie Lantry always needs to rush away to take care of a mysterious elderly woman. They need to share their secrets, but do they dare?

EXTENDED CAPACITY

A small town in Maine wakes up thinking it's just another winter day, but a tragedy has been set in motion by dark secrets from the past and an unfortunate series of recent events. The horror that every town fears is about to come to Hobbs.

RIP TIDE

After the tragic shooting at Hobbs Elementary School, people are trying to get back to normal, but the town and its inhabitants will never be the same. Healers Dr. Liz Stolz and Rev. Lucy Bartlett are used to binding up the wounds of others, but in this book they are hurt by the unintended consequences of their actions

Passing Rites Series

THE IMPERATIVE OF DESIRE

A coming-of-age story that takes a brilliant aristocratic woman from La Belle Époque through a world war, a revolution that outlawed the German nobility, the roaring twenties to the decadent demimonde of Weimar Berlin.

OCCASIONS OF SIN

For seven centuries, the German convent of Obberoth has been hiding the nuns' secrets—forbidden passions, scandalous manuscripts locked away, a ruined medical career, perhaps even a murder.

LIES OF OMISSION

In 1938, the Nazis are imposing their doctrine of "racial hygiene" on hospitals and universities. Margarethe von Stahle has always avoided politics, but now she must decide whether to remain on the sidelines or act on her convictions.

ACTS OF CONTRITION

After the fall of Berlin, Margarethe is brutally raped by occupying Russian soldiers. Her former protégée, Sarah Weber, returns to Berlin with the American Army and tries to heal her mentor's physical and psychological wounds.

About the Author

In addition to the books in the Hobbs series, Elena Graf has published four historical novels set in Europe in the early 20th century. *Lies of Omission*, the third volume in the Passing Rites Series, won a Golden Crown Literary Society award for best historical fiction and a Rainbow Award. The fourth volume, *Acts of Contrition* also won a Goldie and a Rainbow Award.

The author pursued a Ph.D. in philosophy but ended up in the "accidental profession" of publishing, where she worked for almost four decades. She lives with her wife in coastal Maine.

If you liked this book and would like more stories about the people of Hobbs, Maine, write to Elena at elena.m.graf@gmail.com.

Elena Graf is a member of iReadIndies, a collective of self-published independent authors of women loving women (WLW) literature. Please visit our website at iReadIndies.com for more information and to find links to the books published by our authors.

www.ingramcontent.com/pod-product-compliance
Lightning Source LLC
LaVergne TN
LVHW011929070526
838202LV00054B/4561